Gaston Saves the World
Pascal Adolphe
I0714731

Printed in the United States of America

Paperback ISBN: 978-1-956019-68-1
eBook ISBN: 978-1-956019-69-8

Library of Congress Control Number: 2022943510

DartFrog Plus

Published by DartFrog Plus, the hybrid publishing imprint of DartFrog Books.

DartFrog Books
4697 Main Street
Manchester, VT 05255
www.DartFrogBooks.com

For Anais, Lucas and Alex;
This is your heritage.

Acknowledgments

I'd like to acknowledge and thank the following members of the Open Genre Writer's Group at the Writer's Centre, Sydney: Helen Lyne, Matan Elul, Jack Peck, Brian Bell, Helen Grant, Aleit Woodward, Alita Tanswell, Lorraine Bower, Samy Fahmy, Bob Yates, Srinivas Karkenahalli, Zita Fogarty and Filip Rafaneli.

"Inequality is not inevitable; it is a political choice."
—Nabil Ahmed. "Inequality Kills: The unparalleled action needed to combat unprecedented inequality in the wake of COVID-19." *Oxfam.* 17 Jan 2022.

CHAPTER I

The Girl on the Swing

He could feel some pain creeping up his calf muscles and his breath shortening, but he knew it wouldn't be for long. Gaston was well aware of what he needed to do to overcome the initial pain barrier whenever he set out on a long run: deep, deep breaths, inhale through your nose till your lungs almost explode, then exhale gently through the mouth.

It was early evening but Flamboyant Street was deserted, a normal phenomenon in a normal island village. Only the trees swaying gently in the strengthening summer breeze disturbed the silence. Now and then Gaston's loud, laboured breaths took over the soundtrack of the street. He was still struggling but the transition wasn't far away. Soon he became aware of his heavy breathing returning to normal and he felt totally comfortable; running, breathing, and wind blending into one. His running speed slackened and increased at will and he felt as if he could run forever. He was "in the zone".

Gaston discovered jogging in his early teens. Forced to do cross-country running at school, he quickly found he was good at it, and more importantly, it provided some real pleasure in an otherwise mundane life so he took every opportunity to indulge at school and outside. Three or four times a week, he went jogging straight after coming home from school. And he even found his first real friend through jogging: a classmate named Patrick, whose family was so poor that he had to run barefoot until Gaston managed to convince his mother to buy him a new pair of sandshoes for his birthday. Gaston gave his used pair to Patrick, who cried with joy, even though Patrick's big toe protruded through a hole in the right shoe. It was the first present he had ever been given.

Jogging also proved to be the catalyst for Gaston's sexual awakening. Two years on from the onset of puberty and aged sixteen, he had yet to find fuel for his nascent sexual urges. He'd not yet seen a naked woman in the flesh, although he'd come across images of bare breasts and vaginas when, during a visit to his uncle's house, he found a *Penthouse* magazine that had been left inadvertently in the toilet.

. He'd also heard that women were baring their breasts on some of the island beaches but he had yet to witness that on the few occasions—usually during the school holidays—when he spent time at the beach. Images of naked women also would come to him regularly in dreams that only caused him angst and embarrassment when the inevitable orgasm jolted him awake from immensely pleasurable reverie to a reality of sodden pyjama shorts and sheets. After a week where he had to clean up the aftermath of his nocturnal emissions in the middle of the night five times, he took to going to sleep with tissues stuffed inside his pyjama shorts.

As he grew older and stronger, Gaston could jog faster and for longer, and his jogging routine took him farther afield. He naturally gravitated towards the more scenic beachside areas of his home village of Finger Bay, where some of the more affluent island residents—invariably of white European heritage or corrupt government officials—owned luxurious beachside homes.

One bright, sun-soaked summer afternoon, a profusely sweating Gaston experienced a rare stitch that forced him to slow to a walk. He stopped to rub his right side and breathe away the pain outside a palatial beachside home with a substantial front yard protected by a tall wrought-iron fence that allowed passers-by to admire the immaculately manicured lawn and garden. As the pain slowly subsided, Gaston's attention was drawn to a girl laughing and swinging wildly on a homemade swing attached to a huge ebony tree that dominated the garden. She was facing him only a few metres away as she swung seemingly carefree. The girl was actually a young woman but only a few years older than Gaston. She had milky white skin, long flowing dark brown hair, and eyes of brilliant blue. She was wearing a loose, low-cut, off-white linen dress that was pulled up to her waist, showing off her shapely tanned legs from ankle to thigh.

Clutching two of the iron bars and poking his face between them, Gaston looked on, mesmerised. Far from being disturbed by his gaze, the girl giggled mischievously as her eyes met those of her voyeur. She followed up with a big forward swing that took her almost to touching distance (if Gaston had extended his arm fully through the bars). She was the most beautiful girl Gaston had ever seen, and he immediately felt a slight bulge in his tight running shorts that only intensified when, the second time around, she parted her legs as she swung towards him. She was wearing no underwear. The grinning and now completely aroused Gaston had no idea what to do next as her generous mound of pubic hair seemed to overwhelm his vision. For her part she seemed, at once, oblivious and totally aware and enthralled by Gaston's lustful gaze.

"Victoria! It's supper time!" a voice yelled from the house behind.

Gaston heard footsteps ahead of noticing a figure emerging from the house that sent him scurrying behind one of the substantial sandstone pillars supporting the huge, automatic iron gates. Like a detective in a television police drama, he pushed his back against the pillar and drew a couple of deep breaths. When he thought it was safe to look, he peered around the pillar to see Victoria walking towards the house alongside a portly Indian woman dressed in a sparkling blue sari. Victoria seemed to feel him peeking and turned around to catch his eye with a wink and a sweet smile that Gaston impishly reciprocated.

Once she'd disappeared into the house, he set off again but only at a walking pace. Try as he might, he couldn't cleanse his mind of Victoria's vagina, which prolonged an erection that prevented him from running even though his stitch had long since dissipated.

The next day, Gaston was naturally drawn back to her house, where he again found her on the swing, this time dressed in an aubergine-coloured floral skirt and loose, pale green blouse unbuttoned to reveal a hint of her bosom. Her hair was in a ponytail, revealing scattered freckles on her neck. Gaston thought she looked even more beautiful than the day before.

This time, she was just sitting on the swing, her legs tantalisingly apart as if waiting for him. When she saw him, she smiled, got up, and directed him to the right side of the property where, next to a large wooden shed, another iron gate gave the residents easy access to a narrow path down to the beach.

Gaston wasted no time in jogging to the gate. Victoria let him in and held her finger up to her still-smiling lips and took him gently by the hand. She led him on tiptoes into the bare shed, which was bathed in a warm afternoon light courtesy of a small window that gave them a cosy view of the beach. Without saying a word, she pulled down his shorts and masturbated him quickly to orgasm, all the while looking longingly into his eyes. Gaston was dumbstruck with pleasure, but she gave him no time to revel in the afterglow. She took his hand and placed it under her skirt, where again, she was wearing no underwear. She guided Gaston's hands and fingers into pleasuring her until she also came, her moans rising to a crescendo that fortuitously coincided with another loud summons to supper by Victoria's Indian maid.

A still-grinning Gaston hastily pulled up his shorts, and without saying a word, Victoria ushered him out the shed and gate, pointing him in the direction of the beach. She then kissed him gently on the lips and went in to have her supper.

On the third day, Gaston turned up at the beachside house full of sexual expectations. However, Victoria was not waiting for him on the swing or anywhere else. Frantically, Gaston scoured the property from every vantage point that he could but it seemed that no one was home. He returned every day for the next two weeks but didn't detect any sign of life until the day he saw a man hanging up a sign on the front gate, advertising that the house was up for lease.

Many years later, Gaston discovered that Victoria was the daughter of a British hotelier who was visiting the island at the time, hoping to cash in on the boom in tourism development that followed its independence. He had since built three beach resorts on the island. Victoria, at that time, had accompanied him on what was essentially a short working holiday, and the beachside home was owned by the island's tourism minister. By the time Gaston uncovered this information, his lust and desire for Victoria had become nothing more than a distant, blissful memory.

CHAPTER II

Gaston

Some nine years on from the ecstasy of his sexual initiation, Gaston found himself at the lowest ebb of his young life. And again, a woman was instrumental, but this time for his agony.

For the first time in a long time, he thought of Victoria as he stepped out of the beachfront bar and tried to compose himself. That first lust lost did not cause heartbreak. Sure, he'd felt a bit sad for maybe a week, but Victoria was soon forgotten and his emotional equilibrium had been quickly restored. First love lost, however, was proving to be a more ominous emotional challenge. Broken-hearted, Gaston had become a sad, pathetic young man who couldn't remember the last time he was sober in the afternoon. A few weeks, a month at most, but it seemed like a lifetime. Not that he was trying to remember anything. The whole point of being perpetually drunk was to forget, not remember.

He stood motionless for some time outside the bar. The harsh light from the blazing sub-tropical sun caused him to squint, his rapidly blinking eyes struggling to adjust. He could barely see the hordes of tourists sunning themselves on the beach—the very same beach where, as a boy, Gaston and his friends played volleyball during the school holidays; not a tourist in sight, not a hotel within miles; only the singsong sounds of Creole children fooling around, playing, laughing, fighting well into the afternoon and evening. Cousins, friends, and kids from the local villages all joined in.

"Get out of that sun; you'll get sunstroke!" his mother would yell at them every day.

The sub-tropical sun in the afternoon was indeed no place to linger but being coloured or black-skinned made them feel safe. Now, white tourists had invaded en-masse; their voices full of condescension and contempt for non-whites, yet they spent hours on the beach trying to make their skin darker.

Gaston was bemused.

It just didn't make sense, he thought.

What was that expression he had heard over and over again about the British when they ruled the island? Something about only mad dogs and Englishmen go out in the noonday sun!

Crazy all right, these white madmen cooking like roast beef in the sun!

Gaston crossed the road to the beachfront. He stopped at the top end, where a clump of withering Casuarina trees was gently swaying in the light afternoon breeze. He surveyed the beach teeming with people until his glazed eyes settled on a pair of brown breasts browning further in the sun. In a more sober moment, the sight of such voluptuous breasts would have seen his shorts swell in lust, but now the alcohol had severely disconnected his carnal desires from his physical ability to respond to such desires. Besides, women displaying their breasts on the beach were so commonplace these days, even the horny young men selling shells were more interested in making money than perving. That wasn't the case when bare breasts first invaded the island's beaches.

Gaston swaggered a little as he resumed walking. He clumsily tried to navigate his way past a family pack of tourists. A drunken swerve turned him on his heels and Gaston suddenly found himself dizzily staring at their backs as they walked away. He had his own back turned to the rotund man heading towards the roadway in a hurry, a towel draped on his hips and his substantial belly swaying from side to side. The man didn't see Gaston, who was shielded by one of the trees, and collided heavily into him. The man staggered but managed to stay upright. He looked like a freshly boiled crab clamouring to escape a pot of boiling water as his arms flayed about, trying to regain his balance. You could almost see the heat radiating off his flesh, like the undulating heat waves rising off a desert road in the noonday sun. The man's bright pink face was quickly turning red with anger.

"Hey, watch where you're going, you drunken bastard!" the crab man yelled as he pushed Gaston out of his way and brusquely resumed his hasty waddle across the road and up the main street.

Gaston unsteadily walked across the top edge of the beach where it wasn't so populated but suddenly stopped as if the soft, warm sand had set like cement, seizing and trapping his bare feet. He looked out towards the ocean, struggling to keep his eyes open. He could still only manage to squint under the glare of the afternoon sun. He ran his hand through the shock of curly jet-black hair, which had been allowed to grow out of control since the bottle became his master a month or so ago. Seeing his beloved Natalie locking lips with the village "bad boy" had been the final straw.

A tear escaped his eye but was immediately absorbed by the thick black beard, which had grown in harmony with his hair and now covered his face, chin, and neck. A classic Roman nose protruded prominently from the facial hair and provided testimony to the European side of his heritage. Underneath all the hair lurked a handsome, young twenty-five-year-old man with light chocolate skin and large, dark brown (verging on black) eyes, which had been permanently bloodshot from the mix of tears and daily bouts with the demon drink in the past month.

A surprise smile broke through the sadness as a beach volleyball game caught Gaston's eye.

Ahh, those were the days! he thought. *The friends, the beach parties, and of course . . . the volleyball games.*

But the truth was that happy moments were few and far between for Gaston during the holiday beach volleyball games of his childhood. When sides were picked for the game, nobody really wanted Gaston on either side despite him being a competent player. He only got to play when one side was desperately short on numbers, and that usually meant when one of the white kids didn't turn up even though they were all ethnically defined as Creoles—a mongrel mix of European white with varying shades of African and Indian brown to black.

Despite the eviction of colonial rule several decades ago, the apartheid culture it had engendered remained entrenched in the island's social psyche and continued to legitimise racism even within families whose gene pool had been thoroughly shaken and stirred over the years, sometimes through illegitimate liaisons and the odd rape, throwing up both white and black children at random to the same set of parents.

It was no coincidence that many of the black people among the Creole clans were often withdrawn and shy, and some bore terrible psychological scars that made them social outcasts throughout their lives.

Gaston's family was a classic example: five children ranging in skin colour from black to white. His light chocolate skin tone placed him and his sister Rita below the white kids in the social pecking order but spared them from the greater social struggles of the darker folk. At the opposite ends of the family's skin tone spectrum, his blue-eyed, white sister, Mathilde, flourished while his black brothers, Bruno and

Mario, floundered. This was a scenario repeated in countless households among the Creole population.

Bruno and Mario were two years apart in age and rarely ever went out of the house—let alone to the beach on holidays—and languished in all aspects of their lives. Theirs was a life of monotonous regularity and, worse still, no one seemed to notice or care, even Mario and Bruno themselves.

As they grew up, they became reclusive, naturally developing personas and personalities befitting their black skin. By the time they hit their teenage years, they were painfully shy and timid in every aspect of their lives, which had become one of rigid routine whereby they lived each second of every minute of every hour of every day in almost exactly the same way as they did the week before.

Every morning, Mario got up at 6:30 a.m. precisely, Bruno at 6:45 a.m. on the dot. Every weekend, they had chores to do. Bruno was charged with watering the garden at 7:30 a.m. every Saturday and he fulfilled this duty with relish. Even the regular cyclones which pounded the island with torrential rain and severe wind gusts would be no impediment to Bruno's devotion to domestic duty. As one such cyclone lashed the island one Saturday morning in February, Bruno's white-skinned sister, Mathilde, looked on in disbelief as Bruno put on his raincoat, including hat and galoshes, and walked out into the yard, struggling valiantly against the cyclonic gusts of wind, which literally blew him onto his backside several times. It was a scene reminiscent of a Keystone Cops movie.

Oblivious to the laughter of his sister witnessing his folly through the window, Bruno eventually managed to unwrap the hose and turn the water on, only to have the first spray from the hose blown straight back onto him.

Mario's main weekend chore was to clean the bathroom and adjoining toilet, which were separated by a very flimsy wooden wall akin to a public toilet cubicle partition that had been clumsily erected to give the toilet-goer a largely false sense of privacy.

Mario cleaned both areas religiously, starting with the toilet at 7:47 a.m. and finishing with the bathroom at 8:07 a.m. precisely, regardless of whether he still had areas left to clean. Unfortunately, one Sunday morning, Mario's aunty from South Africa experienced an uncontrollable urge to defecate at 7:45 a.m. She had arrived only the night before for a short visit and was unaware of Mario's "devotion" to household duty. As locks were a luxury in the homes of the island's poorer families, Mario simply barged into the toilet just as the aunt settled into position.

Seemingly undeterred, he casually closed the door and headed into the bathroom, annoyed that his routine had been disturbed. Nevertheless, he carried on cleaning the bathroom, oblivious to a plump middle-aged woman straddling the squat toilet and evacuating her bowels within earshot. The aunt was speechless but hostage to her bowel motion. All she could manage was to finish as quickly as possible before fleeing back to her bedroom, certain that the chronic irritable bowel syndrome, which had wreaked havoc with her health regularly since she was a girl, had returned with a vengeance.

For Mario, however, the incident sparked a rare change of routine as from that day on he cleaned the bathroom before cleaning the toilet.

More tragically for two healthy, fit-but-black youngsters, Mario and Bruno never went on holidays to the beach with Gaston and their fairer-skinned siblings.

Even though Gaston was of a fairer skin hue than his black brothers, his brown skin was enough to make him an outcast in a group of the mainly white folk who invaded the beaches during school holidays. Most of the time during the volleyball matches of his childhood, Gaston cut a lonely figure in the background, by the sea's edge, passing the time trying to make seashells skip and dance on the sea surface. Or, he'd sit on the beach and stare out to the reef and dream of venturing beyond to the places he'd read about in *Tintin* comic books—Tibet, the land of the Incas, Sydney, the moon even.

But the beach holidays of his middle teenage years proved more constructive after Gaston befriended a young, white South African man who taught him how to swim. He was no longer disappointed when rejected by his volleyball mates. In fact, a broad smile spread across his face each time he wasn't picked for the team and he immediately scurried away to find his swimming friend. Gaston quickly became a very strong swimmer, and more importantly, his first-ever friendship with a white man improved his general confidence. But that was a long time ago.

Images of those beach holidays persisted as if a cinema projector was reeling the memories through his mind. He watched the swell rise with the wind on the reef and he recalled another favourite beach-holiday activity. But this time, nostalgia coincided much more with reality. In the mornings, the older children would gather on the beach at the water's edge, each on an errand to get dinner, waiting for the fishermen to come in with their daily catch of fish, lobsters, and crabs still alive and dancing in the baskets.

These days, only frozen fisheyes stared at Gaston when he went into the corner store. Occasionally, he would see a fisherman trying to sell supposedly fresh fish from a makeshift stall by the beach. The fisheyes were dull and not one fly hovered around the fish, a tell-tale sign that the fish was not fresh. Lobsters, crabs, and other prized seafood were just a distant memory for the local folk. Yet, as he now looked at the huge waves crashing on the reef, he remembered the crabs, big ones clamouring to escape the even bigger pot of boiling water on his mother's stove. He could almost hear the moribund sound of their death throes as they succumbed to the inevitable.

A warm feeling invaded his stomach; the rum flooding his bladder created an incredible urge to urinate. He quickly headed to another cluster of Casuarinas bordering a popular picnic spot and the main road. He unzipped his fly and let his bladder contents go free. He was oblivious to the gendarme riding his bicycle on the road past the tree just as a spray of urine was caught in the strong gust of wind. Gaston caught the eye of the gendarme at the very moment that the gendarme caught a fine mist of urine over his eyes, causing him to veer off the roadway. The bicycle came to an abrupt halt as the front tyre wedged into the soft sand. Miraculously, the gendarme managed to stay in the saddle, but not for long. He dismounted, threw the bike on the ground, and confronted Gaston while wiping his face with a large, white handkerchief.

"What the hell do you think you're doing?" he hollered.

A few beachgoers, attracted by the commotion, had gathered around the scene, all eyes fixed on the pathetic figure of Gaston Le Clezio—or rather his groin region. Droplets of urine glistened on the end of his flaccid, uncircumcised penis that drooped from an open fly.

"Can you flop it back in, you cretin?" the gendarme said as he slapped Gaston hard on the back of the head.

"Hey, watch it; that hurt," said a startled Gaston.

Jolted into some semblance of sobriety by the blow, Gaston clumsily tucked his penis back into his pants and kept his coloured head bowed in embarrassment. If he had been white, his face would have been glowing as red as some of the sunburnt faces now staring at him.

"All right, folks, there's nothing to see here," the gendarme said to the crowd as he dispersed them, flailing his arms around as if he was directing traffic at the island's main roundabout.

The gendarme grabbed Gaston brusquely by the arm and began to usher him away when he suddenly realised he had left his bike behind. As he let go of the arm to retrieve his bike, Gaston thought of making a run for it. However, his alcohol-infused brain was too slow to translate the thought into action and the opportunity quickly vanished. The gendarme resumed an iron-like grip on Gaston's arm while guiding the bike with the other. Gaston's head remained bowed as he was escorted along the main road to the local police station. Along the way, they came across another gendarme on foot patrol.

"Hey, what have you got there, Winston?" the second gendarme said.

"Some drunken jerk who thought the public beach was a great place to flaunt his brown dick. The filthy bugger, pissing in full view of all those lovely, innocent white ladies," Winston said mockingly while making a shape of voluptuous breasts with his hands.

"Seriously, the idiot even managed to piss in my face. I think he needs a night of our 'hospitality' to teach him some manners. By the way, is that Australian troublemaker still in the lock-up?"

"He sure is," said the second gendarme.

"Well, we're going to have two filthy buggers in the lock-up tonight: one who fucks prostitutes in a picnic area, another who pisses on a public beach. No respect, these fucking clowns. It's typical of foreigners like that Australian fellow, but this boy—one of our own—he should know better."

He turned to Gaston. "You . . . you should be ashamed of yourself," Winston droned on as he gave Gaston another whack on the back of the head.

Gaston was feeling more sober by now but he wished he wasn't. He began to feel pain in his arm where the gendarme maintained a grip. He also wanted to throw up. And throw up, he did. He doubled over and vomited, the edge of a curry-tinged pool of bile splashing against Winston's shoe. For a brief, blissful moment, he felt much better—nausea gone—like the orgasmic feeling when one emerged triumphant following a period of prolonged tension.

But yet another whack across the back of the head brought him back to reality with a thud as his face fell heavily into the vomit pool. The two gendarmes started laughing.

"Hey, Winston, we're going to have to hose him down now and douse him in eau de cologne. Then again, the Australian may like the smell of vomit—probably make him feel right at home."

Gaston felt his body suddenly being lifted up. Two strong gendarme hands had converged on his collar and raised him to his feet. Not quite technicolour, but his face was splattered with bits of green, orange, and dark brown vomit residue.

"Boy, he sure does stink," said Winston. "I better get him back to the station. See you later, Mathieu."

"If you need any help teaching these guys some manners, just give me a call. I'm going off duty but I'm always willing to give up my spare time to educate scum."

As Mathieu departed, Winston reached into the big lunch basket, which straddled his bike, and took out a water bottle. He roughly emptied its contents on Gaston's face, the chill of the water making Gaston jump back onto the road as a car whizzed past, horn blaring and almost running him over.

The vomit cleaned from Gaston's face, Winston again gripped Gaston's arm and dragged him another 500 metres past the fishing boats and to the edge of Finger Bay village.

CHAPTER III

Cailason

The drab, box-shaped police station had seen better days but in mid-summer, it still looked third world, postcard-picture-perfect, flanked by a magnificent flame tree in full bloom. As Constable Winston Duthilde opened the heavy wooden door of the police station, the vibration caused by a sticky door suddenly being unstuck combined with an easterly wind gust to loosen some of the tree's red blossoms, showering them on the pair as they walked in.

"Yo, Cailason, how's it going?" Winston said, feeling inexplicably cheerful at the sight of his old friend and duty sergeant; so cheerful, in fact, he momentarily forgot he had a prisoner.

"Who you got there?" asked Sergeant Cailason. "Isn't that one of Harriet's boys?"

Despite fast approaching his milestone sixty-fifth birthday, Cailason continued to be an intimidating figure when dressed immaculately in standard police uniform, as he was today. The tall, toned, and muscular body of his younger boxing days had been swamped by generous layers of fat, particularly around the gut area—the inevitable result of a high alcohol intake and lack of exercise in recent years. Yet, he still posed an ominous threat to the likes of Gaston and commanded great respect from Winston and his fellow gendarmes. The vestiges of his handsome facial features, the deep-set large, brown eyes, long eyelashes, prominent cheekbones, thick eyebrows, swarthy Latin complexion, and, like Gaston's, the classic Roman nose, were still evident despite the sagging jowls.

The young Cailason had indeed been very handsome, and his position of power as a police officer added to his sex appeal. During his early adult years, he counted many sexual conquests, even among the higher-class white women. But while they were happy to have sex with him, none of the white women he slept with ever contemplated a deeper, more meaningful relationship. As for marriage, that was socially simply out of the question.

Cailason was one of the island's dying breeds; as close as you could get to a native of the island, his family lines dated back to the colony's founding fathers in the early eighteenth century. And he used to know the family connections, liaisons, scandals, relationships, and inter-relationships of every islander since then. That is, who married whom; who fathered and mothered which child, both legitimate and illegitimate; who's had an affair with whom; who's a closet homosexual or lesbian; the sins of the uncle or auntie always talked about in grave, hushed tones; and even the circumstances of every birth and death.

However, the island's social and economic revolution sparked by independence more than thirty years ago had changed all that. No longer tied to the apron strings of its colonial mistress, the island nation had to change to simply survive. The island "village" had enthusiastically joined in the globalisation agenda. The resulting influx of foreigners had led to family liaisons and relationships never seen before (and still resented) by the likes of Cailason: white folks marrying black girls and Chinese girls marrying white and black boys. Racially mixed marriages were still an abhorrent phenomenon to Cailason and other members of his social ilk, and the generation that still clung to the ideas and ideals of an apartheid class structure.

Cailason lamented the direction in which his life, and society in general, was moving since the end of the colonial era.

"Progress, my arse," he'd often say.

Life, for the likes of Cailason, was so much easier to navigate when the British ruled and everyone knew their place in the social pecking order by the colour of their skin. Nowadays, Cailason found himself struggling to work out who among the island's new interracial mix was from a better or lesser class, much to his frustration. Many of the island's traditional social structures were slowly being dismantled and family lines were beginning to blur beyond recognition.

"It's nothing but pollution of the bloodlines," he still cried out at every opportunity.

When his thoughts drifted to this—as they often did—Cailason would always end up with the words of his elderly mother, Chlotilde, ringing in his ears:

You'll burn in hell if you ever marry a Chinese girl; they're not like us!

The ethnic Chinese continued to occupy the bottom rung of the island's social ladder, despite many among them having risen to loftier heights on the island's economic ladder. Like Chinese migrants in other parts of the world, they dominated the island's retail trade and, as a result, many among them were earning a very good income. And they boosted their bank balance substantially whenever islanders, who had managed to escape to a more affluent life overseas, returned to visit family. The cost of goods in Chinese-run shops for them was always three or four times more than for the loyal locals.

Most islanders hadn't had the means to flee the troubled times which gripped the island following independence. The ones who could afford and did leave were branded "traitors" who had abandoned the island nation in its hour of need. As a result, they were viewed with contempt by those who had remained and battled through much economic hardship to forge a nation, which, courtesy of a tourism boom, was now punching above its weight in terms of economic growth.

The island government, too, believed the traitors deserved to be ripped off by the Chinese shopkeepers and simply turned a blind eye to the practice and ignored the many complaints lodged by them.

Cailason's family had never accepted the ethnic Chinese islanders as social equals despite the growing wealth of the Chinese community. Hence, Chlotilde was puzzled when one day, she noticed the Chinese couple who ran the local shop was sitting in the middle pews of the church at the popular ten o'clock mass on Sunday morning.

Chlotilde was a devout Catholic and her life philosophy had been heavily influenced by the teachings of the local Catholic priests, who were all still ethnic white Europeans from France, Ireland, or Britain. And contrary to the Christian ethos, they extolled the virtues of a society strangled in an apartheid straight jacket. From the pulpit every Sunday, they would passionately deliver sermons espousing their warped, racially segregated perspective of Christianity, which was swallowed hook, line, and sinker by the flock of faithful. And the seating arrangements for Sunday morning mass mirrored their enthusiasm for social segregation along racial lines.

Every Sunday, the lambs of Christ from Finger Bay parish would sit in exactly the same spot in exactly the same church pew. And even though human beings were creatures of habit, the church seating habits were no coincidence. Each place on the church pew was determined by the parishioner's capacity to pay, and naturally their capacity to pay was largely determined by skin colour.

Church pews were effectively up for sale and the economically dominant white population naturally were the ones who could afford to contribute the most to the church coffers. However, the increasing wealth of Chinese shopkeepers and traders proved to be a dilemma for the priests. Many Chinese parishioners could now afford generous donations. They were whiter than black but they *"did still look different"*, which made them socially less than white in the view of the priests.

After several meetings, the priests finally arrived at a solution. They simply lied about the donations of the white parishioners when talking to potential Chinese church-going donors. No matter how much a Chinese donor offered, they would be told it wasn't enough to make it past the middle row of pews. This left the Chinese parishioners bemused, particularly the many who now lived in bigger homes and drove more luxurious cars.

For the black members of the congregation, it was standing room only and perhaps the last two rows, if they arrived early enough. As a result, panning from the front to the back of the church at the most popular mass on a Sunday would reveal a gradual, uniform change in the skin colour of the congregation; from white to light and dark chocolate brown, to black with a hint of Chinese—whatever colour they were—in the middle. Cailason's family, being mainly cast in the chocolate brown mould, had never made it past the tenth row from the back in a church that had thirty-seven rows of pews. In the early years of family life, Cailason's mother, Chlotilde, and her husband had found themselves with the black people in the last couple of rows or standing.

Chlotilde never questioned the practices and teachings of the local priests. She was intellectually incapable of doing so. She had had little formal education, as was the case with most women in the colonial times of the mid-twentieth century. She was married at fourteen to Norbert—a much older conservative man—and pregnant for most of the next twenty-five years as she stoically fulfilled her Catholic duty to deliver thirteen children. Her husband, too, never rocked the parish boat because he essentially concurred with the apartheid ethos of the priests.

As husband and wife, Norbert and Chlotilde naturally fell into the traditional roles that were demanded of their era, their religion, and the island's conservative patriarchal society. He was the breadwinner and worked long hours at the local sugar mill five and half days a week. She took care of the house, cooking, cleaning, and looking after the children. In fact, Norbert paid little attention to the children, going off to work in the early hours of the morning before any of them were awake, then eating alone as soon as he got home at 6:00 p.m. While the children had their dinner, he would sit on the porch reading the daily newspaper before retiring to bed promptly at 8:30 p.m. He only ever interacted with the children when they dutifully paraded past him, in line from youngest to oldest, to kiss him goodnight before he went to bed.

This ritual of the children kissing their father goodnight mirrored the passionless manner of their conception. The strong Catholic faith of both Chlotilde and Norbert condemned them to a sex life aimed strictly at procreation. And although they had thirteen children, they would have had sex only some forty times during their twenty-five years of marriage. And those rare sexual interludes were purely perfunctory: always performed in the dead of night, with the lights off, in the missionary position, with Norbert always ejaculating within fifteen pelvic thrusts. Once conception was confirmed, sex was strictly off the agenda. Chlotilde firmly believed that having sex with a child in the womb would harm the child, and besides, one of the local priests had once told her that she would burn in Hell if she ever contemplated having sex for pleasure. And as her brood grew up to be passionate, God-fearing Catholic stock who loved the church as much as she did, Chlotilde was convinced beyond doubt that the local priests were the earthly agents of the good Lord himself.

Like many island folk, Cailason always maintained the façade of being a good Catholic man even though he habitually strayed into the realm of mortal sin, which, according to Catholic doctrine, would condemn him to the flames of Hell for all eternity. Cailason was convinced that his sins could be absolved and his path to Heaven guaranteed simply by contributing generously to his family's household donation to the church. Even after he was married, he continued to contribute to his mother's household budget, thinking this would earn him extra brownie points with God and further secure his passage to Heaven, despite his ongoing religious misdemeanours. And as he progressed through the police ranks, Cailason could afford to contribute more to his mother's household budget than any other family member thereby helping his mother progress through the church-pew pecking order.

Chlotilde considered it a priority to spend as much of the household budget as possible on her church, a priority well above improving the meagre stock of food she had each week to feed her family. After all, she rationalised, her husband and children always had three meals a day, albeit always lacking variety and almost always insufficient in quantity. The family's diet, week in, week out, consisted of bread and occasionally butter for breakfast, the same for lunch with some homemade jam occasionally for the children and for dinner, rice, a vegetable or two, occasionally eggs from the hens in the backyard, and a small quantity of meat on Sunday, usually chicken, which she had to slaughter herself from the backyard stock. (However, killing too many chickens would mean fewer eggs so she had to keep the balance right there.)

As for herself, she was content with the one meal a day the budget permitted and that varied depending on how much rice was left. There were rarely any vegetables or Sunday meat left for Chlotilde and most of her dinners simply consisted of a small portion of rice that she stirred in the leftover oil from the vegetables and/or meat and one hot chili from one of the many chili bushes in the backyard. Very rarely, she would fry an egg but after consuming it, she would immediately feel guilty for depriving the rest of the family of the egg. Her meals, she thought, were totally in keeping with her Catholic duty to suffer through her earthly existence in order to reserve her place in Heaven.

CHAPTER IV

A Pathological Hatred of Drug Addicts

"Harriet who?" said Winston.

Pondering the pathetic figure of Gaston Le Clezio standing in front of him now, Cailason felt sorry for his poor mother, Harriet. Like his own mother, Harriet Le Clezio was a devout Catholic. Cailason was sure of that. Not only did Harriet attend mass every Sunday since he could remember, but any time he glanced at her during the sermons, she was mesmerised, hanging on to every word uttered from the pulpit. Being of the same light chocolate skin hue, Harriet and her family occupied roughly the same patch of pews each Sunday.

"Harriet Le Clezio," replied Cailason. "You know, the lady who's always smartly dressed and very chatty. She's got five children—three of them boys—all still living at home. She's always whinging about it but when her eldest—Gaston, the one now standing before your very eyes, my friend—when he left home for a while to live with his girlfriend, she was grief-stricken and, of course, blamed the girlfriend for turning her supposedly innocent son into a depraved sinner.

"She prayed day and night for the good Lord to pardon his sins. She was so scared that he would burn in Hell.

"When Gaston broke up with the girlfriend, he had no option but to move back into the family home and as soon as he walked in, she dragged him straight to the church for confession. I ran into Mrs. Le Clezio the other day and she told me all about it. She said she'd forgiven Gaston, but he wasn't handling the breakup very well and may even be getting into drugs," Cailason said.

Cailason had a pathological hatred of drug addicts, yet he consumed some four bottles of the local rum a week and, as a treat, a bottle of whisky every weekend. Whenever he arrested anyone for drug offences, Cailason would always employ more force than necessary; the amount of force related directly to how hard or soft the drugs were popularly considered. This meant that those whom he arrested for marijuana would be thrown in jail with a few lumps on the head or body. The ones hooked on heroin would often end up with more serious injuries: broken arms, ribs, legs, and once even a fractured skull, which was, in Cailason's mind, one of his finest moments. He'd arrested a homeless young man on Finger Bay beach who was high on heroin and as usual threw him in the slammer after several whacks with his regulation police baton.

Cailason had been feeling naturally high himself that day. His promotion had just come through, so he showed the drug addict some mercy and the lad's punishment was humane by Cailason's standards. Nothing broken, just a few bruises to match the heavy needle-mark bruises on the young man's inner elbow joint. The next day, no one had inquired about the prisoner so Cailason left him in jail until the evening, when the man began experiencing severe withdrawal symptoms. His distress prompted howls of laughter from Cailason, particularly when the man started hitting his head against the back wall. Fortunately for him, a fellow officer came back from the beat in the nick of time and persuaded Cailason to intervene, but not before the man had fractured his skull. A few minutes more and he would surely have been dead. Cailason was still smirking when the ambulance turned up to take the young man to hospital.

While his treatment of drug addicts induced much mirth and merriment, Cailason found his personal crusade to save his teenage grandchildren from the temptation of drugs not so amusing.

Following the breakup of his thirty-year marriage, Cailason's only daughter, Nicole felt it was her duty to allow him to live with her and her teenage daughters, Sophie and Isabelle. Her husband had flown the family coop a few years earlier after falling in love with his ethnic Chinese secretary, who was barely a teenager and some fifteen years younger than he was. The affair proved so scandalous for the couple that they fled to Europe and severed all contact with island family and friends.

Cailason, as he always did, was listening in one day when seventeen-year-old Isabelle asked her mother for permission to go to the local nightclub with her boyfriend.

"You may as well put her on the pill and give her some drugs to share with her friends!" he screamed.

Nicole blushed but refused to take the bait and get involved in yet another argument about her daughters' social lives.

Cailason believed nightclubs were a haven for drug and sex fiends who preyed on young Creole girls and corrupted them into their evil ways.

But like so many of his misogynistic generation, he was blind to his own hypocrisy. As a young lad, he and his friends would get smashed on the cheap local rum before preying on the local girls, each mate trying to outdo the others in the number of sexual conquests he achieved. The Indian girls were considered sluts and exploited at every opportunity to satisfy their rampant sexual urges. And because of their lowly position in the island's quasi-apartheid social structure, most of the girls didn't complain. Some even saw fraternising with the socially superior Creole boys as a possible passport out of their own miserable lives. Like all testosterone-fuelled boys, Cailason gave little thought to the mother waiting at home for her daughter as he had or tried to have sex with girl after girl after girl in all sorts of weird and distinctly unromantic places, including once in his home garbage pile, which, in his drunken stupor, he mistook for a bed of hay.

On that occasion, he was so engorged with alcohol that he could only muster a half-erect penis that ejaculated before he could get his trousers down. Sperm trickled down his leg, and a small rat who had found his way up his trouser leg copped a load of sperm on the head for its efforts. Cailason's poor female victim could only watch in stony silence for a long time before shame and embarrassment suddenly overwhelmed her and caused her to rush away—crying hysterically.

CHAPTER V

A Musing on Tans

The entire time Cailason and Winston were talking, Gaston's head was bowed. He felt ashamed, the deep shame that regularly overwhelmed him in the transition from drunk to semi-sober. And as usual, his thoughts turned to his mother.

Harriet had been a gentle soul who never smacked her children until alcohol besieged her family life, took her husband Gaetan hostage, and condemned the rest of the family to live on tenterhooks, not knowing when his next alcohol-fuelled rage would erupt.

In their early years of marriage, Harriet and Gaetan were considered the ideal couple, very much in love and openly displaying the affection and passion that saw them produce five healthy offspring. And even though some of their family and friends (in hushed tones) lamented the fact that two of their offspring were black, family life for the Le Clezio family was as idyllic as it could be for a working-class island family; that is, until the day Gaetan, a maintenance worker at the local sugar factory, made a tragic mistake at work. He absent-mindedly left a valve open on an industrial pipe that conveyed boiling molasses to the machine where the molasses was spun off and the sugar retained. His work colleague, thinking Gaetan had done his duty and switched off the valve so he could safely carry out maintenance work, was swept into a vat and drowned in the molasses.

Gaetan never stopped blaming himself for his colleague's death, and despite many months of counselling and regular doses of anti-depressants, he was inconsolable. And one dark April day, Harriet found Gaetan comatose in the lounge room, an empty rum bottle and an equally empty packet of sleeping pills nearby.

Harriet was naturally devastated by Gaetan's death and when anger followed the grief, she started taking it out on the children, smacking them whenever she lost her temper.

The adult Gaston still feared the fury of his mother's hand slapping his cheek whenever he got himself pickled or in a pickle. The same cheek that the maid,

Saganthi, used to smother in talcum powder every morning before he went to school while calling out to his mother, Harriet, "Hey ma'am, this one's a bit too dark; we'll have to make him a bit lighter."

He'd often end up walking to school, oblivious to the fact that he looked like a clown. In summer, it wasn't so bad because Gaston would sweat profusely and as he wiped the sweat off his face, the powder would vanish with the sweat into his handkerchief. The milder winter, though, would often find Gaston arriving at school with powder still intact.

Gaston was by no means black. He had the same light chocolate skin tone that was a source of admiration among sun-baked tourists.

What did the foreigners call it? . . . A tan, that's it, a tan.

As a boy, Gaston used to think a lot about tans and why locals who also had tans—and natural ones at that—were not admired in the same way. As a teenager, Gaston discovered that foreigners often ridiculed locals because of their dark skin, that is, their permanent "tans". This only confused him further. In fact, tans still confused Gaston.

It seemed logical to him that a natural tan had to be better than an unnatural tan that compelled white foreigners to spend hours baking and sweating under the unrelenting sub-tropical sun. Gaston could only spend five minutes in the sun before he started feeling like his body was about to explode. When he asked his white mother about this, she'd just say, "It is as it is!"

Back at the Finger Bay police station, his head still bowed, Gaston once again found himself musing on tans. But not for long. He raised his head only to be met by Cailason's intimidating gaze.

"I'm so sorr—" he began to say.

But he didn't get to finish an apology. Annoyed that his conversation with Winston had been interrupted, Sergeant Cailason silently lifted his finger to his lips, the loud menace in his face enough to instantly silence Gaston.

"Now, as I was saying, Harriet was telling me that Gaston used to be a very happy, talkative kid, but in the last month, he's gone really quiet and she was sure he was getting into drugs," Cailason said.

"She asked me to look out for him, but I haven't seen him for a while until now. So, what's he done?"

Winston outlined the morning's events to Cailason, who kept nodding his head while reflecting on the narrative but never looking directly at Winston. When Winston had finished, Cailason instinctively took hold of Gaston's arms to check for puncture marks on the veins. He seemed relieved when he found none. He would be able to tell Harriet that Gaston, although he'd been a naughty boy for pissing in a public place, at least he was no drug addict. A little overindulgence on rum now and then was nothing to really worry about, although as he pondered this, his thoughts turned to Harriet's tragic loss of her husband.

CHAPTER VI

Planet Utopia

During their mid high school years, Gaston and Patrick became inseparable, spending much of their after-school leisure time together, jogging. Gaston would meet Patrick at the bridge near the bus depot that was roughly halfway between their respective homes. From there, their usual jogging route took them past their school and the local Catholic church, on their way to the local football grounds next to the former army barracks, which military folk from the colonial powers once called home. Since the island gained independence from its British colonial masters, however, the barracks locally known as Casuarina (because of the magnificent casuarina trees which graced the once luscious, landscaped gardens) had been sold off as cheap communal housing and were now a haven for drug addicts and assorted thugs. The dying casuarinas looked on in despair while the thick layer of mulch which once encircled the base of their trunks at the height of the colonial occupation was being replaced by an equally thick layer of bloodstained needles, vomit, used condoms, and assorted garbage thrown recklessly by the hapless population who now lived in equally hapless circumstances.

In winter, it would often be dark by the time Gaston and Patrick arrived at the Casuarina sportsground. If Gaston's mother, Harriet, knew the sixteen-year-old boys were loitering there after dark, she would have had a heart attack. But being full of youthful bravado, they never felt threatened when they stopped to catch their breath, share a laugh, indulge in school gossip, or sometimes discuss more serious issues as they lay on the grass staring at the star-filled sky. And away from the relatively bright lights of the village, they literally were overwhelmed by the stars in their eyes.

"How many stars are up there, you reckon?" Patrick said to Gaston one evening.

"Someone on the radio said there are more stars in the sky than all the grains of sand on all the beaches of the world," Gaston replied.

"Get out of it," Patrick said incredulously. "That can't be right. Have you ever tried counting grains of sand when you're at the beach? I do sometimes when I'm bored. I plunge my hand in some wet sand and try to count each grain. It's impossible. Wow. I just can't get my head around that, Gaston. There'd be billions and billions and billions of stars."

"Makes you feel kind of insignificant, doesn't it?" said Gaston. "I wonder if David Beckham ever looks at the stars like we do."

"Huh! What's David Beckham got to do with us looking at the stars, Gaston?"

"Oh, sorry, my friend, looking at stars like this always makes me think of aliens—" Gaston started to explain.

Patrick, even more puzzled, interrupted with a laugh in his voice: "So that explains it! David Beckham is an alien. That's why he's such a freak on the football field!"

"No, no, it's not that. I know you're joking but please bear with me," Gaston continued in a cheerful tone.

"Given there's a gazillion stars and even more planets, there *must* be aliens out there. Now imagine if they're aliens just like us, but—unlike us—they live a perfect life on a perfect planet. Let's call it Planet Utopia, where everyone is truly equal. They all have enough to eat, a place to live, no wars, no misery, etcetera, etcetera. Now, these aliens from Planet Utopia also have super brains and they make a spaceship to explore the universe. First stop, our earth?

"The Planet Utopia aliens have no idea how we organise our lives so when they get here, what would they think of us and the way we humans live, Patrick?"

"Hmmm . . . I'm not sure. But is this where Beckham comes into it? I get it. They see him play football and see what a genius he is," Patrick said excitedly, sure he'd solved the puzzle.

"Ahh, that's precisely the problem," asserted Gaston.

"Uhh! I don't get it, Gaston!" Patrick said, once again perplexed.

"Well, Beckham's *not* a genius! But like you did just now, lots of people call him a genius. What he really is, is an example of some of the things we do on earth that the Planet Utopia aliens would think is absurd! Look, you know I love football and think players like Beckham have great skills, but he's no genius. What does Beckham contribute to society besides entertainment and stinky perfume? Nothing. Nada. People who actually solve big problems in the world like doctors, scientists, inventors—they're the geniuses.

"Worse still, we make the stupid decision to pay Beckham, and others like him, obscene amounts of money. And for what? His skills at playing a game! Playing a friggin' game! The rest of us are told that we need to work hard to make money, not play a game.

"Yet, if, God forbid, people who actually make a real difference to society, the real geniuses, ask for a pay rise, we call them 'greedy.' It just doesn't make sense."

"You have a point, Gaston. But that's just the way it is . . . isn't it?" asked a bemused Patrick.

"*No, no*, that's the way it is because we just accept that it's the way it is. We don't question anything anymore. We think it's normal for Beckham to make obscene amounts of money. And for what? Not for saving lives. Not for making the world a better place! Not for coming up with new medicines. But for kicking a ball around the park.

"We have the intelligence to change this and make our world more like Planet Utopia but we don't. We've come to accept these things as natural that really aren't natural at all but the result of our choices and stupid decisions."

"So, what can we do about it? You'll never change the world."

"I know. I know it's difficult. But not impossible. We can make the world better by doing very simple things. For example, what if we simply decided to start paying everyone the same and maybe a bit more—but just a bit more—to people who really make a difference to society and our quality of life, like doctors and nurses; surely, we'd have a better world. That's what the aliens from Planet Utopia probably did to create their perfect world. I could go on—"

"I'm sure you could go on . . ."

Despite his tender young years, Gaston Le Clezio had already developed an astute but perhaps naïve sense of the way the world functioned and "dysfunctioned". He had a ferocious appetite for books, especially the *Tintin* comics, which led him to continuously question the way humans organised society.

Why, for instance, did the government spend lots of money on guns for the army when many people on the island lived in abject poverty? Why were "entertainers" like Beckham considered heroes?

Gaston admired their skills but heroes, they weren't.

Now Tintin, he was a true hero, thought Gaston. *He risked his life to fight evil criminals and sometimes saved people's lives. When was the last time a football player saved a life?*

Since Tintin introduced him to a big wide world of stories, Gaston had devoured the written word, whether in books, newspapers, or magazines. And when he wasn't reading, he was listening to the news and current affairs programs on his tiny portable transistor radio, which his uncle from England had given him for his tenth birthday. Six years later, that radio still worked, even though it was covered in paint stains and ingrained dirt, a testament to its use whenever Gaston was charged with doing some painting and other chores around the house and garden. But despite all the stories, news, and information that painted a grim picture of the world and very little hope of redemption for humankind, Gaston remained an idealist.

His outwardly quiet persona also masked a strong sense of self and contentment with his place within that world. Gaston was able to defer to the big picture when considering his own seemingly poor life circumstance. He knew fully well that he could have little to no influence on that big picture until he found a way out of the day-to-day drudgery of life in a working-class family, eking out a meagre existence on an isolated Indian Ocean island. But while his belly was full and he had a roof over his head, he always felt his chance to escape would come and he would change the world. And in Patrick, he had found a true friend and an ally in the hunger for knowledge and the desire for a fairer, better world.

Then, one night, almost two years to the day since they had started jogging together, Patrick had some bad news. Even by Patrick's timid standards, he was unusually quiet and Gaston was quick to notice. And it wasn't long before a tear started rolling down Patrick's surprisingly pale cheek.

"I'm going to live in Australia," Patrick blurted out in between sobs.

CHAPTER VII

Fifi

Nurturing her children's wellbeing and happiness became the mission that liberated Harriet from the chronic grief that consumed her following the death of her husband. But Gaston, her favourite (although she would never publicly admit it), was a source of constant worry. She had no idea of his interest in world affairs and his heartfelt passion for a better world. All Harriet could see was a quiet boy who became chronically quieter as he entered his teenage years, and she started to worry.

One day after his sixteenth birthday, she decided to do something about it and she took him to see Fifi, the local Indian clairvoyant and healer, whose first words upon setting eyes on Gaston was; "This boy knows a lot. Nurture this and he will do great things."

Upon hearing this, Harriet Le Clezio regretted her decision to bring Gaston there, waiting four hours in an overcrowded waiting room to see this woman whose reputation as a clairvoyant was unparalleled on the island.

How could she possibly think that timid Gaston knows a lot? Reputation rubbish—she must finally be going senile, Harriet thought.

Then she remembered the one other time she had been in the presence of Madame Fifi.

Some twenty years earlier, her sister Yvonne had sought Fifi's clairvoyance and Harriet had accompanied her for moral support. Yvonne was hooked on romance picture books and was desperate to know whether she would ever live out her romantic fantasy of meeting and marrying her own prince charming.

At the time, Harriet thought that visit, too, had been a waste of time because Fifi had predicted that her younger sister would marry a distinguished foreigner who would sweep her off her feet and take her away, travelling to exotic places and living a life full of adventure. Upon hearing Fifi's fearless prognostication, Harriet had looked at her sister and thought this clairvoyant was the greatest charlatan she'd ever encountered. After all, at best, Yvonne was plain-looking with a bland personality to match. Besides, her sister had ventured out of the village—to the beach—only once in her twenty years, and that was only after much urging from her mother. Since leaving school some two years before, she had spent her days getting progressively fatter, slouching around the house, reading inane romance novels and picture books, and listening to the radio soapies that had become so popular among the island's housewives and lonely hearts.

Harriet had glared back at Fifi while her fat sister was giggling hysterically. Unable to control herself, Harriet had blurted out sarcastically; "And when is this supposed to happen?" To which Fifi had simply replied; "When you least expect it."

And sure enough, a year later, an American adventurer fresh from a trek through the jungles of Madagascar landed on the island in search of some R & R and happened to venture to the village and happened to run into Yvonne at the local bazaar and happened to fall head over heels in love with her. Within a month, they were married and Yvonne was on her way to America, where she has lived happily ever since while also regularly travelling to exotic places with her American adventurer husband. Just as Fifi had predicted. Six years after their wedding, the happy couple came back to the island for a visit and just like the ugly duckling story, Yvonne had been transformed into a slim, graceful but also worldly and intelligent swan who turned the heads of the honourable island gentlemen wherever she went.

Nevertheless, this time Fifi was surely wrong about Gaston, Harriet thought. What did *he* know a *lot* about? To Harriet, Gaston didn't seem very bright at all. He only got average grades at school and on the rare occasions he opened his mouth at home, he'd say the most stupid things.

One day, Harriet was talking to her sister about the prime minister and his government's plan to raise taxes to rein in an ever-growing budget deficit and prevent economic disaster. Gaston overheard the conversation and responded with; "Why don't they just print more money?" To which Harriet had scoffed; "That's one of the silliest suggestions I've ever heard, Gaston!"

But when Gaston kept pressing for a response, Harriet found she didn't have a logical answer. Money, after all, was deemed to have an intrinsic value or worth that was never questioned, certainly not by the likes of Harriet.

As a teenager, the ever-inquisitive Gaston came to realise that it was sacrilege to think of money purely as printed paper even though, as he had worked out, it only had value through the collective agreement of human beings.

"If I said this shell was valuable and everyone in the world agreed with me, then it would be and I could buy stuff with it. It's the same with the printed paper we call 'money,'" he had said one evening to Patrick as they were walking along the seashore, picking up shells and making them skip on the calm waters of the lagoon.

Gaston lamented the fact that everyone seemed to accept the workings of money and the economy as divine reality. And whenever he tried to question this and another absurd concept he had read about called the "divine rights of kings", he was called a "smartarse".

"So, if the king is like God, why doesn't he eliminate poverty, cure all sick people and live forever?" Gaston asked his mum one day.

Harriet never did answer that question either, again dismissing Gaston as a smartarse. But he found the answer some years later when researching a high school project on the British monarchy. The so-called divine right of kings and queens was simply fiction: for there it was in bold black and white in a history reference book he found in the school library.

"The monarchy was won on bloodshed, not bloodlines!"

It seemed the humans who claimed to be monarchs were simply liars and, worse still, bloodthirsty tyrants. They weren't divine at all but normal people with the most powerful weapons who fought and butchered their way to their alleged divine rule.

That revelation opened up another conundrum for Gaston, and he again turned to his mother for resolution.

"If God is divine and can do anything, why is He (or is it She or It?) so mean and lets so many people suffer so much?"

And once again Harriet had no answer. It didn't occur to her that Gaston's curiosity reflected an above-average intelligence. After all, no one in her family or friendship circle had ever risen to any great intellectual heights.

Fifi took hold of Gaston's hands and cupped them in her own. She closed her eyes and started muttering words that were initially unintelligible to Harriet and Gaston.

"The boy one day will do great things for our island; he'll fight against a great crime and win and become as famous as Tintin," Fifi suddenly barked, startling both Harriet and Gaston.

And twenty years after her first encounter with Fifi, Harriet once again left her clairvoyant parlour profoundly disappointed. She had resigned herself to having a quiet child that would never amount to much, but now Fifi had thrown a spanner in the works with her prediction.

Fifi must be just trying to make me feel better, she thought.

She probably makes the same prediction to all parents about their kids. All parents think they have gifted and talented kids, but surely someone's got to have dumb kids and unfortunately, I've drawn the short straw. She sighed.

Nothing much changed with Gaston and the Le Clezio household over the next few years as Gaston finished school and evolved into a timid adult. He continued achieving average grades and lacked ambition so he decided to get a job, hoping ambition would find him eventually. After an initial struggle, he found work a few days a week at the local Chinese-run shop. Although his mother was initially concerned about his fraternising with Chinese folk, the income he brought in helped her better manage the household budget.

Correspondence from his old friend Patrick had been frequent for the first couple of years after he had moved overseas, then gradually slowed to a trickle and eventually reduced to Christmas cards as Gaston approached his milestone twenty-first birthday. And despite having to interact with customers at the shop, his timid persona lingered. At the same time, he continued to be an avid reader and consumer of current affairs, which prompted him to start writing short stories—philosophical pieces—imagining a simpler, better world, but he never showed them to anyone.

Six months beyond his twenty-fourth birthday, however, the shell that seemed to have suffocated his confidence and personality evaporated almost overnight.

CHAPTER VIII

First Love & Lost

His family was astounded. His mother was even more concerned than she had been about his chronically quiet persona. The change had been so sudden and so radical. But before long, it all became very clear. The trigger that suddenly turned a quiet lad into an emotionally open, chatty, confident young man, but then a year later just as suddenly back into a perpetual drunk cascading towards emotional oblivion, had a name: Natalie.

Harriet was relieved that the source of Gaston's personality transplant wasn't anything too serious. Her immediate diagnosis had been that Gaston was terminally ill and wanted to make the most of what remained of his life. Her relief was short-lived, however. It suddenly dawned on her that Gaston was a young man now who would be snatched away from her by another woman. Of course, she loved Gaston and all her children dearly but found it difficult to physically express that love. Since the tragic suicide of her husband, Harriet had become an emotional introvert who found physical displays of affection difficult, even with her own flesh and blood. She had come to rely on her children to initiate a hug or a cuddle, a duty they naturally fulfilled in pre-teenage years. But as puberty took hold in their teenage years, each child, in turn, just as naturally, withdrew any open displays of affection with their mother. And Gaston, being the eldest, was the first to do so.

Harriet therefore felt pangs of jealousy when she witnessed spontaneous, open displays of affection between Gaston and Natalie. She couldn't remember the last time Gaston had given her a hug. And her misery was complete when Gaston and Natalie decided to live together, a blow only softened by the fact that they settled on an apartment only a few blocks away.

When Natalie dumped Gaston a year later, Harriet was quietly elated but feigned concern and compassion for her heartbroken son, hoping that Gaston would displace some of that sudden void of affection to his sympathetic mother. But her optimism was again short-lived as the misery that enveloped Gaston was as intense as the bliss of Natalie's first kiss. Once again, he fell silent. But this time he also began to drink heavily.

From the highest of highs with Natalie, Gaston now found himself at the lowest of lows: his head bowed, standing in front of two intimidating policemen and still struggling to emerge from a drunken haze but also quickly realising he was in serious trouble. Again, he tried to offer an apology.

"I'm sooo sorry," he spluttered out.

"Keep your fucking mouth shut or I'll sew your fucking lips together," Cailason bellowed. "What's the point of being sorry now, you scumbag? You should have been sorry before you flopped your fucking dick out on the beach."

He turned back to Constable Winston, who still had a firm grip on Gaston's arm.

"Now, where were we?"

"I'm gonna have to go anyway," said Winston. "Gotta get home and cook dinner. You right with this lowlife?"

"What you doing cooking dinner, Winston? You got a missus for that, don't you? Ahh, the good ol' days when women and those fucking Indians knew their place. Men only went into the kitchen when the servant bent their fanny over the stove ready for the ride of their lives and . . .," Cailason said, making a lewd gesture with his hands and hips.

A laughing Winston cut him short.

"Oh, don't give me a hard time. You know times change, faster and faster these days. When was the last time you had that sort of ride in the kitchen?" Winston said, laughing even louder.

"Okay, okay, don't need to make fun of me. Age will catch up with you too one day," Cailason replied light-heartedly.

"But seriously, who would have thought those Indians would be running the country? When I was a kid, they knew their place, you know, in the kitchen, in the laundry, and now and then, a pretty one in the bed," Cailason grumbled. "Now you have to pay them for all that—what a joke!"

Winston nodded. "Couldn't agree more, but what can we do? Listen, my friend, I've really gotta go. You've never seen my wife angry, have you?"

Winston released Gaston's arm, but the pain lingered and he instinctively began rubbing his arm where the constable had held him for what seemed an eternity.

Cailason grabbed a pair of handcuffs and hooked it onto one of Gaston's hands and fastened the other end to a metal railing that ran along the front of the police counter.

"I'd rather not. If she's anything like my ex-missus was, I pity you," said Cailason. "Anyway, I'd better get all the paperwork done for this creep. You know how we like to do everything by the book."

"Yeah, the telephone book," Winston said, looking at Gaston menacingly. Both men then started laughing heartily as Winston began walking away and out the door.

Outside, Winston paused and looked up at the blooming flame tree. He took out his tobacco pouch and started rolling a cigarette. It was a beautiful, sub-tropical day and the flame tree blossoms looked divine, basking in the hues of a bright afternoon sun, the blazing sun being a rare phenomenon on a sub-tropical summer afternoon. Normally at this time of day and year, monsoon clouds would have rolled in and thunderstorms would be lashing the island.

Winston's thoughts drifted back to his youth when, in the summertime, he could virtually set his watch by the onset of the afternoon storms. In recent years though, droughts had been a more regular feature of the island's climate, and some years, the summer's monsoon rains never arrived at all. Winston had heard something about climate change and the threat that it posed to the island's coastal regions, but he didn't really understand what it all meant.

Winston was a poorly educated man. He was only fourteen years old when his father died, and as the eldest boy in the family, he had to leave school to work and help support the family. Thanks to Cailason, he got a job cleaning the jail cells and office at the Finger Bay police station and, from there, eventually forged a career in the police force, but given his lack of education, it was a career that would never rise to great heights.

Winston was the archetypal simple island man at heart, the man with a truly unremarkable life. He had never had to scrap for food like many of his fellow islanders, but he also never questioned his calling in life and his place in the island's social hierarchy. In fact, he considered himself very lucky indeed to have found a secure job that he usually enjoyed and, more importantly, a profession that commanded the respect of the community. Not bad for a man who only had basic literacy skills and who didn't even know the meaning of the word "literate".

Naturally, he owed a great debt of gratitude to Cailason and a conversation with his old friend always put Winston in a good mood. And whenever he felt upbeat, he liked to whistle the tune of his favourite native island song as he did now while rolling his cigarette.

The melody drifted into the station and seeped into Cailason's thoughts, inducing him into a daydream that conjured up images of the local dancers in their flowered frocks seductively shaking their hips for the tourists, drifting into images of the magnificent waterfalls he visited on the neighbouring island the one and only time he'd travelled abroad.

Suddenly, he realised the sound of water falling was actually part of his present reality, and it was coming from the prison cell in the room behind him.

CHAPTER IX

The Power of White

The Australian prisoner was urinating, the stream smacking so hard against the stainless-steel toilet bowl that the noise echoed loudly around the sparsely furnished police station.

As Cailason looked towards the cell, the Australian turned around to face him, laughing, the urine still streaming from his penis and landing on the stone floor of the cell. This made the Australian laugh even harder. When he'd finished, he calmly put his penis back into his pants and zipped them up. He walked to the front of the cell, gripped the bars and defiantly eyeballed Cailason, daring him to take some action.

Cailason rushed towards the cell with a head full of steam and eyes bulging with venom. But as he approached the cell bars, Cailason was stopped dead in his tracks, paralysed like a kangaroo caught in a hunter's spotlight at night in the Australian outback. But in this instance, the spotlight happened to be the glowing white skin of the Australian.

If he had been a dark-skinned local, Cailason would have walked straight into the cell and floored him with one punch. After all, in his youth, Cailason had been the undisputed boxing champion of Finger Bay for five years running, and he had taken out many opponents and the odd lawbreaker with one lethal punch. But none of them had been white. The Australian intimidated him and it had nothing to do with physical strength but everything to do with skin colour. Even though the colonial masters had departed the island more than three decades ago, the power of white skin to intimidate dark skin lingered.

"You can't be serious, you fucking filthy pig," was all Cailason could muster as a feeble vocal response.

He had tried to yell it out but the volume in his voice just didn't match the anger. He could think and even mutter to himself some potentially powerful and even brutal responses to the insolent Australian, but the power dissipated as the thoughts travelled from his brain. And by the time it reached his fists, Cailason simply could not muster the courage to fight back in the face of a white man's arrogance. Such was the power of white skin in a post-colonial outpost where white simply still was might, and Cailason would be long dead before a dark-skinned native ever dared to throw a punch at a white man in anger.

The Australian just laughed—a condescending, half-drunken laugh—before casually sitting on his bunk bed. Stunned by his own inadequate response, Cailason returned to the front counter, cursing and lamenting his powerlessness, and took out his frustration on the milk-chocolate-coloured Gaston.

"I've got a good mind to beat you to a pulp," he yelled, and this time the volume in his voice truly reflected his anger and frustration.

"Your poor mother! If only she knew she had a pathetic excuse for a son who enjoys flopping his big brown dick out on a public beach and spraying his piss on our brave and noble gendarmes.

"Not only have you given me a bad case of indigestion but I've also got to do more fucking paperwork," he continued. "It's lucky for you that you have a good mother who has my respect; otherwise you'd be cleaning up that fucking Australian's piss with your tongue."

Gaston stood cowering, his shoulders drooping farther and farther as each word from Cailason's mouth aroused a more intense fear and loathing of himself and the shame he'd brought to his family. He didn't dare look Cailason in the eye.

"For the official record, what's your fucking name?" Cailason barked.

Gaston felt numb and weary and paralysed by a panic that strangled his vocal cords.

"Gaston," he whispered meekly, still unable to look Cailason in the eye.

Cailason was livid. He moved from behind the counter towards Gaston, who was still handcuffed to the railing. They stood toe-to-toe. Gaston shuddered, still not daring to look Cailason in the eye. The door of the police station creaked open, which made him look up, beyond and behind Cailason. He saw a familiar, menacing hand poking through the opening.

"Speak up, for fuck's sake. Now what's your name and where do you live?" Cailason yelled, almost frothing at the mouth and oblivious to the intrusion behind him.

"His name is Gaston and he lives in Cité Labourdonnais; you should know that, sergeant," a woman's voice boomed as Harriet walked into the station, her hand outstretched as a suddenly meek police sergeant turned to face her.

It was Cailason's turn to feel intimidated again. No doubt she had heard him yell profanities, and when he realised the woman was Gaston's mother, he also felt very embarrassed.

"Oh, madam, please excuse my language. And yes, I do know who he is and where he lives, but I need him to tell me for the official record," he said. "You know we like to do everything properly here, legally I mean . . ."

"No need to apologise, sergeant. Of course, I understand and admire the work of our brave and honest police officers," she said. "As for my son, he probably deserves a good beating."

Gaston again had his head bowed. Surely this was the worst moment of his life, even overshadowing the rupture of his romance not that long ago. His focus again fell on his mother's hand and he thought of the punishment that her hand would surely mete out to him as soon as she got hold of him alone. Despite her advancing years, Harriet was still capable of giving a man-sized Gaston a severe beating, sometimes with the help of the bamboo cane she used when her children had done what she considered a very nasty deed. And this deed would surely rank among the nastiest anyone in the family had ever done, he thought. He almost wished that Sergeant Cailason would throw him in jail rather than release him to face the wrath of his mother.

"I ran into that nice Constable Winston outside the supermarket and he told me that you were 'looking after' my son. What's he done, sergeant?" Harriet asked.

Cailason outlined to Harriet the drunken morning antics of her son on the beach, occasionally stopping to apologise again for his unholy tirade despite Harriet's tacit approval of his fury and stern action in handcuffing Gaston and filling him with the fear of the God, in which they both had a very strong faith.

As Cailason reached the end of the story, he praised Harriet for doing her best to keep her children on the straight and narrow after the tragic demise of her husband, Gaetan.

"But that must be so difficult nowadays, madam, with all the temptations the devil throws their way: the drugs and all those loose Indian and Chinese women," he said.

"In my day, we had respect for the law and our parents and all those other races knew their place. All this racial mixing, it's just not healthy."

"You're absolutely right, sergeant," Harriet replied. "Why, only last week, my Bruno said he wanted to go out with a Chinese girl. Can you believe that?"

"As I've said many times before, madam, it's just pollution of the blood. No good will ever come of that, as we can see by the sins of your son standing in front of you." Cailason lamented, seemingly oblivious to the fact that Gaston's so-called "sins" had nothing to do with issues of race.

"Madam, all you can do is try your best. I am going to let him off with a severe warning this time because I know he's in good hands now," Cailason said as he took the handcuff key out of his pocket and released Gaston, leaving the handcuffs dangling noisily from the railing.

"Thank you, sergeant," Harriet said. "God bless you."

Harriet suddenly raised her hand, and Gaston, still foggy in the head, steeled himself for an onslaught of blows that wasn't forthcoming. Instead, a squeaky yelp escaped his lips as his mother grabbed him by the ear and dragged him outside.

"You should be grateful that the good sergeant didn't beat the living daylights out of you," Harriet exclaimed. "What *were* you thinking?"

She let go of his ear and started walking towards the front door of the police station where Sergeant Cailason stood, having fully regained his composure after the sudden and embarrassing turn of events. He even mustered a lukewarm smile as Harriet approached and warmly shook his hand.

"Thank you, sergeant, for being so understanding," Harriet said. "I'll make sure this never happens again. Does a mother's suffering ever end?

"Thank goodness we still have good, God-fearing folk like us, sergeant, who will one day reap the rewards of eternal paradise. As for those no-good children of mine, they'll burn in Hell if they carry on like this."

Sergeant Cailason didn't hear the end of the sentence as Harriet, with her sheepish son in tow, set off down the main street.

CHAPTER X

Sins of the Father

Harriet was determined that Gaston should seek immediate absolution for his sins of the day. She made a beeline for the Catholic church, hoping that afternoon confession would still be in progress. If it wasn't, she was sure she could convince one of the priests to hold a special session for her son who had strayed so far from the heavenly path. Despite their sins and misdemeanours, she loved her children dearly and now devoted her life to saving them from the eternal fires of Hell. Earlier in the day, she had accidentally walked in on Bruno masturbating in the shower and now this shameful episode with Gaston.

Harriet felt she had already lived a life of martyr proportions so her place in Heaven was guaranteed. But her soul would find Heaven a very lonely place indeed without the souls of her beloved family for company.

Gaston was rubbing his ear and struggling to keep pace with Harriet as they passed the Finger Bay General Store, but he didn't dare slow down even though his head ached and his body felt listless.

"I'm so sorry, Mother," he tried to say, but the words came out garbled in the rush of swishing arms and legs as mother and son raced towards the church as though there was a time limit on Gaston being absolved of his sins.

Harriet pretended not to hear Gaston's attempt at an apology. She didn't want to face him and reveal the tear rolling down her cheek. She kept her head upright and stoically marched on around the corner and into Church Street, with Gaston still struggling to keep pace. He was exhausted. He just wanted to curl up in a ball and fall asleep on the spot but he kept going.

The sight of a life-sized statue of Jesus on a giant cross greeted the pair as they passed through the church gate. As a child, Gaston was terrified of the statue, which, to a young boy, was so lifelike in its display of the bloody wounds Jesus suffered when crucified. The bright red wounds had long faded after many years of bombardment from a combination of fierce sub-tropical sunlight and the almost daily downpour of monsoon rains in the summer.

Gaston did not fear the Jesus statue today, though. He was much more terrified of his mother, whose hand reached out towards him. Gaston flinched in fright again, fearing he was about to be slapped. But Harriet simply grabbed his arm to hurry him up the church stairs.

"Quick, quick," she said. "We're going to miss confession."

As they entered the church, Harriet saw a young altar boy coming out of the confessional.

That seems a bit odd, she thought as the altar boy came out of the middle cubicle of the confessional where the priest normally sat to hear confession. The boy seemed in great distress. Harriet was sure she saw tears rolling down his face. Her maternal instincts took over and she rushed over, hoping to comfort him. But as she got within touching distance of the boy, a priest emerged from the same cubicle and stepped in between them, looking rather sheepish. The altar boy didn't stop. He was almost running as he disappeared quickly behind the altar and out the back door of the church.

The sight of Harriet and her dishevelled son surprised Father Terry, the parish's respected veteran priest.

"Ohh, Mrs. Le Clezio . . . ahh . . . you startled me. I guess you're wondering what Henri was doing in there with me? Well, it was a very quiet afternoon at confession so I was just showing him what I do when I hear confession. He's thinking about becoming a priest, you know."

Gaston knew Father Terry was lying. As a teenager, he had been an altar boy for a very short time, but long enough to bear witness to the sins of the Finger Bay fathers. It was a time when the priesthood had no problems attracting new recruits to the vow of celibacy which most never kept anyway. As a result, Finger Bay, being one of the larger parishes, was home to eight priests with a range of ministerial experience but who all shared an alarming willingness to engage in a range of depraved and criminal sexual practices. And it was only a "stroke" of luck that had saved Gaston from becoming a victim of their depravity.

Father Terry regained his composure, and his defensive tone suddenly turned offensive.

"I really don't know why it was so quiet today," he said brusquely. "It's not as if the parishioners of Finger Bay don't have terrible sins to confess. They're just so lazy. I swear, Mrs. Le Clezio, they will all burn in Hell if they don't repent."

Father Terry realised he was literally putting the fear of God into a cowering Harriet and felt slightly embarrassed.

"I'm so sorry if I'm upsetting you, Mrs. Le Clezio. It's just that I am so passionate about saving the souls of this fine parish. Nothing would please me more than to spend eternal life in Heaven in the company of the fine souls of Finger Bay."

Father Terry's softened tone had the desired impact on Harriet, who felt the fear drain from her.

"I understand, Father," Harriet said. "It must be hard for you. There are so many more temptations for the weak these days. The devil is having a field day. We've been going downhill ever since independence."

Suddenly, remembering the sight of the distraught altar boy running away, she asked, "But why was Henri so upset?"

"Oh, he . . . he banged his head on the door. The door was a bit sticky and it hit him quite hard in the head when he finally managed to get it open," Father Terry said. "But he'll be all right. It was more the shock that upset him, I think."

Father Terry sounded most unconvincing, but Harriet had too much faith in him to think there was anything untoward going on. He was, after all, one of God's agents on earth and incapable of doing any harm.

Nevertheless, the poor boy did look in great distress, Harriet thought.

Father Terry sensed her discomfort and quickly changed the subject.

"You have always been a loyal servant of God, Mrs. Le Clezio. Almost as pure as the Virgin Mary herself. You can't possibly be here for confession?"

"Oh, thank you, Father," Harriet said, blushing. "I certainly have been blessed with absolute faith, but we are all sinners and sometimes I have to wrestle with the devil. Why, only yesterday, our neighbour showed us his new car and I started to feel envy, Father, as if the devil himself was trying to possess my soul.

"But sorry, I digress. I'm here for my son, Gaston, who is straying so far from the holy path. He needs to confess his sins, Father, but after this morning's events, maybe he's too far gone—"

"Nonsense," said Father Terry, cutting her off. "All sinners can be saved if they truly repent."

Sensing the stern stare of the Father suddenly on him, Gaston was overcome with shame and guilt.

"I am truly sorry, Father," he said.

"You see," said Father Terry, "he's already repenting. That's a good sign. Now, if you just give me a minute, I'll hear his whole confession, even though I was going to close up."

Father Terry strode to the doors of the church and poked his head outside to check for any late-coming sinners, but the church courtyard was deserted.

"Humph, it seems that the residents of Finger Bay have been angels this week," he muttered to himself sarcastically.

Yet, Father Terry and the other priests of Finger Bay were completely indifferent to the ghastly sins they regularly committed, like the one he had just committed in the confessional with Henri. So long worshipped and put on a divine pedestal by the Finger Bay congregation, their moral compass had lost all perspective of right and wrong. The local priests had become a protected species in a feudal-style Catholic community that feared the wrath of God. The priests believed they had a God-given right to indulge in criminal behaviour to satisfy their repressed sexual urges or to add proceeds, from what were essentially bribes, to their bulging coffers at the expense of the parishioners, many among whom struggled to put food on the table.

They aggressively preyed on the young, vulnerable boys from the many poor and poorly educated families whose parents often forced their sons into becoming altar boys, thinking it would improve their social prestige in the eyes of others and perhaps discount their way up the church-pew-payment pecking order.

As a result, a growing number of previously gregarious young boys in the parish suddenly started to be more withdrawn and reclusive soon after becoming altar boys, and their parents simply couldn't understand their own complicity in their sons' radical character transformations. The few altar boys who plucked up the courage to make their parents aware of their sexual abuse at the hands of the priests only suffered further humiliation and often further punishment for their "obvious lies" and "disturbing imaginations".

Their God-fearing parents only had one concern: where and how in the hell did their boys learn about the perverted sexual acts which informed their "lies" about the heavenly fathers of Finger Bay? And in their collective minds, there was only one answer: the devil!

But the parents did have different methods of dealing with the devil. Some attempted to beat the devil out of their sons with lashings of the cane, which was the parents' corporal punishment weapon of choice. The few parents who could afford it resorted to the officially condemned but tolerated practice of exorcism, oblivious to the fact that, at times, the very same priests who had abused their boy performed the exorcism for a bit of "pocket money" on the side. Others still, simply did nothing, hoping their sons would naturally return to normal in due course. However, normality for these boys never returned and no one ever investigated why Finger Bay's youth suicide rate and the demand for anti-depressant drugs were higher than the island average.

As he shut and locked the church doors, Father Terry suddenly recalled Gaston's short but memorable stint as an altar boy, a memory which to this day still caused Father Terry great anguish.

At the time, the head of the parish, Father Orton, the legendary priest who had instigated the lucrative church pew pecking order, had finally approved Harriet's request for Gaston to be trialled as an altar boy, much to her delight. After all, Gaston had been on the waiting list for six months.

That same day, Harriet had put on her Sunday best, even though it was only Tuesday, and dragged Gaston to the church for altar boy training.

Father Orton took an instant liking to the handsome young Gaston, as did the other priests, but they were forced to keep their lustful ways in check as Harriet had stayed around for the half-day it took to train Gaston. However, that evening the priests had a fiery discussion about who would be the one to initiate him into their perverted ways. With a lust for Gaston raging among all the five allegedly holy men, they resorted to drawing straws and Father Orton had duly won the prize.

Two days later, the lamb arrived primed for the slaughter at the church presbytery. Father Orton was licking his lips in anticipation as he answered the door and stared lecherously at the innocent bowed head of Gaston Le Clezio.

"Come in, come in, my dear boy; don't be shy," Father Orton said. "We don't have much time. I have much to teach you before you serve at your first mass."

The young Gaston kept his head bowed as he tentatively stepped inside Father Orton's office.

"Relax, my dear boy," Father Orton reassured him. "You have nothing to fear here. We are all God's loyal servants.

"Now, you just stay here while I get changed for mass."

Father Orton stepped behind a bamboo partition, which, Gaston noticed, had the priest's ceremonial robe draped over it. The striking violet-coloured robe worn by priests saying mass during the liturgical season of advent reminded him that Christmas was not far away and the thought instantly calmed his nerves and even made him feel a bit excited at the prospect of receiving presents from Santa and the once-a-year indulgence of Coca-Cola at Christmas lunch. He even began humming to himself his favourite Christmas carol, "The Little Drummer Boy", as he waited for Father Orton to finish changing.

But Gaston's serene daydream about the impending joy of Christmas degenerated swiftly into a nightmare when a naked Father Orton stepped out from behind the bamboo curtain and headed towards him with a large grin on his face.

The shock and horror that Gaston felt as his gaze fell onto the erect penis of the lunging priest found expression in a shrill scream that resonated throughout the church grounds and more critically caused a very surprised Father Orton to literally drop dead in his tracks, the victim of a fatal stroke. He fell at Gaston's feet just as a pack of priests surged through the office door.

The first priest through the door on that fateful day had been Father Terry, and now all those years later as he walked back towards "that murderer" and his "nosy" mother, he sported a similar grin to the one that had graced Father Orton's face as he lay stone-cold dead on the presbytery floor.

Gaston, for his part, had stood there frozen for some time before being whisked out of the room and taken home well before the medical authorities arrived to take away Father Orton's body. He still seemed to have a slight grin on his face, but he was fully clothed and sitting slumped in his favourite armchair. The official account of his death that was circulated among the parish community was that Gaston had been insolent and when Father Orton attempted to discipline him, it had caused a sudden surge in his blood pressure, leading to the stroke.

Father Terry was devastated by Father Orton's sudden death for which he immediately blamed Gaston. The older priest had served as a role model to Father Terry, initiating him to the sinful joy of violating young altar boys; *the one privilege of the job that made living in this God-forsaken sauna of an island worthwhile*, Father Terry thought. Every day, he cursed the island's relentless heat and yearned for the bracing climate of his native Scotland, but the challenge of seducing timid young boys made the heat almost bearable.

Father Terry had prayed long and hard for some kind of revenge since Father Orton's death. But Gaston never returned to serve as an altar boy and was always under the protection of his mother when attending mass. Perhaps delivering Gaston to him on a plate today was God's own mysterious way of rewarding one of his most loyal servants.

It should be easy enough to separate him from his mother. Henri was just the entrée. Gaston will be the main course, he thought.

Father Terry felt a tingle in the boxer shorts under his cassock as his penis hardened slightly at the prospect of finally having his prayers answered.

"All right, my son. When you're ready, I can hear your confession," he said.

"Shouldn't you check on Henri first?" Harriet asked.

"He should be okay," Father Terry replied. "I told him to go put some ice on his wound and I'm sure he's doing that right now. I'll check up on him after I hear Gaston's confession.

"Now tell me, Harriet—may I call you Harriet?"

"Of course, of course, Father," Harriet said, almost blushing.

"What exactly has Gaston done to warrant such an urgent need for confession?"

Harriet briefly recounted Gaston's, at best errant, certainly unlawful, but without doubt sinful behaviour to Father Terry as Sergeant Cailason had described to her earlier. All the while, Gaston simply stood there, almost paralysed, sweating profusely and feeling increasingly embarrassed upon hearing his mother reveal her shame at his sinful deeds.

Father Terry suddenly had a wicked idea that would certainly guarantee revenge.

"May I have a private word with you, dear lady?" he said as he gently grabbed Harriet by the arm and led her away towards the altar.

Harriet felt a flush of excitement at the touch of her favourite priest but almost immediately felt a great shame at the devil's attempt to exploit her weak flesh. She again reminded herself that she must be forever vigilant as, a number of times, the devil had attempted to lower her strong Catholic sexual defences when in the presence of Father Terry. She sometimes found herself almost swooning during his fire-and-brimstone sermons, but she fought very hard and always managed to slay the devil in the end. Upon returning home, she would take out her favourite rosary beads and punish herself by kneeling on the stone-lined path in the backyard in front of the statue of the Virgin Mary, where she would then recite the traditional five decades of the rosary at least twenty times or until her knees could no longer bear the jagged stones.

When she was younger, any encounter with Father Terry would almost always trigger the uncontrollable moisture in her panties. The great shame this caused Harriet had led her to wear absorbent panty liners whenever she thought there was a possibility of running into Father Terry.

When Father Terry was sure that Gaston could no longer hear their conversation, he stopped and, still holding firmly to Harriet's arm, leaned towards her. As his face approached hers, Harriet momentarily forgot where she was and instinctively prepared herself to be kissed passionately like the heroine in the many Mills & Boon novels that adorned her bookshelves. But she was jolted out of her romantic fantasy as Father Terry began to speak. A sombre light prevailed in the church and he couldn't see that Harriet was blushing brightly.

"Perhaps Gaston would like to stay behind after the confession so I could show him how the love of Jesus can penetrate his soul," said Father Terry, his tone rising in vengeful anger. "And make him a man who works for Jesus, not against him."

Father Terry realised he was again upsetting Harriet and possibly letting Gaston in on his plan, as his rising voice could almost certainly be heard at the back of the church where Gaston remained. Father Terry had learnt to theatrically project his voice in the days before microphones became "de rigueur" in churches. Even today, he rarely used the microphone, often positioning himself in front of the altar to deliver his sermons. He felt his message had more impact and was more likely to instil the fear of God in his parishioners, when delivered with the natural tone of a human voice. The many years of delivering sermons this way meant that these days, he was often unaware when the decibel level of his voice rose to sermon pitch.

"I'm so sorry again, my dear Harriet. As I said earlier, it's very hard sometimes to control my passion for reforming the sinners of this fine parish," he said more calmly. "I meant I could give Gaston some counsel and guide him back onto God's righteous path. There are passages in the Bible that would help Gaston. And, if the other priests are up to it . . ." said Father Terry, snickering at his own deviate pun, ". . . perhaps we can all help Gaston see the light."

Wow, Father Terry is taking a personal interest in my family's salvation, she thought.

Harriet was overcome by a surge of affection for her favourite priest. She felt the devil lurking inside her again as she launched herself at Father Terry, letting out a shriek in the process, a shriek that instantly took his thoughts back to the scene of Father Orton's death. And as Harriet threw her arms around him, Father Terry's hatred for the family intensified, hardening his resolve (and his penis slightly) to punish Gaston for his "crime".

For her part, Harriet abandoned herself completely to the uncharacteristic show of affection as she hugged Father Terry tightly, knowing full well that her knees would later bear the brunt of her sins. She would have to exorcise the devil from her soul tonight, but at this moment, she didn't care.

A martyr must suffer and get used to pain, she thought.

Father Terry squirmed, but Harriet paid no attention until she felt a sharp jab in her thigh, causing her to release him immediately. He had become increasingly turned on by the prospect of imminent revenge and his penis was now almost fully erect. Fortunately, the dim lighting masked the prominent bulge in Father Terry's cassock, but he saw the anxiety on Harriet's face. He acted quickly to douse any suspicion. He retrieved from his pocket a bulky set of keys and a chunky gold crucifix, both bound by a sparkling gold chain and held it up very close to Harriet's face.

"My apologies, dear Harriet," he said. "I always keep this in my pocket. I hope it didn't hurt you."

Before she had a chance to reply, he moved away from her and headed back towards Gaston at an ambling pace that would hopefully give his erection time to subside. Harriet dutifully followed, falling into line with the snail's pace set by Father Terry. When they finally reached Gaston, the evidence of Father Terry's excitement had all but subsided. The high sexual emotion now was replaced by the calm reason needed to execute his plan.

There will be ample opportunity for sexual excitement later, Father Terry thought as he approached Gaston with as much of a sympathetic look as he could muster. He coolly placed an arm around Gaston's shoulder and led him towards the confessional.

"Now, my dear boy, I'll give you a few moments to seriously think about the events of this morning and whether you're ready to repent," Father Terry said in a fatherly, gentle tone.

"I can already sense that you're very sorry for your sins, but God Himself needs to hear that in my sacred confessional. And mark my words, He'll know if you are not truly sorry. And if you're not, you'll burn in Hell."

Again, Father Terry had to check his burning passion for revenge.

"I'm sure that the all-merciful God will forgive you, after you've done your penance, of course."

As they approached the confessional, Father Terry announced that following confession, he would be counselling him in private to make sure that he would not re-offend. Gaston was suddenly gripped with the same fear he had felt earlier today when Sergeant Cailason was screaming at him. But he felt powerless to stop Father Terry from steering him into the confessional, and, like a dutiful Catholic, he instinctively knelt on the cushioned kneeler and waited for the priest to slide the screen and hear his confession.

Gaston was visibly shaking. He felt trapped. If he tried to flee before confession, his mother, let alone God, would never forgive him, as was the case following his childhood encounter with the depraved fathers of Finger Bay. On that fateful day, the priests had sent him home in the care of a gentle, caring nun, Sister Edith. But despite her best efforts, he arrived home still in great distress and unable to say a word. He had been rendered mute by the continual flashbacks to Father Orton's erect penis. However, as the emotional scars healed and gradually faded over the next few weeks, he regained his voice and managed to find the courage to tell his parents his version of the events in all its sordid detail. When he had finished, Harriet said nothing. She took a deep breath and raised her hand. Expecting some consoling words and a gentle caress or hug, a sobbing Gaston eagerly moved closer to his mother but was stopped dead in his tracks when Harriet slapped him hard across the face. He stopped sobbing immediately and just stood there in shock, and once again, he was rendered mute.

Harriet refused to believe that God's loyal servants could be guilty of such heinous crimes.

Where on earth did he learn how to make up such a fanciful, sordid story?

And when Harriet heard the priests' version of events the following day, it only confirmed her worst fears. No doubt about it, the devil had been busy, invading Gaston's soul and filling his mind with perverted thoughts. She contemplated calling her sister Marie-Noelle who knew of a rogue priest who performed exorcisms. But Marie-Noelle was such a gossip that within days, Harriet would have been the laughingstock of the Finger Bay parish.

There goes the woman who gave birth to the depraved devil child. Evil surely breeds evil.

For some time after, Harriet dreaded any encounter with the parish priests but true to Murphy's Law, she managed to bump into several of the Finger Bay fathers in the village centre over the course of the next week. But to her very pleasant surprise, she found that each of the priests, despite grieving the loss of one of their own, had shown great compassion, which, she felt, had absolved her from any responsibility for Gaston's sinful behaviour.

"Boys will be boys," they had said. "It's not his fault. Father Orton had a serious heart problem anyway and probably wouldn't have lived much longer."

Harriet was relieved and even more so when Gaston apologised, confessing that he had made it all up. For his part, Gaston had realised that no one was ever going to believe his story and as time went on, he himself began to have doubts that it had really happened. And over the ensuing years, he gradually buried the memory into the nether reaches of his subconscious, hoping it would never resurface, but now the revelation that Father Terry would be "counselling" him had brought a nauseating impression of the memory back to the surface. He was scared, sweating, kneeling, thinking that Father Terry was plotting some kind of sinister revenge.

Outside the confessional, Harriet, head bowed, was coincidentally also thinking of the events surrounding Father Orton's death.

Exorcism all those years ago may not have been such a bad idea and may have saved us many years of heartache, she thought.

The extended hand of Father Terry suddenly burst into view near her belly button, startling Harriet and causing her to look up straight into Father Terry's eyes, then down again in embarrassment. He took her hand and held it gently.

"I suggest that you leave us now so that I can give Gaston my full attention," Father Terry said, feigning compassion. "Trust me, dear lady, after I've finished with Gaston, he'll be a new man, one who will serve the Lord with gusto."

A reassured Harriet raised her head and confronted Father Terry's deceptively warm smile with a genuinely warm one of her own.

"Oh, thank you so much, Father. I'll leave Gaston in your capable hands and look forward to welcoming him home a new man, as you promised, and free of sin," she said. "Thank you so—"

Before Harriet could finish her sentence, Father Terry snatched his hand away from her "loving" grip and walked towards the main church door to let her out. Harriet took the cue and followed him, and as she arrived at the church doors,

Father Terry had already taken the set of keys out of his pocket and was fiddling with the creaky lock.

"Voila!" he triumphantly exclaimed as the ancient lock succumbed. He held the door open for a still blushing Harriet to scamper through, murmuring her gratitude once more to the priest who was no longer listening. However, he did instinctively grab her by the waist as she passed by to hurry her exit. Harriet subconsciously mistook this for a display of affection and, once again, felt a surge of sexual excitement and even a hint of moisture in her panties, something she hadn't felt for a long time.

"Is there no escaping the evil work of the devil?" she quietly cursed as she moved quickly down the church steps and headed home.

Father Terry wasted no time in re-locking the door and heading back to the confessional, rubbing his hands with glee and laughing internally.

CHAPTER XI

Revenge in the Name of the Father . . .

As the screen slid open, Gaston opened his eyes. He realised they had been closed since he knelt at the confessional waiting for his confessor to materialise, his thoughts surprisingly having drifted to food. He hadn't eaten since breakfast and he was very hungry. But the calming reverie of his mother's delicious curried octopus suddenly dissolved into the reality of Father Terry's glare through the lattice of the screen opening.

As their eyes met, Gaston immediately felt intimidated and looked away and down at Father Terry's feet. Although the screen mesh combined with the darkness of the confessional to obscure his view, Gaston could just make out the page of a magazine under Father Terry's feet depicting a naked body. He also saw a crumpled towel on the floor next to the magazine with some darkish stains on them. Gaston was sure they were bloodstains.

In a split second, a myriad of thoughts flashed through Gaston's head.

Perhaps, Father Terry had been telling the truth after all and Henri had injured himself in the confessional and even drawn blood! But what's that magazine with the naked body doing there? Maybe it's not a naked body?

"Now, my boy, what do you have to confess?" Father Terry suddenly barked.

Gaston immediately replied, "Bless me, Father, for I have sinned. There's been . . ."

Gaston surprised himself by his instinctive reaction to the confession ritual, even though it had been many years since he had graced the confessional with his sinning soul. Yet now he stumbled because he simply could not remember when he last went to confession.

"Well, get on with it, my boy," Father Terry said impatiently, then instantly checked himself. He wanted to win Gaston's trust and lull him into a false sense of security to make it easier to lure him into his perverted trap.

"Ehh, I'm sorry, my boy. I imagine, like all young men and women in this increasingly Godless world, it's been some time since you've been to confession. Now as

God knows everything, He'll remember the last time you went to confession so we can proceed," Father Terry said.

Father Terry's deceptively merciful tone had the desired impact and made Gaston feel more at ease. He instinctively resumed the confession ritual by prefacing the account of his morning's sins with the standard "and here are my sins" and terminating his sorrow-laced narrative with, "and for these sins, I am truly sorry".

Father Terry expertly feigned interest in hearing Gaston's sins as he did with most of the confessions he was forced to endure. The sins of his parishioners frankly bored him unless it gave him an opportunity to add to the church coffers or identify a potential target for sexual exploitation. Why, only yesterday, he had heard the confession of the delicious Martine Latois, a shapely brunette with normally sparkling, seductive brown eyes who had arrived at the confessional dripping with tears as she confessed to feelings of extreme sexual frustration and bouts of being "tempted by the devil to pleasure herself" because her husband of several months had been unable to consummate the marriage. Father Terry had made a mental note to follow up on that. Although he preferred the frisky boys, he rarely passed up an opportunity to "help" a God-fearing, horny woman. He would visit her as soon as possible on the premise that Jesus and the Holy Spirit had heard her howls of frustration in the confessional and could not bear to witness the suffering of such a dutiful servant of God. And as such, they had instructed Father Terry to "ease her pain". It worked every time.

"Now, my son, as I will be giving you my personal counsel, God, no doubt, would want you to have a lighter penance than would normally be the case for such serious sins," Father Terry said. "I think three Hail Marys and two Our Fathers should do it."

As he realised that revenge was drawing ever closer, Father Terry began to feel that primitive sexual excitement that often accompanied a surge in adrenaline. And again, the excitement manifested itself in a growing erection.

"I have to do something about this; otherwise, it'll give the game away," he said to himself.

All in the very same instant he sensed Gaston still peering at him through the confessional window, seemingly waiting for permission to go.

"Ahh, my boy, yes, please go and wait for me at the presbytery," he said to Gaston. "It's locked at the moment, but you'll find a bench by the front door. Just wait for me there. I'd like to say a few prayers and thank our Lord almighty, as is my custom at the end of each confession session. Besides, it'll give you an opportunity to say your penance."

The gentle tone of Father Terry's voice convinced Gaston that maybe he'd misjudged the Father's intentions.

"By the way," Father Terry added. "Could you also check up on Henri if he's still around? I did tell him to wait for me. I want to make sure he's recovered from that nasty accident with the door this morning."

This concern for Henri further reassured Gaston and as he walked out of the confessional smiling inside, he had a genuine feeling of liberation from his sins of the morning. He even began whistling his favourite hymn, "Ave Maria", as he felt a sense of normalcy return to his life.

Meanwhile, Father Terry had already begun to take steps to ensure his plot for revenge was not betrayed by the present difficulty in controlling his sexual urges. He surely would have time to masturbate and release some sexual tension in the confessional before letting the other priests loose on Gaston. He had thought about leading the revengeful pack against Gaston, but his hatred of the boy was so deep he felt repulsed by the thought of having to touch him. The younger priests, who had not been around when Father Orton died, would have no such qualms and Father Terry would simply take great delight in seeing the murderer punished for his crime.

The boy needs to suffer as much as I did, he thought to himself as he raised his cassock above his knees and took hold of his rock-hard penis. With his other hand he reached under the seat for the pornographic magazine he had used earlier in "initiating" Henri to the sins of the Finger Bay fathers.

Meanwhile, Gaston had made his way out of the church through the side door and was heading down the dusty pathway to the presbytery when he felt the urge to urinate, an urge that only intensified when he spotted the public toilet to his left.

As he stepped inside the toilet block, Gaston noticed an altar boy's robe scrunched up on the ground. *That's a bit odd,* he thought. It hadn't been lying there for long. The robe was still very clean except for one bright red spot, which stood out in stark contrast to the whiteness of the robe, a much darker red than the traditional red collar which adorned the robe.

Should I pick it up? thought Gaston.

But he'd had enough angst for one day and didn't want to jeopardise the upward swing of his mood following the forgiveness of his sins. Gaston carefully stepped over the robe and went into the toilet cubicle, where he was confronted by another dark red blob on the toilet seat. And again, Gaston decided against being concerned. Deep down, he knew it was blood, just as the red stain on the altar boy's robe was also a blood stain. And he was fairly sure that the robe was Henri's. He had a quick look into the other three toilet cubicles but found no further sign of Henri.

He must have gone home, thought Gaston, who was quietly relieved. He had enough problems of his own.

When Gaston emerged from the toilet block, he'd successfully managed to forget about Henri's robe and the bloodstains and his inner smile had even found its way out. He made his way to the bench by the front door of the presbytery and sat down, adopting a meditative-style pose to say his penance. He didn't want to risk any more of Father Terry's displeasure and God's possible wrath.

Despite his penchant for sinning throughout his life, even straying into the mortal variety in recent times, Gaston still believed in God, a merciful God who would forgive him if he genuinely repented but would also punish him even more severely if he didn't. There had been many examples of him feigning repentance for his sins and God punishing him soon after; the most harrowing instance being when he had been tempted by the devil (in the guise of the beautiful and extremely sensual Natalie) to lose his virginity and well before he'd given any thought to marriage. The parish priests had often and loudly proclaimed the evils of having sex outside the sanctity of the marriage bond. Gaston felt duty-bound to confess his sins but he wasn't the least bit remorseful.

His first sexual encounter had been such a great thrill and immensely pleasurable, even though he had been extremely nervous at first. Surely a loving and merciful God wouldn't consider the most intense, loving, and pleasurable act that he'd ever experience a serious sin, despite what the parish priests said?

But a week after his pretend confession, he lost his prized handmade gold bracelet. And despite promises to St. Anthony that he would hand over the contents of his meagre bank account to the poor should he help him find the bracelet, he never found it. A few months later, Gaston suffered an even greater loss. Natalie dumped him unceremoniously only a week after looking deep into his eyes and professing great love for him. He never again doubted the power of God to punish the sinners who tried to fool Him. He wasn't going to risk such great loss again, even though earlier in the day, he felt he really had nothing left to lose.

Five minutes went by with Gaston, eyes closed, happily muttering his penance when he felt one of his eyelids being pried open gently and the image of his mother's face gradually filling the gaze from his slowly opening eyelid. Gaston was surprised that he was so relaxed he hadn't been startled by his mother's unexpected appearance.

"I'm just saying my penance as Father Terry instructed me to do, mother," Gaston said.

"Yes, I could hear that," Harriet replied. "But where's Father Terry? I've brought him some curried octopus, which I had left over from last night's dinner, as a thank you. I know he loves it, and curries always taste better the day after."

"He's just finishing up in the confessional," Gaston started to say when he and Harriet suddenly heard a muffled moan emanating from the church. Harriet almost dropped the casserole dish containing the curried octopus while Gaston opened his remaining closed eye instantly. They both rushed back into the church. The moans grew louder as they approached the confessional.

Concerned for Father Terry's health, Harriet opened the door of the confessional with her free hand just as Father Terry unleashed the loudest of moans that heralded the ejaculation of semen, most of which landed evenly between Harriet's breast and the casserole dish. Harriet was shocked but also instinctively excited at the sight of Father Terry's still-erect penis glistening in the soft evening light filtering through the stained-glass windows. A primal part of her being wanted to take him into her mouth and suck him dry. She felt the dreaded moisture between her thighs return. Gaston was oblivious to Harriet's repressed inner sexual demons but totally in tune with the outward shock and outrage, which found expression in her delayed ear-piercing scream.

CHAPTER XII

Patrick

Patrick bit his lip and held his breath. A vote was imminent, the vote that he thought would propel him onto the world stage as its saviour and his image onto the front page of every Australian newspaper and perhaps even media abroad. He felt very guilty about looking forward to seeing his face on the front page but he couldn't help it. The thought of it made him feel very good indeed. He was human, after all, and he justified the feeling as being his one concession to ego.

Patrick, after all, had remained essentially humble in the face of bourgeoning political popularity and a steady stream of praise from his constituents. He'd had a stellar start to his political career, fuelled by supporters who seemed to warm to his idealistic policies and his heartfelt passion for creating a more just and equal society where so-called celebrities and elite athletes were not worshiped like the false idols they were.

"It's absurd that we seem to value our entertainers, not just a little, but obscenely more than those who save lives, look after our children and work to improve our lives," Patrick had concluded.

The seed of such rebellion against the established order had been planted through his friendship with Gaston, but that wasn't immediately apparent to Patrick. It had been many years, and so much had happened and changed in his life since Gaston introduced him to David Beckham, aliens, Planet Utopia, and income injustice under the stars at the Casuarina sports grounds.

But like Gaston, Patrick was not content to accept the powerful force the cult of celebrity wielded on the market economics of capitalism, which, he believed, distorted market forces and led to gross injustice in income distribution and the ever-increasing wealth gap. And he quickly became convinced that he could be the agent for radical change to make the system fairer, which, in turn, he was equally convinced, would make everyone happier and the world a much better place.

In the lead up to his quest for council office, Patrick had designed a radical socio-economic doctrine which he subsequently introduced to the townsfolk via a series of amazingly well-attended political rallies during his campaign for the council elections.

Patrick's doctrine was driven by his simple interpretation of a Marxist philosophy designed to make everybody as equal as possible, socially and economically.

"The true heroes are the workers who actually make a difference and contribute to society's progress and wellbeing," he would holler with great passion at the beginning of every rally.

At his first rally, the crowd erupted in equally passionate cheers even before he had finished the statement, which surprised Patrick, but as the reaction was similar at subsequent rallies, he soon began to believe that the electorate was indeed ripe for revolution.

"Entertainment has become the new religion," he would preach at every rally.

"Just like the so-called divine rights of kings and queens, which had once legitimised the rule of a pompous bunch of bloodthirsty monarchs and allowed them to keep the serfs oppressed and in servitude, it seems the divine right of celebrity is doing a similar job on the unthinking homogenous masses these days.

"But just as the more enlightened societies abolished the monarchy, we now must stop worshiping celebrities. It's the medical professionals—the doctors, the nurses—and others, like our emergency workers, inventors, police, teachers, childcare workers—those who devote their lives to the common good and our society's welfare—they are the ones worthy of celebrity. Yet, what do we do when they ask for a pay rise? We call them 'greedy.' But when David Beckham, the Kardashians, and others of that so-called celebrity ilk demand more and more money for their so-called work—to the point where these people earn probably more than the GDP of the poorest nations—we call it market forces! That's just wrong, my dear people, and it has to change, and with your support, it will change!" Patrick roared on, again to be met almost always with rapturous applause and wild cheering.

"We have created this unjust, unfair system prone to corruption and abuse of the weak by the powerful. So, surely, we can uncreate it. My policies will elevate the status of society's real heroes—and hence their incomes—while relegating the status and brutally slashing the obscene financial benefits that we now bestow upon the elite sports people, entertainers, and other so-called celebrities.

"And you, fat-cat chief executives of greedy multinationals, your days of obscenely fat pay cheques are numbered. We are sick of you exploiting the many for the benefit of the few bloated shareholders and executives. Why should the poor count their blessings while you count your money? Under my regime, your ridiculous pay packets will be re-distributed to provide all workers with the same, very comfortable standard of living."

The cheers and applause were at fever pitch as Patrick reached the end of his call to arms and moved to the front of the stage to shake the many, usually female, hands that lurched forward, eager for the faintest of touches from their apparent saviour.

However, to put his ideas into practice would involve a revolution beyond any Marxist standard that had gone before him. A healthy victory at the ballot box had further emboldened Patrick, who, upon election to office, had wasted no time in introducing his radical political agenda to his fellow councillors.

Lulled into a false sense of confidence by the seemingly passionate voter response at the rallies, Patrick failed to realise that his supporters were primarily women who were not necessarily reacting to his ideas. Fresh in their memory was Patrick's extended role on a high-rating reality television program where he had achieved celebrity status. And the qualities—his youthful exuberance, good looks, and thoroughly engaging personality—that had won him many fans among viewers and turned him into a celebrity had also endeared him to his local council electorate, particularly the female voters.

For his part, Patrick had failed to see the irony of his own celebrity reaping him a great reward—albeit not financial in his case but a major step towards achieving his political ambitions.

However, those who had voted for him, women and men alike, had also been well aware that his political impact would be severely limited in a council dominated by conservative councillors. In the meantime, they believed the council spin-doctors would be able to exploit the vestiges of Patrick's television popularity to freshen up the image of a jaded, apathetic, and dull council.

At his political rallies and community meetings, the men of the town had enthusiastically claimed it was "time to give the young people a go". Even if they all thought that his policies were "loony tunes", they desperately needed a young and charismatic local political figure to be a role model and perhaps help stem the exodus of young folk from the region.

In a town where patriarchy ruled, most women paid scant attention to the cut and thrust of local politics until Patrick came along. His coffee-coloured skin, rockstar looks, and sex appeal attracted drooling women en-masse to his rallies. He also had a constant flow of women through his office.

Often, Patrick would arrive at work to find a line of seductively dressed women, each patiently waiting to see him to express an alleged concern about an alleged important council issue. But more often than not, the women quickly became more concerned with seducing him when they found themselves alone with Patrick.

One morning, Patrick arrived at his office earlier than usual so he could get some much-needed work completed before the expected onslaught of his lady constituents. But not early enough, it seemed. Standing outside his office was Beatrice White, the attractive wife of a local publican. She was wearing a skimpy, clingy red dress, which amplified her already ample cleavage and showed off her well-preserved, shapely figure and legs. It was a dress that would not look out of place adorning a brothel madame, Patrick immediately thought.

At the same time, he understood why the pub operated by Beatrice's husband, Bob, was the vastly more popular of the town's two pubs. Beatrice regularly helped out as a barmaid wearing similar outfits, he had heard. She grabbed his arm as he opened the front office door and approached his ear with her luscious red lips exclaiming in a loud, seductive whisper: "I have something urgent to discuss with you, councillor."

Don't they all, thought a smirking Patrick, who was unable to shift his focus from her cleavage, much to Beatrice's delight.

Ever conscious of not offending a potential voter, Patrick politely feigned interest in her concerns.

"Let's talk about it in my office, Mrs. White."

"Oh, please call me Beatrice, or Betty, as all my close friends do," she said.

Patrick guided her into his office with a gentle touch to her lower back, which made Beatrice erupt in goosebumps. Patrick, too, could not help but feel aroused and he was suddenly grateful that he'd chosen to wear his baggy suit this morning. Despite her approaching middle age, Beatrice was still a very sexy woman. And she smelt very good indeed. Patrick had always been sexually vulnerable to women who smelt good, even though what defined a "good" smell that turned him on would vary wildly depending on the situation; from one woman's sweaty pungent body odour and lack of feminine hygiene in bed, to another's natural scent or the succulent aroma of a delicate perfume gracing her skin at other times. But when lust beckoned them to the bedroom, like Napoleon, Patrick preferred his Josephine unwashed.

Beatrice's scent mixed a hint of body odour with the subtle perfume of the essential oil he recognised as patchouli, a scent that often graced the perfect skin of a former love, Gemima. Beatrice's skin was not so perfect, exhibiting the lines and scars of impending middle age, but she still turned him on.

Nevertheless, he refused to be tempted by the sexual allure of Beatrice White. He couldn't let anything compromise his political ambitions, despite the slight bulge in his baggy trousers trying hard to convince him otherwise. Any scandal, especially one involving a married woman who was well known in a conservative town, would surely derail those ambitions and certainly end his quest to be the saviour of the world.

Once inside his office, Patrick took immediate steps to quell the smells that were fuelling his sexual urge. He blew his nose hard into his own handkerchief and kept his nose covered for some time, inhaling the strong Christian Dior aftershave that laced it.

As he sat down at his desk, Patrick started to feel the sexual excitement subside and fortunately the only other seat in his office was an armchair which was currently positioned some distance away from his desk near the office window. Patrick had placed it there yesterday afternoon so he could take advantage of the fading natural light while reading the evening newspaper. Surely Beatrice wouldn't have the strength to move the armchair closer to his desk? And he certainly wasn't going to offer any help.

But before he had the chance to settle into his office chair, Beatrice had managed to push the armchair towards Patrick's desk. Although surprised by her apparent strength, Patrick nevertheless still felt protected from Beatrice's sexual advances thanks to the large solid oak desk that provided a safe barrier between them. But also surprising was the fact that she hadn't pushed the chair right up to his desk, instead leaving it at least a metre away but directly in Patrick's line of vision.

Beatrice kept him on tenterhooks. She remained standing still behind the armchair for some time, staring at him, then breaking out in a cheeky seductive smile and running her fingers delicately across her breasts while subtly moistening her lips with the tip of her tongue. When she felt that Patrick had her undivided attention, she made her way around the armchair to sit down. Try as he might,

Patrick couldn't take his eyes off her, and as she sat down, he soon realised why she had positioned the chair at viewing distance from his desk. Patrick's eyes were naturally drawn to her shapely legs draped in that short and slinky red dress which she lifted slightly (but very deliberately) to reveal her sexy, lacy, crotchless underwear. Knowing she had his eyes where she wanted them, she slowly crossed her legs to cut off the titillating spectacle.

"Are you enjoying the view, councillor?" Beatrice said cheekily as Patrick's eyes rose to meet her seductive wink.

Clearly blushing through his coffee-coloured skin, Patrick was briefly lost for words, caught between his primitive sexual desires and his resolve not to let anything impede his political ambitions. He was, however, at the peak of his sexual powers that wanted to ravage this sexy woman who was clearly expressing her own wish to let him have his way.

Yet, a voice of reason managed to fight through his raw sexual emotion and hunger to fuck Beatrice White. He had much bigger fish to fry and certainly didn't want to take the sexual bait, which, as he reminded himself again, in such a small conservative town, could end up poisoning his great political ambition.

Patrick took a couple of deep breaths, followed by an exaggerated clearing of his throat that echoed a clearing of his mind from any thoughts of having sex with Beatrice and guided his councillor persona towards the business at hand.

"Now, Mrs. White . . ." he started saying, only to be interrupted by Beatrice, who tried again to steer relations towards the sexually suggestive.

"Please, dear councillor, call me Betty," she said. "I'd like us to be friends, friends who may come with great mutual benefits."

Patrick began to think he would never be able to escape Beatrice's lecherous clutches. Then he suddenly remembered being confronted by a similar situation not long ago. That time it had been Sylvia Halloran, the wife of a local real estate agent who had tried to seduce him in a similar fashion. He called her bluff and came onto her very aggressively, which immediately had her retreating.

Maybe it'll work with Beatrice as well, he thought.

Patrick suddenly rose from his chair and subtly grabbed his groin region as he made his way quickly to Beatrice, who was surprised by his sudden movements.

Without a moment's hesitation, he placed a hand on her knee and slowly began moving it up her thigh.

"Now, Betty, what sort of benefits did you have in mind? Or should I be more blunt and ask how you want me?" Patrick said as a cheeky grin overwhelmed his face.

"Personally, I'm very partial to anal sex. The smell turns me on," he said forcefully. "How about you? What are you offering? By the way you're dressed and your behaviour, you're obviously aching for me to pound you senseless."

As he said this, Patrick tightened his grip on her upper thigh, thinking he had the battle won. But to his surprise, Beatrice simply looked him even more lustfully in the eye as if begging for him to carry on.

"Now you're talking, counsellor . . . I thought you'd never ask," she said with a sensual softness. She then drew her lips closer to his, convinced that she was about to feast on Patrick's lips as the entrée to a delicious sexual smorgasbord.

Patrick began to panic. Sylvia Halloran had backed off as soon as he touched her, apologising profusely to Patrick as if he "had somehow got the wrong idea". Sylvia certainly hadn't worn such a seductive outfit but had flirted outrageously with him and had given him every impression that she wanted to have sex with him. Patrick had simply called her bluff.

"What would be the *right idea then, Sylvia*," Patrick had bellowed, to which Sylvia could only reply with a nervous apology before hastily retreating.

This situation with Beatrice was obviously different.

The crotchless panties should have been a clear warning sign that she was determined to go all the way, Patrick thought.

But he still had an ace card up his sleeve or, to be precise, his trousers.

Just as their lips were about to touch, Patrick backed away.

Without saying a word, he undid his belt and trousers and let them fall down around his ankles exposing, despite his best efforts, an obvious bulge in his tight fighting briefs.

He was suddenly grateful that he had chosen to wear briefs rather than his preferred boxers, as they maximised the exposure of a symmetrical pair of birthmarks, which lined his upper thighs, stretching up to his groin on each side.

At times, unlike now, when he actually wanted to have sex with a woman for the first time, exposing the birthmarks inevitably led to an awkward moment and a quick explanation and sometimes the need to produce recent blood test results. They looked like a rash, which, given their location, could easily be mistaken to be the result of some kind of sexually transmitted disease.

And that seemed to be exactly what Beatrice was thinking as the lustful joy, which had flooded her face as she locked eyes on the bulge in his briefs, turned into subdued horror as she shifted her gaze to the birthmarks.

Patrick's relief was palpable.

"Ohh, that, please don't worry, Betty. I've always been very careful; a stickler for safe sex, I am.

"I know what you're thinking, but I get checked out regularly and I can prove to you that it's not what you're thinking," he said as unconvincingly as possible.

It worked. Patrick struggled to keep a straight face as he watched panic swiftly spread across hers and her body tense up. She stood up, straightening her dress as she backed right away from him.

"What kind of girl do you think I am, councillor?" she blurted out.

"It's not that I don't believe you but I . . . I really can't take a risk," she said. "I . . . I did actually come to talk to you about a very important issue. My husband and I . . ."

And at the mention of her husband, she found a sudden comfort and security.

"Well, we're struggling a bit at the moment; what with the economy in trouble and all that, we . . . my husband and I . . . were wondering whether you could help us increase the opening hours of the pub."

Patrick was only half listening, but he did manage to catch the gist of her lie, enough to respond, as he pulled up his trousers.

A triumphant Patrick smiled warmly at Beatrice before telling her that although the drinking laws were a state government matter, he would speak to his political friends in the city about the issue. Patrick had no real intention of doing so, but it seemed like the answer she wanted to hear.

Without another word, Patrick went over to open the office door. Beatrice took the cue and quickly walked out the door, muttering an insincere "thank you" as she left.

CHAPTER XIII

A FAIR Plan for All

Now, as he waited for the vote, he was certain he would reap the rewards of his steely will power in resisting Beatrice and many other temptations to keep on track and on message about his radical policy to "save the world".

At community consultations following his election victory, Patrick had received subdued praise—which he falsely interpreted as a ringing endorsement—for his vision of a future society that would impose a tax of 80 percent on advertising and sponsorship money that went to the sport, leisure, and entertainment industries while advertising and sponsorship to hospitals, schools, universities, emergency services, and other organisations that added value to society would be tax-free. He wanted to make the doctors, nurses, teachers, paramedics, inventors, etc., the stars and higher wage earners of any future society. He would personally take charge of a panel, comprising a broad cross-section of the community, who would determine where each profession would be ranked on the scale of value to society.

He dubbed his radical, political, and socio-economic manifesto, FAIR, an acronym for Formula Advancing Income Revolution or, in his own mind, "Fucking Awesome Income Revolution".

Under a regime governed by FAIR, Patrick envisioned that all workers, regardless of industry, would earn the same generous basic wage that would enable them to have a very decent standard of living. The first crucial step in his manifesto would see the State, naturally under the leadership of trusted, ethical men and women, take total control of the wage system, just as Marx had envisioned with his "Dictatorship of the Proletariat" concept. And also, as Marx had postulated, eventually the responsibility for distributing wages would devolve to the community or regional level. But unlike Marxist doctrine, from the outset, small wage bonuses would be distributed to those who contributed most to the progress and wellbeing of society. As a result, Patrick envisaged that the "true heroes" of any society would be marginally at the top of the wage-earning scale.

The other significant policy initiative of his manifesto would be a law to direct that business profits, which weren't ploughed back into the business generating the profit, be handed over to the State for use in funding essential services like health, education, and transport.

Patrick would start small, naturally, with his policy to be implemented within his own council organisation and any businesses under council control, but he had no doubt that momentum would build and eventually all human societies would embrace the FAIR doctrine and Patrick would be hailed as one of history's greatest political reformers.

"Young Councillor La Malettie is a role model, a fine upstanding young man who has mesmerised us with his idealistic political vision and passionate speeches in recent times. While we may not agree with some of his ideas, he has every right to air them and we need to respectfully listen. But Mr. Mayor, I cannot vote for his motion to pay our garbage men and our senior managers the same basic wage. In fact, if we say yes to Councillor La Malettie's plan, our garbage men would probably end up with his proposed 'valuable society contribution' bonus, which means they would be earning more than the senior managers. Mr. Mayor, that is absurd."

Gentle calls of "here, here", not dissimilar to what Patrick had interpreted as a chorus of approval for his earlier speech in support of the motion, resonated around the council chambers in response to Councillor Gary Adams' closing remarks. All the other councillors, regardless of their political hue, were vehemently opposed to Patrick's motion. But they also didn't want to upset the public relations plans for their rising star, so they had adopted a "softly, softly" approach to Patrick's "crazy" motion, essentially to keep him on their side.

The aging, world-weary councillors were eager to tap into Patrick's youthful charisma and undoubted intelligence and use him as the face and voice of a progressive, vibrant council which, in turn, would attract positive publicity and more dynamic, modern businesses into the local area. Start-ups had become the buzzword in business circles and, while to most councillors it remained a foreign concept, they realised they had to attract some start-up "action" to their region in order to keep pace with the modern world. And in Patrick, they thought they had the ideal councillor to achieve that ambition.

They had all met the day before to plot a strategy for the council meeting that would ultimately reject Patrick's motion, but hopefully without upsetting him too much. They had agreed that only Councillor Adams and Councillor Iain Mainwaring would speak against the motion before it was put to a vote and their objections and inevitable rejection would be understated. The councillors were certain that Patrick's idealism was "just a passing phase" and, soon enough, like all before him, the trappings of power would seduce him and turn him into "one of their own" who would willingly acquiesce to council's generally conservative policy agenda.

For his part, Patrick was totally ignorant of the councillors' strategy and somewhat oblivious to the action on the council floor. He remained blissfully unaware that his motion was doomed to failure. After all, none of the councillors had raised an objection to his reform during previous discussions with them. Mind you, none of them had openly supported it either, and Patrick had understood their silence to be tacit approval for the plan.

The proposal to pay council garbage workers the same as council managers was the first plank of his grand vision for the FAIR manifesto. He'd even pulled off a public relations coup, or so he thought, which fifteen minutes earlier, he had outlined to council. And his PR coup, Patrick thought, would be the story that would accompany his picture on the front page of every newspaper in the country the next morning.

Patrick had an objection to public relations as an industry but he was willing to make an exception in this case as it was for the greater good.

He believed he had a verbal agreement that the most popular rock band in the country, Count Ability, would play a short gig in the town later on in the year as a show of support for Patrick's proposal to equalise the pay of garbage workers and senior managers, and the band had accepted to be paid the same basic wage that a FAIR worker would earn in a week. It was a token gesture, no doubt, but it would be the first small step in changing the world for the greater good. Count Ability usually earned twenty times more per gig than the annual salary of the council's general manager and more than forty times the annual salary of council garbage workers.

"Given the money they respectively earn, we value our entertainers so much more than our garbos. That's just obscene and needs to change," he had argued passionately on the council floor.

The other councillors and a packed public gallery had kept a respectful silence throughout Patrick's impassioned speech, with only an occasional swoon coming from some of his female admirers.

"Imagine if we had no garbage workers? Our quality of life would be severely diminished. But if those obscenely paid pop stars were paid less, we'd still have entertainment, arguably better-quality entertainment, and no egocentric star tantrums we see in the press every day. More importantly, we'd also improve our quality of life. The advertising and sponsorship money they get, under my policy, would be diverted to the industries that make a difference: health, education, and emergency services."

But little did he realise that he had been dealing with a junior staff member at the Count Ability office who was even more idealistic than he was. Seduced by the idea of a truly just and equal society outlined by Patrick, the office junior had promised Patrick that the one and only Count Ability would no doubt love the plan and Patrick had interpreted his enthusiasm as a done deal. It was a quantum leap, but one so easily made when the world was in such need of a saviour.

"Mr. Mayor, there's no doubt that Councillor La Malettie, as Councillor Adams mentioned, is a man of great intelligence, a man whose heart is in the right place and who has a passion for social justice. But, like Councillor Adams, this so-called FAIR plan is nothing of the sort. While we recognise the great work done by our garbologists, it is still unskilled work. People who rise to the managerial ranks are skilled professionals, Mr. Mayor, with university qualifications that have demanded many years of hard work, learning, and personal sacrifice in order to now earn the incomes they thoroughly deserve."

Councillor Mainwaring's monotone delivery had resulted in Patrick totally tuning out of the debate, his thoughts visualising the more just, and less absurd, society of the future. He saw doctors' white coats and nurses' uniforms emblazoned with advertising logos and symbols. When the patients were well enough, doctors and nurses could even secure some extra sponsorship income for themselves and the hospital by spruiking the various services that would help in the post-hospital life of the patients. Naturally, any bonus sponsorship income would be capped to ensure that disparity in wealth was kept to an absolute minimum. Also, they would only be allowed to accept sponsorship income from an ethical business and Patrick had plans to establish a new council department that would be charged with investigating and recommending such businesses. He would not only create new jobs for the local towns but ethically meaningful occupations.

But that was for the hopefully not-too-distant future, thought Patrick as he tuned back into the debate to hear Councillor Mainwaring praise him for "his courage and his conviction".

Deluded by the praise and still believing that all was going to plan with his motion, Patrick once again plunged into contemplation mode.

He had a flashback to the days when he and his teenage friend Gaston would lie on the grass in the park after a sweaty jog, stare at the stars and discuss a wide range of social, political, and economic issues in a depth that belied their age and simple upbringing.

That seems like a lifetime ago. And the story about aliens, Planet Utopia and David Beckham . . . that was it. The heart that gave life to my political plan!

Patrick suddenly realised his FAIR manifesto had its genesis in that park where the sweet smell of the dew on the grass on a sub-tropical summer evening challenged the stench of used tampons and condoms dumped under the nearby trees. Perhaps that memory subconsciously triggered a desire to make the council's garbos the first beneficiaries of his policy. Patrick stifled a chuckle at that thought.

When his family first emigrated to Australia, Patrick had every intention of keeping in touch with Gaston forever. But the thrilling new distractions and opportunity-filled lifestyle of a first-world nation combined with success in his studies and a blossoming political career to ambush his ambition. Those first few years in Australia also coincided with a momentous stage in Patrick's life: the transition from clumsy—but cute—adolescent to handsome, sexually alluring adult surrounded by a new coterie of ambitious and equally attractive friends and lovers. This all conspired to quickly relegate his former best friend to the realm of a pleasant but distant memory. The weekly trip to the local internet café to write emails to Gaston detailing every facet—the good, the bad, and the ugly—of his new life soon became a once-a-year electronic birthday card, and within five years, no communication at all.

Such was the overwhelming "memory loss" of his friendship with Gaston that Patrick hadn't realised, until now, that Gaston had, indeed, been the architect of the FAIR manifesto. The Beckham-Planet Utopia story, among others, had obviously lurked in his subconscious and surfaced when he surprisingly found himself in the political position to formulate his revolutionary policies, and even more surprisingly, to potentially put them into practice.

Wow. Soon Earth will be Planet Utopia Mark II. And a humble young man, with the great help of his former best friend, both from an insignificant third-world island nation, will be responsible for the greatest economic reform in history and possibly save the world from socio-economic catastrophe.

Fond memories of Gaston, the curious child who had introduced him to "big ideas" and the exotic world of Tintin, now came flooding back. Like Gaston (or thanks to Gaston), Patrick, too, had developed a hunger for knowledge beyond the socio-economic straitjacket of his native island, a hunger that he had been able to nurture beyond his wildest dreams living in Australia. He remembered the two of them being simultaneously fascinated, bewildered, and sometimes repulsed by the stories of (what they thought was) absurd human behaviour they'd heard about in the media.

For example, why on earth do so many people still worship the Queen of England as if she and her dysfunctional family were superior beings? Worse still, why is she still sponging off the public purse and being given gifts wherever she goes, even though she's one of the richest women in the world?

And why, oh why, do poor countries like India and Pakistan spend so much money on building nuclear bombs when so many of their people are starving?

These types of stories just didn't make sense to Patrick and Gaston then, and they still didn't make sense to Patrick now as he sat waiting for the councillors to finish the debate on his FAIR reform.

Unusually, perhaps, for teenage boys, they'd also devoted some of their leisure time to dissecting some of the world's major problems and devising (what they thought) were obvious solutions. What struck them at the time was that the obvious solutions seemed to be simple ones.

"Why are some people poor, some people rich, and others not poor and not rich?" Gaston said out of the blue one evening as the boys were trying to regain their breath after a vigorous jog.

"Well, Gaston, some people are more intelligent or have better skills—" Patrick began to reply.

"I know, I know all that," Gaston interrupted impatiently. "It was a rhetorical question!"

"Huh?"

"It's a question that's also the answer," Gaston said.

"Double huh?"

"I mean, it's a question that makes a statement without really expecting an answer . . . ahh, never mind!" Gaston said.

"The point I'm trying to make here is that there are individuals with enough money to live a thousand lifetimes in luxury while many others don't have enough to buy food or have a home. It's a stupid system, isn't it? Why don't we as humans devise a system where we can make sure everyone has at least enough money for the basic things? Surely that can't be difficult?"

A news story Gaston had heard on the radio earlier in the day sparked his train of thought. The story was about an African mother who blamed poverty for forcing her to sell her twelve-year-old daughter to a brothel where the girl was kept like a prisoner and raped by three to six men a day.

"It's so unfair. How can anyone not be angry after hearing that story, and why isn't a rich man helping her?" Gaston said angrily after relating the story to Patrick.

And he was convinced a problem like that had a very simple solution: the world's money needed to be shared around more evenly. After all, humans had created the system of "money" so they could surely and easily fashion a new system where everyone would have a similar amount of money and, thus, a similar standard of life, he explained to Patrick, before concluding that human beings simply needed food, water, a roof over their heads and some love for a decent life.

"Everything else is a bonus. Besides, all humans end up eventually equal anyway; equally dead, that is," he had added half-jokingly.

"But seriously, why or why can't we all be equal in living? Surely that would make life easier and more pleasant for everyone."

Cocooned from the complex social, economic, and political power structures which ordered the global village beyond their island, the teenage Gaston was certain that one day he would convince his fellow human beings to see the sound reasoning behind his simple solutions to save the world.

Little did he realise that a young Karl Marx had been reasoning along similar naïve lines almost two centuries before them, and little did Gaston realise at the time that Patrick would one day actually be in a position to follow through on some of these ideas they had discussed as teenagers.

The adult councillor, Patrick La Malettie, was now, indeed, nervously waiting for the vote and confident that the spark lit by Gaston was about to burst into a flame that would spread like wildfire throughout the world, and it would only be a matter of time before every human on the planet would see the wisdom of their idea for a FAIR-er world and Patrick and Gaston would take their rightful, heroic place in history.

I wish Gaston was here. He would be so proud.

Patrick was watching Councillor Mainwaring speak, but he was so engrossed in the memories of his friendship with Gaston that he heard nothing of the councillor's restrained condemnation of his FAIR plan. If he had been listening, he probably wouldn't have noted on the council papers in front of him a reminder to give Gaston due credit when he announced the practical plans for his FAIR council reform at a press conference he had already scheduled for tomorrow.

CHAPTER XIV

Lessons in the Not-so-fair

"How much money does the Pope have, miss? I bet he doesn't have as much as David Beckham."

Miss Stanislas had her back to the class while she was writing her lesson plan on the blackboard. But she didn't have to turn around to know who had posed the question.

It's Gaston Le Clezio, she thought, rolling her eyes before turning around to address the inquisitor.

"I read in the papers that David Beckham gives a lot of money to charities," Gaston continued as Miss Stanislas met his gaze. "Does the Pope do that too, miss?"

Visual arts—and sometimes religion—teacher Gisele Stanislas, in her late thirties, was a petite, pretty woman with big brown eyes shielded by stylish spectacles and long jet-black hair that was always tied up in a rigid bun as mandated by the Finger Bay Catholic High School.

Since her year-ten religion class began its mandatory curriculum exploration of the Vatican earlier in the week, Gaston had become obsessed with the wealth of the Pope and his Catholic Church. And he continually questioned why they weren't using their money to help the poor.

"Isn't that what Jesus taught us, miss? That you have to give all your money and stuff away to get to Heaven?" he had asked early on in the first lesson after it was revealed that the Vatican, indeed, was one of the wealthiest institutions in the world.

It was a question that momentarily had flummoxed Miss Stanislas: a feeling she was now revisiting with Gaston's current line of inquisition.

Before she could respond this time, Gaston's friend Patrick chimed in with a statement that momentarily baffled the whole class, including Gaston.

"Those Vatican folk are going to be like a camel if they don't give away their money," Patrick said.

A collective "huh" reverberated around the classroom.

"Sorry, my thoughts are a bit jumbled," Patrick said, chuckling to himself. "Recently at mass, the priest said that Jesus warned the rich people that 'it would be easier for a camel to pass through the eye of a needle than for a rich man to enter the kingdom of God',

"So, if these guys at the Vatican spend money on themselves or hoard it away instead of spending it to make the poor less poor, the hungry less hungry, and the homeless less homeless, they'll never go to Heaven, right?"

Miss Stanislas was lost for words but couldn't help letting a wry smile escape and assuage the initial irritation at the interruption to the flow of her lesson. Despite the challenges, she was pleased to have Gaston and his friend Patrick in her class, two teenage boys who questioned the workings of the world rather than toe the establishment line and swallow, hook, line, and sinker, everything the ruling class proposed. They had brought back fond memories of her younger days at the Sorbonne, where she undertook her visual arts and teacher training. Even though she was a Creole, she had been "blessed" with white skin and above-average intelligence. As a result, she managed to secure a scholarship to the prestigious Paris university. Having a French father had no doubt also helped her cause.

All through her four years of training she had often engaged in fierce debates in the university courtyard in summer and in the local cafes in winter on the greed and corruption which plagued the planet, particularly its political and religious institutions. Like many of her peers, Miss Stanislas, at the time, had been optimistic that her generation would eventually change the world for the better, only for her to now end up a committed cynic with a sense of realistic hopelessness in the face of a heartless establishment that would never change without a global collective will to do so.

But that was as likely as Arab-Israeli peace or the Ku Klux Klan embracing Martin Luther King, Jr. as an American hero! she thought.

Nevertheless, the Berlin Wall had come down the year before Miss Stanislas graduated from university. Who would have thought that possible even a few years before it actually happened? And now there was even talk of a black man in the American White House at the next election.

Surely that's pure fiction—written by a deluded black American. Miss Stanislas chuckled inwardly at the thought.

She had much sympathy for the views of Gaston and Patrick on the Vatican seemingly hoarding its wealth while many of its flock starved. She knew the boys weren't being smartarses but were genuinely curious about such things, as she once had been. In her younger days, she, too, had questioned the vast wealth of the Vatican and the "greed is good" cultural norm of the 1980s in the western world, only to be branded "idealistic", a label she wore as a badge of honour at the time.

But now, in her professional capacity as a teacher of religion and a representative of a Catholic school, which paid her well by island standards, there was little room for questioning the modus operandi of the Vatican and its leader. Her personal views or any remnants of youthful idealism were irrelevant. As the teacher of impressionable young Catholics, she had a duty to uphold and defend the faith and all who served it.

"Now, as you may be aware, the monetary system is much more complicated today than in the time of Jesus, and I'm sure the Vatican people work very hard and spend a lot of money helping the world's poor," she unconvincingly reassured the class.

But Gaston sensed that Miss Stanislas's sympathies lay with him and Patrick, so he decided to press the issue. He demanded an example of the Vatican helping the poor or giving money away to the less well-off. Again, Miss Stanislas, deep in nostalgic thought of her own youth, could not immediately come up with evidence that would placate Gaston and Patrick.

Therefore, for homework, she set the class the task of finding a good news story about the Vatican or the Catholic church and, in doing so, she was sure someone would come up with a glowing example of the institution's charitable heart.

But true to form, Gaston found the opposite. The next day he presented a piece of news that demonstrated the cold heart of the Catholic church.

According to a news report1 that Gaston had found on the internet, in 1982, an Italian priest was saying mass in Rome in what the article described as a "gold-plated church near the Spanish Steps".

Reporter Greg Szymanski said in an article he wrote in 2006 that "the priest was about to give his sermon when in stormed a street beggar screaming at the top of his lungs".

"Give me the money and give it to the starving people like me," the beggar had cried. "All criminals at the altar, especially you, Father, with all those golden rings and chalices!"

---

[1] The story written by Greg Szymanski in March 2006 is headlined "Vatican Wealth is 'Truly Astonishing.'" https://rense.com/general70/wealth.htm

Several church ushers rushed to remove him from the premises, but while being pushed out of the church like a piece of garbage, he made one last plea to those attending Holy Sunday Mass.

"Don't give him the money; please don't give it to him! I need to eat. So do many others. All they do here is steal your money while many die in the streets!"

The article concluded with the reporter saying that "the unknown Italian street beggar wasn't given any food that day from the fat cats of the church. In fact, the golden doors were slammed shut on his face as the man walked off, disappearing down the narrow and cobblestoned Rome streets".

But surprisingly, Miss Stanislas found that she was not angry, annoyed, or even frustrated by Gaston's continuing rebellious behaviour—quite the opposite. His challenge to the Vatican orthodoxy had touched a raw nerve and led her to revisit the humanitarian principles and beliefs that had shaped her university years, still the best days of her life. She had long abandoned those values and surrendered to the mainstream ethos of working and consuming your way to happiness. In doing so, not only had she betrayed her true self but also lost the only love of her life to date. Although deep down she knew it all along, Gaston had made her realise that moments of true happiness had been rare since she joined the capitalist "flock", and even more rare since the conversion to a more conservative worldview and lifestyle triggered an acrimonious split from her French boyfriend Remy Francois.

The progeny of an artist couple who had manned the barricades with other art students during the 1968 Paris riots, eighteen-year-old Remy was imbued with the same anti-capitalistic fervour as his parents when he met Miss Stanislas, who was the same age and newly arrived in Paris. And true to the spirit of counterculture and revolution, they had met at the Café Deux Magots, where Remy, armed with a writing pad and paper and fuelled by strong black coffee, spent several hours every day striving to channel the spirit of his literary heroes—Ernest Hemingway, Jean-Paul Sartre, and Albert Camus—to pen his own revolutionary philosophical novel.

It was love at first sight. Both were struck by the proverbial thunderbolt when Remy locked eyes with the wide-eyed Miss Stanislas, who could hardly believe she was in Paris, sitting in and savouring the ambiance of one of the world's most famous cafes.

Wow, Pablo Picasso may have drunk from this very same cup, she was thinking as she looked up to meet the sparkling, smiling blue eyes of Remy Francois.

The couple soon discovered they not only had a strong physical connection but were also intellectually very compatible. They were both studying creative courses at the Sorbonne, Remy in writing and Miss Stanislas in visual arts. They were also mutually seduced by each other's artistic projects: Miss Stanislas's clumsy, cubist-styled paintings depicting scenes from her native island created in homage to her artist hero and Remy's philosophical novel centred on the establishment of a new, humanitarian world order that referenced the pitfalls of Cambodian despot Pol Pot's horrific attempt to wind the clock of human history back to Year Zero.

"Now, Pol Pot had one good idea. But *only* one. The need for human civilisation to stop and start all over again. Everything else Pol Pot did wasn't a revolution but just plain revolting. He was a vile man. I'm the opposite. A good guy who simply wants everyone to live a peaceful life in perfect harmony with one another and nature," Remy had explained, the perfect smile slowly spreading across his face as Miss Stanislas stared at him in awe.

"I know, I know what you're thinking. I'm a crazy, idealistic dreamer. But someone's got to be," Remy said, his smile suddenly evaporating.

"This world is rapidly heading for extinction and evil will prosper if good guys like me do nothing.

"We have to start human history again. That's the premise for my book. But I'll have to call it something else, not Year Zero, obviously."

As their relationship intensified, Miss Stanislas became increasingly seduced by Remy's ideas and his quixotic literary vision. They spent the next few years together sharing a cosy studio apartment in Avenue Rapp in the shadows of the Eiffel Tower, him working on his novel in one corner, her at an easel armed with oil on canvas in another, and the two coming together regularly on the sofa bed in the centre of their one and only living/bedroom, plotting the next "revolution" between steamy sessions of lovemaking. There was also much discussion and agreement about not conforming to the system or compromising their shared values as artists and revolutionaries.

"The revolution is inevitable," Remy confidently predicted many times during the early days of their love.

"And my book will be the bible for the new revolutionaries. Just as the Christian bible stories laid down the rules on how Christians should live, the disciples of the upcoming revolution will use my stories as the philosophical and moral framework on which they will build a fairer world," he confidently boasted.

In Miss Stanislas, Remy had found a disciple. She hung on to every word he spoke and wrote and was even more convinced than Remy of the inevitability of the revolution, which would herald world peace and societies where love, kindness, and compassion reigned. And as their university years rolled on, that was easy enough for them to believe. The couple lived the clichéd classic love story in arguably the most romantic city in the world, in a state of bliss largely cocooned from the economic demands of the real world thanks to Miss Stanislas's scholarship and a generous French welfare system that valued students and artists. And as the end days of their respective studies loomed large on the horizon, Remy remained confident that the bliss would survive when the State inevitably withdrew its "charity". After all, he was about to write the final chapter in what he was convinced would be a bestselling novel. Theirs would be an enduring love story, he thought: *the modern-day Sartre and De Beauvoir.*

It took Remy almost a year to write that final chapter and, in that time, they had finished their university studies. This meant that, long before he had penned the final sentence, the financial well of the State, which had sustained their idyllic lifestyle, had run well and truly dry.

But still infatuated with Remy's visionary ideas, Miss Stanislas decided to find a job to support them both while the love of her life completed his opus. She had excelled in her university studies and managed to find a teaching job through the French Ministry of Education. But in keeping with the ethos of the department to send the least experienced teachers to difficult schools, she ended up with a job at a lycée in the troubled Parisian suburb of St. Denis, where the reality check of teaching in one of the roughest schools in Paris soon evaporated her infatuation with Remy's vision.

They both began to experience something new in the relationship: almost daily arguments about money. Remy seemed indifferent to their financial circumstance and certainly lacked empathy for her challenging job and the sacrifices Miss Stanislas was making in order to preserve their love.

"Look, Remy, you sit here on your arse every daydreaming up these kooky ideas that have nothing to do with the grim reality that I'm living every day," she screamed at him one evening after he had brushed aside her desire for him to find a job so that she could leave hers and take time to find something better.

"I'm just a counselling and reform service for a bunch of budding juvenile delinquents—the spawn of alcoholic, drug-addicted, or abusive parents. They turn up to school hungry and justifiably angry every day, making life hell for teachers and their peers alike," she continued, her anger rising with every syllable.

"It's a wonder they manage to negotiate the day safely without killing each other . . . or themselves . . . or *us*!"

As her anger reached a crescendo and she found herself accusing Remy of being "deluded", she immediately realised there and then that the relationship was over. And in the weeks that followed, the breakdown of the relationship was mirrored by the failure of Remy's literary ambitions. A stream of Parisian publishers rejected his novel and by the time he realised that self-publishing was the only option left and not easy in the pre-internet era, Miss Stanislas had long left their Parisian nest and was already on the teaching staff at the Finger Bay Catholic High School.

Living back on an island where inequality and class privileges were the norm and ingrained into the psyche of the population, she was even more certain that Remy's quest for revolution to a better world was nothing but a futile ambition. She assumed that Gaston and Patrick would come to a similar conclusion—eventually. But she never would have guessed that Patrick would one day be in a position to attempt to take a practical step towards that better, fairer world she and Remy had believed was inevitable.

CHAPTER XV

Humiliation & Exile

Patrick's FAIR manifesto was now on the launchpad with the debate officially over. Even though it was quite cold in the council chambers, courtesy of an air-conditioning system set to "blizzard", Patrick began to sweat profusely. So convinced that history was about to be made and that he would be hailed as a modern-day prophet, Patrick had been oblivious to the mayor's call to finalise votes on his motion.

"All those in favour, say 'aye'," bellowed the mayor.

A moment of deathly silence ensued before Patrick realised what was happening. When he did, he leapt out of his seat, almost yelling his approval. But his confident, high-pitched "aye" quickly retreated into a sheepish silence when he realised he was the only one who was supporting the motion.

"Those against?" And in almost the same chorus that all other councillors voiced their muted "nay", the mayor went on to declare the motion lost.

"I thought I had your support . . ." Patrick mumbled through tears as the councillors quickly moved out of the chamber, avoiding eye contact with a sobbing Patrick, who had slumped back into his seat. Some of the councillors gave Patrick a pat on the back as if to say "well done" as they passed him, but none stopped to console him.

He was right on one count, at least. The next day, the two regional newspapers and even one national newspaper picked up the story. They all had in common some very unflattering headlines. In fact, the one newspaper that graced its front page with the story had the most unflattering headline: *"Council Casts off Commie Councillor"*, the Daily Mercury hollered to its readers. And that really hurt. It was the leading regional newspaper and one he had expected would be a staunch ally in helping him to win over the hearts and minds of his local constituents.

In the weeks that followed the vote, there were no more queues outside his office. His public humiliation and a weakening of his power on the council floor seemed to also trigger a sudden loss of his sexual power over the women of the town.

He was an outcast and inconsolable. At subsequent council meetings, he didn't utter a word and spoke to no one apart from exchanging the unavoidable polite greetings with his fellow councillors, none of whom could look him in the eye again.

Within three months, Patrick La Malettie had not only fled the town but also the country; so deep was his grief of having his political ideas rejected so emphatically in front of what he had believed to be his loyal constituents. He was less than a year into a three-year council term, yet his humiliation was so complete that he immediately resigned his position as councillor, fuelling an unwelcomed by-election that further estranged him from his council cohort. He quietly organised a move back to his native island without telling a single soul in town.

CHAPTER XVI

Compensation

At about the same time that Patrick's plane began its descent into the island's airport, not too far away over the rugged volcanic mountain range that cut the island almost exactly in half, Harriet's piercing scream reverberated around the Finger Bay Catholic Church.

Shellshocked by what they had just witnessed, Gaston and Harriet remained frozen for seemingly an eternity. Harriet's grip on the casserole of octopus curry had not been able to withstand the assault from Father Terry's semen. It had fallen heavily on the concrete confessional floor, scattering the curry far and wide and terminally damaging Harriet's favourite casserole pan.

Alerted by her distressing scream, four of the Finger Bay fathers rushed into the church to be confronted by Gaston's consoling arm around his hysterically sobbing mother. Behind the pair, the priests caught sight of a sheepish and dishevelled Father Terry staggering out of the confessional, their eyes drawn to the damp patch rapidly spreading on the front of his cassock.

One of the senior priests, Father Thibault, quickly grasped the gravity of the situation and took charge. He took a firm hold of Harriet's elbow and ushered her and Gaston, whose arm was still fastened around his mother's shoulder, out the side door of the church, insincerely apologising all the way.

"I'm so sorry, my dear lady," Father Thibault said with feigned compassion. "Rest assured, Father Terry will be punished for this. God knows the devil strikes when you least expect it."

As they all stepped outside the church, the fresh air of a breezy sub-tropical afternoon seemed to slap the clinging duo out of their emotional stupor. Harriet even managed to find some semblance of voice.

"Thank ... thank you, Father," she muttered. "But why? Why? How can the devil possess such a divine man? The holiest of men?" Harriet added, her voice regaining strength and composure with each syllable.

Father Thibault guided them towards the same seat, where, fifteen minutes earlier, Gaston had been saying his penance and recovering well from the ordeal at the police station. The trio remained standing, Gaston and Harriet both seemingly in a trance.

Now fully sober, Gaston suddenly felt a surge of inward anger, but anger that was only partially directed at Father Terry's wicked deed. He was more incensed at his own apathy, inaction, and the alcohol-induced emotional depths he'd plummeted into over the past month or so. He had long known about the criminal behaviour of the Finger Bay fathers. After all, he himself had narrowly escaped becoming a victim of their depravity. Gaston also knew deep down that Henri had been sexually abused by Father Terry earlier today. He had seen the evidence in the public toilet. Yet he had consciously chosen to ignore it and take no action. If he had, he might have saved his dear mother from bearing witness to Father Terry's depravity. While he could be excused for repressing the memory of Father Orton's shameful death given his youth, there was no excuse for not taking action today.

Why didn't I do something? But what could I have done?

Gaston suddenly thought of Tintin and a wry smile escaped his face. Tintin certainly wouldn't have started the day downing a bottle of rum like he had and Tintin would certainly have fought back when confronted with such evil. And at the end of the day, Tintin would have been triumphant and the bad guys would be in jail. Even Tintin's dog Milou would have put up a braver fight than Gaston had today.

Still on autopilot, Gaston and Harriet sat down, but Father Thibault remained standing as he continued talking to the pair. But neither Harriet nor Gaston could register what he was saying. Mother and son stared blankly ahead, occasionally blinking or closing their eyes, each absorbed in processing their respective level of harrowing emotion stirred by the events of the day.

"I'm sure we can find a way to compensate you for your suffering today, my dear Mrs. Le Clezio . . ." Father Thibault said.

The word "compensate" vaguely penetrated into Harriet's consciousness, and when it was swiftly followed by a reference to "mass seating arrangements", Harriet suddenly snapped out of her trance. She lifted her head, a hint of a smile breaking out and rapidly spreading across her face as she heard clearly Father Thibault's assurance that the third row of church pews would be reserved for the family from now on at ten o'clock mass every Sunday for the rest of the year, regardless of the donation the family offered.

"Of course, that guarantee is conditional upon you being discreet about what you've witnessed here today," Father Thibault continued. "After all, we don't want to cause any alarm in the community about this very isolated event. As you said yourself, one never knows when the devil will strike so we must remain vigilant always.

"Rest assured, we will ensure that Father Terry's demons are exorcised and he will once again be the fine priest that he's always been, one who cares very deeply about his parishioners. But as you can appreciate, dear Mrs. Le Clezio, any hint of scandal may jeopardise his recovery, so I think it's best you don't tell anyone about what happened today, and we'll be here to welcome your family to the third row on Sunday."

Gaston, however, remained oblivious to Father Thibault's monologue, his thoughts still focused on the evil deeds of the Finger Bay fathers and his own failings.

Who would have thought a woman could wreak such havoc on my emotions and set me down a path of self-destruction? he thought.

A tear trickled out of his left eye, only to be instantly swallowed up by the mass of facial hair. But Gaston wasn't feeling sad, just somewhat sorry for himself. At the same time, he could also feel an emerging resolve to arrest his downward spiral.

Gaston clenched his fists and opened his eyes wide. A wicked smirk slowly spread across his face as he perceived Father Thibault's crotch at eye level and within kicking distance. He felt the urge to lash out savagely with his foot and strike not only a personally painful blow to Father Thibault but also a symbolic body blow against the sins of the Finger Bay fathers.

But a flashback to the harrowing events of the morning quickly quelled his desire to physically hurt Father Thibault. He would risk ending up once again a "guest" of the intimidating Sergeant Cailason and this time, facing an even more serious charge of assault. The thought of standing toe-to-toe again with the aggressive police sergeant sent shivers up his spine and caused him to lessen the tension in his leg and foot that had been poised to strike.

Instead, Gaston suddenly rose from the seat and made a beeline for the toilet block where earlier he had conveniently evaded the evidence of Henri's abuse. He didn't know why he was heading there; he just knew he had to get away from a situation where his rapidly rising anger might have set him on a course of action that he would regret. Unlike earlier this afternoon, when alcohol was a barrier to better judgment, he was now thinking clearly.

Harriet was now so immersed in conversation with Father Thibault that she didn't even notice Gaston's departure. She had regained her composure and general good humour. The thought of her dramatic elevation up the church pew pecking order courtesy of a "devil's deed" was proof to Harriet that God indeed worked in a very mysterious way. As Father Thibault spoke, Harriet was looking into his eyes like a dewy-eyed schoolgirl seduced once again by the power of the good Lord undoubtedly speaking through his dutiful earthly servant. The harrowing but also unnervingly arousing events of the afternoon had all but vanished from her thoughts.

Wow! The third row at the most popular mass of the week. My neighbours will be impressed. The whole village will be impressed, were the only thoughts that now occupied Harriet's mind.

CHAPTER XVII

Veiled Threats and Nostalgia

Gaston arrived at the entrance to the toilet block and hesitated. He looked back to see his mother and Father Thibault still deeply locked in conversation. It was nauseating to see his mother smiling, blushing, flirting with yet another evil Finger Bay father. But what could he do?

The situation was seemingly hopeless. He certainly wasn't going to find a way to bring the wicked fathers to justice in the toilet block. But just as the chasm of hopelessness was about to swallow him up, Gaston suddenly remembered the bloodied altar boy robe he had avoided earlier.

That robe, if indeed it was Henri's robe as Gaston suspected, surely contained evidence that could be used against Father Terry. He had seen enough crime films where the evidence of a bloodstained garment had been used to convict evildoers.

If Father Terry had indeed abused Henri, his fingerprints too would surely be all over that robe, he thought.

And then there was another type of evidence they used these days to convict bad guys.

What was it called again? Ahh, yes, DNA evidence. Surely Father Terry's DNA would be all over that robe.

Gaston knew that DNA had something to do with genetics from his vague recollection of biology classes at school. He hadn't really been interested in any kind of science then and certainly was none the wiser now, but he did know that special police units used DNA evidence to identify criminals and link them to the scene of the crime. He just didn't know how. He also knew that Father Terry and most of the Finger Bay fathers should be in jail and a bloodied robe, infested with Father Terry's DNA and fingerprints, could be the piece of evidence that would put at least Father Terry there. If that happened, surely it would only be a matter of time before the other evil priests followed him.

Although serious crimes like murders, assaults, and armed robberies were still not as common on the island as in what native islanders called the "big countries", they had been on the rise since the end of colonial rule, another sign that some of the more malevolent tentacles of the global village were fast encroaching upon the island. Gaston had read stories in the newspaper where crimes on the island had been solved using DNA evidence.

He remembered one particular case when a rapist was identified and convicted because his DNA had been extracted and detected from the fingernails of the victim.

Gaston felt a sudden surge in adrenaline that set his legs in motion. He ran into the toilet block in anticipation, but the robe had vanished and, with it, his momentary ray of hope.

He looked up and saw himself in the mirror. He recoiled in horror at the ape-like face that stared back at him.

"How on earth did I let myself get to this point?" he gasped.

He almost didn't recognise himself. Before the breakup with Natalie, he was always clean-shaven. He detested facial hair, mainly because when he first experimented with growing a moustache in his late teens, a girl he wanted to date told him the moustache made him look more Indian. And given the island's social climate of silent apartheid, Gaston took offence and, at the time, vowed never ever to grow any kind of facial hair.

He turned on the tap and cupped his hands under the water. He bent his head down towards the basin and splashed his face with the cool liquid. He felt instantly refreshed, his mind buzzing with thoughts of revenge.

Gaston felt disappointed that the robe had vanished, but at the same time, he realised that it was a long shot anyway. After this morning he was certainly no friend of the local police, which was the obvious place to find someone to analyse his evidence. Also, Gaston had heard many rumours that corruption was rife among the police force, so his quest for justice through the bloodstained robe may have been short-lived anyway.

Who else could have helped him investigate the evidence? A scientist? A private investigator? A lawyer? He didn't know anyone in or connected to those professions. He certainly couldn't afford to pay anyone to investigate. This rush of thoughts erased his disappointment at not finding the bloodstained robe but also reopened the chasm of hopelessness.

Gaston suddenly felt suffocated, knowing outside he was surrounded by many Finger Bay fathers who would be distressed with Father Terry's apparent fall from grace. Such an event risked having their sexual exploits scrutinised and possibly exposed to the general public—and even criminal prosecution.

Gaston had vaguely heard Father Thibault mention "compensation" to his mother as long as she didn't reveal anything about the afternoon's scandalous events to anyone. He knew that his mother would comply with Father Thibault's wishes, but he was under no such obligation to obey. He wanted nothing short of bringing them to justice and an end to their depraved behaviour. But he also knew the priests would quickly realise the potential threat he posed to their morally deviated fiefdom. And they would stop at nothing to extinguish that threat. Father Thibault's sudden generosity to his mother in elevating her in the church pew pecking order was a clear warning sign. Gaston knew they would also try to buy his silence, but in his case they would not be so generous. They would be more likely to threaten or brutalise him into silence.

And given their lack of moral boundaries, the risk of serious injury or even death was a distinct possibility.

He winced at that last thought and had the urge to flee as quickly as possible.

As he emerged from the toilet block, Gaston suddenly remembered his old friend Patrick who, unbeknownst to him, had only minutes earlier felt the sensual assault of the warm, humid island air for the first time in ten years as he set foot outside the island's airport terminal.

Gaston had heard that his old friend and teenage jogging partner had become a "big shot" abroad. He certainly could use a good friend right now. He stood on the toilet block porch staring straight ahead but saw nothing. He found himself reminiscing about his close friendship with Patrick, founded on a love of books and political discussion.

But Gaston's reflection on the more pleasant times with his teenage friend soon transformed into the unpleasant reality of facing his foes again. As he started walking back towards his mother and Father Thibault, they suddenly stopped their conversation and turned their eyes towards him. Gaston could see the venom in Father Thibault's stare, which unnerved him. But he had no choice. He had to walk past the two to make his escape.

As he approached the pair, however, Gaston was stopped dead in his tracks by the foreboding figure of Sergeant Cailason striding up the presbytery pathway towards them all, concern glowing in his eyes.

"Is everything all right, Father?" Cailason bellowed as he stopped in front of Father Thibault, who had taken a few paces back and away from where Harriet still sat, momentarily silent.

"I ran into Mrs. Kisnorbo as I was walking out of the station to go home and she said she'd heard a terrifying scream when she was walking past the church . . ." Cailason explained.

Before Father Thibault could answer, Cailason noticed out of the corner of his eye that Gaston was looking at them both.

"That fu—err, scumbag—excuse the language, Father—he's not the cause of this trouble, is he?" Cailason asked menacingly, his tone rising markedly with every syllable.

"No trouble here at all, sergeant," Father Thibault calmly replied. "Gaston came to confess his sins like the good Catholic man that he is. And his dear mother, Harriet . . ." he continued, nodding acknowledgment to Harriet still sitting on the seat in the ever-growing shadows of the afternoon light, ". . . came to support him like the good Catholic family that the Le Clezios are, sergeant."

Cailason hadn't noticed Harriet sitting on the bench until now. And once again, he felt embarrassed by the aggressive tone and language he had just employed, unaware that a lady was present.

For his part, Gaston was surprised that he was no longer fearful, as he looked first at Father Thibault then Cailason directly in the eyes with a steely stare that reflected more his anger and desire for justice.

Father Thibault and Cailason were standing side-by-side, silent, staring back at Gaston in a scene that reminded him of the duels he'd often seen in his favourite American western films.

Suddenly, Gaston's gaze was distracted by movement behind Cailason and Father Thibault. A group of priests was walking out of the church in a choreographed huddle, with Father Terry in the middle shielded from view and making their way to the back entrance of the presbytery. Gaston could see that they were silently laughing as they strolled, trying not to draw attention to themselves.

If he'd had a grenade, Gaston would have happily lobbed it over Father Thibault and Cailason into the huddle and rejoiced in the revenge of obliterating a significant number of his foes in one devastating blow.

Alas, only a daydream in the fading afternoon light, thought Gaston, laughing inside.

Meanwhile, Cailason felt obliged to apologise to Harriet for the second time today.

"I am again so sorry, dear lady, I didn't realise you were there," he spluttered out.

Cailason was uncomfortable addressing his apology directly to Harriet so he continued with his gaze drifting between her, Gaston, and Father Thibault, all the while flailing his arms around before they found a resting place with both hands on his hips and his thumbs inserted into his regulation police belt, cowboy style. The palm of his right hand covered his holstered pistol.

"Given Mrs. Kisnorbo seemed very frightened by the scream she heard, I thought there may have been a crime in progress so I rushed over here, and when I'm stressed like that, my language can be a bit colourful."

Cailason suddenly remembered that the scream had yet to be explained!

"Father, please, who was responsible for the scream that caused such alarm for Mrs. Kisnorbo? And why?"

Before Father Thibault had a chance to reply, Harriet rose from her seat and approached the two men.

"It was me, sergeant," Harriet explained. "Just as I walked into the church, I saw a huge rat run out of the confessional, heading straight for me. It moved so fast I didn't have time to get out of its way. It ran between my legs, touching them on the way through. That's when I screamed. Worse still, it caused me to drop and shatter my favourite casserole dish, which had a delicious octopus curry I wanted to share with the fathers."

Harriet felt no guilt at all in lying to Sergeant Cailason, despite lying being a sin. In her mind, it was her heavenly duty to protect God's representatives on earth: the divine Finger Bay fathers who had just promoted her up the church pew pecking order.

And the third row . . . the third row! Wow!

Confession and prayer would absolve her of her sin, although for confession to have effect, she would need to feel remorseful of her sin, which she didn't. Surely, she would receive God's forgiveness for such a "little white lie" after an hour or two of suffering, kneeling in prayer on the stone pathway in front of the Virgin Mary at home.

"I'm very sorry I caused Mrs. Kisnorbo such distress and for you to come running all the way here in such an anxious state, thinking that a crime may be in progress," Harriet concluded.

"It's no problem, madame," Sergeant Cailason replied. "It's all part of the job. You don't need to apologise."

"And there's no need *for you* to apologise for your tough language, sergeant. I understand perfectly well," Harriet said. "We're lucky to have such a good man protecting the good citizens of Finger Bay."

Cailason was indeed relieved there was no crime or violent criminal. Some days, he simply felt too old and tired to take on criminals and this was one of those days. He was still incensed at his feeble capitulation in the face of the arrogant Australian "arsehole" wielding his weapon of "white". And to complete the humiliation, the arsehole's father had turned up in the company of the island's chief police inspector just as he was about to head home, demanding that his son be released immediately. And again, Cailason had no option but to capitulate and comply with his "white-arsed" demands. The inspector made it very clear that failure to do so would not only risk a major diplomatic incident but also a potentially great economic loss to the island. The father, it turned out, was a very wealthy resort developer who was planning to build the island's first six-star resort, which would be worth millions of dollars to the national economy but more importantly, also create hundreds of ongoing jobs for local workers. Apparently, the son had fallen in love with a beautiful island girl and they were planning to marry and manage the resort.

What was he doing fucking a prostitute on the beach, then? Cailason had thought but wisely decided to keep the thought to himself.

Given the way the inspector was fawning over the "big shot" Australian developer, he quickly realised it would potentially have been a career-ending move. As the trio left the police station, heading towards the father's luxury car parked arrogantly in the "Police Vehicles Only" parking bay in front of the station, Cailason saw the father discreetly hand over an envelope to the inspector. Cailason knew that bribes had been a routine and regular part of police business on the island for a long time. Most islanders knew it too.

And Cailason himself was certainly no saint. He used to have a suitcase full of cash stashed under his wardrobe at home, courtesy of the "grateful" learner drivers who had been granted their driving licences despite obviously failing their driving tests. During his earlier days in the police force Cailason worked for the island's police roads and traffic unit, which was responsible for issuing all driving licences on the island and it was part of his duties to conduct driving tests. Many of the female learner drivers were particularly generous to the then handsome young Cailason. And if they couldn't offer money, he was more than happy to accept their offer of payment "in kind", the kind that usually involved a sleazy midnight rendezvous in an equally sleazy, flea-bitten hotel on the other side of the island.

Harriet went over to Gaston and took him by the hand.

"Come, Gaston, I think we've had enough excitement for one day. It's time we went home," she said.

Father Thibault continued to view Gaston menacingly as he and his mother moved towards the pathway that led out of the church grounds.

As they drew level with the two men, Father Thibault gently touched Gaston on the elbow, which was a signal for them to stop. Gaston sensed a threat was imminent and steeled himself for it.

Father Thibault chose his words carefully so as not to give Sergeant Cailason any cause for suspicion.

"Now, my dear boy, before you and your dear mother head home, I'd just like to give you a bit of advice that may help you maintain a holy path," Father Thibault began.

Gaston was surprised by Father Thibault's compassionate, gentle tone, which belied his menacing look.

"When you get home, I'd like you to reflect long and hard about the experiences you've had today and what you've seen and heard," he continued.

"As a good Catholic boy, or should I say a fine young Catholic man, you know that God indeed has the power to forgive even the most evil of sinners. If I were you, I'd be very discreet about the events of today, and in doing so, like your mother who is blessed with absolute faith, you, too, will reap great rewards here and an even greater one in Heaven.

"However, if you choose a different, perhaps contrary path, God will find you out, and like all sinners, I have no doubt that life on earth will be hell for you and certainly Hell will await you when you die."

While Father Thibault maintained the veil of compassion and gentleness throughout, Gaston nonetheless sensed the underlying threat contained in his counsel.

For his part, Cailason listened pensively to Father Thibault, thinking that the Father's advice to Gaston was in response to his earlier drunken transgressions that almost landed him in jail. He was unaware of the most recent scandal involving Harriet, Gaston, and Father Terry so the advice seemed perfectly reasonable to him and raised no suspicion whatsoever.

"Well said, Father. Good advice for any God-fearing Catholic soul," Cailason said, conveniently ignoring his own lack of remorse at the litany of mortal sins, crimes, and misdemeanours he'd committed throughout his life, which would surely reserve him a first-class ticket to Hell when he died.

Cailason gave Gaston an intimidating look that rapidly transformed into an insincere smile when he noticed that Harriet was looking at him.

"I'm sure young Gaston has learnt a good lesson today, madam, and I don't expect to have him as my 'guest' again," he said.

"Thank you, sergeant," Harriet replied. "Now, if you'll excuse us, we really need to get home. It's been a very trying day indeed."

Still leading Gaston by the hand, Harriet moved towards Father Thibault and Cailason, who realised that they were blocking their path to the exit, but like a pair of automatic doors, the pair reacted simultaneously, moving their bodies side-on to allow Gaston and Harriet to pass. Gaston could not bear to look at them as he passed but could sense the dagger of their insincere smiles accompanying them all the way out of the church grounds.

Just before exiting, Gaston turned around to see Father Thibault with his arm around Cailason's shoulder, guiding him towards the presbytery. Gaston realised there and then that, to exact revenge, he would have to take on and conquer two of the most powerful forces on the island. Little did he realise that within weeks, there would be a third force lining up against him.

CHAPTER XVIII

Idris

Gaston heard Idris before he saw him. He was a good ten metres away from the familiar red and white twirling pole outside Idris's barbershop when he heard the clickety-clack of scissors competing with Idris's booming voice ear-bashing a customer, as was his custom.

Idris didn't notice Gaston walking into the barbershop; he was so absorbed in his mission of cutting hair and even more so in vehemently condemning the prime minister for adding yet another storey to his mansion looming on the scenic hills just outside Finger Bay.

"That good-for-nothing crook is building a palace just like all those tin pot despots in Africa," Idris bellowed. "And he always has a police escort, even when he goes to the beach in his chauffeur-driven car! Worse still, have you noticed wherever he goes, they switch all the traffic lights to green for his car so it never has to stop? They say it's to prevent terrorists from getting to him. Terrorists, my arse. He's the only fucking terrorist on this isla—"

Idris was suddenly rendered mute and his scissors still as he looked up in the mirror and caught Gaston's reflection behind him. Gaston had quietly taken a seat, waiting his turn. He was reading a magazine when, instinctively, he felt Idris's gaze, which made him look up and break out in a broad smile.

"Wow, monsieur Gaston, all that hair!" Idris exclaimed as the booming voice returned to full volume. "What have you done to yourself? I almost didn't recognise you."

It had been a couple of weeks since his harrowing encounter with the Finger Bay fathers and Gaston had spent most of that time sleeping and laying to rest the ghost of his heartbreak. His sleep was peppered with nightmares of the Finger Bay fathers, including one which, upon awakening, initially caused him distress but then gave him an idea. The nightmare was set inside the Finger Bay church. Gaston was dressed in a classic medieval executioner's outfit, complete with a leather mask. He was wielding a curved, large, bladed sword similar to the one carried by Sinbad, one of his favourite childhood book and cartoon characters. One by one, the priests were tied down on the altàr with genitals exposed, legs spread and dangling off the end and over either corner of the altar.

Gaston would castrate each one with a swift blow of his sword, which unleashed two testicles and a gush of blood that swallowed the (also) severed penis. The testicles bounced onto the floor only to be scooped up and eaten by a giant rat. Each priest's castration followed the same script as if the same scene was on a continual loop through Gaston's sleeping mind, although each time Gaston recognised it was a different priest. He woke up in the clichéd cold sweat of nightmares and howled softly. Sleepily, he switched on his bedside lamp which also seemed to trigger an equally clichéd light bulb moment.

That's it. I need to find a way to castrate the priests, he thought.

In his half-sleep, Gaston was suddenly buoyant—excited even by the prospect of justice by castration—and managed to fall back to more blissful sleep. But several hours later when fully awake and walking to Idris's barbershop, he recalled the nightmare and quickly realised that the idea of castrating the Finger Bay priests was pure fantasy. He dismissed the thought with a snigger and shake of the head, but it nevertheless seeped into his subconscious.

"I haven't seen you for a very long time, Monsieur Gaston," Idris said, now smiling broadly and revealing a mix of crooked, rotting, missing, and tar-stained teeth—testimony to the poor dental hygiene and high smoking rates that plagued the island's low socio-economic classes.

The poor health of his teeth was also a scar on his otherwise handsome features whenever he laughed or smiled. Idris was a tall man of obvious African descent, dark brown in skin colour and crowned in a classic short-to-medium length afro hairstyle, which was always immaculately styled and groomed, and a natural, enduring promotion for his prowess as a hairdresser.

Idris's once-thriving business had witnessed a steady decline in recent years mainly through natural attrition, that is, the older clientele dying off and also many of the younger ones fleeing the country in search of a better life for their children abroad. Nevertheless, Idris was still managing to make enough money to sustain a modest lifestyle. Being a single man with no family ties who lived alone helped, although it also fuelled continuous rumours about his sexuality and hushed tales of "strange young men" allegedly visiting his modest corrugated iron home at all hours of the night.

Gaston paid no attention to those rumours. Idris had always been a great sounding board for the good, the bad, and the ugly of his life's journey so far, and he considered him a friend. His father, Gaetan, had introduced him to Idris when he was a teenager.

"What have you been up to besides growing hair? Surely your girlfriend's not happy with your look? How is the beautiful Natalie?"

The smile on Gaston's face evaporated at the mention of her name, which, in turn, caused Idris to pause and witness the gloom that descended upon his friend's demeanour. He quickly realised he'd ventured into territory that Gaston no longer inhabited and did not want to revisit.

"Oh, I'm very sorry, Monsieur Gaston. I didn't know that you and Natalie had . . . you know . . . you were such a lovely coup—"

Suddenly lost for words, Idris knew he was only compounding Gaston's sorrow, but at least he had an explanation as to why his friend was consumed in facial hair.

But Gaston quickly moved to put his friend at ease.

"I'm okay, Idris. I've probably dodged a bullet. It was getting too intense really . . . you know . . . still too young to get so serious," Gaston said unconvincingly.

The outward melancholy and forlorn tone in his voice betrayed the inner peace that he now felt after two weeks off the demon drink. He had finally come to terms with the fact that Natalie was gone, forever. And now a haircut and shave from his good friend Idris would surely help him deal further with the ever-waning emotional residue.

"I'm really sorry to hear that, Monsieur Gaston," Idris said with genuine compassion. "I won't be much longer and then if you need to talk . . ."

"Take your time, Idris," Gaston replied. "I'm in no hurry and happy to wait."

The clickety-clack of scissors resumed, but this time minus the bellicose monologue from Idris, who felt sincerely sorry for his friend.

They were such a lovely couple—an ideal couple, he thought.

Gaston looked around the spartanly furnished barbershop that accommodated one standard barber chair, which had seen better days, two bright orange plastic chairs for waiting clientele, and a small coffee table on which sat a dozen or so magazines and a newspaper. He went to return the magazine he'd been reading to the pile when his eyes fell upon the front-page newspaper photo that caused him to gasp in horror.

"Croc Mauls Finger Bay Boy to Death," screamed the headline that was accompanied by two photos, one of a seemingly smiling crocodile and the other of a chubby-faced young boy whom Gaston instantly recognised.

"Oh my God!" Gaston murmured to himself. "It's Henri!"

Gaston snatched the newspaper off the table and began to read, his hands shaking as he did so.

The newspaper reported that a young Finger Bay boy, identified as Henri Laroche, had accidentally fallen into the crocodile pit at the island's wildlife park and was instantly devoured by a crocodile. Apparently, there had been no witnesses so the authorities were left to ponder as to how and why the boy had come to be within the enclosure in the first place. A solid, two-metre wire fence surrounded the crocodile enclosure, and for further protection of the public, the three medium-sized crocs were accommodated in a pit that was about a metre and a half below ground level of the enclosure. The authorities could only speculate that the boy had climbed the fence, then lost his footing and fallen into the pit while trying to get a better view of the crocodiles.

"After all, boys will be boys. They are risk-takers who often don't realise the danger until it's too late," the reporter had editorialised, which Gaston thought was a touch insensitive.

Looking mournfully at the angelic, smiling boy beaming back at him from the front page, Gaston felt a tear welling in his eye; then he suddenly remembered the bloodstained altar boy robe he had seen in the church toilet block. He felt a shiver down his spine. What if Henri's death wasn't an accident? Gaston wanted to instantly dismiss the idea, but it lingered. It was nauseating to contemplate that Henri could be so traumatised by his abuse at the hands of Father Terry that he would take his own life. And if that was indeed the case, Father Terry was nothing short of a murderer.

"I know I'm jumping to conclusions, but it does seem rather coincidental that Henri should have a fatal 'accident' so soon after being abused by Father Terry," Gaston silently reasoned. "And what was Henri doing at the wildlife park on his own? The report said there had been no witnesses."

Although Gaston didn't know him very well, Henri had come across as a shy boy and not an obvious "risk-taker".

Gaston was anxious and angry but most of all determined to get to the truth—straight after a shave and a haircut.

CHAPTER XIX

A Not-so-pleasant Memory

"Monsieur Gaston . . . Monsieur Gaston, I'm ready for you."

Gaston was shaken out of his trance-like state by Idris's summons to the barber's chair. He'd been so lost in grief and contemplation over Henri's death that he hadn't noticed that the previous client had already paid and left the shop.

"Are you okay, Monsieur Gaston? You look like you've seen a ghost," Idris said. "Are you thinking of . . . you know?"

Gaston looked up to be greeted by the sympathetically smiling face of Idris and he felt instantly less grief-stricken.

"Sorry, Idris . . . no, no, it's nothing to do with Natalie. I am really fine about her now. Did you hear about the boy who was eaten by a crocodile at the wildlife park?" Gaston asked.

"Ah, you knew the boy?"

"Yes, yes. Not very well, but I knew him," Gaston replied.

"Oh, I am so sorry to hear that, Monsieur Gaston," Idris said. "I heard about that poor boy on the radio this morning before reading about it in the newspaper."

By this time, Gaston had settled into the barber's chair and Idris had fastened the collar of the regulation barber's cape tightly around his neck and wrapped the cape itself around his body to catch the expectant deluge of hair.

"Please, Idris, stop calling me monsieur. It makes me feel uncomfortable," Gaston said. "I saw him, Henri, that is, not long ago. I can't believe this has happened."

"Yes, such a terrible accident. His poor mother," Idris said.

"That's the problem, Idris. I don't think it was an accident," Gaston interrupted.

"*Mon dieu*! Monsi—my friend, you can't be serious?" Idris replied. "What else could it have been?"

Gaston realised he'd let the cat out of the bag somewhat and felt obliged to recount the story of Henri's apparent sexual abuse at the hands (and God knows what else) of Father Terry. But despite feeling that he could trust Idris explicitly,

Gaston stopped short of telling him about his mother's confrontation with the masturbating Father Terry.

"So, what do you think, Idris? Could it have been suicide?" Gaston asked. "It's a grisly way to do it, but effective!"

Idris pondered the question while spraying Gaston's hair with water in preparation for cutting.

"Yes, effective indeed, my dear friend, but I doubt he—"

A sudden memory emerged to render Idris mute. As a fifteen-year-old teenager, he'd had a crush on his cousin Mariel, who was of similar age. However, Idris was a very shy boy so whenever she came over with her family for a visit, he'd break out in a cold sweat and remain in his room until his mother, Irene, shamed him out with loud pleas for the visitors to excuse her "ill-mannered son". He was then forced to greet the five members of Mariel's family with a kiss on both cheeks. The first time he remembered having to kiss Mariel, he was visibly shaking and felt so embarrassed when his cold sweat dripped onto her cheek that he fled back into his bedroom and didn't emerge again for the rest of the evening. He subsequently made sure he had a handkerchief handy every time the family came over in case he had to wipe his face before greeting them.

When she came over for family celebrations like birthdays and Christmas, Idris would worship her from afar, almost stalking every move made by the confident, gregarious heartbreaker-in-waiting who would flirt outrageously with the older male members of the extended family. Mariel also loved to showcase her singing talent and would entertain the family on such occasions with impromptu renditions of popular island songs.

No doubt about it, she's way out of my league, Idris had thought, then reconciled his disappointment with the fact that Mariel was also his cousin, so any romantic relationship would have been taboo anyway. Nevertheless, his pubescent lust for her found some relief in his first experiences with masturbation.

But, about a year after Idris's lustful infatuation with Mariel began, she suddenly stopped coming when her family visited. Idris simply assumed that she'd found a boyfriend and, although disappointed at first, he felt some relief from the pressure of having to be sociable in the face of her sexual intimidation. He did notice, however, that the demeanour of Mariel's parents, Markus and Delilah, had changed markedly. They had been cheerful, extroverted types but now seemed inconsolably sad and only stayed briefly before making some excuse as to why they needed to rush back home. When she also didn't show up for Christmas, Idris knew there was something drastically wrong.

"Why doesn't Mariel come anymore?" Idris asked his mother as she was doing the dishes after Christmas lunch.

"You're too young to understand, darling," Irene had replied.

However, a few days later he heard his mother mention Mariel's name as he was about to enter the lounge room to say goodnight to his parents, who were having a cup of herbal tea before bed. It made him stop short of the lounge room door, out of sight but within earshot of the conversation.

"It's all so sad, Eric," he heard his mother say. "That poor, poor girl. I just can't imagine anyone could do that sort of thing to such an innocent child. And her own uncle, her own flesh and blood."

"So where is she now?" asked Eric.

"They've taken her to the Jung Clinic," replied Irene.

"Isn't that where they put crazy folk?" asked Eric, alarmed.

"It certainly is," replied Irene. "Markus didn't know what to do after she tried to kill herself."

Idris couldn't contain his shock at the news. It found expression in a muffled squeal that alerted his parents to his presence. A few minutes later, he was sitting on the sofa between his parents and in tears, wanting to know more about what had happened to his cousin. Both parents had their arms around him, trying to reassure him that Mariel was in good hands and that she would be okay.

"But why did she try to kill herself?" Idris kept asking.

"Well, err—" Irene began.

"He may as well know the truth. He's nearly sixteen," Eric interrupted before turning Idris towards him.

"Well, son, you remember Mariel's uncle, Harold, Markus's brother? It turns out that he's been doing things with Mariel that he shouldn't be doing . . . err . . . evil things that only horrible men do," Eric said. "Not only that, but he also brought her to some of his friends who did the same thing."

"What did they do?" asked Idris, who knew deep down but wanted it confirmed by his dad.

"Well, they did adult things to her, forced her to . . . you know. We've had that talk about the birds the bees . . . err . . . sex . . . and that's fine if it's between two adults who love each other but never with a child . . ."

In the days that followed, Idris found out that Mariel had attempted to slash her wrists with blunt razor blades, which proved her saviour. She would have no doubt succeeded if the razor blades had been sharp.

The moment spent in reminiscence of Mariel's fate allowed Idris to finally form the opinion that Henri had probably taken his own life.

If sexual abuse had triggered a suicide attempt by a previously well-adjusted girl like Mariel, it was entirely plausible that the sexual abuse Henri suffered may have led him down a similar path. And unlike Mariel's razor blades, those crocodile teeth *were* razor-sharp.

Nevertheless, he kept silent as he started cutting Gaston's hair.

"Well, my dear friend, it does seem a very odd 'accident', so suicide is a real possibility. But wow, what a gruesome way to go," he finally managed to utter.

"I know, I know, Idris," Gaston replied. "The more I think about it, the more I'm convinced that Father Terry is a murderer."

"Then you'll have to go to the police and tell them what you know. You owe it to your friend Henri," Idris said.

"I can't do that, Idris." Gaston quickly replied.

Gaston was reluctant to recount the misdeed that landed him as a guest of the Finger Bay police force. He still felt so embarrassed by the incident.

"Let's just say I don't trust the police. And they'd never believe me anyway," Gaston said. "I wouldn't be surprised if they already know what the priests are doing, but like everyone else, they're powerless to do anything or don't want to do anything."

"You know, Gaston, it all makes sense now," Idris said.

"What do you mean?"

"Well, my sister Monique works in the presbytery kitchen, and I remember her saying that she sometimes hears boys screaming," Idris said. "One day she asked one of the priests about it and he just said it was the television."

"Well, now you know the truth, Idris," Gaston said.

Both men felt an equal sense of anger and helplessness that plunged the salon into silence except for the sound of the scissors continuing the slick journey through Gaston's thick head of hair.

Idris only used scissors to cut hair. He had tried using an electric trimmer once but found it difficult to control, resulting in the occasional slip and a divot-like intrusion into otherwise perfect haircuts. Fortunately, his expertise managed to cover up the mistake without most customers realising.

"Well, I've got a solution for you, my dear Gaston," Idris said with such serious conviction that it gave Gaston a fleeting moment of hope.

"I'll just tell my sister to put rat poison in their food and kill them all!"

Gaston immediately realised Idris's "solution" was in the same realm of flippant fantasy as his earlier dream to castrate the Finger Bay fathers. But like the whacky dream, the equally whacky idea of poisoning them also seeped unknowingly into his subconscious.

"Wishful thinking indeed, Idris, wishful thinking," Gaston said.

CHAPTER XX

An Old Friend and New Job Prospects

Once again, the salon was plunged into silence as Idris contemplated the finishing touches to restoring Gaston's hair to its former, familiar style: short back and sides and a little longer on top to allow the curls to form. All that was needed was a quick snip at the front, which Gaston also liked to keep a little long so that the curls would cover his forehead.

"Now for the beard, Gaston. Surely you won't find a replacement for Natalie with a beard like that," Idris said, smiling.

Within ten minutes, the beard was gone, an initial scissor trim followed by a close shave with the cutthroat razor.

The lightening of the facial hair load on Gaston seemed to mirror a lightening of the mood in the salon and a welcome change of conversation topic. In keeping with the barbershop ritual, Idris held up a mirror for Gaston to inspect the haircut at the back of his head and nod his approval.

"Hey, Gaston, your old friend Patrick came in for a haircut yesterday," said Idris.

"Really, Idris? Wow, I didn't know he was back!" replied Gaston. "Did he leave a contact number? I'd really love to see him again."

"Yes, yes, he did because he wants to catch up with you too," said Idris. "That was the first thing I was going to tell you about but all this horrible business with abused boys, suicide, and crocodiles almost made me forget."

Idris ran off into the back room and quickly returned with a glossy gold-embossed business card with Patrick's contact details on the front. On the plain white back of the card, Patrick had written his local address.

"My old friend must be doing all right," Gaston said, smiling as he looked at the address. "He's living in a very ritzy part of the island."

Patrick was living in the affluent west coast village of Palm Waters, home to the most desirable and pristine of the many reef-bound, turquoise-coloured lagoons around the island. As a result, developers from all over the world had flocked to the area since independence and erected a number of multi-starred hotels, which, in turn, had become a magnet for the world's filthy rich and sometimes famous.

Gaston recalled that Palm Waters had been the centre of local (and even some international) media attention in recent times because an Australian developer had won approval for the island's first six-star resort hotel to be built in the village. But he'd courted controversy over his plans for a multi-storey resort building that would defy a long-standing development convention for island resort hotels. Since independence, hotel development had been governed by an unwritten law that prohibited any coastal resort building higher than the tallest coconut tree—a law to which developers had voluntarily adhered until now.

The Palm Waters regional council had initially rejected the development proposal but the island government had stepped in to veto the council decision, despite howls of protests from locals that continued to the present day—even though the massive framework of the resort building was already towering over the tallest coconut trees.

The prime minister had personally intervened in the matter, repeatedly saying that the project's economic importance, both in terms of jobs and capital investment, was in the national interest and should not be subject to an unwritten, antiquated convention that was not in keeping with a twenty-first century, progressive island nation.

But the prime minister's fervent and very public support for the project only fuelled rumours that approval had only been secured through a trail of bribes leading all the way to the upper echelons of government. And the circumstantial evidence only served to add credibility to the rumours. Work on a third storey of the prime minister's already palatial residence began coincidentally close to the resort's approval. The treasurer had also suddenly been able to afford a lavish swimming pool, sauna, and spa at his mansion, complete with cascading waterfalls, luscious, landscaped "jungle" surrounds, and an entertainment and stage area capable of accommodating one hundred or more party guests and a small orchestra.

And the island's third most powerful politician, the police minister, had been caught on camera by the paparazzi unashamedly driving around in a brand-new Mercedes-Benz a month after the approval.

Gaston had followed news on the project's progress with an equally fervent zeal and vested interest, although his motives were somewhat more ethical. A few weeks before his breakup with Natalie, his mother had come across an advertisement in the newspaper calling for expressions of interest from people who wanted to work at the resort.

Gaston had not been able to secure a proper job since leaving school, much to the frustration of his mother. He fancied himself as a writer and also had a keen interest in politics; however, a career path involving either discipline was not obvious to a simple village boy living in an island community that still coveted careers in white-collar industry sectors like the civil service, banking, and finance where the jobs not only provided superior salaries but more importantly, also bestowed a more prestigious social status upon the worker.

In more recent times, however, the influx of luxury hotels had seen jobs in hospitality, service, and hotel public relations join the white-collar sectors at the summit of the island's economic and social hierarchy, making them also desirable career options for the island's job seekers. As a result, competition for these jobs was fierce, and Gaston's mother, Harriet, prayed long and hard for a "miracle" that would land Gaston a plum job in the hotel sector. Her other sons, Mario and Bruno, never figured in those prayers for a miracle. Harriet, like many parents who had a mix of white, brown, and black children, remained blissfully unconscious of their desire and open support for the whiter children to succeed. The children, for their part, just accepted this without question. It was the norm in the quasi-apartheid world they inhabited.

The day after an hour of intensive prayer for Gaston kneeling on the stones in front of her Virgin Mary statue, Harriet stumbled upon an advertisement from the new resort looking for workers across a number of hotel service areas. She saw it as a sign from God. After all, she rarely read the newspaper.

God, no doubt, rewarded his worshipers according to the principle of no pain, no gain, she thought.

Harriet didn't mind which job Gaston secured as long as it was a white-collar occupation. Blue-collar professions such as cleaners, builders, plumbers, electricians, etc., were still considered low status, despite salaries for these jobs being on a rapid rise. The boom in building and construction since independence meant that blue-collar wages were now almost on par with white-collar ones. But the level of workers' wages was not going to break down the class structure of island society in the foreseeable future.

Gaston, for his part, had enthusiastically embraced his mother's plans for him to apply for a job at the new resort hotel. He desperately wanted to start earning a regular income so that he and Natalie could one day escape the island and embark on adventures just like Tintin. At the same time, he also thought that his chances of landing a job at the resort had been minimal at best. Nevertheless, he had put in his application with the enthusiasm his mother expected but when he hadn't received a response after a few weeks, his pessimism seemed validated. And the heartache that engulfed him soon after cast any memory of the application deep into his unconscious, only to resurface the day after his encounter with Sergeant Cailason and Father Terry when, much to his surprise, he received a letter from the resort asking him to come in for an interview. At the time, he was still feeling somewhat shell-shocked by his traumatic encounter with Sergeant Cailason and Father Terry so he hadn't fully grasped the good news potential of the letter.

But after some much-needed rest and recreation, Gaston re-read the letter a week later with fresh eyes and a clear mind.. And he quickly realised that this could be the perfect opportunity for a fresh start. The letter had also provided him with the motivation for the haircut and shave. With unkempt hair festering over his face and cascading haphazardly onto his back and well over his ears, the slim chance that he had of landing a job at the resort would have evaporated to no chance at all.

"You've done a great job, as usual, Idris," Gaston said. "Thank you so much for being a good friend."

"It's my pleasure . . . as always, Monsieur Gaston," Idris said.

Old habits die hard, Gaston thought but decided that this time, he would not remind Idris of his discomfort at being called "monsieur". After all, he felt no discomfort at all, only contentment that he hadn't felt for some time in the presence of a good man and friend like Idris.

Things are definitely looking up, he thought, a beaming smile overwhelming his face as he stood up and reached for his wallet in his back pocket.

But as he tried to lift the wallet out of his pocket, Idris gently grabbed his arm, preventing him from doing so.

"Ah, non, non, Monsieur Gaston," Idris said, shaking his head and grinning. "This one's on me. It gave me great pleasure to restore my friend to his former handsome self."

With the grip on his arm tightening ever so slightly, Gaston knew that he would not be able to convince Idris otherwise, so he lowered the wallet back into his pocket, causing Idris to immediately let go of his arm.

"Well, thank you very much, Idris," Gaston said. "You're not only a wonderful barber but also a good friend."

And as he said this, Gaston made a mental note to buy Idris the best bottle of rum he could afford and leave it on his back doorstep before he got home from work.

"Till the next time, Idris," Gaston said finally as he headed out the door, only to have the smile vanish instantly from his face as he saw Father Thibault walking rapidly towards him.

CHAPTER XXI

A Funeral Yields an Ally

Gaston held his breath and instinctively turned towards Father Thibault as he approached, summoning up the courage for *"God knows what"*?

Another hostile threat, perhaps? He certainly wouldn't physically harm me in broad daylight on a busy street.

Whatever his intentions, Father Thibault certainly wasn't going to be the harbinger of good news for Gaston, who braced himself for a verbal onslaught of some sort.

To his great surprise, the Father walked straight past him as if he wasn't there. He didn't even acknowledge Gaston's presence or make any attempt to make eye contact. For his part, Gaston's gaze never left the priest as he walked away from him at a brisk pace.

Gaston realised his shave and haircut had possibly rendered him invisible to Father Thibault. It was certainly a very different-looking Gaston Le Clezio who had locked horns with him two weeks ago. He let out a sigh of relief and his good mood, which had been cultivated as the hair fell off him in Idris's salon, immediately returned.

He waited for Father Thibault to disappear from sight before he started heading back home in the same direction. His thoughts turned to the job interview scheduled for the next day, which had also been the catalyst for his head and facial transformation. No doubt about it, he was looking forward to getting his life back on track and a job at the new resort—as unlikely as that was—would certainly be a step in the right direction.

Gaston even started whistling a happy tune as he walked past his favourite bookshop. He stopped to look into the display window, his attention attracted by a colourful array of Tintin and Asterix comic books in one of the two display windows. Gaston loved the hardcover editions of Tintin and never tired of seeing the images on the front. His uncle Cyril had the full series, and as a child, Gaston looked forward to his weekly visits there, where he and his cousin, Pierre—also a

Tintin addict—would lock themselves in Pierre's bedroom and gorge themselves on their hero's adventures.

Those delightful memories lifted his spirits even more until he made the mistake of casting a glance at the other display window. The unsettling cartoon image of a gigantic, grinning crocodile, mouth agape in excitement at the prospect of devouring a gang of children, instantly evaporated Gaston's cheerful mood. The image graced the hardcover of the classic children's book *The Enormous Crocodile*, which was the centrepiece of the shop window's display featuring the work of Roald Dahl in honour of the twenty-first anniversary of the author's death.

Poor Henri, I hope he didn't suffer much, Gaston thought, but looking at the crocodile's huge teeth in the cartoon drawing on the book's cover conjured up an image of a real crocodile's teeth gnashing into the still-growing soft bones and tissues of the hapless Henri. And despite himself, Gaston couldn't stop his thoughts drifting to whether the crocodile would have actually detected the unusual variety in his diet. He immediately chided himself for even thinking of such a thing.

He turned and walked quickly away. He mechanically crossed the road, paying scant regard to the traffic, which fortunately was light. But just a metre from the safety of the opposing footpath, he narrowly avoided being hit by a bicycle carrying one of the island's ubiquitous street food vendors and his cargo of freshly made parathas, curry, and assorted condiments housed in a purpose-built, wooden and glass box strapped to the back of his bicycle.

The vendor had begun ringing his bicycle bell well before reaching Gaston, but the timid tinkling of the bell was hard to distinguish from the usual daily cacophony of noise on this (and almost every) island street. Gaston had simply marched on at the same brisk pace, oblivious to the impending danger. Survival instincts kicked in just in time for him to sense the threat, pause, and allow the slightly swerving bicycle to pass a hair's breadth away from him. So close did the bicycle pass by that Gaston caught a generous whiff of the bike rider's pungent body odour mixed with the bad breath–laced spray from his mouth as he swore at Gaston.

Despite the close call, Gaston was not distressed by the near-miss. He felt only relief to have escaped the harrowing image of the crocodile. The sadness that had swamped him at the shopfront window was replaced by equally overwhelming anger at Henri's "murder". Without realising, he pounded a clenched fist into the palm of his other hand. He had to find the truth behind Henri's death, and if, as he suspected,

Henri took his own life because he was sexually abused at the church, Gaston was determined to find a way to bring the heinous Finger Bay fathers to justice.

But where do I start?

He walked on, still largely oblivious to his surroundings, deep in thought and now well away from the congestion of the shopping district and on autopilot towards home. He turned down Flamboyant Street, only a block away from home, where he was stopped in his tracks and roused from his stupor by a disorderly but steady crowd of mourners emerging from one of the humble homes on the street and the sound of moaning and weeping peppered by an occasional ear-piercing wail emanating from within the property. The procession of black-clothed bodies headed towards Gaston, who had to mould himself into a bamboo fence to allow the mourners to pass. And then he saw it: a small white coffin draped in an ever-diminishing array of colourful flower petals being progressively blown off the coffin by the warm afternoon breeze.

Gaston knew what remained of Henri lay in the coffin, which was only half the size of the living, sobbing boy he and his mother had encountered only a week ago. There could be no open coffin for Henri, as was the custom on the island. Gaston could not help but wonder what bits they had managed to retrieve from the crocodile and the poor souls tasked with recovering those body parts and putting them back together into some semblance of the boy who once lived and breathed.

Once again, he felt angry at himself for the macabre train of thought. Thankfully, he was soon distracted by a middle-aged woman who was being physically propped up by two burly men and sobbing into a dark handkerchief while being conveyed by the tide of the procession behind the coffin. Gaston had no doubt she was Henri's mother. Eventually he would tell her the truth behind Henri's murder and hopefully he would, at the same time, reveal that he had a plan to avenge the boy's untimely death, with or without the help of the relevant authorities. But for now, his heart bled for the poor woman and he felt a tear roll down his cheeks and flow into the corner of his mouth.

Gaston recognised many of the faces in the crowd, some of whom he hadn't seen for a long time. The dwindling cohort of village natives continued to come out of the woodwork for momentous local events of pain and pleasure, like funerals and weddings, even if they were only remotely acquainted with the respectively bereaved or festive family. And for the duration of such an event, the island reverted to earlier times, the air filled with familiar expressions of condolences or congratulations, tears of grief or joy, laced with mournful renditions of traditional hymns or colourful, rhythmic native beats but poignantly, there reigned an ambiance of genuine care, kindness and compassion or hope, happiness, and celebration for the respective grieving or happy families involved.

As the last of the mourners passed him by, Gaston made eye contact with a woman he immediately recognised as Idris's sister, Monique, even though he hadn't seen her for some time. She was the spitting image of Idris, but happily without the missing or nicotine-stained teeth which scarred Idris's otherwise handsome features. Monique, on the other hand, retained the attractive smile that her brother was now unable to produce. Only two years separated them in age and many mistook them for twins. Even her haircut was similar: a short Afro immaculately styled. Gaston had no doubt that Idris was the craftsman responsible for her slick coiffure.

As Monique drew level with Gaston, he detected a faint, respectful smile of recognition which he instinctively took for a cue to join her in the procession of mourners. She was walking alone with only a few rows of distracted mourners behind her, so Gaston felt he could comfortably engage her in conversation without showing disrespect to the grieving crowd ahead of them. Besides, the crying, wailing, and howling of the close family and friends continued unabated at the front of the procession rendering any chatter at the back relatively mute.

"Hello, Monique; that is Henri there in the casket, isn't it?" Gaston asked in a heightened whisper, to which Monique gave a nodding reply.

"Are you a close friend of the family?"

Monique hesitated before replying, causing Gaston some momentary emotional discomfort.

"Not really. I'd make small talk with his mother sometimes when she dropped him off at church. And I'd see Henri too when he came in to do his altar boy things. He'd often have to come into the kitchen to get something for one of the priests," Monique replied in an equally hushed, respectful tone.

"He was such a sweet, good-looking boy, but very timid and at times very nervy. I tried to talk to him a couple of times but he kept his head bowed and would answer with only a word or two. It's all a bit mysterious, really. What was he doing on his own at the crocodile park? Really can't understand that, but it's all so very sad. His poor mother . . ."

Gaston suddenly remembered that earlier today Idris had mentioned that Monique worked in the church presbytery kitchen where she sometimes heard strange screams while she was working.

Did she know any more? Gaston thought. *It wouldn't hurt to probe a bit more.*

"How well do you know the priests, Monique?" Gaston asked.

"I really don't have much to do with them. When they do come into the kitchen, they rarely talk to me. Now and then I bump into one of them when I'm coming into work or leaving work and it's just chit-chat. Why do you ask?"

"Let's just say that I think they may have had something to do with Henri's death and—"

"*What*?!" exclaimed a stunned Monique, louder than she had intended, causing the mourners immediately in front of her to suddenly turn around and inflict a searing look of condemnation.

Monique turned her head away to avoid eye contact until she sensed that they had resumed looking towards the front of the procession.

"You can't be serious," she said, this time in a more respectful tone, her hand shielding her mouth as an additional sound barrier.

Monique looked up at Gaston and quickly realised that he was indeed serious.

"But, but . . . what makes you think that?" she asked, still in disbelief. "Surely it was just a tragic accident, like everyone says?"

"I'm not saying the priests actually killed him, but I think he committed suicide because of things they did to him," Gaston said.

"*No, no way . . . That can't be true*!" exclaimed Monique even louder than before, but fortunately this time her voice was drowned out by the sudden ringing of the church bells as the procession entered the church grounds.

"Look, Monique, I'll tell you all I know and you can make up your own mind. Are you going in?" Gaston asked as they approached the church steps with most of the procession inside the church and the coffin already positioned in front of the altar.

"Yes, I was planning to stay for the service, but I'm not going to the cemetery," she replied.

By this time, they were halfway up the church steps and Gaston resigned himself to attending the funeral service with her. He desperately needed an ally and he sensed that Monique might just fit the bill, given her regular contact with the priests. He didn't have a plan at this stage but felt that one would emerge. He had no doubt she would be eager to join forces with him once he revealed to her the details of the priests' sordid deeds, including Father Terry's abuse of Henri just days before his death.

But as he approached the church doors, Gaston detected the foreboding figure of Father Terry lurking inside, greeting the mourners with the solemn demeanour that the occasion commanded, his whispering words and compassionate gestures befitting a priest providing spiritual comfort to his parish flock in a time of great sorrow. Gaston instinctively thought of fleeing, but it was too late to turn back without disrupting the orderly procession through the church doors and drawing attention to himself. As he got closer to the priest, Gaston detected smugness in his look beneath the outward display of sympathy for the mourners. He wondered whether any of them could discern the dishonesty.

No doubt about it, Father Terry has mastered the art of masking his indifference to his parishioners, whether in times of grief or celebration, he thought. *His so-called rehabilitation has been remarkably swift.*

Even though Monique was by his side and closer to Father Terry, Gaston kept his head bowed as they walked past him. But Father Terry paid no more attention to Gaston than to the rest of the mourners. Perhaps, like Father Thibault earlier, Father Terry had simply not recognised a freshly shorn and clean-shaven Gaston.

Safely seated in the back row of the church next to the aisle, Gaston poked his head out a little to get a better view of the coffin, which had completely shed its covering of colourful flowers. Positioned on solid iron supports at the front of the church, the coffin's bright white colour now stood in stark contrast to the prevailing funeral-standard black clothing of the congregation. It looked lonely and vulnerable, just as Henri no doubt would have felt as he approached that crocodile pit and contemplated his fatal destiny. The thought provoked a feeling of intense grief, and once again, Gaston felt tears welling in his eyes.

The sight of Father Terry emerging from behind the altar, decked out in Catholic funeral finery black with generous hints of white and violet, immediately added a layer of disbelief and anger to Gaston's grief. He hadn't kept track of the priest's movements since entering the church.

Monique felt Gaston's agitation and anger brewing.

"Are you okay?" she whispered.

"Not really," Gaston replied. "Look, I can't stay. Can you meet me at the Tropicana Café after the service? I need to get out of here."

Gaston only faintly heard Monique's reply of "yes, see you there" as he moved with almost military precision out of the church pew, instinctively genuflecting and crossing himself facing the altar before turning around and heading out the church doors and running down the steps.

CHAPTER XXII

A Plan . . . of Sorts

For the first time in a week, Gaston was tempted to order a drink—or three. But his rehabilitated common sense prevailed. He had to keep a clear head, not only for his imminent strategy meeting with Monique but also for his job interview the next morning.

Outside the Tropicana Café, daylight was quickly fading. Gaston was perched on a small stool at a table by the wide glass window panels at the front and looking out, mesmerised by the sun slipping away from the heavy canopy of clouds that had just dumped the habitual tropical volume of afternoon rain. The fiery sun, fluctuating in colour from red to orange and yellow, dipped between two mountain peaks, pursued by wisps of cloud that seemed to have escaped the main mass. As the sun finally disappeared over the horizon, it cast out rays of golden light across the darkening skies.

"It's like a stairway to Heaven," muttered Gaston to himself, once again invoking the memory of Henri, this time as an angel ascending the golden, sun-shaped pathway to eternal paradise.

Gaston had managed to score the prized table by the window at the Tropicana, having arrived during the lull before the evening stampede of workers who stopped by for a quick drink or two and the complimentary tapas-like snacks known on the island as *gajak*. It was traditional for island bars and cafés to also provide *gajaks* whenever alcohol was consumed. On the *gajak* menu tonight were traditional island specialities like *gateaux piment* (dahl chilli cakes), *baja la cervelle* (calves brains fried in spicy batter), and *gesier poulet* (chicken giblets with garlic, bacon, and onion, served with paratha bread). No native island drinker, even the alcoholics, would ever contemplate having a drink at a bar without *gajaks*.

Outside, the first star of the evening (or was it a planet) had risen and shone in a sky still in transformation from a dark blue to purple hue. Soon total darkness would take over and invite other stars and planets to emerge.

Gaston looked longingly at one of only two customers sitting at the bar, sipping on a drink and munching hungrily on a *baja la cervelle*.

I don't know if I'll be able to control myself much longer if Monique doesn't turn up soon, thought Gaston.

Gaston was beginning to feel the evening hunger pangs, which usually also kindled his appetite for an aperitif. His line of vision followed his thoughts to the row of spirit bottles behind the bar dominated by rum but also comprising two bottles of scotch whisky, which was his aperitif of choice.

Surely one drink wouldn't hurt, he thought.

But just as he stood up and started walking towards the bar, the café door opened and in walked Monique with her brother Idris in tow, the couple suddenly blocking his path to the bar. At the same time, a traditional cuckoo clock hanging on the wall behind the bar came to life. A dishevelled brown cuckoo staggered through the bird door seven times, each time producing a dissonant, feeble call, which became more dissonant and more pathetic with each call. Only the clock's small hand remained, which meant that patrons only had a totally accurate measure of the time on each hour.

The cuckoo's call of seven o'clock also seemed to be the signal for a portly man with a bushy moustache to suddenly rise from his stool at the bar, leaving his half-finished drink behind as he barged his way through the middle of the trio on his way out the door. Idris recognised the black Creole man as Serge Lacroix, who had acquired a reputation as the village drunk and a slave to a rigid routine whereby every night, he would frequent the three bars of the village, arriving and leaving each bar—whether he had finished his drink or not—at precisely the same set time before heading to a friend's house for a final drink where, again, he often left behind a half-finished glass of rum.

"I hope you don't end up like him, Monsieur Gaston, after your recent problems. We need to find you another beautiful woman to take your mind off the booze," Idris said facetiously.

"Very funny, my friend," Gaston replied. "But you really don't have to worry about me becoming a drunk or finding me another woman.

"You see, I'm not even thinking about having a drink," he lied, pointing to his almost empty glass of soda water on the table by the window.

"Would you like another drink? I've already started telling Monique what you told me earlier," Idris said.

"Sure, Idris, but I think I'll move on to the stronger stuff," Gaston said, subtly winking to Monique, who broke out in a wry smile while Idris's own smile retreated.

"I'm teasing you, my friend; a Coke would be great," Gaston lied again.

He certainly would have preferred something stronger, but once again he thought better of it. Even though Gaston knew deep down he wasn't an alcoholic, he was still troubled by the fact that he had automatically taken refuge in the bottle following his heartbreak.

"I'll have the same, Idris," Monique said as Gaston gently grabbed her elbow to lead her to the table while Idris went to the bar.

"I hope you don't mind that my brother's here too," Monique said as they sat at the table. "I just dropped by his salon after the funeral and we started talking about you and what you think may have happened to that poor child, so when I told him I was on my way to meet up with you, he wanted to come along."

"No, I don't mind at all, Monique. The more allies I have, the better, and I know both of you are good people who may be able to help me find a way to do something about these criminals. They certainly aren't the holy men they profess to be. I had a close encounter with them myself, which I hadn't thought about for many years until recently."

Gaston went on to tell Monique about the incident surrounding the death of Father Orton, in which he had almost become another casualty of the Finger Bay fathers' lust for young boys.

"You know, I really convinced myself that it never happened. But what else do you do when your own mother doesn't believe you and calls you a liar?"

Gaston and Monique sat for some time in silence.

Gaston then moved on to recount more recent events leading up to Henri's death, beginning with his heartbreak and subsequent battle with the bottle. Pangs of shame re-emerged as he told Monique about his errant behaviour—urinating on the beach—which led to his arrest and humiliation at the Finger Bay police station. But Gaston ploughed on, regardless, and told her everything he and his mother had experienced that day, including him finding blood on the toilet seat and a bloodied altar boy outfit in the church's public toilet block that he was convinced belonged to Henri. And just as he started telling her about him and his mother witnessing Father Terry's act of onanism in the confessional, Idris arrived, juggling three glasses of Coke, his own paler in colour due to the generous infusion of white rum, which he almost dropped as he sat down with a look of disbelief in his eyes.

"You didn't tell me about that, Monsieur Gaston!"

"You took your time, Idris?"

"Sorry, I had to go to the toilet and, if you haven't noticed, my friend, it's happy hour at the bar. But never mind all that. Tell me more about this sex-fiend priest. He didn't actually do that, did he? In the church? In front of your poor mother? That's really sick!"

"Yes, I'm afraid he did, Idris, but my mother will never testify that anything untoward happened because she's a faithful servant of the good Lord,'" Gaston said in a tone mocking his mother's devotion to her faith. "And they've also bribed her," he added more seriously.

"How much did they give her?" Idris asked.

"Something much more precious to her than money. Something that will guarantee her silence."

"But what could that be, Monsieur Gaston?"

"You obviously don't go to church much, do you, Idris?"

"No, I must confess, I've never set foot inside *that* church, and I never will if what you've told me about the priests is true. My mother used to take me to church when I was a boy and we lived in Les Cascades, but since then . . ."

"Well, that's another scandal. The priests ask, or should I say demand, that their devoted parishioners donate to the church coffers, and whoever contributes most gets to sit closest to the front of the church. closer to God, they believe," Gaston explained, again mocking the faithful flock of Finger Bay.

"Obviously, we don't have the means to give much, so my family's had to sit towards the back of the church ever since I can remember. But now, my mother's been offered a seat in the third row, and for her, it's like winning the lottery. She's so thrilled that her memory 'lapses' when you bring up the sordid episode with Father Terry."

"We know corruption—you know, money, bribes, and stuff like that—is everywhere on the island so that's no surprise and not good, of course. But sex with children . . . well, that's just, just—and now, one of them is dead because of what they did to him. That's . . . that's . . ."

"Evil; that's what it is, Idris! They are criminals of the worse kind. Sexually abusing children is evil enough, but now they've added murder to their list," Gaston said.

"But I still can't believe it. You really think they had something to do with Henri's death?" Monique suddenly chimed in.

"Every day, I'm in that kitchen making food for them, surrounded by these disgusting men. I had no idea this was going on; although, as I've said to Idris, I have heard some strange screaming noises from time to time. But it seemed perfectly reasonable when they said it was coming from the television. There's so many of those ugly crime shows nowadays."

"It was perfectly reasonable of you to think that, Monique. Who would have thought that priests, of all people, would be capable of such monstrous acts?" Gaston reassured her.

"And yes, I do think Henri committed suicide because of whatever Father Terry did to him in the confessional that day. And I shudder at the thought of what that might have been, given the bloodied robe."

"Agh . . . it makes my skin crawl just thinking about being in that kitchen again," Monique said, shaking her body as if her skin really was crawling.

"I don't know if I can face going back to work there."

"But you must, Monique," Gaston said.

"You're our best hope of finding some way to bring them to justice. With you there in the kitchen every day, maybe, just maybe, we can find some way to trap them or get some evidence for the police. But then again, I don't think the police will be much help."

"What makes you say that, Gaston?" asked Monique.

"I think some of them at least are well aware of what goes on but turn a blind eye to it," Gaston replied.

"I should put poison in their food and kill them all. That would fix the problem," Monique said with venom in her voice and tone suddenly rising, causing heads at adjoining tables to turn towards them.

"Oops, sorry," she said in a more muted tone.

"I know, your brother already suggested that you could poison them—effective but not very practical," Gaston said. "When are you working there again?"

"I don't have a shift until next Monday," Monique replied. "The priests gave all the kitchen staff the rest of the week off after Henri's death.

"All right then, let's see if we can come up with a plan before then, but I think, for the time being, the only thing we can do is for you, Monique, to keep your eyes and ears open for anything suspicious. And if you hear the screaming again, perhaps you can investigate further. But you have to be very careful, of course. They're really capable of anything, and I certainly don't want you taking any risks which may put your life in danger. What do you think, Idris?" asked Gaston.

"I'm with you, Monsieur Gaston. I think Monique is our best hope of doing something—whatever that may be. But as you said, these people will do anything to protect their patch so you need to be very, very careful, Monique," Idris said.

Gaston was about to gently remind Idris that he felt uncomfortable being called "monsieur" when the bar once more echoed with the sounds of the cuckoo clock, this time heralding eight o'clock.

It's obviously a hard habit to break and really it doesn't hurt anyone, Gaston thought.

Gaston decided to let the matter rest, and instead he suddenly rose from his chair as if summoned into action by the call of the cuckoo clock.

"Sorry, folks, but I must get going," Gaston said.

"What's the rush?" Monique asked.

"I need to eat and get some rest. I've got an important job interview tomorrow," Gaston replied.

"Besides, I also want to check whether we have any rat poison at home that you can feed to the priests when you go back to work next week," he said jokingly with a wink in his eye before kissing Monique on both cheeks and heading home.

CHAPTER XXIII

Booze, Brothel, and Another Embarrassing Blow

Patrick drew back the heavy black curtains, instantly transforming darkness into bright daylight as the brilliant rays of the early afternoon sun gushed into the bedroom. His head was sore and his mouth parched. He struggled to open his eyes. The fact that, once again, he had been up late drinking didn't help his cause. He couldn't even remember where he had had his last drink but he knew it was a strong, dark local rum that certainly finished him for the night. He had been drunk too often since his return to the island.

He blinked profusely in an effort to exorcise the lingering fatigue from his vision. Eventually, his eyes adjusted sufficiently for him to open them, at first narrowly, then wide, as his gaze fell upon the tranquil, translucent waters of the lagoon. And as blinking, too, resumed a more normal pace, he looked out further where the habitual summer afternoon storm, even more intense than usual, was brewing and stirring up the seas, generating wild four-metre waves that were lashing the reef.

Patrick had always loved the contrast (the yin and yang, he called it) that the reef created in its relationship with the ocean waters. The serene, gentle turquoise lagoon waters within, and beyond the reef, the almost always angry, dark blue sea that was like a throbbing vein exploding onto the reef with a continuous wall of white water. Much of the island's appeal to overseas tourists was the sea-life-rich, protective band of coral that encircled almost the entire island. The only significant breaks in the reef were at Port Marcel that gave birth to the island's capital and in neighbouring La Cuvette beach, which Patrick could see in the distance if he leaned his head out the window and looked right.

La Cuvette was a magnet for surfers who came from all over the world to experience the often perfect, pounding swells. An unpredictable and ever-changing rip there made it particularly dangerous for swimmers, some of whom nevertheless ignored the two large panels, featuring skulls and crossbones, warning them of the ever-present danger. Some of them never made it out alive.

Patrick wasn't too worried about his current binge on booze. He knew it wouldn't last but it was a necessary evil to completely obliterate the memory of the humiliation he had suffered on the council floor in what seemed like a past life in Australia. It had been nearly four months now, but the emotion was still raw.

What worried him more was his first-ever visit to a brothel a couple of nights before, which had also ended in humiliation. Patrick had always been fascinated by brothels but never seriously contemplated going to one. He had had no need. His charisma and position of political power meant that, for most of his active sex life to date, he had had sex on tap, although always judicious and discreet in how he turned the tap on and off.

While he was a councillor, finding true love was not on his agenda as he believed a serious romantic relationship would just as seriously jeopardise his political ambitions. However, he was also a young man with a rampant libido that needed to find a sexual outlet. Therefore, to safeguard his reputation and ambition, he insisted that any prospective sexual partner sign a pre-sexual agreement that would make him a very rich man while bankrupting the other party should the agreement be breached and details of their sexual dalliances ever publicly revealed. Even though it sometimes temporarily killed the mood of the moment, such was his sexual allure that only one woman had ever refused to sign. But Patrick hadn't been too disappointed. From the moment he had met her at the local pub, he had been suspicious of her motives anyway.

He had been tempted to visit a brothel a couple of times when drunk in Australia, but sanity had prevailed on each occasion despite the devil of alcohol fighting a raging battle against the God of reason. But back on his native island, where he was just another brown face among the island's rainbow racial mix, the God of reason was missing in action and the devil of alcohol had been given free rein to lead Patrick into the Harlot No. 1 "massage suites" where he had the choice of a bevy of surprisingly beautiful "masseuses" representing the island's varied racial mix. He even found one with his ideal sexual fantasy mix of red hair, blue eyes, and freckly skin.

Nevertheless, he had felt very nervous as the masseuse, allegedly named Cherie, led him down the dimly lit corridor and through a doorway that had a lit, green bulb above it. Once inside, she flicked a switch, which simultaneously extinguished the green light and illuminated a red one above it. She closed the door and led him towards a four-poster bed that dominated the room.

Patrick started shaking as Cherie stopped near the bed, turned around to face him and began undressing, revealing a pair of well-proportioned freckled breasts that Patrick felt were just the right size—that is, big enough to cup in the palm of his hands. As she quickly removed her one remaining garment—whore-standard, frilly, G-string knickers—she smiled and twirled around like a model showing off her wares.

"Do you like?" she asked with a seemingly sincere smile.

She was either a very good actress or genuinely happy to have me as a client, Patrick thought.

The truth lay somewhere in between. While Cherie wasn't too thrilled about her profession, which essentially funded her son's private school fees, she found Patrick very attractive and a welcome change from her usual clientele of overweight, boorish men.

"Yes, I like very much," Patrick replied as he moved towards her and gently grabbed her around the waist before letting his hands slide over her bare, curvaceous bottom.

Patrick experienced a surge of sexual urge as his hands gripped Cherie's butt tightly before letting a finger glide up and down the generous cleft in her buttocks. But he soon began to panic, as his brain wasn't able to convey that sexual excitement to his loins, leaving Patrick's penis at "half-mast". He was struggling to get a viable erection. Worse still, Cherie was already undoing his pants and expertly had them and his underwear around his ankles in next to no time. But as her mouth approached his semi-erect penis, the mix of nerves and intense sexual emotion caused Patrick to lose control and he ejaculated all over her face.

Embarrassed into some semblance of sobriety, Patrick quickly pulled up his underwear and trousers, reached into his pocket, and pulled out a handkerchief with which he clumsily wiped as much semen as he could off her face. He apologised profusely, even though Cherie seemed unperturbed by the incident. Nevertheless, Patrick continued apologising as he took a few notes out of his wallet and placed them into her hands (as if a generous tip would alleviate his embarrassment) before making a rapid getaway. He was grateful that he had paid in advance so he only had to stop to dispose of the handkerchief in the bin near the reception desk before fleeing out the front door, vowing never to return.

CHAPTER XXIV

Back on the FAIR Track

Despite the brothel incident Patrick felt he had made some progress, two weeks after his return to the island. He had only been drunk four times and it was Monday again. The whole first week had disappeared in a drunken blur.

A few days ago, Patrick had his first alcohol-free day since leaving Australia and travelled back to his home village of Finger Bay, intending to track down Gaston and catch up with the news and gossip of the past ten years. The logical place to start was their mutual barber, but unfortunately Idris too hadn't seen Gaston for some time and even expressed some concern for his wellbeing. It was uncharacteristic of Gaston not to have his hair cut at least once every two months, Idris had told Patrick.

An earlier search of local phone books and the internet had revealed no clues as to Gaston's whereabouts. Patrick now wished he had kept in touch, but somehow his studies and then blossoming political career had intruded on his initial resolve to keep in contact with his island friends. During his ten formative years in Australia, Patrick had thought very little about the island and his teenage friend Gaston.

But, in the days following his demoralising defeat on the council floor, Patrick continued reminiscing about his political initiation with his teenage comrade-in-arms, and these flashbacks, which intermittently brought some relief from his intense grief, were the key influence in his decision to flee back to his native island. Nevertheless, he remained committed to his FAIR manifesto despite its resounding rejection by his fellow councillors.

Surely decent human beings can see the logic in it? I need an ally maybe . . . and a village, a town, an island to give it a go and I'm sure it will spread like wildfire.

But as Patrick continued to stare at the waves pounding the reef, he wondered whether the adult Gaston had maintained the rage and still had a passion for radical political change.

In the more sober moments between his heavyweight championship bouts with the booze since returning to the island, Patrick had begun researching the island's political structures and party machinations with a view to infiltrating the local political scene and introduce his FAIR doctrine to the island community. He had already established that corruption was a minor problem in government circles, although democratic conventions like a regular election cycle since independence had always been respected and seemingly conducted freely and fairly. This gave him hope that the island could provide him with a potential political platform to spread his FAIR message.

Worryingly, however, Patrick noted that recent press articles about the prime minister and his cronies suggested that the present government was showing signs of a regime trying to dismantle the rugged democracy that (perhaps surprisingly) had been embraced by all racial and political factions following independence. Given the quasi-apartheid society that had reigned during colonial times, the rest of the world believed the granting of independence would inevitably see the island consumed, at best, by large-scale political instability and, at worst, by racial conflict and extreme violence ending in a dictatorship so common among the island's African neighbours who had undergone a similar transition from colonial rule to independence. Many islanders, too, had been fearful of the post-independence future, and those with the financial means had voted with their feet, leaving the island in droves for the seemingly safer political climes of their first world, former colonial masters.

The island still had a free press, which further encouraged Patrick. Journalists were still able to scrutinise and criticise the machinations of government and expose any potential corruption. This demonstrated to him that the government was still accountable to the people. And it was precisely a series of articles about a dodgy deal between the government and an Australian billionaire developer, Jack Wright, to allow him to build the island's first six-star resort which had led Patrick to take up residence at Palm Waters, where he hoped to get involved in local politics at a time when the village was very much the focus of the national political spotlight.

Local news over the past year had been dominated by stories of alleged national government corruption, which allowed Mr. Wright and his son Tom to quash local community dissent and build the resort, which contravened the island's long-standing tallest coconut tree building convention.

Patrick believed the local politicians and community, who were raging against the Wrights' resort development, would provide fertile ground for the radical ideas of his FAIR manifesto, whose overriding principles aimed to wipe out greed and create a fairer social structure where "rich bastards" like the Wright family would never again be given free rein to trample over the will of the people simply because they were rich.

His policies would eliminate obscene individual wealth in one fell swoop. Only workers whose jobs were deemed to contribute a social benefit to the community would be allowed to earn a bonus income over and above the generous living wage to which every adult would be entitled. Therefore, these workers would not only be deservedly richer but only by a small amount, thereby eliminating the growing disparity in wealth, which was the uncontested, absurd norm in modern capitalist societies. Patrick was convinced that, eventually, everyone would have a full belly, a roof over their heads, and enough left over for life's little luxuries.

Patrick stuck his head out of the window and looked left to the picture-postcard-perfect lagoon and white sand beach of Palm Waters and, across the road, the metallic frame of the Wrights' development, which had already surged past the tallest coconut tree and subjugated the beachfront. Outrage among the local community and politicians over the development had continued despite construction being well advanced; anger that was further inflamed by the posting of a veritable army of police personnel to keep protesters away from the development site in the early stages. The seeming ease with which the Wrights could call on the taxpayer-funded police force to protect them was another disturbing sign of government corruption. There had already been several violent clashes between protesters and police, including one incident that saw police fire tear gas and a protester suffering a minor injury. It was a story that sparked outrage throughout the island and even made international headlines.

Patrick believed he was ideally placed to take up the fight against the Australian nemesis of the Palm Waters community, despite all signs that it was far too late to stop the resort development. He had the great advantage of having lived in Australia, but more importantly, he would be able to draw on his experience as a local government councillor who often had to navigate stormy political waters and protect local community interests against the rampant greed of powerful developers like Jack and Tom Wright.

CHAPTER XXV

The Good Australian Samaritan

Patrick could hardly believe the good fortune that had allowed his family to "escape" to Australia; the good fortune on which he was able to capitalise to rise to a position of some influence and power in his local Australian community.

Patrick's mother had worked as a maid for the wealthy owner of an island sugar estate, an expatriate Australian named Matthew Perkins, who, over the years, had become very fond of Patrick's family. Mr. Perkins had inherited his fortune and a natural career path in the sugar industry from his own family of sugar barons in Queensland. But he decided to move to the island and buy a sugar estate there after falling in love with a local woman, Angelique Joffret, whom he had met at a conference. The couple had a son who was the same age as Patrick, and when he reached high school age, Mr. Perkins decided to sell his island sugar interests and move his family back to Australia, where his son would be able to get a better high school education. But he also wanted Patrick's mother to continue working for him, so he offered the whole family the opportunity to come with them to Australia. He gave Patrick's dad a job at his family's Australian sugar estate, which had been kept under family control during his absence. He even paid for Patrick to attend the local public high school.

Despite his wealth, Mr. Perkins had never felt comfortable with the silent apartheid which ruled the island's socio-economic structure. Within his own sphere of influence around his sugar estate, he ensured all workers were treated equally and promotions were solely based on hard work and merit, not skin colour. His was the only sugar business on the island that had black men in managerial positions and a Chinese woman in charge of the IT department.

"It's called a 'fair go,'" Patrick would often hear him say. "It's how we do things back in Australia, and that's what I'm going to do here too."

In fact, the word "fair" seemed to punctuate so many of his conversations Patrick overheard in the sugar factory. Patrick's family lived on the sugar estate—albeit in a much humbler abode than Mr. Perkins' luxury homestead—so Patrick would often wander over to the sugar factory to gaze in wonder at the machinery turning the cane into sugar or simply to hang out with Mr. Perkins' son, Lex.

Besides "fair go", Patrick would often hear Mr. Perkins utter the expression "fair dinkum", which confused him because Mr. Perkins used it in so many different situations. Mr. Perkins tried to explain the various connotations and appropriate use of fair dinkum to Patrick, but the nuances of meaning escaped him until many years later when the expression popped up regularly in his own vocabulary during conversations with his Australian country constituents.

Feeling comfortable with the Australian version of the English language had been instrumental in Patrick forgiving his parents for snatching him away from his friends and familiarity of his native land. And that only took about six months after the family's arrival in Mackay, Queensland. A year later, Patrick surprised everyone when he secured an academic scholarship to board and complete his Higher School Certificate (HSC) at the prestigious Brisbane Grammar School.

Patrick only decided to tackle the exam for the HSC scholarship after Mr. Perkins had resolved, despite wrestling long and hard with his egalitarian ethos and philosophical objection to an elitist school system, to send his own son Lex to Brisbane Grammar. Patrick and Lex had become good friends, and with the loss of his cherished island friend Gaston still relatively fresh in his memory, Patrick did not want a repeat of that miserable experience with his new best mate. However, his parents certainly couldn't afford the fees for the prestigious private school. And when it was made clear that Mr. Perkins would not extend his generosity to pay for Patrick's fees, the scholarship exam was a last-ditch effort and, much to everyone's surprise, including Patrick's, he was one of only five students throughout Queensland to be granted a scholarship.

CHAPTER XXVI

Political Baby Steps

Two years later, Patrick achieved an outstanding Higher School Certificate result that placed him among the top five percent of students in Queensland; a result that enabled him to indulge his passion for politics through a university pathway majoring in law and political science. Patrick also found political allies at the University of Queensland Socialist Club, where the words "fair" and "unfair" continued to swirl through his psyche in the vigorous debates among his comrades. The Socialist Club also indoctrinated Patrick into the Marxist ideology which provided the political legs that supported and set in motion his own FAIR doctrine.

Patrick managed to graduate from university within two and half years instead of the standard three, driven not only by his above-average intelligence but also by a keen desire to initiate political action in the real world.

Emboldened by his university comrades' acclaim for his "revolutionary vision", Patrick immediately joined the Australian Labor Party upon graduation, convinced the party would welcome him as a messiah. After all, he had *the* radical and FAIR Socialist agenda Labor had been seeking throughout its political history. The FAIR manifesto, Patrick believed, would be the spark for that "light on the hill" invoked in the 1949 speech by Labor titan and Prime Minister Ben Chifley, as his vision of an egalitarian society based on selflessness, compassion, and social justice. Patrick was certain that, by instantly closing the ever-growing wealth gap, the FAIR manifesto would finally deliver a society in which Labor's true believers could once again believe.

However, the naïve idealism which had reigned within the confines of his university socialist club did not translate into the real politick of twenty-first century Australia. The competing ideologies, which had once defined the respective policies of the two major political parties—the Labor and Liberal/National coalition—no longer existed. The left and right wings of Australian politics had merged towards the centre in the pursuit of the popular vote. It never, ever occurred to Patrick that the policy framework of his FAIR manifesto was on the radical left of the political spectrum and was, therefore, unlikely to appeal to a largely affluent electorate and it struggled to gain traction, even among the extreme left wing of the Labor Party.

Patrick's next political pit stop was the Greens, a party gaining in popularity as Australia entered the twenty-first century. Among the idealists and social justice ideologues who inhabited the Greens, Patrick finally found many who supported his FAIR manifesto and this gave him some (false) hope. If he had paid closer attention to his admirers within the Greens, he would have found them to be primarily women who were more attracted to the man, not the policy framework. They wanted to sleep with him, and Patrick took full advantage, thinking it would help him forge a path to popularity in the party and also project him into the party hierarchy.

While an egalitarian ethos prevailed within the party, a hierarchy was indeed essential to the efficient and effective organisation of the "inevitable revolution". Patrick was comfortable with this. After all, even Marx had concluded that a dictatorship of the proletariat would be necessary for the transition from an unfair capitalist system to a communist utopia.

However, Patrick soon became extremely uncomfortable with the lack of tolerance for any dissent against Greens party policy. Like any other mainstream political party, there was an expectation that Greens party members would faithfully toe the party line. Although the Greens' power brokers didn't expel members who voted against party policies, as the mainstream parties did, they nevertheless made it clear that Patrick would be ostracised and never rise to any great heights in the party if he voted against any ratified Greens policy. And this came to a head over two issues: the Greens policy on same-sex marriage and a bill, which came before the state parliament, designed to outlaw the right of people to protest outside abortion clinics.

While his FAIR manifesto was a product of revolutionary thought, Patrick's upbringing in a strict Catholic household had made him a very conservative thinker on the issue of gay rights and abortion.

When the question of marriage equality raised its controversial head in mainstream Australian politics, it was immediately embraced by the Greens, but not by novice Greens candidate Patrick La Malettie. He simply could not join in the Greens' call to arms to fight for same-sex marriage. That was simply out of the question for the Catholic faithful.

He wasn't homophobic, but the thought of two men having sex or living as man and wife made him physically ill. He remembered seeing the film *Midnight Express* some time ago and almost vomiting when, for the first time, he saw two men kissing passionately on the screen.

At the same time, he'd always felt somewhat ashamed that the thought or sight of two women kissing had the opposite effect. Like most heterosexual men, girl-on-girl sex turned him on immensely, and he struggled to reconcile this instinctive biological betrayal of his Catholic faith. In the end he simply accepted that it was an unfortunate hangover from the caveman days lurking within the heterosexual male subconscious. But he designed his own way of fighting this demon. He blessed himself and said three Hail Marys each time he found himself fantasising about women kissing or having sex.

As for abortion, it was always murder, he thought. *And a mortal sin to boot!*

Patrick could certainly understand—and perhaps even tolerate—abortions for women who had been raped. However, using abortion as a method of birth control or to correct an error of judgment in the intoxicated throes of passion, or as a culling method for defective babies, was morally wrong, according to Patrick. He simply could not support a bill that would restrict morally courageous folk from protesting outside clinics that *"murdered innocent babies"!*

As for the mortal sin aspect, one of his lovers pointed out that sex before marriage was also a mortal sin.

"That can't be right," Patrick had replied. "Which of the ten commandments says you can't have sex before marriage? The commandment about adultery is only about having sex with married women . . . right?

"Having consensual sex with a single woman isn't harming anyone. Quite the contrary, so it must be fine . . . No, much more than fine. Sex gives people great pleasure and it's healthy. God surely can't punish people for something that makes you feel so good and keeps you healthy? Besides none of us would be here without sex."

"So, you belong to the small 'L' liberal brand of Catholicism," the naked woman, sitting on the bed and stroking a visibly aroused Patrick, had replied, smirking and tightening her grip. "You, as a *dirty, dirty* Catholic boy, can do anything you like, as long as it doesn't cause any harm and—"

Patrick didn't let her finish the critical, albeit playful, analysis of his convenient Catholic faith. He was feeling so incredibly horny that her comments fell on deaf ears. Instead, he simply pushed her gently over on the bed and made love to her with great passion and without a further word.

Nevertheless, the gay rights and abortion issues had made it very clear to Patrick that party politics did not suit his modus operandi as a politician.

"How could everyone have the same view about every single issue—political or otherwise?" he mused. "It's impossible!"

The only option he had left was to be an independent. However, Patrick also realised that an independent candidate had little hope of being elected without having a high public profile in the electorate. He was convinced he had a political manifesto that would set him apart from the crowd of wannabe politicians promising more of the same and rarely delivering to an increasingly cynical, disengaged electorate. But without major political party backing or "celebrity" status, his cause was lost.

He also twigged that in the twenty-first century, reality television had become an orthodox path to celebrity for people of little to no real talent beyond the ability to woo viewers with on-screen charisma. Patrick was handsome, full of youthful bravado, and best of all, he oozed sex appeal, the ideal character blend for reality television fame and celebrity and, more importantly for him, a sure-fire shortcut to achieving his political ambition.

But he couldn't sing. He couldn't dance, and he hated renovation programs. Cooking was his only option. After all, he enjoyed cooking. He had even (only very briefly) contemplated a career as a chef after being so disillusioned with his party-political experience. And his friends, family, and regular lovers always praised his traditional island dishes. One casual lover had been so impressed with his sea cucumber soufflé and black pudding curry that she had insisted on "rewarding" him. She had served herself a share of the strawberries and cream dessert on parts of a naked, blindfolded Patrick spread-eagled on the bed among sexually clichéd red satin sheets. His hands and legs were tied to the bedposts, leaving his body erotically prone and primed for her carnal desires. But not before she had hungrily devoured a healthy portion of dessert off his naked body.

And soon enough, Patrick had become the talk and toast of the "water cooler" in offices around the country as he found himself progressing through the rounds of the popular *The Chef Rules OK!* television series.

The foodies would dissect his recipes and cool cooking style, while many of the women and the odd gay man would openly drool over his telegenic good looks and charisma while expressing a desire (in hushed tones, of course) to be his kitchen slave dressed only in a slut-standard apron.

Patrick was well on his way to raising his public profile to a level that he felt would enable him to be competitive in a political arena when he became embroiled in a *The Chef Rules OK!* scandal.

Extremely grainy paparazzi pictures surfaced in a leading women's magazine of a couple closely resembling Patrick and an attractive female celebrity chef and *The Chef Rules OK!* judge frolicking at a secluded out-of-town beach in various states of undress. The accompanying story detailed an alleged "intimate private dinner" at a nearby beachside shack that had been allegedly rented by the couple. The writer of the story even alleged that Patrick had illegally imported some rare tenrec meat from his native island, which he had cooked up in a curry that "tasted like chicken with a sewer after taste" but also "as spicy as the bedroom romp which followed".

Given the blurry nature of the photos in which the people were barely recognisable, Patrick and the judge had at first confidently denied the allegations and even threatened to sue. However, some days later a copy of a credit card receipt signed by Patrick as payment for a sex shop item emerged, which placed him in the vicinity of the same beachside town on the exact dates alleged by the magazine story. Dismissing the revelation as "pure coincidence", Patrick and the judge continued to deny the allegations.

The producers of *The Chef Rules OK!*, however, wouldn't bear the risk of bias—perception or otherwise—towards any competitor on the part of the judge, particularly after newspaper stories covering the scandal began highlighting examples of the judge's "extraordinary praise" for Patrick's cooking and the "obvious on-screen chemistry between them".

Patrick and the judge were evicted from the show in an emotionally charged episode designed to extract a deluge of tears from viewers and every last rating point from two flawed heroes who, polls showed, had continued to enjoy the support of most viewers despite the scandal. And the strategy was a resounding success, with ratings reaching the dizzy heights that saw it crowned the highest rating television program of the year.

But when the ratings for subsequent episodes in the series plummeted just as dramatically, the program's executive producer began to question the wisdom of the decision to evict them and even explored possible avenues to bring them back into the series. Working on the adage that "any publicity was good publicity", the executive producer was convinced the inevitable negative media backlash from their return would translate into ratings gold. But no way could be found to legitimately or morally restore them to *The Chef Rules OK!* fold without incurring the wrath of the remaining contestants and a possible implosion of the whole series.

Meanwhile, the same any publicity is good publicity philosophy was also propelling Patrick into action on the political front. He wanted to cash in on the flame of momentary television fame, which still flickered. Fortuitously for him, local council elections were looming and he seized the opportunity to run for office, shrewdly using his newfound notoriety to procure the money he needed to fund his campaign.

And well before the last word had been uttered about the *Chef Rules OK!* scandal around the office water cooler, Patrick La Malettie had become a local councillor and, in his own words, "taken a big baby step towards saving the world". With his FAIR manifesto always at the vanguard of his campaign for office, he mistakenly believed that voters were seduced by his extreme political agenda. But yet again, it was primarily the body, not the mind, of the candidate which proved to be an electoral magnet, with 95 percent of women voting for a political manifesto that maybe 5 percent actually understood.

CHAPTER XXVII

The Perfect Day to Die

No doubt about it, the weather was closing in. From the vantage point of his apartment window on the fourth floor of the complex, Patrick could see a huge mass of menacing black clouds rolling in belligerently over the reef. In its wake, the shifting shades of blue, green, and turquoise in the usually crystal-clear lagoon were transformed into a uniform, angry dark blue sea capped with abundant windblown wisps of white water. Waves were leapfrogging the reef and rolling onto the shoreline five hundred metres away, albeit only a tenth of the size and much less powerful.

There had been talk in the past week of a moderate cyclone threatening the island and that threat was now imminent.

Looking out into the increasing gloom, Patrick's vision was drawn to a sight that would not be so unusual if the weather wasn't so foul. A woman was stripping down to a bikini and heading into the water. Testimony to the ever-growing strength of the wind, the woman's long black hair was blowing at nearly right angles to her body as she walked calmly into the sea.

Not the best time for a swim but each to their own. I hope she's a good swimmer, Patrick thought.

Patrick went to a cupboard to fetch a pair of binoculars. When he returned and refocused on the scene, he quickly realised swimming wasn't the objective of this beautiful young woman. She walked on into the lagoon; her progress slowed by a strong current. And as the waterline reached a point whereby swimming would be the natural mode of navigation, she continued walking, her head bobbing up and down between the rolling swells and churning sea as if her natural survival instinct was locked in a fierce battle with her apparent desire to drown herself.

Patrick was paralysed with fear and trepidation, his mind still slightly foggy from the previous night's binge. He remained rooted to the spot by the window, looking out onto the tragic scene unfolding before his eyes, as if he were watching a film.

Surely this isn't happening. Why is she doing this?

And just as he found the necessary motivation to leave the cinema and head down to the beach to perhaps effect a happy ending, he saw a young man dressed in a suit run onto the beach, rip off his tie, jacket, shirt, and shoes and dash into the water. The man swam towards the woman whose progress had been somewhat arrested by the ever-increasing swell.

Fortunately, the man was a strong swimmer and managed to navigate the waves and swirling white water to reach the woman quickly. However, as he tried to grab her to bring her back to shore, she seemed to make an attempt—albeit a feeble one—to resist. The man easily managed to subdue her resistance, hook his arm around her and swim back to the shore. Patrick held his breath as he saw the woman's limp body being carried out of the water by the man who placed her gently down on the beach, well away from the raging sea. She lay there motionless and for a brief moment, Patrick feared she had achieved her objective. Compounding his fear was the fact that the man was giving her mouth-to-mouth resuscitation.

Patrick couldn't help thinking that if someone had just stumbled on this scene, the couple might have been mistaken for lovers, although certainly the weather was far from ideal for any spontaneous expressions of love. With his binoculars firmly focussed on the drama unfolding on the beach, Patrick didn't notice a luxury car skidding to a halt on the roadway by the beachfront, not far from the couple.

Moments later, he breathed a sigh of relief as the patient began to stir. Even though he didn't know the woman, Patrick was thankful to have escaped bearing witness to a potentially tragic event. And now he had the urge to investigate further. He quickly put on some appropriate clothing, including a pair of galoshes that had been growing cobwebs in the closet, and went down to the beach. Despite the rain, Patrick found a few people had gathered around the scene of the rescue. The woman was sitting up and being comforted by a well-dressed, older man and reacting with a forced smile to whatever he was saying to her.

No doubt, still in a state of shock, thought Patrick.

In the meantime, her rescuer was forcibly taken some distance away by a couple of burly security guards who handed him over to a white man. And to Patrick's great surprise, instead of being lauded for his bravery, the young Creole man found himself immediately under assault from the white man whose kick thankfully missed the mark as his opponent swayed his head back in the nick of time. He instantly recognised the Creole man as his old friend Gaston.

CHAPTER XXVIII

To the Rescue

Gaston was feeling uncomfortable. His legs were itching. For the first time in his life, he was wearing a suit, one of his late father's old suits, which had been adjusted by the local tailor to fit him. His mother had almost swooned before he walked out the door, heading for his job interview in Palm Waters.

"Oh my, you look so handsome. Your father would have been so proud," Harriet had said, with a tear in her eye, while using her moistened palm to pat down the one patch of his hair that refused to conform to his otherwise immaculately coiffured head of hair.

While the 1950s-styled suit was cut of fine quality cloth and was therefore well preserved, the fabric made his skin itch. He had an old pair of pyjama pants he would normally wear under a pair of his own trousers made of such fabric, but he couldn't find them. Just before leaving home, he remembered that the last time he had worn those trousers—and the pyjama pants—was at Natalie's place, which put him in a bad mood. He again felt resentment rising, although memories of Natalie no longer made him feel sad. Grief had now given way to anger, which was a preferable emotion to the misery that had overwhelmed him after the unexpected breakup.

As he walked out the door, he exhaled an audible sigh of relief and set off towards the bus stop at almost a jogging pace in an effort to shake off the irritation he was now feeling. A brisk walk or jog almost always had a positive effect on his frame of mind. And sure enough, by the time he reached the bus stop on the main road, a genuinely warm smile graced his face and his pace had slowed to a more jaunty stride. His legs didn't even feel so itchy anymore. And best of all, thoughts of Natalie had retreated to the deepest recesses of his subconscious.

The arrival of the bus coincided with a huge gust of wind which sent a garbage bin flying across the road. Fortunately, there was no traffic in its trajectory and it landed safely into a bamboo fence on the other side of the road, scattering its contents on the ground, which, in turn, were immediately picked up by the swirling gusts of wind and flung violently to various parts of the street and surrounds.

Gaston was relieved he could take refuge in the bus, which was carrying only a handful of passengers. No doubt the weather was having a dampening effect on commuter numbers and the general traffic, which normally would be much busier at this time of day. And as Gaston sat down in the seat directly behind the bus driver, he tuned in to a voice emanating from a transistor radio perched on the bus dashboard in front of the driver's steering wheel. The radio announcer was relaying a warning from the weather bureau that an alert number two was now in place for a cyclone that had been meandering around the region for about a week. In coming days, the announcer said, it was highly likely that the alert level would be raised to number five, the highest possible threat level, which would halt public transport, close all schools, shops, and offices, and compel residents to secure their homes and stay indoors or take refuge in a government-sanctioned emergency centre.

As he settled into his seat on the bus, Gaston thought once more of Patrick, which made him feel even more cheerful. He was planning on using the opportunity of being in Palm Waters to track him down after the interview, but the cyclone might just wreak havoc with his plans.

Gaston had no idea what to expect from the interview, only that he had no expectations. It was going to be his first-ever formal job interview, after all. He didn't even know what job the resort owners had in mind for him. The letter summoning him to the interview had only revealed that he would be considered for a pool of either office workers, food and beverage staff, or manual labourers. Gaston wasn't too fussed. He'd even be happy with a manual labouring job. He was already a decent home handyman and enjoyed the few times he'd been called upon to help maintain the garden.

"I'll take any job that gives me a bit of money and also time to do some more writing," Gaston had told his mother, who, while not wanting to crush his dreams, believed his writing ambition was nothing but a futile one. She hoped Gaston would be able to secure a job for life at the resort. That was her dream. And in the week leading up to the interview, she had spent many hours scarring her knees, praying to the Virgin Mary for her dream to come true.

But in recent days, Gaston had made a move to test his potential as a writer. He had sent an article he had written, an opinion piece, to the island's main newspaper, the *New Express,* in the hope of having it published. That hope came courtesy of a chance encounter at the corner shop a few days earlier with an old school friend,

Emile, who also shared Gaston's passion for *Tintin* comic books. Naturally, the conversation quickly turned towards their beloved hero.

"Guess what, Gaston?" Emile had said enthusiastically. "I'm going to be a reporter just like Tintin.

"My uncle has just been appointed as editor of the *New Express* and he's agreed for me to get some work experience there. He says they're always on the lookout for new talent and he liked some of my writing I showed him. Are you still writing?"

"I haven't written anything recently," Gaston confessed. "I haven't felt inspired, to tell you the truth."

"That's a shame; you were a really good writer at school. I liked some of your kooky ideas. Positively kooky, I mean," Emile said in a friendly tone matched with an equally friendly smile.

"A story expressing some of those ideas would be great for the newspaper. My uncle's a real progressive type. Says he wants the newspaper to have more stories that shake up the establishment. My dad says he's a communist, and maybe I am too 'cause he likes my writing."

"Yeah, maybe I'll get back to it," Gaston said unconvincingly.

"Hey, my friend, you really should. Say, if you can write something interesting in the next couple of days, I'll pass it on to my uncle. I'm seeing him on Friday. As I said, they're always looking for new talent," Emile said before scribbling down his phone number on a ragged piece of paper and handing it to Gaston.

And lo and behold, in the days that followed, Gaston had somehow managed to summon the necessary inspiration and perspiration to produce a story about an alternative island community he had visited with Natalie some six months before.

The residents of Choisyville, a village in the remote south of the island had gone tribal, largely cutting themselves off from mainstream island society and creating what was essentially a socialist enclave whereby all villagers had agreed to pool ninety per cent of their incomes into one community bank account from which they provided the basic necessities of life for all villagers—that is, home, food, and energy utilities. A committee of chosen elders administered the account and organised recreational activities and other social events like weddings and funerals, drawing on the community bank account to cover the costs. As a result, no one went hungry, everyone had a roof over their heads, children played safely on the streets, and genuinely happy souls and laughter seemed to pervade the community environment.

The Choisyville community insisted that their new socio-economic system be called the "Common Sense Collective Plan" to avoid any association with the socialism that had universally acquired a bad name.

In his story, Gaston had argued for other island villages to emulate the example of Choisyville, citing, in particular, the "seemingly content villagers" and the "refreshing lack of advertising pollution in the village". Gaston had worked through the pangs of angst that inevitably surfaced when evoking the memory of that visit to Choisyville with Natalie to produce a story that, he felt, was as good as anything he'd read in the *New Express*.

However, before submitting his story to the newspaper, he wanted a second opinion, so he made the trek to his old school to seek out his former favourite teacher, Miss Stanislas. She had seemed very pleased to see him and happily agreed to critique the article, and much to Gaston's delight, her feedback had been extremely positive, saying something about his writing "reminding her of an old boyfriend".

Gaston was contemplating the praise of his former teacher and dreaming of his article being published on the front page of the *New Express* as the bus left Finger Bay behind and ploughed on along the picturesque coastal route to Palm Waters. He felt quite relaxed and in good spirits now, despite the ominous wind gusts and occasional flurries of rain. He looked out the bus window in awe at the massive, cyclone-generated swell that was pounding the reef in the distance and the almost deserted beaches which, on a normal sunny day, would be packed with swimmers, sun, and sea worshippers. Gaston did spot a few brave hearts on surfboards enjoying the rare experience of surfing island waves inside the lagoon.

The worst of the cyclone is still probably a day or so away, plenty of time to get home after the interview, thought Gaston.

As he spotted the bright orange and yellow sign in the shape of the sun, which heralded the bus's arrival into Palm Waters, he began to feel nervous, and even more so when the giant metal skeleton of the new resort development came into view. Gaston wondered where the interview would be conducted, as the only address he had been given was the site of the resort development, which, at this stage, was not fit for that purpose. That question was immediately answered as he stepped off the bus and saw a large group of people huddled together under a temporary awning that snaked around the corner of the construction site leading to a demountable building at the back, which had been surrounded by sandbags, no doubt heeding the call of authorities to take the necessary precautions against the impending onslaught of the cyclone. The building, nevertheless, still looked rather flimsy as it visibly shook with the now regular strong gusts of wind, some even significantly bending the palm trees on the beach promenade.

He had been the only one of three passengers who alighted from the bus to head in the direction of the beach. He wanted to take a few moments to survey the progress of the impending storm and gather his thoughts for the interview. The two others had fled in the opposite direction as fast as they could to escape the rain and take refuge among the people under the awning awaiting interviews. The rain didn't deter Gaston. It only added to the splendour of Mother Nature's fury, which was about to be unleashed on the island. Besides, he had an umbrella which he had deployed and was strong enough to resist the strong wind gusts . . . for now.

He looked out over the lagoon and saw a mass of black clouds still beyond the reef and moving towards the coast at a leisurely pace. And as his gaze shifted downwards, from the sky to the shoreline, it was immediately drawn to the odd sight of a woman, all alone on the beach, stripping down to her bikini and casually heading towards the water. Unbeknownst to Gaston, his old friend Patrick was watching the same scene from the vantage point of his apartment building across the road near the construction site.

Swimming in this weather—she's bonkers!

A sense of disbelief momentarily paralysed Gaston, and, like Patrick nearby, he felt as if he was viewing the scene unfolding in front of him through the lens of a camera. Yet, a beautiful woman was indeed walking into the angry sea with some determination to end her life. As Gaston fully grasped the seriousness of the situation, he sprang into action.

He threw down his umbrella and ran towards the shoreline. He could now barely see the head of the woman bobbing up and down in the sea, even though she wasn't too far out. He wasted no time in tearing off his jacket, tie, shoes, and shirt (suddenly grateful that he had listened to his mother and put on his best boxer shorts) before fearlessly jumping into the water. Gaston knew he was a strong swimmer who could navigate the cyclone-fuelled currents and swell. Nevertheless, his progress was slow and at one stage he lost sight of the woman only to realise she had fully disappeared under the water, but fortunately only a few metres away.

As he reached her and attempted to grab her around the upper torso, she seemed to awaken from a trance-like state and resisted Gaston's attempt to save her.

She managed to wriggle out of his grip just as a powerful wave rolled over them. Gaston, however, persisted and was soon able to grab her again and, this time, her resistance was merely a token effort. Fortunately for Gaston, she had also passed out, although for a brief moment he feared she had passed away. He gently wrapped his arm around her neck to elevate her head and keep it above the water then placed his other hand on her neck and detected a faint pulse. Relieved, he started making his way back, which proved a much easier task with the breaking waves working in his favour to propel them back towards the shore.

As Gaston reached a water level that allowed him to stand and walk, he held the unconscious woman in his arms and carried her limp body out of the water in a style reminiscent of Hollywood movies. Rain was still falling steadily as Gaston placed her on the sand not too far from the roadway. He tilted her head back, pinched her nose and pried open her mouth to check her breathing before planting his lips on hers and blowing firmly but not too hard. He was suddenly grateful he had taken the time in his teenage years to complete a first aid course. The South African friend of his teenage years, who had trained him to be a strong swimmer, had also regularly preached the benefits of learning first aid.

Gaston was soon completely immersed in his resuscitation efforts despite the strong wind squalls blowing in all different directions and occasionally driving rain horizontally into his face as he came up for air. He failed to notice a luxury car pull up suddenly on the roadway immediately in front of them, its tyres slipping and sliding on the wet road as it stopped abruptly, causing the car to swerve and park at an angle to the kerb and propelling the rain that had accumulated in the gutter onto the footpath and beach.

Inside the car, Tom Wright pressed his face against the back window and couldn't quite believe his eyes. The anguish turning to anger was visible on his face as he watched his fiancé seemingly engage in passionate kisses with a handsome stranger who seemed somewhat familiar to him.

This is surreal, thought Tom. *How dare she betray me? And in this fucking weather! She's insane! And the guy is dead. No one does this to Tom Wright.*

He was furious, the rage mounting with every second of inaction. And it was only fifteen or so seconds before he and his two burly car companions—a chauffeur and a security guard—stepped out of the car on a mission to teach "this mother-fucker" a lesson.

CHAPTER XXIX

Almost a Fatal Attraction

Gaston certainly didn't have any conscious erotic thoughts as his mouth covered the mouth of Solange Dubois, fiancé of Tom Wright. Yet, he became sexually aroused as he administered mouth-to-mouth resuscitation. Parting her voluptuous lips and the touch of her smooth skin combined with the surge of adrenaline to pull the sub-conscious sexual triggers, which resulted in an inconvenient bulge in his boxer shorts. Later, he would read that sexual arousal in a crisis situation was not an uncommon experience.

It only took a matter of minutes for Solange to regain consciousness, coughing and spluttering to life and causing Gaston to recoil in surprise. She opened wide her sparkling grey-blue eyes, which met and lingered on his long enough for both to feel the proverbial thunderbolt, despite the distinctly inappropriate setting for any thoughts of romance.

Gaston hardly had time to reflect on the moment of undoubted mutual attraction as he was suddenly grabbed by the arms and lifted off Solange, his feet dangling and swinging wildly, suspended in mid-air.

"*What the* . . ." was all that he had time to scream before he found himself being whisked away and flung to the ground. He landed face-first into the sand with an audible thud and lay flat on his stomach. Momentarily in shock, he nevertheless managed to lift his head and immediately began coughing and spitting out the sand that he'd ingested when he hit the ground open-mouthed. And, as he struggled to open his eyes through the veil of sand plastered on his eyelids, he vaguely detected a pair of expensive Nike jogging shoes right under his nose.

"Get up, you fucker! You're going to pay for messing around with Tom Wright's girl," Gaston heard through the faint bells that seemed to be ringing in his ears.

Although he had trouble understanding the man's accent, Gaston quickly caught on that the woman was his girlfriend.

Why's he trying to kill me, then? He should be thanking me for rescuing . . .

Gaston wasn't able to complete that thought as he instinctively felt the shape of a Nike shoe hurtling towards his head. He managed in the nick of time to avoid being struck, but the momentum of jerking his head back unexpectedly caused him to lose any semblance of balance he'd achieved while trying to get to his feet. He again found himself flat on the ground, but this time lying on his back and looking at the very angry face of Tom Wright through a veil of light, steady rain.

"Come on, get up. What did you do to her to make her want to fuck you on the beach in this weather, you weird, crazy sonofabitch? You must've drugged her, you sick fuck!" Tom barked.

While, again, he couldn't completely understand what Tom was saying, he did now understand the reason for his fury, which, in reality, was a complete misunderstanding.

Or was it? Gaston thought as, despite his perilous position, he had a flashback to that moment when their eyes met.

Surely, she too had felt that spark of attraction.

"What the fuck are you doing, mate? Fair dinkum, this bloke's a hero."

It was a voice that sounded vaguely familiar to Gaston, but the accent was similar to his assailant. The broad Australian accent also took Tom by surprise and caused him to abort another attempt to land a blow to Gaston's head with his foot. Still lying on his back, Gaston seized the opportunity to roll over, away from the immediate danger. He even found the strength to stand up, but his vision was still a bit blurry and he felt wobbly on his feet.

His attention was immediately drawn to Solange, who was now sitting up on the beach and being comforted by a well-dressed older man who had wrapped a bright floral pashmina around her. A security guard shielded them from the rain with a huge umbrella and from the scene of conflict with his massive body. A few other people from the resort construction site, umbrellas also deployed, had been lured to the commotion on the beach but were keeping their distance as the skirmish unfolded and the angst level rose. And in Tom Wright's line of fire, Gaston soon realised he'd been replaced by his old friend, Patrick.

CHAPTER XXX

The Black Kid

"They're offering how much?"

"Five hundred thousand Australian dollars. How much is that, Harry?"

"It's more than enough for all of us to live like kings for the rest of our lives. You sure you heard right? They want to give us five hundred thousand Australian dollars for this dump?"

"That's what Tom said, dear. He said they need it to finish building the hotel. But tell me, will we be able to spend Australian dollars here?"

"Don't be so stupid, Marie; he'll give it to us in our type of money," Harry said condescendingly before muttering under his breath.

"How on earth did I marry someone so fucking dumb?"

Harry Dubois hadn't always felt such enmity towards his wife. In fact, he had been very much in love (or was it lust?) with Marie when they married some twenty-five years ago. Who wouldn't have fallen in love with those beautiful big, blue-grey eyes and velvet smooth white skin, which, however, had also blinded him to her limited education and life experience?

Marie's curvaceous body, too, had been a delight to explore in those early years. Harry didn't like skinny women. Her slightly bulging tummy and her full, well-shaped buttocks had turned him on enormously. But the couple's frequent passionate and, at times, kinky sexual encounters did nothing to make them more intellectually compatible. And little did they realise that the sexual thrill of golden showers and the odd excursion into bondage and even anal sex was always going to have a limited lifespan.

Nevertheless, in the colonial world ruled by silent apartheid, scoring a beautiful white woman had also been a passport to much social and business success for a plain Creole man like Harry, who was graced with an "acceptable" light chocolate skin hue.

Harry had become the region's rock star stonemason who had built (or as Harry put it, "crafted") the fences of many island politicians and several stone beach houses for island celebrities. Most significantly, he'd also worked on the refurbishment of two prominent churches: the island's biggest in the capital and one in Finger Bay.

And when Solange was born three years into the marriage, bearing the same milky white skin and exquisite eyes as her mother, Harry was the happiest and proudest man alive. He was also relieved that Marie's libido had remained largely unaffected during most of her pregnancy and shifted quickly back into overdrive following the birth of Solange.

But the "black kid" had changed all that.

Marie gave birth to their second child, Francois, five years later, and much to Harry's shock (and internalised horror), his skin was black as the pit-deep hole that masqueraded as a public toilet in the village square.

Where the fuck did he come from? Harry had muttered to himself as he left the hospital dejected the evening after the birth and headed home, where he quickly guzzled half a bottle of whisky before passing out on the sofa.

The morning after, Harry woke up with a slight hangover, convinced that Marie had slept with a black man. After all, he couldn't think of anyone that black within his extended family. That would give him an escape route, a religiously viable excuse to send them both packing and to file for divorce without incurring the wrath of God. But there was one major stumbling block to his plan. His son was the spitting image of him, barring the skin colour, of course. The brief moment he had looked into Francois's face, he'd seen himself staring back at him.

All the way to the hospital that morning he still hoped against all hope that the maternity staff had been guilty of a terrible mix-up. But he had been right there when that black head had emerged from Marie's enlarged vagina. His wife had been standing upright to give birth while bracing herself against a large chest of drawers. Harry had been in awe of her ability to withstand the incredible pain that she must have been feeling after more than twenty-four hours in labour. And just as she was entering the final phase, the midwife had called him over to look up his wife's vaginal passage to see a massive crown of black hair that was about to emerge from the birth canal. He remembered chuckling inside and immediately thinking that the child would be so beautiful, blessed with such lovely black hair and fair skin. But he was left dumbstruck moments later when a healthy but jet-black baby boy announced his arrival into the world with the stock-standard piercing scream of a newborn.

If he had traced his family tree, Harry would have found the black skin probably came courtesy of an illicit relationship between his playboy great-grandfather, Chester, and the family's African maid, who was sacked for allegedly stealing food some weeks after he had slept with her. As a result, Chester was unaware of the baby until one morning when the maid turned up at his house and attempted to barge her way in using a baby as a battering ram. His wife, Millicent, had answered the door that day and upon seeing the baby realised immediately why the maid had returned. The baby bore a striking resemblance to her husband. The horror of that realisation made her react in an equally horrific way. Millicent repelled the maid's vigorous attempt to enter the house then followed her outside, where she grabbed her firmly by the arm and dragged her through the yard before aggressively throwing her out the front gate. The maid was crying hysterically, the baby perched precariously on her shoulder as she stumbled and almost fell. But Millicent showed no mercy, warning her that she would call the police if she ever came back before slamming the front gate shut and locking it with a chain and padlock. A week later, however, the maid did return but, in the dead of night and, only to leave the baby at their doorstep before fleeing and seemingly disappearing off the face of the earth.

Chester's wife, like so many wives of high-society white folk in early twentieth-century British colonial outposts, had immediately forgiven her husband for his sexual indiscretion, in order to maintain the privileged lifestyle to which she had become accustomed. By the time she found the baby on her doorstep, she had also reconnected with her more compassionate self and immediately resolved to keep and raise the child. After all, Millicent was in her late thirties, childless and in a marriage that was unlikely to ever produce children. One had to have sex with one's husband for that to happen, and sex had become an increasingly rare event in what had essentially become a "marriage of convenience".

Millicent believed adopting the child would also endear her to her Christian circle of friends and perhaps even win back her largely estranged family. She told everyone that the poor child's mother had died in childbirth and, given that the late mother had been a cherished former employee with no known family in the village, it was her Christian duty to adopt the orphaned child. She also believed that God would forgive her for lying, given her selfless, charitable action. Of course, she was never privy to the whispers and oblivious to the rumour and innuendo which flowed among the many who couldn't help but notice the child's amazing resemblance to Chester.

The child went on to be the grandfather whom Harry never knew because he had died long before he was born. Harry, therefore, had no idea that he shared an unusual bond with the child's father, Chester, in each having a black child who looked so much like their respective dads.

Harry also inherited life in a society that had made little progress since Chester's day in accepting people of black skin as the equal to those of white. This was especially so in the inward-looking island mountain village of La Montaigne, that the Dubois family called home. It was no coincidence their family and friends failed to follow up on their initial visits to the hospital after the birth of Francois. Excuses were always found as to why many of them, especially the white folk, couldn't visit the family home or attend the Christening. Yet, when Solange was born, there had been an endless procession of well-wishers and visitors to the family home for many weeks after, and the whole village had turned up for her Christening party.

From the time they were married, Harry and Marie had always been a popular couple on the village social scene. But the constant flow of invitations to parties, weddings, dances, and other social events, which had surged following the birth of Solange, suddenly dried up after Francois's birth. Harry would often hear about an event the day after, from someone who expressed some expertly feigned surprise that he hadn't been invited or aware that it had been on.

The "black kid," in fact, became the scapegoat for every negative twist of fortune or ructions within the life of the Dubois family. Harry even blamed Francois when the lust in his relationship with Marie inevitably began to wane. By that time, some fifteen years had elapsed in their marriage and Harry resigned himself, like many of the island's Catholic "martyrs", to suffer through an essentially loveless and lust-less marriage in order to reserve his place in Heaven.

But Harry, like so many others, was a convenient Catholic. He didn't see any risk to him booking his eternal place in Heaven when he began flouting another hardcore Catholic commandment, sex outside the marital bond. After all, the declining lust in his relationship with Marie hadn't reduced his libido, so it was only natural for him to seek another sexual outlet courtesy of the local brothel. And he was convinced that when the day of judgment came, God would surely forgive him for doing what came naturally. Most men were slaves to their primal sexual urges and Harry had often heard the priests say that God had "created man in His own image". He had therefore deduced that God, in his human incarnation, Jesus Christ, probably experienced and even acted on the same primal sexual urges.

"After all, the son of God and part of the holy trinity was rumoured to have had a lover in prostitute Mary Magdalene," Harry conveniently reasoned to justify his own sexual peccadillos.

His Catholic beliefs did have one very positive influence, however. It compelled him to love the black kid despite all the trials and tribulations. He desperately wanted to hate him or, at the very least, dislike him but he simply couldn't. After all, God surely would not forgive a father who didn't love his own flesh and blood no matter what the skin colour, would He?

Besides, Jesus was a native of the Middle East so he must have been a coloured man; the only real argument was just how dark! Harry thought.

But Harry didn't blame the black kid for the affair. According to him, that was Marie's fault. No doubt about it. It was her failure to remain sexually appealing to him that made Harry vulnerable to the sexual charm of a new client—a wealthy, attractive but fanatically bored housewife of one of the island's leading businessmen. And unfortunately, the other significant female in his life, the imminent teenager Solange, couldn't escape being caught up in the wake of Harry's guilt which almost overnight turned him into a controlling bully with a very short fuse. He began to bark orders and demand that Marie and Solange acquiesce to his every whim and if they didn't, he'd scream them into submission. Marie did not have the intellectual fortitude to fight back and was soon too scared of Harry to even attempt to leave the marriage. When Harry began staying longer at work, Marie suspected that Harry was having an affair but she didn't care. She was relieved that she didn't have to tread on eggshells and always be on guard should the bully's fuse be lit by some minor dispute.

Solange felt helpless, too immature to know how to respond to such a radical personality transformation in a father whom she still loved dearly. She was obliged to accept and obey in the face of frequent intimidation. She, too, started feeling happier when she didn't see him for days on end, with Harry leaving for work before she woke up in the morning and getting home well after her bedtime.

Harry's affair didn't last a long time, though. He quickly lost interest in the routine, unadventurous sex. When he ended it, he simply resumed visiting the local brothel where he could once again indulge all his kinky carnal desires. However, the affair had irrevocably tarnished his personality and temperament. And while he became less of a bully, Solange and Marie remained wary and forever alert to anything which might upset Harry or provoke a fit of rage.

The end of the affair also seemed to trigger a sudden decline in the demand for Harry's services. Harry once again was tempted to blame the black kid, although he quickly realised that the claim had no substance given that Francois was now nearly nine years old and the workflow had only slowed to a trickle over the past year.

Little did he realise that his sudden rupture of the affair had greatly irked a narcissistic lover with an overinflated ego, a vindictive nature, and powerful connections. And her revenge was swift. She urged her bevy of influential contacts in the local area to boycott the services of Harry the stonemason, claiming that, despite his previous stellar reputation, alcoholism had withered his professional powers. She even went as far as paying a close friend and amateur tradesman to knock down the flawless stone fence that Harry had built for her and replace it with a shoddy one, then inviting any connections who doubted her claim of his fall from grace to "come and see for yourself".

Her plan worked a treat. Before the affair, Harry had more work than he could handle, often toiling six—and sometimes seven—days a week to keep up with the demand. But only a month after the affair, he was lucky to work two or three days a week. He was struggling to put food on the family table when he decided, as a last resort, to advertise in the local paper, something he'd never had to do before. Only two new clients, who'd just moved from the coast and had yet to be tainted by his former lover's network, responded.

Harry saw little option but to move as far away from La Montagne as was geographically possible or face death by starvation or boredom, whichever came first. While his two new clients didn't provide him with the financial lifeline he had required, they did determine his choice of a new home village. Both clients coincidentally had moved to the hills of La Montagne from Palm Waters, where his stellar reputation seemingly remained intact given they had hired him to build new fences solely on the recommendation of friends and family there.

Within a month, Harry had managed to sell his substantial family home in La Montagne, from whose proceeds he could only afford to buy a habitable shack in Palm Waters. While this meant the children would have to share a bedroom, at least they would have enough to eat. And within two months, they had set up a new home there and within three, Harry's business had returned to a sustainable level. Even the family's initial anxiety at living in a much smaller, less comfortable home had been assuaged somewhat by the seaside village ambiance and its proximity to the beach, a two-minute walk away.

Although expensive by La Montagne standards, their Palm Waters shack had been purchased in the nick of time, a year out from a significant boom in beachside real estate propelled by the Wrights' controversial six-star resort development. The Dubois's shack had suddenly become a prized piece of land. But it still wasn't worth the ludicrous amount the resort owner's son and daughter's boyfriend was now offering. While Harry wasn't thrilled at the prospect of moving again after only eighteen months, they really had no choice. With five hundred thousand Australian dollars in their pocket, they would be able to afford a decent home in Palm Waters . . . and more.

Surely, it's too good to be true?

"What's the catch, Marie?"

"Uhh, what do you mean, Harry?"

"Come on, Marie; why would the Wrights pay so much money for this dump? Look around you. This place is worth nothing near that! And Tom's never mentioned anything to Solange about buying our place. Unless she's kept it quiet for some reason.

"They must want something in return."

"Well, Tom said they really need the land here for the hotel so they're willing to pay, he said, a 'fair amount'. But if you think he's paying too much maybe we should offer to sell at a lower, fairer price? After all, Tom's almost family now," Marie said with a satisfied expression on her face as if she had made a brilliant suggestion.

Harry simply rolled his eyes and looked at his wife with some disdain.

"Are you insane? We have a chance to make enough money to live the rest of our days in luxury and you want to pass that up?"

And I'll be able to afford the kinkiest, most glamorous whores in Palm Waters, Harry also thought to himself.

"To these guys, that amount is just pocket money."

"But Harry, Tom can't be that rich. When he came to see me yesterday, he was wearing jeans that had a big rip on each knee. I thought it was funny that the rips were both on the exact same spot and you could see his knobbly knees. But I also thought it was a bit strange that the rest of his jeans, and his shirt too, seemed brand new."

"You obviously haven't been shopping in the designer stores lately, have you?" Harry said condescendingly. "Or doing much thinking, for that matter," he muttered under his breath.

"What's a designer store, dear?"

"Oh, never mind. Did Tom say when he's coming back?"

"He'll be here tonight to pick up Solange, but he won't have time to talk to us about the house then. They're going out to dinner. He says he'll come back tomorrow evening to talk to all of us about his plans for the house. But he must have been feeling a bit confused when he left.

"He called me mum!"

CHAPTER XXXI

Solange

Solange Dubois was not in love with Tom Wright. And she certainly didn't want to marry him, so much so that it drove her to attempt suicide, and if it hadn't been for that "handsome stranger", she would have succeeded.

But where's he gone?

Solange still felt somewhat dazed and confused, as she had been ever since she came to, save for a few moments of absolute clarity when their eyes met. She'd never experienced that before.

Was it love? Surely not?

Solange had always been sceptical of all that romantic palaver about love at first sight. Falling in love was complicated and couldn't happen in an instant. It took time and great effort. Sure, there had to be an immediate physical attraction, but an alleged "lightning bolt" moment that sparked true love and happily-ever-after was pure fantasy, reserved for that make-believe realm of movies and romance novels. Yet, here she was, front and centre of a near-tragic scene unfolding among the natural chaos of a looming cyclone and his eyes seemed to penetrate deep into her heart and soul to melt her despair and desperation, replacing it with a warm inner glow, a feeling of complete exhilaration flowing through her whole being.

But as soon as her saviour abruptly vanished, the demons had swiftly moved back in. An overwhelming feeling of hopelessness and gloom took control once again, causing her to start shaking. She paid scant attention to Jack Wright's attempt to warm and comfort her by wrapping her tightly in a pashmina.

His son, Tom, had been the catalyst for her descent into a deep depression. Her relationship with him had also been living proof that physical attraction did not always blossom into love, no matter how hard you tried.

No doubt, Solange had found Tom physically appealing from the moment they first met in her lounge room just over a year before. He'd come around to advise the Dubois family that his father had recently acquired the property in front of their home—a ramshackle, abandoned warehouse complex on a prized location across the road from the beach, which they were planning to demolish to build a luxury resort complex. The Dubois family was still in the process of settling into their shack, having moved from La Montagne only two months before.

At that first meeting, there was no mention of any plan to acquire the Dubois's home. Tom had simply said that it was a courtesy call from a good neighbour who was concerned that the family might be inconvenienced somewhat during the construction phase of the resort. However, he had also assured them that he would do his utmost to minimise any disruption to their lives.

Over the ensuing six months, construction on the resort development started and proceeded at a seemingly express pace. Tom was overseeing the work and often visited the Dubois's, allegedly to ensure the family was coping well enough with the construction work while also assuring them that the development would bring many benefits to the village, including a huge increase to the value of their property.

However, his true intentions soon became clear. He was infatuated with Solange and, at first, she offered little resistance. Flattered by the attention, the regular gifts and occasional bouquet of flowers that would mysteriously appear on her doorstep, Solange immediately felt that Tom just could be the man of her dreams. He was, after all, a "great catch". In her mind, she simply had to wait for that physical attraction to bloom into love as she believed it naturally would. Solange was also fascinated by Tom's world, which was so different from hers and seemed so glamourous. And he appeared to be equally as enthralled by the simplicity and innocence of her world. But in reality, he had been captivated by her extraordinary beauty, and from the moment he had set eyes on Solange, he was determined to make her his bride. And what Tom Wright desired, he had always achieved, no matter what the cost.

His plan was to woo her slowly, content with kisses and cuddles and holding hands on romantic moonlight walks on the beach. It didn't matter to Tom that Solange refused to have sex with him. He assumed that being a good Catholic girl, she was hellbent (or more Heaven-bent) on saving herself for the man she married and Tom was convinced that would be him—the man to whom Solange Dubois would pledge at the altar to cherish, love, and above all, obey.

Besides, Tom already had a ready and steady supply of women of all colours eager to fuck a rich, white foreign man who, in their mind, might just provide them with a whiff of an opportunity for a better life. Occasionally, Tom also sought sexual consolation from prostitutes, largely for the thrill of it.

Solange, of course, had no idea that Tom was sexually misbehaving. For some time, she remained convinced he was her "prince charming". He was always affectionate, well-mannered, respectful, and forever compliant to her wishes, and from very early on, he had professed an ever-deepening love for her, which she too initially believed would have its ultimate expression in marriage.

But no matter how much Solange longed to fall in love with Tom, it just didn't happen. She tried everything, including soliciting divine intervention. She began a ritual of going to church every odd day of the week to pray wholeheartedly for love to bless their union. But when God failed to answer her increasingly desperate pleas, she blamed herself. After all, he was perfect—a charismatic, handsome, rich, worldly, intelligent foreigner.

What is wrong with me? Any island girl would kill to be in my place!

After six months, Tom started to grow impatient. He was unable to penetrate the protective shield that Solange seemed to have wrapped tightly around her emotions. His regular affirmation of deep and enduring love for her, and her only, was met with long pauses followed by a throwaway response such as "that's sweet" or "you're really a lovely man" and a rapid change of subject, which only served to compound his frustration.

But Tom felt he still had the ultimate circuit breaker up his sleeve: a marriage proposal.

How could any island woman resist the opportunity to marry someone who can guarantee her a life of ultimate luxury, although not fidelity? Tom thought.

To guarantee success, Tom had organised the most romantic scenario possible: dinner and champagne (Krug, of course) at the most expensive restaurant on the island, followed by a romantic walk along the beach and a proposal on his knees by the light of a full moon where he would produce the obscenely expensive diamond engagement ring.

In the highly unlikely event that his foolproof plan failed, Tom still held an ace card. He had managed to persuade his billionaire father, Jack, who was also very fond of Solange, to buy the Dubois family home for an outrageous price on the premise that it was needed for the hotel development. And there was a sound method to the madness of such a ludicrous offer. Tom had broached the subject of marriage with Solange many times and each time, she had tried to avoid the issue, claiming to be an old-fashioned girl who needed the consent of her father to marry. So, he had simply come up with a way to bribe the father.

For her part, Solange had been trying to buy time, still under the illusion that she would eventually fall in love with Tom. In the meantime, as she was only twenty years old, she was confident that her father would, at the very least, insist on a long engagement should an official marriage proposal ever be forthcoming.

Plenty of time for love to blossom, she thought.

Even though the Dubois's property wasn't essential to the completion of the resort complex, the extra land would be useful to its public relations campaign. Jack had agreed to use the land to create an exotic public park and gardens, which would be peppered with "smart" video billboards continually peddling the allegedly idyllic lifestyle of a resort guest. Tom was even investigating the possibility of creating a mini petting zoo in the park populated by as many iconic Australian animals—kangaroos, koalas, emus—as the space would permit.

Such a park would also offer an olive branch to the community who had reacted with rage and howls of protest against the resort development proposal, which was on a scale above and beyond any island standard.

Tom was smiling broadly as Solange opened the door. She was more radiant than ever, although something about her was not quite right. And Tom quickly realised what it was. She looked "off-balance", with the one pendulous earring on. Instead of coming forward to greet him, Solange had backed away after opening the door to put on the other earring.

As he stepped inside, the now balanced Solange kissed him worryingly on the cheek. (He had expected at least a more affectionate meeting of the lips.) But he had little time to reflect on his disappointment as Harry emerged from the back of the house and warmly shook Tom's hand.

"Good to see you, Tom. I hope my little girl is looking after you," he said.

"Would you like a drink before you two lovebirds head off?"

Solange hadn't seen her father so warm and hospitable to anyone for some time. In the previous six months that she and Tom had been dating, he'd been polite and made small talk before quickly finding an excuse to retreat to the back room. He had certainly never offered him a drink.

"I hear you're coming back tomorrow night to talk business?" Harry said with a wink, facing away from Solange.

"What business?" Solange asked, turning towards Tom.

"Uh, it's no big deal, darling. I've just got a small business proposal for your father . . ."

It's not a big deal; it's a really huge deal, thought Harry, grinning from ear to ear.

"But Tom, you've never mentioned anything to me before about a business deal," said Solange.

Solange's aggrieved tone made Tom a touch anxious. He wanted to sail smoothly through the evening and land the girl of his dreams at the end of it. But they were suddenly drifting towards potentially troubled waters, so he had to steer the conversation quickly and safely away from the danger.

"You look so beautiful tonight, darling . . ." he blurted out as enthusiastically as he could muster.

But he realised that Solange wasn't buying the compliment, despite the obvious sincerity with which it had been offered. She continued to glare at him, causing Tom to be momentarily lost for words. He knew he had to deal with—and hopefully bury—the vexed issue of the business proposal.

"I haven't had a chance to tell you, my darling, and was saving it up as a surprise. I promise I will tell you and the whole family about it tomorrow. Tonight's a time for pleasure, not business," said Tom nervously.

But a glance at Harry's smiling face instantly dissipated his anxiety. It was the face of a father who would give his blessing to their marriage. Tom was sure of that now. Even though he still believed that Harry's consent could be achieved without the offer of money, there was certainly no harm in taking out an "insurance policy". The sum was a small fortune to the likes of Harry and Marie, but peanuts to the Wrights, whose family wealth was in the billions.

"Thank you for the offer of a drink, Harry, but we really must get going," Tom said.

Before Harry had time to reply, Tom gently put his arm around Solange's waist and guided her out the door, bidding a hasty goodbye.

CHAPTER XXXII

Love Fails to Materialise

A day later, Tom found himself once again knocking on the front door of the Dubois residence feeling once more anxious and emotionally vulnerable, despite the dinner and proposal going more or less to plan.

The "more" was Solange's mood, which swiftly shifted to upbeat once they had hit the road. At dinner, too, and on their moonlight walk along the beach, Tom had been surprised by her frequent random acts of love and affection. She had called him "darling", held his hand tightly as they walked, and hugged him at every opportunity. She had even stroked his hair as he got down on his knees to launch into the marriage proposal. (Tom loved having his hair stroked, and Solange knew it but had only rarely indulged him.)

The "less" had been Solange's lukewarm response to the proposal, which seemed to prompt an immediate change in her demeanour to downbeat and distant, and her indifferent reaction to the exquisite diamond-infested engagement ring, which was worth almost as much as what he was offering for her family home.

For her part, Solange had not been surprised by the marriage proposal. Her intuition had kicked in as soon as Tom pulled into the carpark of the Filao Restaurant, the finest restaurant on the island and one only frequented by wealthy tourists and the island's elite. But the idea of an imminent marriage proposal had also scared her into being more affectionate than usual. It had made her realise that she would soon be running out of time to fall in love with Tom Wright. And by forcing herself to be more affectionate, she thought it might somehow spark the flame of love that had eluded her so far in the relationship. At the same time, she really had no idea what love actually felt like.

When he finally did pop the question on the beach, it felt surreal, even though Solange had rehearsed it in her head many times before. Worse still, it had the opposite effect to what she had anticipated. Instead of feeling love for Tom, she had felt instant repulsion which immediately checked any further effort to be affectionate. She had managed to coolly nod her approval but found it impossible to actually say the word "yes" and almost immediately resorted to playing the "daddy must approve first" card, as Tom had expected.

Tom was naturally disappointed that her conditional consent hadn't been accompanied by any gesture of passion, as would be the norm for an eager and willing bride-to-be. Nevertheless, he took solace in the belief that he would be dealt the winning hand in the end.

And as Tom heard footsteps approach the front door on a luminous late summer evening with a quasi-full moon rising on the horizon, he certainly felt he had the ace card up his sleeve, or in his hands to be precise, in a contract—lovingly wrapped in a pretty red ribbon—for the sale of the house which would surely also secure the "sale" of Harry's most precious possession.

Harry's beaming face as he opened the door only served to allay any residual fear of failure. His obvious joy was contagious, causing Tom to break out in an equally broad smile as the pair warmly shook hands.

"Very good to see you, Tom. I trust all went well last night and Solange was well behaved?" Harry said with a sly wink and definite twinkle in his eye.

Tom was sure that Solange had not told Harry about the marriage proposal. She had promised to wait for him to do the chivalrous deed of asking her father for her hand in marriage. The prospect of becoming a wealthy man was obviously the reason behind Harry's fervent greeting. Tom couldn't blame him, really. If he was honest about the motivation behind most of his and his father's work, greed would usually be on top of the tree.

Before Tom had time to reply, Harry's partner in greed, an equally excited Marie, ran out, almost screeching in delight at seeing Tom and hugged him tightly. By contrast, a sheepish-looking Solange followed timidly in her mother's slipstream. Her palpable lack of passion as she stepped into the aura of her new fiancé instantly wiped the smile off Tom's face. He was suddenly grateful that he had taken out the "insurance policy".

Francois had been sent to a friend's place for a sleepover. While they both openly claimed the reason behind this was that Francois would be "bored with all the financial talk" and "it was the school holidays after all", Harry and Marie simply didn't want the black kid around. Deep down, they thought his presence might somehow jinx the deal. They had even managed to convince themselves that he had been invited for a sleepover by his best friend, Jacques. The truth, however, was that

Marie had rung Jaques's mother, Juliette, and engaged her in a conversation about how much Francois "loved spending time with Jacques" and "how it'd been such a long time since he had had a sleepover there", leaving Juliette with little option but to invite Francois over.

Marie really shouldn't have bothered. Tom had paid scant regard to Francois since entering the lives of the Dubois family and certainly hadn't noticed his absence tonight. Solange was the one and only object of his desire, and he was on the brink of satiating that desire.

Solange didn't even look Tom in the eye as she approached and kissed him lightly on the cheek, as a child would dutifully kiss a parent. This only compounded Tom's concerns, causing his grip on the contract to tighten, which reassured him that despite her current attitude, as always, Tom Wright would get his way.

Harry, too, picked up on Solange's frostiness towards Tom but the misogynist in him immediately attributed her sombre mood to being "no doubt, that time of the month". He ignored her, and Marie for that matter, and placed his arm around Tom as if welcoming home the prodigal son before steering him away from the two women and towards the back veranda. Tom glanced back at Solange as he was being led away, only to be further disheartened by her sullen demeanour. She looked as if she could burst into tears any minute.

"Now, Tom, before we get down to business, can I offer you some whisky? I've only just put the champagne on ice, so it needs some chilling time. Besides, we'll enjoy that a bit more later, I imagine," Harry said, grinning like the proverbial Cheshire cat.

Champagne? Maybe Solange had spilled the beans about the proposal, thought Tom.

Harry had indeed bought a bottle of very expensive French champagne and an over the top expensive bottle of single malt Scotch whisky in anticipation of a deal that would make him a man who could easily afford such luxuries. He had also splurged on new crystal whisky glasses and champagne flutes, snacks, and a take-away banquet dinner from the most expensive Chinese restaurant in Palm Waters. And Harry had gone on his spending spree without even checking whether Tom would be willing or able to stay for drinks and dinner. As he had a shower in preparation for Tom's visit, it dawned on him that he had spent a month's wages on these luxuries before any official offer was on the table for the sale of his house.

Consequently, in the moments before Tom's arrival, Harry had begun to feel somewhat anxious.

Was Tom pulling Marie's leg? It's so much money for such a hovel. Maybe she'd misheard Tom's offer? She's not the brightest tool in the shed, had been the thoughts replaying in Harry's head before Tom's knock on the door that had only heightened the tension.

However, his fears were allayed when Tom had walked in clutching the rolled parchment, bound with a red bow, which Harry immediately assumed was the contract for the sale of the house. Therefore, as they walked towards the veranda, Harry's mood was on the upswing.

The veranda at the back of the house had seen better days. It was enclosed in a rotting (and in many parts, fully rotten) frame crowned in flyscreens, which also served as de-facto windows. They had miraculously withstood many years of battering from, at times, cyclonic winds, but naturally they were dilapidated and peppered with holes so big that giant butterflies often found their way in. As Harry and Tom walked onto the veranda, a multi-coloured specimen was resting on the table, its exquisite rainbow of colour providing a striking contrast to the pristine white tablecloth draped over the table. It was Marie's favourite tablecloth, a gift from her aunt that she only used on special occasions.

The distinctive aroma and some wispy threads of smoke from a mob of mosquito coils rose from under the table as the pair sat down opposite each other. Dusk was fast approaching and without the coils operating in overdrive, the veranda would have been a no-go zone at this time of day. No one noticed the butterfly meander away, languidly flapping its wings and expertly finding its way through one of the holes in the flyscreen.

Tom placed the contract in the middle of the table just as Marie and Solange walked in with a tray of drinks and snacks, which they positioned symmetrically, one on each side of the contract.

The offer's now officially on the table, Harry thought, his eyes bulging with expectation.

Without asking, Harry poured out a generous amount of Scotch into one of his new crystal glasses and pushed it in front of Tom.

"Ice or water?" Harry asked.

"Just a bit of ice, thanks," Tom said distractedly.

Solange and Marie had taken a seat at the table, but again disappointingly for Tom, Solange settled in a chair next to her father while Marie had sat next to him and edged her seat as close to his as she could possibly get, which unnerved Tom.

But looking across at Solange, Tom was somewhat relieved when he saw her smiling.

A clearly happier Solange gave him the confidence to get straight down to business, but not the business Harry had been expecting.

"Now, Harry, you know how I feel about that beautiful daughter of yours," Tom began, taking a sip of the scotch.

"But just in case you've been hiding under a rock, let me say that I love her more than anything in the world and, as someone who likes to cut to the chase, I would like to make Solange my wife. So, it would be an absolute honour, sir, if I could have your permission to marry your beautiful daughter," Tom spluttered out, getting surprisingly more nervous with each word he uttered but managing a sincere smile at the end.

Harry had never been called "sir" before and was more surprised by that than being asked for his permission for Tom to marry Solange.

"I gather you've already asked Solange?" Harry asked calmly.

"Yes, I have, sir . . ."

There it is again; I could get used to this, Harry thought.

"And it's a credit to you, Harry, and—" turning to Marie "—you too, Marie, that Solange is still an old-fashioned kind of girl, obviously well brought up. She insisted I seek your approval first," Tom said.

Well, no longer a "sir," but it was good while it lasted, Harry thought, chuckling inside.

"I take it that Solange said 'yes'?"

"She did, but of course, she insisted that it would *only* be with your consent," Tom said.

Harry paused to take a sip from his own glass that he'd filled with whisky, ice, and water, his expression blank. This caused Tom's heart to flutter with fear. At the same time, Solange, despite herself, couldn't help but feel a flash of hope that her dad might object to the marriage. (Later she would recall the emotion she felt there and then as a bit of an epiphany, the moment she knew for sure that she would never fall in love with Tom Wright.)

Her optimism was short-lived, as a broad smile promptly foreshadowed Harry's response.

"How could I say no . . . *son*?" Harry said.

He rose from his chair and walked around to the other side of the table and extended his arms out. Tom took the cue and got up and timidly hugged his future father-in-law. Marie couldn't contain herself any longer. She rose, squealing, and joined them in a group hug.

But Solange remained seated. It suddenly dawned on her that the last obstacle to her becoming Tom Wright's wife had been vanquished. And she felt terrified. A wave of goose bumps invaded her skin and prompted her to also rise from her chair to plead for a "stay of execution".

"Papa, Mama, of course I said yes. But I think we shouldn't rush into marriage. I am only twenty, remember, so there's no need to hurry. I'm sure Tom won't mind a long engagement so that I can at least finish my studies first," Solange said.

Solange was in her second year of a teaching degree in English at the island university, her entry to the degree being facilitated by her white skin, no doubt, even though she certainly had the intelligence and aptitude to be a fine teacher. She had two years remaining before graduation.

Her voice was trembling but she felt compelled to speak her mind. As the same time, she was still wary of saying or doing anything that might upset Harry, even though he was no longer the ogre he had been in the aftermath of the affair.

Tom went to his fiancé and put his arm lovingly around her shoulder.

"Of course, I *am* happy to wait, darling, but when I reveal the business deal, you know, the one you wanted to know about yesterday, I'm sure you'll change your mind and realise that we'd all be better off if we set the marriage date for sooner rather than later, especially for your parents who've worked so hard to get where they are and have done such a magnificent job of raising you and Francois."

Solange had forgotten about the business deal but she was no fool and wasn't going to fall for such an obvious attempt to butter up her parents. However, the slight menace in Tom's tone of voice also made her feel uneasy.

"What? What difference will it make to them when we marry?" Solange said, almost in a panic.

Tom let go of Solange and walked around to the other side of the table. He was now facing the trio of Dubois's, two of whom were grinning with expectation, the other gloomy with despair inside but trying to maintain a brave, cheery face.

Tom picked up the parchment and undid the bow-tied ribbon. He rolled it out on the table facing it towards Harry and Marie, who immediately moved in to scrutinise its content.

Harry's eyes skipped immediately to the bottom of the parchment and there it was in bold, black ink: five hundred thousand dollars. He was almost drooling as his eyes skimmed over the rest of the contract.

"Well, Harry, it's all there. It's the deal of a lifetime, as I explained to Marie," Tom said.

"No catch . . . although . . ." Tom weighed up his words carefully before proceeding. He had not been planning on resorting to what effectively was blackmail, but Solange's demand for a long engagement had left him with little option.

"We do need to have the sale settled as quickly as possible—within three months at the most—for the hotel construction to meet its budget deadline," he lied.

"And ideally Solange and I should be married within that time. Don't you agree, Harry? You and Marie can then be free to find a home that would better suit your smaller family, and you'd be able to afford something more luxurious and probably have extra money to spend on travelling or a luxury car."

Money to pay for today's indulgence first, thought Harry.

"You won't have to worry about your Solange. She'll be living a life of luxury and be well looked after, loved—no, adored—by me and my family. All her needs will be met.

"But of course, if it doesn't happen this way, I'll have to reconsider the deal. We really can't afford to have a delay in the resort development, Harry, and even though it's not directly related, it would make a lot of sense to settle everything at the same time, including the marriage."

Turning to Solange, he said, "As for your studies, darling, you'll be free to do anything you want and better still, you'll be able to fully concentrate on your studies, even though you won't have to work at all if you don't want to once you marry me. You can lead a life of extreme leisure. You won't need to worry about menial tasks like shopping, cooking, cleaning. We have staff for that.

"So, what do you say, Harry?"

Harry turned to Solange with an intimidating look that forced her into responding with a lukewarm smile. He didn't have to look at Marie. She was still beaming and contemplating a lifestyle of travel to exotic destinations.

"Where do I sign?" Harry roared.

Solange realised any further protest was futile. It was a done deal. She only had three months to find a way to dodge the proverbial bullet.

CHAPTER XXXIII

Calm Heads Before the Storm

Two months later, the bullet was travelling at breakneck speed towards its target. An increasingly desperate and depressed Solange had reached a point where she felt there could be no escape from the fatal shot which would pierce her heart and effectively kill off any hope of ever finding true love. Instant death seemed preferable to a death of a thousand cuts, entombed in a loveless marriage.

But little did she expect her suicide attempt would be the agent of love. Yet, here she was, filled once again with a warm inner joy despite still feeling rather woozy from her near-death experience. She couldn't stop thinking about that moment when their eyes met.

Surely that was pure love.

Solange was being escorted back to Tom's car, supported by Tom's father and one of his bodyguards. She glanced back over her shoulder to see that Gaston was now on his feet, standing behind another man who was arguing with Tom, and curiously she noted that the man had a similar accent to Tom's.

Tom had calmed down somewhat but was still squaring off against Patrick and Gaston, who was keeping a safe distance behind his old friend.

"I ain't got anything against you, mate, so get out of my fucking way so I can . . ." Tom said with some venom.

"Listen here. I saw the whole thing happen. The woman was trying to kill herself and my friend here saved her. He's a hero. Sorry, the truth is pretty hard to take because obviously she's your girl and all . . ." Patrick said, almost pleading to be believed.

"That's bullshit," Tom interrupted. "You're fucking insane. We're about to be married. It's the most joyous time of our lives."

And true enough, since her engagement Solange had given the outward appearance of a woman seemingly in love and eager for the wedding to proceed. She was too petrified of her father's—and Tom's—reaction if she acted otherwise. For his part, Tom was high on the narcissistic spectrum and empathy was a foreign concept to him. As a result, he was very much out of tune with the emotional roller coaster his fiancé had been enduring in the lead-up to the pending nuptials. Once he had secured the "trophy" firmly in his grasp, he had paid scant attention to Solange's emotional wellbeing. He wasn't even aware that she had been a regular patient of the local psychologist who had prescribed anti-depressants after wrongly attributing her unhappiness to a passing phase of pre-wedding jitters. But the pills had only accelerated her emotional spiral downwards. They overwhelmingly made her feel numb with the occasional high, which was inevitably followed by an extreme low and a just as inevitable return to numbness. She would later describe the experience of being on anti-depressants as being "an observer in your own life rather than an active participant".

"Wake up to yourself, mate. Who would be mad enough to go for a swim in this weather? Only someone with a death wish, that's who," Patrick said, noticing the wind getting considerably stronger. The cyclone was approaching.

"All I know is that I saw the two of them kissing on the beach. He must have drugged her or something. I didn't see her in the water," Tom said as if suddenly trying to convince himself.

"Well, I did, mate. And if my friend didn't bravely go in and rescue her, you'd now be planning a funeral, not a wedding," Patrick said calmly but firmly.

"But, but . . . why would she do that? We're about to get married, the happiest time of our lives. There must be some logical explanation . . ."

Patrick could see that the truth was beginning to sink in. Tom, consequently, assumed a less aggressive stance and a more moderate tone of voice. Patrick suddenly felt sorry for him. He also could sense that it was safe enough to approach and place a hand on the shoulder of a man who was now bowing his head and fighting off tears.

"Look mate, I'm sure there *is* a logical explanation. Who knows what goes on in a woman's head sometimes, even when she should be happy?" Patrick said with genuine compassion.

"I know it's tough for you right now but I assure you, my friend Gaston wasn't kissing your girl. He's a fair dinkum hero and without him your fiancé would have drowned."

Gaston could understand what Patrick was saying about him "not kissing" Tom's girl, but he had become increasingly convinced this might not be the whole truth. It had become a kiss at some point. He was sure of that. Nevertheless, he now felt safe enough to also approach the pair. The burly security guards had backed right away from the whole scene.

A tear or two was flowing down Tom's cheek as he looked up and turned towards Gaston, extending a hand out to him.

"Mate, I hope you can understand this but I am truly sorry. I really thought you had done something nasty to my fiancé and that you two were making out on the beach," Tom said sincerely.

Gaston remained cautious, unable to fully understand all that Tom was saying, although there was no mistaking the contrite tone of his voice. He shook Tom's hand warmly.

"Thank you, and if there's anything I can do for you to thank you properly, let me know. Just drop around to my office at the new resort development there," Tom said, pointing to the construction site where the palm trees in the front were now swaying wildly in the wind.

Tom had been intrigued by Patrick's accent given he looked like a native islander, but he was simply not in the right frame of mind for a friendly chat or to delve into the possible quirks of Patrick's personal history, which had led him to acquire an Australian accent.

Patrick translated Tom's words to Gaston in the local Creole dialect just to ensure that Gaston got the message. Gaston was impressed that Patrick still spoke the local language like a true island native. But there would be plenty of time to catch up on old times and perhaps plan some future adventures. The cyclone was definitely closing in and they all simultaneously seemed to realise that it would be in their best interests to seek shelter as quickly as possible.

"Thank you very much," Gaston said in almost perfect English. But as he suddenly remembered that a job interview at the construction site had been his original destination, he felt compelled to add in a mixture of Creole and English, "I will drop by the construction site as soon as the weather clears up," which Patrick, in turn, translated to Tom.

"Great, mate. I'll see you then," Tom replied as his thoughts suddenly turned to Solange, who was in the car and could be in need of medical attention. And if he didn't leave now, he would run out of time to get her to the hospital, if need be, before the cyclone made the trip a life-threatening venture.

Patrick and Gaston were now alone on the beachfront. The rest of the crowd had long scattered. Despite the weather, they stood still for a few moments and looked at each other with the affection of long-lost lovers, a broad smile on each face struggling to break through the cyclonic wind and torrential rain now lashing them both.

"It's good to see you again, my friend," Patrick had to scream in order to be heard.

"Yes, it's been a long time," said Gaston as a large coconut dropped from a nearby tree and was caught in a gust of wind that propelled it towards the pair. The flying coconut missed Gaston's head by a whisker. It was a warning of the danger fast approaching and a timely cue to flee the scene. But not before Gaston rushed onto the beach to retrieve his discarded shoes and clothing, which fortunately had not been carried away by the wind. The driving rain had half-buried his suit and shirt in the sand, creating a firm, sandy doorstop which had held the items firmly in place.

CHAPTER XXXIV

A Cunning Plan

Still dressed only in his multi-coloured boxer shorts and hugging tightly the cargo of clothes and shoes to his bare chest, Gaston followed Patrick across the road hugging the beachfront. They didn't even bother checking for traffic as the village was now akin to a ghost town. Any sensible resident had long headed home or to one of the many reinforced concrete buildings, usually schools or community halls, converted into makeshift cyclone shelters. They were a refuge for almost half the island population who lived in housing that turned deadly when battered by winds of cyclonic force.

Gaston and Patrick were running as fast as they could and dodging an assortment of debris being flung haphazardly by the swirling cyclonic winds.

Just like the good old days, thought Gaston, although he couldn't ever remember jogging with Patrick in such horrendous weather conditions. Their parents would have never allowed it anyway.

Fortunately, they had the wind at their back so they reached the safety of Patrick's apartment quickly. Although it was early afternoon, darkness had descended on the village courtesy of the heavy blanket of menacing clouds. Patrick found the button to switch on the apartment foyer lights but had no joy when he pressed it. The cyclone had no doubt followed the traditional path of its predecessors and knocked out the island's power supplies, thus once more showcasing Mother Nature's unrivalled force and her absolute contempt for the essential tools of mere mortals. Fortunately, there were a number of windows in the building which allowed in just enough natural light for them to easily find their way up the stairs to Patrick's fourth-floor apartment,

Like most islanders, Patrick kept a cyclone survival kit handy during the late summer months when the risk of the potentially violent and destructive storms was at its highest. The rough weather associated with a cyclone rarely lasted more than a day or two but its impact on life's essentials and essential services was always longer; how long naturally depended on the severity of the cyclone. Candles and matches, together with supplies of drinking water and tin food and—most importantly—a battery-powered transistor radio and a supply of spare batteries, were the standard components of any such kit. But Patrick also kept bottles of rum in his kit and after lighting a candle, he immediately reached for one as he noticed Gaston shivering uncontrollably.

"Get this into you, my friend," he said, opening the bottle and handing it to Gaston, who instinctively took a big swig. He hadn't had a drink since the abrupt end to his Natalie-fuelled drunken binge, which landed him in trouble with the law. The calming effects were almost instant. The warmth travelled seemingly throughout his entire body and erased any residual trauma from the ordeal of the immediate past. Enhancing his sudden lift in mood was another flashback to that meeting of lips. The soporific effect of the alcohol also filled him with a momentary but intense feeling of love . . . *for her, no doubt,* Gaston thought.

"Whoa . . . go easy on that, Gaston. We only have a couple of bottles and who knows how long we have to sit this one out," Patrick said, laughing.

Gaston was also laughing as he handed the bottle to Patrick, who took an even bigger swig. He put the bottle down, went to his bedroom and emerged moments later with a towel and a change of clothes.

"Here, dry yourself off and put these on. It's probably time I paid you back for those holey running shoes you gave me all those years ago," said Patrick, still grinning from ear to ear.

"It is really good to see you. You haven't changed that much at all except that you're perhaps more handsome, you bastard," he said, laughing once more.

"Look who's talking. I hear you're a bit of a celebrity in Australia. So why did you come back?"

"You, my friend, are a big part of the reason I came back. I only realised in the last few months before my return what a huge influence you've had on my life."

Patrick went on to tell Gaston his whole "life in Australia" story, his monologue peppered with exclamations and expressions of disbelief from Gaston. And as he approached the end game; the tale of his demoralising defeat on the council floor, Patrick didn't hold back on his feelings of utter humiliation, confident that Gaston would be sympathetic and totally on his side.

Gaston was more than on his side. He was in awe of his friend's achievements and very flattered that he had had such a large impact on Patrick's political philosophy and career.

"Well, Patrick, I hadn't thought much about those days, and the things we used to talk about, until recently when I was writing a story about Choisyville. Have you heard about what's going on down there?"

"Can't say that I have," said Patrick.

"Sorry, I forgot that you haven't been around for a few years. It's a village in the south, you know, a village of fishermen and unskilled labourers, corrugated iron shacks and the like. A picture-postcard fishing town with a deep harbour port but not good for tourist development. It has shingle beaches, too much wind and is hard to get to by land. Well, it's a village that's seen the light, my friend," Gaston said and went on to tell Patrick about the mini velvet revolution which had transformed the economy and lives of the Choisyville inhabitants for the significantly better.

"It's the kind of society we used to dream about, remember? I still think the only way we can save the world from rack and ruin and, goddammit, the only way to make a whole lot of people a whole lot happier is to have more places like Choisyville and preferably a Choisy *world*!" Gaston concluded, feeling simultaneously blissful and animated from the combined effect of the rum and the stimulating discussion with his long-lost friend.

Just like old times, yet different and better, Gaston thought.

"Glad you still think that way, Gaston. I haven't given up either, and I certainly could use a partner in crime."

By this time, Gaston had dried himself off and put on the clothes that Patrick had brought him: a designer label T-shirt and shorts, which fitted him perfectly well. They were sitting on the couch and hardly noticed the cacophony from the tempest raging outside—the howling wind, the occasional cracking of tree branches and the thud of a flying object smashing against a wall. Patrick's apartment block was a fairly new building designed and constructed to resist the onslaught of most violent tropical storms.

They had consumed half the rum, taking turns in swigging straight from the bottle before Patrick stumbled his way to the kitchen to fetch two glasses and some food. He was suddenly grateful he had stocked up on parathas and dal puris from his favourite street vendor the day before.

Back on the couch he poured a more conservative nip of rum into each glass. Patrick surprised himself with his desire to enjoy a drink with his old friend without getting seriously drunk. He was intoxicated enough by the conversation with a kindred spirit.

Gaston hungrily tucked into a chicken curry paratha wrap as Patrick started telling him about his plans to resurrect his FAIR agenda on the island, but suddenly stopped mid-sentence as he had a flashback to their earlier confrontation with Tom Wright.

"Say, that's the developer family I've been reading about, isn't it? The ones who bribed the government to get permission to build that monstrosity down the road. I hope this cyclone flattens it. It's just pure greed, mate, and my . . . I mean . . . our FAIR policy will drive away all those greedy bastards like the Wrights and turn this whole island into a caring, sharing Choisy island," he said.

"But obviously there's some trouble in paradise. I wonder why his fiancé was trying to kill herself? Soooo beautiful and seemingly everything to live for, really. But like I said, who knows what goes on inside a woman's head, isn't that right, Gaston?"

Gaston had been listening attentively to all Patrick was saying until the mention of Tom Wright's fiancé, which, once again, sent him off into a reverie.

"Yes, yes, indeed, who really knows . . ." was all Gaston could muster in response, all the while hoping that he had given her a reason to keep on living. She had certainly given him a new lease of life.

"Well, enough of my life. So, what's been going on in your world, apart from the story of Choisyville? By the way, why did you write that story and what's happened to it?"

Gaston managed to refocus on the present and told Patrick about his newfound determination to be a writer, which had led him to write the story about Choisyville.

"You were . . . *are* a very good writer, Gaston, and of course, always full of great ideas. What took you so long to get serious about it? I bet it was a woman?" Patrick said jokingly.

But Gaston didn't laugh. He didn't feel sad either, just surprised that Patrick had hit the nail on the head.

"You may have been gone a long time but you still know me well," Gaston said. "Her name was Natalie."

It was Gaston's turn to reveal the good, the bad and the very ugly of events of the recent past which culminated in an epiphany of sorts: the embarrassment of his arrest, bearing witness to the vile behaviour of the Finger Bay fathers that had shaken him out of his general stupor, having Idris and Monique join forces with him in a desire to avenge Henri's death, then the chance meeting with his old friend Emile that had rekindled his ambition to be a writer. Finally came the surprising offer of a job interview that had brought him to Palm Waters.

Were these sudden positive developments in his life the result of pure coincidence or his more buoyant outlook on life attracting more optimistic outcomes? And perhaps the best was yet to come—true love, emerging rather unusually from the ashes of a near-tragic episode. Nevertheless, the Solange "thunderbolt" was one thing Gaston was reluctant to share with Patrick for the time being. He didn't really know why. Perhaps, he wanted to reassure himself first that the moment actually happened. Thinking back on it now, admittedly through a slightly rum-fuelled haze, it seemed rather surreal, although the emotion was very real and lingering, no doubt about that. He still felt something that could only be described by that romantic cliché of love at first sight. For now, it would remain *their little secret* but if the relationship somehow developed further, Gaston had no doubt that Patrick would be the first to know.

Patrick reacted with a combination of shock, horror, and grief as Gaston recounted the events of the past month.

"But Gaston, we have to do something about this. We can't let them continue torturing and now killing kids," said Patrick.

"I know, I know, but what? I've racked my brains to find some way to stop them and bring them to justice. We certainly can't go to the police, the obvious place you'd go in a normal country. And the only plan put forward so far is to poison them all. I'm sure you'll agree, not a great plan," Gaston said.

The pair sat in silence for some time, occasionally taking a sip of rum but continuously staring straight ahead, both seemingly searching for inspiration. A sudden thud interrupted their musing and drew their eyes simultaneously to the windows at the front of the apartment. Liberated from its iron latches by a tropical strength gust of wind, one of the apartment's wooden shutters had flown open, exposing the glass window it had been protecting to the full force of the cyclone. The shutter started banging violently back and forth, causing a strobing effect inside the darkened apartment. Miraculously, the glass window remained intact for long enough to give Patrick time to get to the front of the apartment and refasten the shutter, which he managed after a short but intense scuffle with some volatile cyclonic winds.

As he made his way back to the couch, he broke out in a broad smile, which almost frightened Gaston. His grinning face came into his aura of the candlelight.

"Poison is not a bad idea, Gaston," Patrick said, now laughing.

"What! Have you gone completely mad, Patrick? I think you'd better stop drinking!" Gaston said.

"No, no, sorry, I should explain. I mean, poison their sex drive, chop off their balls, kill their cocks . . ." Patrick said, with much mirth and merriment evident in his tone of voice.

"Come on, you're not taking this seriously," Gaston said in frustration.

"How do you suggest we do that? Or, have you been channelling one of my nightmares? I had one about the priests being castrated by having their genitals chopped off with a huge sword. When I woke up in the middle of the night, I thought it was a brilliant plan."

"That is a funny dream. And sure, it's pure fantasy but I *do* have a serious plan which will have a similar result," Patrick said.

"When I was on the council in Australia, we had an issue with a convicted paedophile who wanted to move to our town when he was released from jail. Well, as you can imagine, when the townsfolk found out, there was a huge outcry. Anyway, to cut a long story short, this guy volunteered to be castrated to prove that he wouldn't be a threat and—" Patrick began.

"What! He agreed to have his balls chopped off?" Gaston said, wincing at the image that popped into his head

"No, no, no. They can do it with chemicals. They give paedophiles a drug that kills their sex drive so they no longer pose a threat to children."

"Wow—that's a great idea," said Gaston.

Chemical castration of the Finger Bay fathers sounded like a perfectly reasonable and achievable plan to two men who had just polished off a bottle of rum. But adding flesh to the skeleton of the idea proved beyond them. Where would they find the necessary drugs? How would they administer the drugs? These questions were left unanswered as the rum was also having its comatose impact on the pair. Soon after, they succumbed to the inevitable and went to sleep still convinced that they had finally found a way to exact revenge and free the Finger Bay children from the sexual tyranny of their Catholic clergy.

CHAPTER XXXV

Reality's So Hard . . .

Patrick woke up with a start, a furry tongue, a fuzzy head, and sweating profusely. He wasn't sure whether the catalyst for his sudden waking was a nightmare or the errant wooden shutter which had once more shaken off its latches but was banging more gently than the night before. The cyclone had abated but the wind was still blowing occasionally at gale force.

Patrick had very kindly allowed Gaston the luxury of sleeping in his bed—the only bed in the apartment—while he crashed on the couch. He enjoyed a very deep sleep despite the heavy alcohol intake. Normally, drinking so much would have sent him quickly off to sleep, only to wake up a few hours later when the sugar kicked in and thwarted any effort to resume normal slumber. But not last night.

Maybe I hadn't drunk as much as I thought.

That theory was instantly laid to rest as Patrick cast his eyes on an empty bottle of rum and another with only half left. He shrugged his shoulders.

Who knows? Maybe the excitement of seeing my old mate somehow diluted the impact of the alcohol.

His thoughts drifted to the closing conversation of the previous evening and his smile turned into a chuckle.

Then again, we must have been pretty drunk. What an insane idea—castrating priests with chemicals! Patrick shook his head, got up, and walked to the bedroom.

Gaston was still fast asleep so Patrick had a shower, grateful that the passage of the cyclone hadn't cut the water supply as these types of storms often did. He needed the recuperative power of a shower to lift the vestiges of the fog that lingered in his head. He emerged refreshed and still musing on the previous night's conversation. But he was no longer laughing.

He rushed to his bookcase, where he meticulously kept all the paperwork from his days as a Councillor. The bookcase was still in the dark even though it was positioned next to a large window that looked out onto the western beachfront. Patrick opened the window and liberated the wooden shutter, letting in the sunlight, which was obfuscated somewhat by big fluffy white clouds being propelled by vigorous wind squalls across ever-lightening skies.

Patrick grabbed a large folder filed under "P". All the council papers and personal research on the paedophile incident in Australia were there. He could hardly contain his excitement as he flicked through the documents and finally came across one that detailed an assortment of natural products which could be used to suppress libido. Plant products like Chasteberry, hops, and valerian would be hard to find on the island. However, Chinese herbs like Rehmannia, Ligistrum, or Skullcap should be easy enough to procure, given he knew some influential Chinese merchants who could certainly get some for him, no questions asked.

But procuring the herbs would be the easy part.

How the hell are we going to give the priests the "treatment"? he thought.

Patrick was staring blankly out the window, looking at, but not seeing, the assortment of council and government workers busily clearing up the post-cyclone debris. He was far too deep in thought, contemplating a plan of action.

Gaston walked out of the bedroom, eyes half-closed and yawning. He bumped into the coffee table, causing the empty rum bottle to tumble over the edge. The noise of the bottle hitting the tiled floor startled Patrick out of his trance-like state. Fortunately, the bottle remained intact and bounced towards Patrick, who picked it up and placed it absent-mindedly back on the table. He looked at his friend, who started to apologise timidly while also appearing somewhat befuddled by unfamiliar surroundings.

"Ah, no need to apologise, my friend. No damage done although looking at you, there may be some damage to a few brain cells," Patrick said, smiling.

"Yes, I know. I haven't drunk that much for some time. But, how come you're so cheerful and, it seems, not the slightest bit hungover?" Gaston asked.

"Well, mate, I am still feeling a little seedy, but I've had a shower which helped to clear the fog a bit. More importantly, I think I have a plan to stop those evil bastards," Patrick said.

Gaston stood there momentarily mute, trying to process what Patrick was saying through the lingering haze in his cognitive faculties. It took him a few moments to register that the "evil bastards" to whom Patrick was referring were the Finger Bay fathers and a few moments more to recall the previous night's conversation.

"Right, so we talked about chemically castrating them. Seemed like a good idea at the time, but most ideas do when they're washed down with copious amounts of rum," Gaston said, laughing.

"Please tell me you've thought of another plan. I can think of a few drawbacks to last night's plan, as great as it sounded then. Minor things, really, like where we would find such chemicals. I gather the local pharmacies don't stock them. And even if we did get some, there's the teeny-weeny problem of feeding it to the priests," he added somewhat sarcastically.

'No, no. Same plan, Gaston," Patrick said enthusiastically.

"But . . . but, you can't be—" a clearly disappointed Gaston started to reply.

"Yes, I am indeed very serious, my friend," Patrick interrupted.

"I'd forgotten about some research I did about this whole chemical castration thing back in Australia. No surprise I had a few holes in my memory given the amount of rum we drank, but there it is! Or there it was last night. But this morning it all came back to me. Gaston, we don't need chemicals to castrate the priests. We can do it with herbs which I can get from my Chinese contacts, so that problem's solved. But yes, finding a way to give it to them remains a challenge, to say the least."

Gaston closed his eyes for a moment and his thoughts immediately drifted to Monique and an image of her stirring a big pot in the Finger Bay presbytery kitchen. When he re-opened his eyes seconds later, he also had a wicked smile on his face.

CHAPTER XXXVI

Paparazzi

By mid-afternoon, the construction site at the Wright's resort development was once again a hive of activity. Across the road on the beachfront, a swarm of council workers was also hard at work. It had only been a couple of hours since the cyclone's last hurrah in the village; a 190-kilometre gust of wind that had lifted the roof off the Palm Waters gymnasium and dumped it onto the beach, where it had shattered into numerous large pieces on the very same spot which, only the day before, had been the scene of near tragedy and confrontation.

Under a burning sun and brilliant blue sky, Patrick and Gaston stopped for a moment to watch a crane being manoeuvred into position to help clear the remnants of the gym roof from the beach. Two big trucks stood by, engines idling, ready to cart the roof debris away. Once that was completed, there would be very little sign that the cyclone had ever happened.

Patrick and Gaston were on their way to the construction site office to suss out whether Tom would honour his promise to compensate Gaston for yesterday's "misunderstanding". Their mood was buoyant. While they would have preferred for the priests to be hanged, drawn, and quartered or, at the very least, thrown in jail for their crimes, they were convinced they had at least found a way to stop the abuse of the Finger Bay children with minimal disruption to the parish community.

They had gone on to discuss Patrick's desire to revive his political ambition and Gaston had pledged to be his comrade-in-arms on the frontline in their bold mission to save the world from the ravages of economic injustice. But that would take some time and an equally bold plan of action. For now, he had to put his life back on track after it was almost critically derailed by Tom Wright's misplaced aggression. That potentially agonising encounter had evolved into a potentially lucky break which, Gaston hoped, might serve to catapult him to the head of the queue for a job at the resort. He had resolved to accept nothing short of an opportunity to work there as compensation and preferably in a respectable white-collar job that would hopefully draw on his writing skills and, most importantly, make his mother proud.

Gaston was wearing one of Patrick's best suit, tie, and shirt combinations after his own had suffered irreparable damage from exposure to the ravages of the cyclone on the beach. Patrick had decided to accompany Gaston to help him negotiate with Tom, given his experience of Australians and his familiarity with the Australian nuances in the English language. He also wanted to hopefully talk privately to some of the workers on the site. He had heard rumours that they were being underpaid and working longer hours than legally allowed and regularly toiling in dangerous situations without access to the required safety equipment. He realised the rumours had been fuelled by protestors opposed to the development, but he thought it wouldn't hurt to investigate. After all, he'd been presented with another silver lining from the potentially dark clouds of yesterday's events: the privilege of access to the site, which, according to the protest group, had been denied to the unions. But his motivation for exposing any possible worker exploitation was not entirely altruistic. If he did uncover evidence of worker abuse, it might just provide him with the ideal issue to garner the community support he needed to drive his quest to enter the island's political fray.

Patrick and Gaston made their way through the group of council workers who seemed to be properly attired and safely equipped for their job at hand. Patrick and Gaston—stylish, clean-cut, and handsome—stood in marked contrast to the workers adorned in grubby, fluoro safety vests and hard hats and busily loading the trucks with the remaining debris.

Like Patrick, Gaston, too, had an ulterior motive for wanting to visit Tom as soon as possible: the burning desire to see the damsel in distress again. Procuring a job at the resort could have waited, but snaring the possible love of his life couldn't. Nevertheless, he had already steeled himself for intense disappointment: envisaging a likely scenario of Tom and his fiancé in an affectionate embrace, kissing even, a happy couple resuming their preparations for the happiest day of their lives. Every minute that passed, Gaston was becoming more and more convinced that the thunderbolt moment had been simply an illusion.

When they finally arrived at the site's security gate, they noticed a group of photographers and journalists loitering, smoking cigarettes, and chatting under the shade of a large coconut palm nearby. The pair assumed they had come to cover the story of the cyclone and its aftermath. But as they got within detection distance, the eyes of the whole media pack turned towards them in unison and someone yelled something from which Gaston and Patrick only heard the word "hero".

Moments later, they were mobbed by the media contingent, cameras flashing, a cacophony of questions hurled towards them. Two reporters holding microphones pushed their way to the front of the group, their accompanying television crews hot on their heels with cameras poised and ready to record the action.

It turned out that one of the few witnesses to Solange's suicide bid and its aftermath had also recorded proceedings on a mobile phone, which he had sent to various media organisations hoping to make a bit of money given the involvement of the "notorious" Tom Wright. Word had rapidly spread among the small media circle on the island despite the inclement weather. They had instantly recognised Tom from the blurry mobile phone vision. After all, he and his father, Jack, and their controversial development, had become a regular feature of their news stories in recent times. As soon as the danger of the cyclone had passed, a dozen journalists and two television crews had descended upon the construction site.

But Tom had refused to be interviewed and denied the news hounds access to the site. But the journalists were more interested in the story of the hero and his sidekick anyway so they had set up camp outside, hoping the main protagonists would eventually return to the scene of the crime. And here they were and, as a bonus for the cameras, they were already dressed like celebrities.

Unaccustomed to the spotlight Gaston instinctively started to back away. But the media-savvy Patrick quickly realised a golden opportunity and suddenly stepped confidently forward, causing the pack to stop their advance.

The questions came fast and furious.

"Which one of you rescued the girl?"

"Did you know the girl?"

"What was the fight about?"

"Hey, hey, hey—hold on to your horses," said Patrick.

"We're happy to answer your questions but one at a time, please," he urged, glancing at Gaston, who was shyly looking at the ground.

"My friend Gaston here is the hero. He saved the girl but as you can see, he's not used to having cameras in his face."

"Gaston, what's your family name and are you a local?" one journalist asked.

Gaston looked up and answered the question. His voice was crackly at first but grew in strength with every syllable.

"What were you doing in Palm Waters during a cyclone?" the same journalist inquired.

"Well, I was here for a job interview at the new resort development and I'd just got off the bus when I noticed the girl on the beach...."

Gaston went on to detail the events with an eloquence that surprised Patrick, and himself even more so.

Another journalist interrupted Gaston's narrative to ask him whether he'd been afraid for his own safety given the stormy seas.

"Not really. I didn't really have time to think. I knew I was a strong swimmer and the cyclone was still in its early stages so the sea wasn't too rough," Gaston replied, then took the opportunity to praise the South African friend of his youth who had taught him to swim.

One of the journalists turned to Patrick and asked: "So what's your role in all this?"

"I'm just a close friend who happened to witness the whole thing. I'm so proud of him as we should all be, gentlemen. He risked his own life to save a life. Gaston is a hero, no doubt about that."

By this time, many of the workers on the construction site had abandoned their tools and headed down to the front wire fence to check out the media-fuelled commotion.

"If Gaston is such a hero, what was the fight about then?" one sceptical journalist asked.

"It was a simple mis—" Gaston began to answer only to be interrupted by Tom Wright, who had barged his way through the throng of construction workers, momentarily pausing to order them back to work, before putting on a plastic smile and joining in the impromptu media conference. He recognised this might just afford him an opportunity to win over some of the local community who had been so hostile towards the resort development.

"What my friend, err—" Tom started to say suddenly realising that he'd forgotten Gaston's name.

But Patrick sensed this immediately and came to his rescue.

"Gaston, Mr. Wright. His name is Gaston," he said.

A slightly flustered Tom continued, a phoney smile still plastered to his face.

"Yes, yes, as I was saying, what my friend . . . err . . . Gaston was about to say is that it was all a misunderstanding and I take full responsibility for that. I thought he was kissing my fiancé when he was really giving her life-saving mouth-to-mouth resuscitation. You see, I hadn't witnessed the rescue but, of course, I thank God that . . . err . . . Gaston was there. And I intend to make sure that he is generously rewarded for saving the life of my beloved fiancé."

"What sort of reward are we talking about?" one journalist asked.

"That's between Gaston and me," Tom was quick to reply.

"As you would appreciate, I almost lost my most precious poss—err—precious fiancé. It's been a very distressing time so I'm sure you'll understand if I don't go into any details now. Suffice to say that no financial compensation would be enough to express my appreciation of what Gaston has done," Tom said with feigned sincerity, fully aware that the lights on top of the television cameras were flashing and the journalists hanging on his every word.

"Now, if you'll excuse us, I'd like to invite Gaston and . . ." Tom paused again realising he didn't know Patrick's name either but wasn't going to wait for someone to rescue him this time around.

"... his friend to come to the office so I can thank Gaston properly and work out what we can do for him."

"What was your fiancé doing going for a swim in such filthy weather anyway?" one intrepid journalist finally dared to ask the question that everyone else had uppermost in their minds but were too intimidated to ask given the power and influence that the Wrights seemingly yielded among the island's power brokers including their media bosses.

There had hardly been a bad word written or spoken in the island's media about the Wrights, even in the handful of progressive publications. A recent editorial in the island's most influential and popular newspaper in fact lauded the Wright family for their "immense generosity and vote of confidence in the island's economic development, which was mirrored in their multimillion-dollar investment and visionary resort development rising majestically above the tallest coconut trees of Palm Waters".

The brave reporter and the rest of the media entourage were left hanging for the answer as Tom turned his back on them and steered Gaston and Patrick towards the security gate. Although he had heard the question, which had instantly wiped the smile off his face, he had no intention of answering it, not only because he hated the media and would never discuss such an intimate matter with "those vile bastards", but the reason behind her suicide bid still remained a mystery to him. He hadn't been able to talk to Solange since the incident. She'd been heavily sedated upon being admitted to the hospital for observation and was still in no condition to talk to anyone. Tom had spent most of the previous night by her bedside, holding her hand and combing his heart, soul, and rational mind for an answer. But none came. Narcissism absolved him of all blame and responsibility.

"Surely it must be something in her nature which knocked a screw loose. Perhaps it was a severe case of pre-wedding jitters. Maybe it was like post-natal depression, such a common thing that happened at a time when a woman should be happy!" was all Tom could come up with.

His father had taken up the relief at the hospital while Tom had gone home, showered, and returned to the construction site to make sure that the workers were not slacking off. Tom had regretted his offer of a reward to Gaston and had hoped that he wouldn't take him up on it, at least not until Solange had fully recovered. He was exhausted, mentally and physically, and really not in the right frame of mind to deal with such trivial matters, at least until he could get to the bottom of Solange's moment of madness.

He had locked himself away in his office. He had postponed scheduled interviews for jobs at the resort for at least a week. But he had been forced to act when alerted to the media ambush of Gaston and Patrick. He cursed himself for not having allowed the journalists onto the site earlier and granting them an interview. Once the cameras started rolling, he had little choice but to intervene and begrudgingly assume the role of the grateful fiancé and generous, benevolent boss, a role he had to continue playing now as he led Gaston and Patrick to the office still in view of the cameras and suspicious glare of the journalists.

"How is your fiancé?" Patrick asked with genuine compassion as the trio walked side-by-side to the demountable office at the back of the construction site.

"She's still recovering," Tom answered brusquely.

He wanted to get rid of these emotional intruders as fast as he possibly could. He really was in no mood to talk to anyone. And he certainly wasn't going to reveal any more information about Solange. He had no new information anyway apart from the fact that she had suffered no physical harm from her ordeal but the jury would be out for some time on the emotional residue.

As they walked into the office, Tom ushered Gaston and Patrick to two uncomfortable orange plastic chairs in front of a large oak desk while he sat in the decidedly more comfortable, cushioned, brown leather chair behind the desk.

"I'm glad you came over," Tom lied.

"And Gaston, I hope we can find some way to thank you properly for saving Solange's life. I am indeed very grateful for your heroic effort," he continued, this time with some sincerity.

Gaston's ears pricked up at the revelation of her name. Patrick on the other hand had no vested interest and the first mention of her name didn't especially register with him. He had immediately felt sorry for Tom's fiancé—and Tom for that matter—despite the aggression. The times he had reflected on Solange and the incident since, he had merely pondered on what trauma or possible catastrophic episode would cause a beautiful young woman, about to be married to a rich and handsome man, to attempt suicide.

"Thank you, Mr. Wright," said Gaston. "I'm sure it's been a very distressing time for you and . . ."

"Please, please call me Tom," said Tom.

"Yes, err, Tom. As I was about to say I certainly don't want to make this any more upsetting for you. But I was on my way here for a job interview when I saw your fiancé on the beach."

Alleluia; thank God! Tom thought as he realised he would be able to get rid of them quickly. After all, he had the power to grant him his wish. As a bonus, he would be able to earn some much-needed public relations brownie points when the media resumed their pursuit of the "Gaston hero" story, as he was in no doubt they would.

"Say no more, Gaston. I'll make sure there's a job for you at the resort. Just send me your resume and I'll get the managing director of the resort to get onto it straight away and find something suitable for you.

"Is there anything else I can do for you?"

Patrick's Australian accent once again crossed Tom's mind and fleetingly made him curious to question Patrick further, but the desire to hastily purge the pair from his presence was a more urgent need. He stood up precipitously and politely gestured towards the door, hoping they would take the obvious hint.

"Now, if you'll excuse me, gentlemen. I need to urgently finish up some paperwork before heading back to the hospital."

"Of course, of course, we—" was all Patrick was able to utter before finding himself and Gaston on the veranda of the demountable office building, looking towards the front of the construction site and hearing the office door close quickly behind them.

CHAPTER XXXVII

Cailason Gets a Dose of His Own Medicine

Even though he had spent his entire life living in a sub-tropical climate, Sergeant Cailason still hated the sapping heat and humidity of the summer months. Following the passage of a cyclone, it was even worse. The heat visibly rose from the sodden roadways drying under the sub-tropical sun and in some areas a walk meant navigating a sauna, the waves of steam floating up from the asphalt causing pedestrians to sweat profusely as they went about their business. In most parts of the island, walking on the roadway was still the only option for travel by foot as footpaths were still a rarity outside the three major towns. The only road with a footpath in Finger Bay was the shopping strip opposite the beach-fringed bay, which ran from the police station on the northern edge of the village to the Samsara bar and disco on the southern edge. In between lay a half a kilometre of shops, a handful of restaurants, two cafes, and a medical centre and pharmacy complex.

It had been an exhausting couple of days for Sergeant Cailason, who had been on police duty for most of that time. While everyone else battened down the hatches during the passage of a cyclone, emergency personnel were mobilised to deal with any crisis situations and for police, their main job was to look out for any looters. And if Sergeant Cailason ever caught a looter, he would deal with them as he did with drug addicts: applying the fullest physical force of the law he could get away with. He despised looters almost as much as he did drug addicts. Occasionally he hit the jackpot, snaring a looter who was also a drug addict. It was then almost impossible to contain his rage. The poor dual offender almost always ended up unconscious in hospital, the official cause of injury invariably being that the looter had been mysteriously struck by a solid object, such as a large flying tree branch or coconuts while trying to make good his escape.

Fortunately, this cyclone had not been severe and caused minimal damage to buildings, thereby depriving looters of any opportunity to ply their nefarious trade. Cailason's workload had been relatively light; no major crisis and certainly no looters sighted. Nevertheless, the sleep deprivation had taken its toll and as he left the police station after knocking off work in the early afternoon, he donned a pair of sunglasses to protect his heavy eyelids and weary bloodshot eyes from the harsh glare of the post-cyclone sun. He decided on a fifteen-minute walk home rather than the five-minute bus ride. The exercise might serve to refresh him, he thought. Besides, in the aftermath of a cyclone, bus operators were slow to regain the rhythm of their normal timetable and he certainly didn't want to be waiting at a bus stop for too long. He was desperate to heed the call of his comfy bed. His decision was immediately vindicated as he passed a very crowded bus stop populated by commuters alternating anxious looks between their watches and the road ahead from where the bus obviously hadn't materialised for some time.

Cailason was dressed in a black suit, white shirt, and his favourite red and blue patterned tie as he ambled up the main street, occasionally stopping to wipe the steady stream of sweat pouring from his brow with a large, monogrammed blue handkerchief. He often changed into civvies before heading home from work and, although there was no official requirement for him to wear a suit when not in uniform, he took great pride in his appearance when in the public eye.

After being cooped up in their barricaded homes for a couple of days, the villagers of Finger Bay were out in force, resuming the routine business of a normal working day. Cailason begrudgingly found himself obliged to return the greetings of the many villagers who recognised him as they passed by, despite him being out of uniform. After all, he had been a highly visible presence and dominant figure in the village community for a very long time and was now, for better or for worse, one of Finger Bay's most familiar characters.

For his part, Cailason paid scant attention to the village citizens who saluted him as they crossed his path. In his sleepy state, he hardly recognised any of them. However, as he reached the edge of the shopping strip, three young men walking abreast towards him attracted his attention. They were talking loudly, laughing and occasionally breaking out into a choreographed dance move. It made Cailason yearn for the halcyon days of his own youth—long gone now, but certainly not forgotten. A hint of a smile breached his face.

Cailason was sure he knew one of the men but couldn't quite work out where they might have met. As the men got within a few metres of Cailason, the "familiar" man walking in the middle of the trio suddenly attempted a clumsy pirouette, a la Michael Jackson, no doubt in response to the music even Cailason could now hear blaring out of his headphones. And as he regained his balance and forward position with one arm raised in seeming triumph, the man couldn't avoid bumping heavily into Cailason, who stumbled but managed to stay on his feet. Looking fleetingly at his face, Cailason now had no doubt they had previously met but still couldn't recollect the situation or time of their encounter.

All three men were profusely apologetic and immediately rushed to help the stumbling Cailason regain his balance and composure. For his part, Cailason was too tired to even be annoyed by the intrusion. All he could think about was the blissful slumber that awaited him at home, only a few minutes away.

"Are you okay?" they asked.

"Yes, yes, I'm fine," Cailason replied rather brusquely, which seemed to take the trio aback, causing them to instantly break their physical contact with Cailason. They resumed their journey, still apologising as they walked away.

Cailason stood there for a short time, still feeling a bit winded. He took a couple of deep breaths before slowly heading off in the opposite direction. However, something didn't seem quite right and after walking only a few paces his hand instinctively reached into the inside pocket of his jacket to find his wallet missing. Cailason quickly realised he'd fallen for the oldest pickpocket trick in the book. The collision had not been an accident.

He felt a surge of adrenalin which instantly roused him out of his sluggish state. He quickly turned around, raised his sunglasses to rest on his forehead and looked in the direction where the petty criminals had made their getaway. His bleary eyes blinked profusely, straining to focus into the distance, all the while convinced that they would be out of sight by now. But suddenly, his vision cleared sufficiently to see a head with a set of prominent headphones turning and disappearing down one of the cross-streets not too far away. If he hadn't been struggling with exhaustion and taken a moment to reflect, Cailason might have considered it strange they hadn't fled the scene of the crime as quickly as one would expect thieves to do. He simply hadn't noticed that they were walking, not running, unlike Cailason now, who somehow summoned the energy to take off in pursuit of the "thieving scoundrels".

Cailason turned into the cross-street and was surprised to find two of the alleged thieves, including the "head-phoned" one, only metres ahead. But he was so intent on retribution for the wrong they had done him that he didn't immediately register the fact that they were standing still, facing him and smirking. But as he came to a halt only inches away from the pair with every intention of reading them the riot act, it did cross Cailason's mind that the three were now only two.

"Say, where did the other guy go?" he wondered.

He didn't have to wait long for an answer. He suddenly felt a cold, hard object press heavily into his back, his years of experience as a police officer instantly telling him that it was a handgun (or something doing a very good job of imitating one).

"Just stay still, don't say a word and keep calm or I'll splatter your guts all over the footpath," a voice whispered loudly in Cailason's ear.

It was a cue for the other two to come forward and position themselves on each side of Cailason. They grabbed him gently by each arm and started to lead him away. Cailason no longer felt the gun on his back and momentarily thought about trying to make an escape. But the two who were holding him must have sensed his intention because their grip tightened markedly.

"What the fu—" Cailason started to say, but his voice was throttled to mute by the gun being thrust into his back once again but with much greater venom than before.

"I told you to shut the fuck up, grandpa, or else!" the third man whispered violently.

The gang had obviously done their homework, thought Cailason. The side street they had chosen was sparsely populated with people or traffic. It was not much more than a laneway flanked at the intersection by two substantial concrete buildings with few windows giving onto the streetscape. Nevertheless, they had been careful not to arouse the suspicions of the few passers-by, keeping the weapon concealed and any talk to a menacing minimum and heightened whisper. Although his anger was mounting with every step, self-preservation overruled and Cailason wisely kept his mouth shut, the gun still poised in his back, albeit with a more gentle touch as they walked.

They've got my wallet—what else do they want? And where the fuck are they taking me? Cailason pondered.

He tried to cheer himself up by thinking of the brutal punishment he (and his police pals) would mete out to these "fucking insolent punks" once he managed to escape. He'd have to be judicious, though, in exacting his revenge. Any injuries they suffered (and boy, they *will* suffer!) would have to be officially "accidental and unavoidable" when inflicted in the course of the thieves violently resisting arrest, an offence seemingly committed by most offenders arrested by Cailason.

But as they passed an old, deserted warehouse, fear suddenly crept into Cailason's emotional armoury and challenged anger for supremacy. He suddenly realised they were reaching the outer limits of the Finger Bay village where already there were no other villagers or cars in sight. Ahead lay acres of sugar cane plantations which miraculously seemed to have survived the cyclone largely intact. The harvest was still a couple of months away so the densely packed field of sugar cane plants could provide a perfect cover.

But cover for what?

An ideal place to murder a cop, perhaps? They wouldn't dare!

Cailason felt the sweat drip profusely from his forehead, with some beads lodging uncomfortably in his eyes. Yet, he was paralysed by his mounting fear and impotent to alleviate his discomfort either with his hand or his customary blue handkerchief boldly embroidered with the letter C. He had a two-week supply of such handkerchiefs in various colours stored in one of his bedside table drawers. If only he could be lying on his bed looking at that drawer now. He blinked rapidly, hoping the action would restore his slightly blurred vision.

They crossed the road and headed down a narrow, rocky dirt track that dissected two fields of sugar cane. The track was very muddy and many of its abundant potholes were still full of water. Cailason's prized leather shoes were already caked in mud which, in normal circumstances, would have made him livid. But fear was now triumphant and gloating. He was even beginning to tremble.

Cailason spotted a large tailless Madagascan tenrec (known on the island as Tandrac or Tang) scurrying out of the cane fields, which momentarily distracted him from his tricky predicament. He hadn't seen one in the wild for some time, let alone eaten a delicious Tandrac curry which was one of his late mother's specialities. After her death, he had tried many times to cook the dish himself but, despite being a very good cook and following his mother's recipe to a tee, it never quite tasted the same.

They turned into a narrow pathway crossing the main track and penetrated further into the heart of the cane field, the pace of the pack seemingly quickening like racehorses entering the home straight. Cailason was struggling to keep up and almost stumbled a couple of times but quickly regained his balance after feeling a sudden sharp jab from the gun into his back.

They came around a bend that yielded suddenly to a small clearing from which they had a choice of four different even narrower pathways leading even deeper into the seemingly endless cane fields. The gang leader, who was at the head of the pack, abruptly stopped and raised his right arm, signalling for the others to do likewise. He turned around and walked up to Cailason waving a red polka dot bandana he had dug out of his pocket.

Without saying a word, he wrapped the bandana around Cailason's eyes and spun him around to disorientate him. He needn't have bothered; Cailason was feeling so tired that he was already largely unaware of exactly where he was even though he had walked, patrolled, chased, and caught many crooks in and around the Finger Bay cane fields regularly throughout his long police career.

The pack resumed their march with the finish line now in sight, a ramshackle building in a clearing ringed on three sides by the cane fields and a forest of bougainvillea nestling the building itself. The dense vegetation of its surrounds would render the structure invisible to all but those who could view the landscape from the air. Although it looked diminutive from afar, as they approached, the building loomed larger, its substantial back rooms shielded from view by the canopy of bougainvillea.

A blindfolded Cailason was now extremely concerned for his welfare but also in some way relieved as he felt the pace of the group slowing, which probably meant that he could stop walking soon. His energy reserves were almost spent and he had all but surrendered to whatever Fate had in store for him.

The front section of the building was really a façade created to douse suspicion should anyone stray by. It looked derelict, made of grey wooden planks—rotting in parts—and a thatched roof that had seen better days. It was flanked on all sides and on top by flourishing bougainvillea blooms that further camouflaged the structure. Despite the recent passage of the cyclone, they were still heavily ablaze with colourful flowers in various shades of pink, red, burgundy, and white.

Cailason almost fell as he was shoved through the unlocked front door and into a hallway but quickly steadied himself as the gang leader ripped the bandana blindfold off his head. On autopilot, Cailason started walking down towards the back section of the building and was confused to see a thick steel door at the other end marking the entrance to a modern concrete structure.

"Sorry pépère, we don't have time for a grand tour of the premises," a laughing gang member said before violently latching onto the tail end of Cailason's jacket and hauling him back.

Cailason found himself standing face to face with the gang leader, the rage glowing in his eyes in equal proportion to the fear in Cailason's. The gang leader suddenly laughed, loud and menacingly. This only compounded Cailason's terror, which found expression in a stifled whimper.

"My, my . . . you are very curious, aren't you, pépère? If we showed you what was behind the steel door there, we'd have no option but to shoot you," the gang leader said, a malicious grin consuming his face.

"But because I'm feeling suddenly very cheerful, I'm going to be a gracious host and let you in on our secret and satisfy your no doubt burning curiosity about what we do here."

He grabbed Cailason roughly by the hair and turned his head to face away from him and towards the back of the building.

"You see, pépère, behind that door is my little factory. We make things that make a lot of scum very happy and high and me very rich. Can you guess what it is? I bet you can, given all those years on the beat," he said, laughing once more.

"Well, we've got the best fucking drug lab in this part of the world, pépère. Ganja zamal, you know, dope, Mary Jane. Call it what you like; that's been our staple for many years. You can always sell that stuff. It's natural after all, isn't it, pépère? That's what the junkie kids think and they're willing to pay me well for it. So, we have two rooms full of the best fucking quality ganja you can find anywhere in the world.

"But like any commercial enterprise, you have to diversify, don't you, pépère?" he said, suddenly letting go of Cailason's hair, causing his chin to drop violently onto his chest.

The gang leader moved in front of Cailason and lifted his face to once again stare threateningly into his eyes.

"As I was saying pépère, to keep up my profits and keep me in the lifestyle I have become accustomed to, I had to expand my business. For many years, everyone wanted speed, speed, and more speed but now they all want ice, you know, crystal meth. It's the drug du jour, pépère. So, as a good businessman I must keep my customers satisfied, and trust me, I have very many very satisfied customers, including some of the island's most honourable and prominent citizens."

The gang leader cast his gaze behind Cailason and winked at the gang members standing behind him. It was a signal for them to move and grab Cailason brusquely by the arms and carry him back towards the entrance.

He was flung into a room to the right of the hallway, where he fell to his knees. The room was dimly lit and damp-infested, furnished only with an old-fashioned, padded armchair and a small coffee table next to it. Laid out on the table were a few small, coloured sachets containing some kind of powder, a small beaker of water, and various items, which Cailason instantly recognised as an injecting heroin user's traditional toolkit. A syringe completed the artistic arc of implements, its needle sparkling from a thin shaft of sunlight shimmering through a hole in the roof. On the floor in front of the chair was a coil of thick rope similar to the type Cailason had seen in the cowboy films he liked to watch.

Still on his knees, he was too exhausted to ponder his fate. He was now their ragdoll, mentally and physically numb and completely vulnerable. As he struggled to get up, his only thought was how comfortable the chair looked and he longed to just collapse in it and fall asleep. It wasn't long before he was granted part of his wish. Two of the gang members lifted him off his feet, ripped off his jacket, tie, and shirt and dumped him into the armchair. But they had no intention of indulging his desire for sleep.

They held him down in the chair while the gang leader bound him tightly to the chair with the rope. He needn't have bothered. Cailason was incapable of making a run for it. Hugged by the comfort of the armchair and despite the rope cutting into his ample gut, he was struggling to keep his eyes open. He found himself immediately drifting off to sleep and felt a fleeting moment of pure bliss.

"We'll have to prop them up with matchsticks, pépère," the gang leader said, smirking menacingly and prising Cailason's eyelids open with his fingers.

He moved his face close to Cailason's, penetrating his gaze deep into his eyes, which were now wide open and exhibiting a fear that he had never experienced before.

"I want you to see something, pépère," the gang leader continued, this time with some venom.

He parted his thick long, black hair to reveal a prominent scar that ran along the top of his scalp, almost from ear to ear.

"Any idea how I got this?" he said, rubbing his finger along the scar.

Cailason wanted to say something but nothing came out, his vocal cords paralysed by a flashback to a teenage drug fiend banging his head against the wall and lapsing into unconsciousness at the Finger Bay police station prison cell while Cailason looked on laughing hysterically.

"Well, you see, I've had a real struggle deciding what to do with you, pépère. On the one hand, you nearly killed me, leaving me to go cold turkey and getting your rocks off watching me batter my head against the wall, you fucking piece of shit.

"Result? Fractured skull, many months in the hospital, and some years later, an aneurysm, which I think happened because of the fractured skull, but the docs can't say for sure. Luckily, they got to it in the nick of time."

Shell-shocked by fear, Cailason began preparing himself to meet his maker. His thoughts turned to the Hail Mary and its concluding line, "pray for us now and in the hour of our death".

"If that was all there is to it, you would have been dead a while ago. You see, while you did your best to kill me, you also saved my life, a fucking cruel and sadistic way to do it and it wasn't your intention, but God or whoever pulls the strings on us mere mortals does indeed work in mysterious ways," the gang leader continued.

Cailason suddenly felt a ray of hope.

"If you hadn't arrested me and made me go through hell in the police station and even greater pain after, the heroin would have finished me off for sure. I literally had the fucking addiction bashed out of me. Who would have thought? But there it is. And I've never touched the stuff since, probably also 'cause I realised that I could have a much better life selling that crap to the fucking lowlife junkies rather than be one myself.

"So, you see my dilemma, pépère, don't you? I really don't want to kill you. That would be ungrateful," he said, smirking once again.

"But you still must be punished, and I've had a long time to think about an appropriate punishment while I've built a nice little business empire with more than a little help from some of your best mates in the police. And let me tell you, some of the highest flyers in the force are some of my most regular clients, and they've come to realise it's in their best interest to look after me."

Despite his precarious circumstance, Cailason was shocked. Conveniently ignoring his own corrupt practices as a police officer, he couldn't believe anyone in the police force would help this merchant of death peddle drugs, let alone consume his vile substances.

"But I do want to see you suffer and enjoy watching you suffer as you did with me. I've had a lot of pain in my life but nothing as bad as the pain you made me go through, you fucker. And I don't mean the head injuries. So, I thought to myself, if I could just get you to experience that pain, you know, reverse roles?

"And so, here we are, my friend. I think you can guess what I have in mind," he said, looking at the coffee table and laughing.

"It's so hard to get your hands on heroin these days. Everyone wants ice, ice, and more ice. That's good for my business, not good for my revenge plans. But, as always, you can rely on the good old Chinese shopkeepers. You can get anything from them."

The gang leader reached over and grabbed a piece of a bicycle inner tube which was among the various implements on the table and threw it to one of his gang members. A third gang member came over to physically pin down Cailason to the chair even though the rope was, by and large, doing its job. Cailason tried in vain to resist the inner tube being applied to his upper arm as a tourniquet. He knew very well what was about to happen, but even without the effective physical restraints, he simply had no energy left to resist.

The gang leader wasted no time emptying the powder from one of the sachets onto a spoon, dissolving it with water, and heating it up with a cigarette lighter. He was glad they had employed the tourniquet; otherwise it would have been difficult to find a decent vein in Cailason's flabby elbow joint.

The gang leader had lost none of his skill, although it had been many years since his last injection of "horse". The needle went in without a hitch and Cailason very quickly found himself captive to the heroin rush, a blissful warmth flowing through his body and a state of unparalleled contentment and relaxation, no doubt exacerbated by his extreme fatigue.

But this was only the beginning of Cailason's pain for the gang leader's pleasure. For the next week, Cailason was kept on a continuous heroin high to turn him into an addict who would then have to endure the immense suffering of withdrawal. He was naturally oblivious to his evolving addiction and to the media frenzy beyond the well-camouflaged hideout which had been sparked by the "mysterious, out-of-character disappearance of Finger Bay's finest police officer".

Exactly a week after Cailason received his first dose of heroin, the gang stopped administering the drug to him, then watched him go cold turkey and gradually be subjugated to the effects of withdrawal over the next twelve hours or so. The clichéd cold sweat, nausea, and vomiting caused the gang leader to erupt often into raucous laughter, particularly in one moment when he literally rubbed Cailason's face in his vomit. It gave him a greater satisfaction than he could ever have imagined and one he'd been craving for so long. And to make that revenge even sweeter, just as Cailason was emerging from the worst of the withdrawal some five days later, the gang again tied him down and fuelled him up once more with heroin before brazenly dumping a "heroin-high" Cailason in front of the Finger Bay Police Station.

CHAPTER XXXVIII

Gaston the Celebrity

Gaston was startled by the bank of huge television screens, all screening the same blurry, close-up footage of Sergeant Cailason writhing in a gutter outside the Finger Bay police station in great distress. Although the scene was shot on a mobile phone in the middle of the night, there was no doubting the identity of its star.

Gaston was already feeling very nervous and being bombarded by the unnerving vision of Sergeant Cailason as he entered the lobby of the island's main television station only added to his anxiety levels.

The barely audible voice of the newsreader was explaining how mystery still surrounded the disappearance of one of the island's preeminent law enforcers who had then suddenly turned up just as mysteriously, high on heroin, outside the Finger Bay police station in the middle of the night.

"Constable Winston La Malettie had been on night shift dozing in the back room of the police station when a screech of tyres startled him wide awake. When he went to investigate, he found his boss high as a kite, lying on the ground outside and speaking in gibberish. It's believed that Sergeant Cailason had been dumped there, but this has yet to be confirmed," the newsreader was saying.

Gaston could hardly believe it.

Surely Cailason was no drug fiend? If he was, then what a fucking hypocrite!

These thoughts rushed through his head and only served to heighten his anxiety before he felt the reassuring arm of his friend Patrick around his shoulder, leading him away from the screens and towards the station's receptionist.

Gaston had been invited to the station for an interview with one of the island's most popular television personalities, the host and creator of the celebrity talk show *Encounter*, one of the highest rating programs on the island's one and only commercial television network. It had only been two weeks since he rescued Solange and, in that short space of time, Gaston had already become somewhat of an island celebrity. Sometimes exaggerated tales of his heroics—battling monstrous swells and miraculously bringing Solange back to life—had attracted media attention from every corner of the island and even the international press. Gaston had to run the gauntlet of paparazzi in the first few days after the rescue. The fact that he handled it all with the aplomb of a professional, true celebrity, further endeared him to the hearts and minds of the island population.

The presence of the media-savvy Patrick by his side throughout it all no doubt helped Gaston adapt to his newfound fame and the demands of a media keen to explore every angle of a hero's story. Yet, as he had done when confronted with the media pack at the construction site after the rescue, Patrick rarely encroached on Gaston's media spotlight. He didn't need to. Gaston was a natural—good-looking, articulate, and intelligent—who had the journalists hanging on his every word and the odd female reporter audibly swooning.

For his part, Patrick was ecstatic. He knew from past experience that, while Gaston's celebrity would most likely be fleeting, it would also favourably serve their immediate political ambitions. And, as the island's most famous television personality, Julien Benoit, personally came out to greet them in the lobby, Patrick was once more content to play the sidekick. He lingered a few metres behind him as Benoit greeted Gaston with a warm smile and a firm handshake. Gaston was hoping that Benoit hadn't noticed his sweaty palm.

"It's a pleasure to have you here at last, Gaston," Benoit said. "I've been looking forward to this interview for some time."

Gaston was still distracted by the ongoing vision—this time a photo of a younger, smiling Cailason in uniform at the Finger Bay police station—rolling on the screens behind Benoit, who could sense this and fleetingly turned around to check the source of Gaston's distraction.

"Ahh yes, it is very big news, hey," Benoit said. "But it's also very strange. Two of the biggest news stories ever on the island happened in the last two weeks. Your heroic rescue, Gaston, and now one of the island's best police officers found high on heroin outside his own police station. Who would have thought? What's next? They do say things come in threes!

"Did you know him?"

"Ahh ah, no, not really. Of course, I know who he is. He's from the same village as me, but I haven't . . .," an increasingly nervous Gaston was suddenly lost for words.

For the first time, Patrick felt obliged to intervene to put Gaston at ease and ensure his star continued to sparkle for the sake of their FAIR agenda. Patrick was well aware that Gaston would need to be at the top of his game for a live television interview.

"Monsieur Benoit, it's a pleasure to meet you, sir. I'm a big fan," Patrick lied, extending his hand to Benoit. He had heard of Julien Benoit but had never seen a frame of his work on television. However, being a politician and having encountered a number of celebrities during his *The Chef Rules OK!* experience in Australia, he knew how to massage their egos.

"I'm Patrick, Gaston's best friend. I saw the whole thing. It's the bravest thing I've ever seen. That girl wouldn't be alive today if it weren't for Gaston."

Gaston was grateful for his friend's intervention, and he started to feel less anxious despite Sergeant Cailason still looming large on the screens.

Benoit guided Gaston and Patrick to the reception, where they signed in before he led them through a security door and into the engine room of the station. The building was an old warehouse that had been converted into a modern television station complex. Gaston was enthralled as he walked into the biggest room he'd ever seen, featuring large wooden beams crisscrossing the high ceilings and dominated by a large open-plan office space, which was a hive of activity. Many worker bees were swarming around the office while a few sat, buzzing in front of their computer screens. A multitude of glass-panelled offices lounged the perimeter of the room, bar one corner where a substantial space was devoted to a news studio, also encased in soundproof glass so staff and visitors could witness the action. The "On Air" warning light was flashing deliriously above the closed entrance to the studio.

Gaston looked on in admiration at the newsreader doing her job, seemingly oblivious to those watching her through the glass wall. She was immensely telegenic, bearing beautiful big brown eyes, luscious lipstick-stained red lips, and high cheekbones. She was immaculately attired and her long flowing black hair stylishly coiffured. However, she was also somewhat of a pioneer, being the first woman and coloured person to ever grace the island's television screens in such a prominent role.

Up until recent times, island television presenters and news readers had been exclusively white men, usually on-air talent who had failed to make the top grade in Europe. Julien Benoit was a classic example. He was a man consigned to reading the late-night news bulletins for nearly a decade in his native France before a holiday visit to the island set him on a pathway to local television stardom. He fell in love with the lifestyle and climate and impulsively decided to take up residence. Serendipitously, at the time, the island's television industry was unsophisticated by world standards and the two fledgling networks, one public and one private commercial channel, were in desperate need of a more professional approach and innovative content. And Benoit brought both via his years of experience in French television and also a pitch for a new talk show, a then foreign format to island viewers. With Benoit at the helm flouting a charming French accent and newfound charisma which he had seemingly acquired on the migration path to the island, *Encounter* was an instant hit and, over its fifteen-year history to date, had organically evolved into a celebrity interview program, although politicians and accidental celebrities like Gaston were also regularly featured. The instant popularity of the *Encounter* format caused the head of the rival government network to scramble to put together a similar format which had never reached anywhere near the dizzy heights of rating success that *Encounter* still inhabited.

Gaston couldn't take his eyes off the newsreader.

She's a stunning looking woman, no doubt about that.

Yet, he wasn't attracted to her at all. He could admire her beauty, but he was simply not turned on by darker-skinned women. Maybe it was the contrast with his own skin colour that stirred his loins. He had never really given it much thought and hadn't even noticed that his girlfriends to date had all been white or "off white" in skin colour. He was still staring at the newsreader when she suddenly stopped talking to the camera and turned to chat with a man sporting headphones who had approached her desk. The "On Air" light was no longer flashing.

Gaston turned his attention to the screens broadcasting the network's output which were seemingly ubiquitous throughout the space. Live vision of the newsreader had been replaced by a field story about the price of vegetables rising as a result of the recent cyclone.

"Now's our chance," Benoit suddenly said, grabbing both Patrick and Gaston roughly by the arm and leading them into the news studio.

Benoit ushered them past the newsreader and her producer, who paid them no attention at all. They made it through the back door of the news studio a moment before the newsreader resumed her gaze towards the camera, whose red light was once again glowing on top.

Gaston and Patrick found themselves in the network's main studio and in the heart of the familiar colourful set for *Encounter*, which had only had some minor changes in its fifteen-year history. The studio's high ceiling was cloaked in rows of lights, some spinning wildly and others strobing as pre-production was in full swing for the recording of the program. Heavy black and red curtains surrounded the back and sides of the set. Four cameras and their operators were swirling around the front of the set under the direction of the floor manager. Benoit's throne-like presenter's chair and the well-worn couch, where his guests were always quizzed and occasionally grilled and their egos often massaged, were populated by unknowns undergoing camera and lighting checks.

Benoit left them alone and headed to the control booth to speak to the program's director. Gaston once again started to feel nervous and turned towards Patrick, who gave him a reassuring smile.

"This is it, my friend. I know it's a bit scary but you can do it," Patrick said. "It's a great opportunity, Gaston. This show is seen by virtually the whole island."

Realising a huge audience would be watching did little to ease Gaston's nerves, and Patrick quickly realised he shouldn't have mentioned it.

"Oh, I'm sorry, Gaston. I didn't mean to make you more stressed. Look, you've done a fabulous job so far and I'm sure you'll be fine. The people love you. A man who selflessly risks his life to save the life of a beautiful woman. Who doesn't love that? The fact that Solange is so beautiful has a huge impact on this story. Don't forget that. It's TV, mate. Sex and beauty still sell.

"You're a hero, my friend, and trust me, they'll hang on to your every word. It's the perfect platform to tell them about our plan to make the world a better place."

All the while, Gaston nodded. He grasped the wisdom in what Patrick was saying, which helped calm his nerves to manageable.

"Now, you don't want to give the whole game away, and I don't want you to say anything that may risk your job at the resort."

Tom had been true to his word and offered Gaston a job at the resort, and one that had exceeded his expectations. Tom had had every intention of giving him a menial office job, but as he noticed Gaston's star rising among the island media and general community, he also realised Gaston's celebrity could be harnessed and exploited to spruik the benefits of the resort development and, more importantly, quell the still very hostile public opposition to it. Hence, Tom had summoned his marketing manager, Edouard Manilal, and ordered him to fast-track Gaston's "indoctrination" into the world of modern public relations and set the stage for "Gaston the Hero" to evolve rapidly into the marketing face and brand that the community would readily identify with the resort.

As a result, Gaston was thrown into the deep end of the resort's public relations pool, where he was initially tasked with writing formulaic media releases about the resort construction. But he was also promised potential rapid progression to a much more prominent role should he find public relations to his liking. Tom had not elaborated on what that role might be, which, at first, had caused Gaston some consternation. The only hint Gaston was given was that he would be required to do a screen test in the next week or so. He wasn't even sure what a "screen test" was however, Tom had reassured him that it would be a ticket to a quick promotion and a job that would be well within his capabilities.

Tom spoke with such genuine enthusiasm about having him on the payroll that Gaston's fears were soon allayed. Patrick, too, was convinced that Tom was sincere and certainly a markedly different man from the aggressive brute they'd encountered on the beach and the perplexed, agitated husband-to-be in the office the day after.

"Perhaps Solange is back to her old self and the wedding is once again on track," Patrick had said to Gaston, which had instantly soured his mood.

When Gaston told Tom about the offer of the *Encounter* interview, which would require him to take almost a full day off work, Tom was ecstatic. This surprised Gaston, who had been nervous about asking for the time off, given he'd only just started working there and wasn't yet aware of Tom's marketing plans. But Tom had also not-so-subtly hinted that he should do his best at some stage in the interview to steer the conversation towards the resort and the many benefits it would bring to the local community and the island economy and also to avoid any discussion of the misunderstanding which had led Tom to act "out of character".

"If Benoit starts talking about the incident on the beach, you need to make sure that he, and the viewers, understand that it was a complete and understandable misunderstanding," Tom had said to Gaston almost threateningly.

Tom had heard that Benoit only ever sketched questions for his interviews and usually allowed the conversation to take over. More importantly, the man wielded much power and influence in manipulating community opinion on the critical issues of the day. And there weren't too many issues occupying the public mind and eye more than his controversial resort development.

On Tom's orders, Mr. Manilal had spent several days coaching Gaston on the likely line of Benoit's questioning and how Gaston should respond.

"You can set the record straight on the resort project," Tom had said. "Look, you're working with us now so you're obviously on our side.

"And, of course, Gaston, it's also a golden opportunity for you personally to secure a potentially very rewarding future working with us," Tom had concluded with a wink, but also a vaguely menacing tone in his voice.

Tom's words echoed in Gaston's mind as a broadly smiling Julien Benoit emerged from the studio control booth.

"Ha, Gaston, makeup's ready for you," Benoit said, gently touching his elbow to guide him towards the makeup room.

"Please, my friend, you can relax," he continued noticing that Gaston was visibly nervous.

"Everyone thinks the show goes out live, but really we record it as if it is a live broadcast but really it isn't. That means if you do make a mistake, we can just stop and do the recording all over again. You see, so there's no need to be nervous . . ."

Realising that Patrick hadn't moved with them, Benoit stopped and turned to face him.

"Please . . . err, Patrick, isn't it?"

Patrick nodded.

"Please, dear Patrick, follow us. You are more than welcome to accompany your friend to makeup," Benoit said.

As the powder was being lavishly applied to his face, Gaston suddenly had a flashback to his beloved maid Saganthi, and a resultant chuckle startled the makeup artist.

"Err mm, I'm sorry, madam," he said sheepishly as if Saganthi herself had chastised him.

The very solemn-looking middle-aged makeup artist resumed her work without changing facial expressions or saying a word. Gaston stayed as still as he could for the rest of the time it took to apply his makeup and he, too, remained silent throughout. Once finished in makeup, he was taken straight onto the set. Patrick only had time to pat Gaston affectionately on the back and wish him "good luck" as he passed by on his way to the comfy guest sofa. Gaston let out an audible sigh as he sat down and was surprised to find the nerves had dissipated and he was once again smiling inside.

CHAPTER XXXIX

Thunderbolt Strikes a Second Time

Her head nestled comfortably on his shoulder; she yearned to feel something, anything—most of all, love.

But numbness still reigned supreme.

For his part, one arm was wrapped affectionately around her shoulder, the other occasionally roaming across her chest to form a gentle hug.

Tom and Solange were snuggling on the couch and watching television. A voyeur, in the form of a chirping gecko eyeing the couple from the safety of the ceiling, could be excused for thinking it had stumbled across a scene of pure domestic bliss. But as had been the case throughout their relationship, appearances were highly deceptive.

It had been a difficult couple of weeks since her attempted suicide, and while physically Solange was now in reasonable shape, the psychological wounds were still raw and, at times, openly bleeding. She had fits of uncontrollable sobbing and often felt estranged from a man she would soon marry and live with, "happily ever after".

Tom was somewhat relieved when Solange had offered a viable reason for her suicide attempt: a spectacularly adverse reaction to anti-depressants.

"I'm so sorry, darling. I really don't know what came over me. It felt so weird. I couldn't feel anything, just an overwhelming numbness which made me feel like I was watching myself doing all this, not actually doing it," she had said to him, a crushing sadness in her voice.

In the first week after the suicide attempt, Solange was obviously still too fragile to be quizzed further, so Tom resolved to let it rest and willed himself into being more upbeat by focusing on the wedding preparations and plans for his mini petting zoo on the expanded resort site. But to his surprise and great delight, Solange seemed to get caught up in his positive slipstream and was soon talking about the wedding again with genuine enthusiasm. As a result, Tom indefinitely abandoned any plan to revisit motives or emotions surrounding her suicide attempt, fearing it might once more unleash the demons.

Little did Tom realise that she was going to excruciating lengths to make herself cheerful. He and others in their social circle remained blissfully unaware that she was drawing on every ounce of emotional reserve to hide her pain. A more sensitive, perceptive man would perhaps have detected the hollowness in the laugh, the tears in her smile. But Tom was not such a man.

Solange's apparent return to her normal self only served to revive the narcissistic traits in Tom's personality, further compounding her misery. This made her resort to finding any excuse to be unavailable to spend time with him. Fortunately for Solange, she was still living with her family in the same house next to the resort. Even though the sale of the house had been finalised and the money handed over to the Dubois family, Tom had taken out an extra "insurance policy", allowing them to stay in the house rent-free until they found another suitable home. However, they had been given a deadline of the wedding day, which had been pushed back by a month. Living with her family enabled Solange to use her "family responsibilities and duties" as a legitimate reason to be otherwise occupied and brushed aside any objections from Tom with a reassuring, "we'll soon have all the time in the world, darling".

But every time she uttered such words, it immediately evoked a vision of her future with Tom, which only increased her anxiety levels. She had some relief from having to come up with excuses when he was compelled to spend longer at work as construction of the resort was in overdrive. This meant less time she would have to spend pretending everything was fine. Nevertheless, she quickly found herself once again on a trajectory towards the type of emotional collapse which had triggered the suicide attempt. She was only just holding on and desperately needed a circuit breaker.

"It's about to start, darling. They say every cloud has a silver lining and this could be it," Tom said cheerfully.

"Let's hope that Gaston is 'on message,' as Mr. Manilal would say."

Solange smiled, but a different smile to the perpetually forced, plastic one which had adorned her face in Tom's company in recent days. It was a rare, genuinely warm smile, subconsciously triggered by the mention of Gaston's name and the fact that she was about to see him again for the first time since that fateful day on the beach. As the familiar opening soundtrack to *Encounter* filled Tom's lavish living room (he had, of course, installed the latest in surround sound technology, which was on high volume for the broadcast), Solange realised she was actually looking forward to something for the first time in a very long time. She felt a tingle of excitement invade her being in anticipation.

"Tonight, ladies and gentlemen, you will meet a true-life hero, a man who selflessly risked his own life to rescue a damsel in very great distress," Benoit's voice boomed, seemingly bouncing off the walls and marble-tiled floor and transforming Solange's tingle to a surge.

The camera cut to a close-up of Gaston, whose smiling eyes, opened wide, seemed to fill the screen as he fleetingly looked directly into the camera. Solange couldn't believe it. Even through the filter of television transmission she felt his fleeting look penetrate deep into her soul as it had done on the beach. All was well again in the world. Tom didn't exist and there was no wedding on the horizon. Pure bliss.

"Well, he certainly looks the part, doesn't he?" Tom said brusquely, bruising but not breaking Solange's reverie.

Her eyes remained glued to the screen and the bliss lingered as Gaston spoke humbly, playing down his courageous deed. Solange was in love, no doubt about it, and somehow she was certain he felt the same way. Tom paid his fiancé scant attention, even though he still had his arm around her. They were, to all intents and purposes, "alone" watching the same screen. The apparent intimate snuggle on the couch was just that, apparent and lacking any emotional connection whatsoever. Both were fully immersed in the interview, albeit for vastly different reasons. Tom was waiting anxiously for the conversation to turn to the aftermath of the rescue. He didn't have long to wait.

"To be honest, Monsieur Benoit, I would have probably felt the same way if I had suddenly seen my girlfriend on the beach looking like she was kissing a stranger. He didn't see me rescue her, so what else could he have thought? Look, once Mr. Wright realised what really happened, he calmed down straight away and my friend Patrick and I were able to convince him that I was saving her life, nothing else," Gaston said with great sincerity.

"But you know what, Monsieur Benoit, he then proved to me that he was genuinely sorry for losing his cool. He kept his promise and gave me a job, and not just any job but one of the better jobs in the company. He didn't have to do that."

Tom suddenly let out a triumphant squeal. On national television Gaston had exonerated him of any blame for the altercation on the beach and even painted a picture of Tom Wright as a benevolent, understanding man.

But he once more held his breath when Benoit began to probe Gaston on possible motives behind Solange's reckless behaviour in going for a swim with a cyclone almost in full fury, the line of questioning leaving viewers to draw the only conclusion possible, that it was an attempt to kill herself.

"Why would a beautiful young woman, with seemingly everything to live for, do that, Gaston? Do you have any idea?" Benoit asked.

"Well, Monsieur Benoit, from what I understand, she'd been on some medication that caused her to go a bit crazy, you know with the stress of the wedding and all that; it just pushed her over the edge. It could happen to anyone under that sort of pressure. After all, Mr. Wright is no ordinary man, as we all know, and this wedding is going to be big—very big.

"But I can assure you, Monsieur Benoit, that Solange is now back to good health. She's obviously not taking the medication anymore. She's busy with all the wedding preparations and, I believe, feeling much happier and very much looking forward to marrying the boss," Gaston said, following Manilal's instructions to the letter.

He felt much of his good humour instantly dissipate in almost equal proportion to the lift in Tom's mood as he had a vision of Tom and Solange exchanging wedding vows at the altar. Tom on the other hand let out an audible sigh of relief, then leapt off the couch, punching the air, beaming with delight.

"That's my boy," he cried. "Manilal's done a great job. I'll make sure he gets a decent pay rise for doing this."

Solange remained rooted to the couch and oblivious to Tom's joy. She simply folded her arms, annoyed that Tom was blocking her full view of the television screen until she realised that the network had cut to a commercial break anyway.

"And that Gaston, well, I must say he's a real surprise packet. Who would have thought? Obviously, a quick learner. We have big plans for him, but I wasn't sure he was really on our side . . . but after this . . .?"

"Maybe we should have him around one night for dinner?

"I've been thinking about that for some time but wasn't sure whether you'd be up to it. And to tell you the truth, I haven't really been up to it, either—until now. What do you think, darling?"

Solange had not tuned in to what Tom had been saying until the mention of Gaston's name. She felt her heart rate immediately quicken and her body flush with a warm glow.

"Oh my God . . . Gaston . . . here!" she shrieked internally, silently.

Solange wanted to leap off the couch too and say, "*Yes, yes, yes* . . . get Gaston here as soon as possible!"

But the only expression of her true emotion was one corner of her mouth lifting in a half-smile. The words which then flowed out of her mouth betrayed her inner joy.

"I don't know. I guess it would be nice to have . . ." she meekly started saying.

Tom wasn't listening anyway and cut her off abruptly. He had made up his mind and was in no doubt that Gaston was now a team player, and no ordinary player but a true-life hero whose ever-rising celebrity could be harnessed to turn around the hostile community sentiment towards the resort.

"I wonder if he's got a girlfriend. I've never asked him. Well, if he has, she can come too. If not, he can bring his friend Patrick," Tom continued, buoyantly pacing across the room in front of the very wide-screened television.

Solange's half-smile dissolved at the mention of "girlfriend". While Gaston had been obsessively on her mind since the rescue, she'd never contemplated the possibility of him having a girlfriend until now!

Such an attractive man, surely he would have women chasing him all the time, she suddenly thought, casting a slight gloom on the upward momentum of her mood.

Tom paused and turned to face Solange. He was too focused on his dinner plan to notice Solange's blank stare at him.

"So that's settled, darling; we'll have Gaston and maybe his girlfriend over for dinner as soon as possible. I'll ask Manilal as well. I think he's married, so that'll be a plus one. I'll get one of the chefs we recently hired for the resort to cook for us, and I'll make sure a couple of the maids are here as well, so you won't have to do a thing."

The *Encounter* theme took over the surround soundscape of the room, signalling a return from the commercial break. Tom sat down again, mechanically looping his arm around Solange's shoulder as passionlessly as before.

"So, Gaston, now that you're probably the most popular man on the island, what are your plans for the future? I imagine you can do anything you want. Does being prime minister have any appeal?" Benoit asked light-heartedly.

"Ahh, Monsieur Benoit, I know you're teasing. I just did what I would imagine most people would do in the circumstances. And since then, I've been very happy working for Mr. Wright. It's my first real job and it's a very good one, so I really want to concentrate on doing a good job for the boss. But, down the track, I do have a plan to save the world, you know," he said, the huge smile in his voice materialising in a cheeky grin.

"Really, Gaston, tell us more," Benoit said playfully.

"Well, in all seriousness, my friend Patrick and I do have some ideas that, we think, could make a big difference and improve life for islanders and, who knows, maybe the whole world. And to put those ideas into action, well, I imagine you can only do that if you're part of a government, right?"

"Wow, Gaston, so you have political ambitions and maybe a plan to save the world?" Benoit said again playfully.

"Well, when you look at the way things are around the world, it does need some saving, doesn't it?" Gaston said, this time taking on a more serious tone.

"And we think our ideas are a good start. You know the saying, 'the only thing necessary for the triumph of evil is for good men do nothing', and there sure is a lot of evil around, isn't there? And not enough good men—and women—doing something about it. So, we think, as good men, we need to act. Our ideas, I guess, are really simple and we'd like to think a bit of common sense.

"Ever since we were kids, we've been interested in, you know, finding ways to make the world a better, fairer place; maybe one day we'll grow out of that," Gaston chuckled.

"Is that right? I wonder what would make two island kids start making plans to save the world?"

"Well, Monsieur Benoit, it's a story that starts with David Beckham, the universe and aliens visiting planet Earth, and ends up with a fair and just society where everyone is happier."

"Fascinating, Gaston. Can you give us some idea of how you aim to achieve that—dare I say—Utopia? Many have tried before but failed."

"I can, Monsieur Benoit, but then I may have to shoot you," Gaston replied, this time laughing wholeheartedly.

Benoit, too, broke out in genuine, generous laughter.

"Intriguing! Who would have thought? You really are a surprise packet, Gaston," Benoit said.

"I'm sure we'd all love to know more, but unfortunately we've run out of time. I'd like to thank my guest, Gaston Le Clezio, for sharing the story of his brave rescue but also for giving us a fascinating insight into his future plans. And who knows, we may see you here again one day as Prime Minister Le Clezio."

Tom picked up the television remote from the extravagant glass table-top sitting on a support structure fashioned from a patterned frame of real elephant tusks, the ivory having been illegally acquired by a Finger Bay furniture importer. Tom had had no compunction about buying the table and paying an exorbitant amount of money for it; much more, in fact, than the twenty-five thousand dollars he'd outlaid for his home entertainment system. He fell in love with the lattice design of the tusks as soon as he laid eyes on it in the back room of a furniture shop in Palm Waters. He rarely acted on impulse when buying anything but didn't hesitate to make this purchase. The table had not been on open display to the public primarily because the shop owner would have risked prosecution, but also few islanders could have afforded the hefty price tag.

Being one of the island's wily Chinese shopkeepers, he had immediately recognised Tom from the recent media frenzy surrounding Solange's rescue and realised that he was one man who had ample means to buy the table.

Tom pushed the mute button, causing the surround sound of the television to suddenly go silent and his own voice to reverberate around the room, startling Solange.

"Did you hear that, darling? Gaston wants to save the world. Well good for you, mate. You can start by saving me from those fuckwits in the media and the community who are against my resort.

"Really, what a fucking bunch of Neanderthals these islanders are," Tom began to say before realising Solange was all ears.

"Oh, present company excepted, of course, darling," he humbly blurted out before the tone lifted once more as he resumed his rant.

"Can you imagine being so hung up on a convention that you don't build higher than the tallest coconut tree? What a fucking joke! I understand that was useful in the old days, but we can build things now that can weather any bloody storm. Fucking primitive thinking, that's what it is. Thank God, they've got a few sensible heads in the government who can see beyond that. Mind you, applying a liberal dose of grease to some of those Neanderthal palms didn't hurt, either," Tom said, chuckling.

"That'll be a wake-up call for Gaston if he does ever get into government. Everyone has his price, even you, Gaston, and that's why the world will never be fair and his plans are doomed to failure, isn't that right, darling?"

Solange disguised her repulsion to what Tom was saying with a forced, lukewarm smile. She could feel the anguish return. Gaston was no longer on the television and Tom was . . . well . . . "just being Tom".

She had always known that beneath the charm offensive of their early months together, he was an arrogant—even ruthless—man, thin on compassion, deficient in empathy and devoid of any morals whatsoever.

"Why did I let myself get into this situation? Obviously, I had a price too and he paid," she thought.

She was in a hurry to leave.

"I'm sorry, darling, I'm starting to feel rather tired. It's been a big week," Solange said in desperation.

Tom suddenly realised that Solange indeed was looking paler than normal, although not for the reason he was led to believe.

"Oh darling, it's me that should be sorry," he said with sincerity. "I got a bit carried away—well, actually relieved more than anything—with the great job Gaston did on the show and also excited about him working for us."

"I understand, but could you please take me home, Tom? I'm really not feeling well," Solange almost pleaded.

"Of course, of course, darling. I hope you'll be okay by the weekend so we can have Gaston over," Tom said with sincerity.

The mention of Gaston immediately lifted Solange's morale once more, a touch of colour returning to her cheeks as she pictured him once more looking lovingly into her eyes.

On the short drive to Solange's home, they both remained contemplative and silent, but Tom did notice the alternating flashing and strobing lights of the Angels Massage Suites as he drove past and knew he would be making a pit stop there on the way back.

Sure enough, at about the same time he was ejaculating into one of his regular "angels", Solange was hunched over the toilet bowl, ejecting the bile that had quickly built up as she contemplated a life as the wife of Tom Wright.

CHAPTER XL

Soup, Sleuth, and Chastity

Monique reached into her large, black, faux-leather handbag and took out a chunky, clear plastic pouch bearing black Chinese characters.

She was intrigued by the plan Patrick and Gaston had outlined to her and Idris at the Tropicana Café. Over a light lunch, they had every so often simultaneously and separately lurched over the table and spoken in hushed tones, just like in a spy movie. Monique had initially been apprehensive, but she fully trusted Gaston and Patrick and was easily convinced that she would be doing the community a great service in carrying out their plan.

Patrick's hunch had also proved spot on. He had easily procured the necessary herbs—Rehmannia, Ligustrum, and Skullcap—from his Chinese contacts and bought supplies of all three in case one didn't work or seemed to work better than the other two. He and Gaston wanted to experiment with all combinations until they found the ideal formula. The spare bedroom of his apartment was now stuffed with big cardboard boxes filled with hand-sized pouches of the herbs. He had procured an ample supply for at least six months. Patrick was certain that by that time, they would know for sure whether the herbs were having the desired impact. Patrick didn't inform the seller of what he was going to do with such a large quantity of libido-reducing herbs, and the seller hadn't enquired either.

However, Patrick and Gaston soon realised that finding a way to measure success or failure would be a challenge without sending in some form of alluring "jailbait" to assess whether the priests had reined in their libidos. A handsome young boy would be ideal; however, should the herbs fail to work, the boy would find himself vulnerable and in a potentially perilous position at the mercy of the lascivious priests.

The pot of soup had been bubbling away for an hour or so and Monique was finally alone in the presbytery kitchen. Her kitchen aide had finished the washing up and headed home. Monique had accompanied her to the front door of the presbytery, as she often did, hoping that the aide didn't notice that she was trembling with trepidation. Outside the front door, Monique had waved her goodbye and lingered on the porch for some time until she disappeared from view before going back inside, fully resolved to carry out her part of the plan.

Before entering the kitchen again, she had checked the adjacent rooms to make sure none of the priests were back. After serving at masses in the morning, they all liked to head into the village centre, supposedly to have a quiet coffee among themselves or engage socially with their parishioners before coming back to the presbytery for lunch. However, over the years parishioners had allegedly seen the odd priest disguised in civilian clothing entering an establishment of ill repute. No one, of course, had the audacity to further investigate or report them. They knew no one would believe it, given the power the priests wielded over the Catholic faithful of Finger Bay. Instead, they ended up convincing themselves that they had imagined it all or joked to their family and friends about the "doppelgänger" of their beloved parish priest they had seen entering the brothel.

Monique knew they could be back any minute, so time was of the essence. Her hands were still shaking as she scoured the pouch for a sign of the opening, only to find a small symbol in one corner indicating that scissors were needed to liberate the contents. And just as she opened a drawer to get the scissors, she heard the front door open accompanied by a raucous laugh echoing down the long corridor. She still had time if she worked quickly. Within seconds, she had crossed herself before opening the pouch and emptying its contents into the pot of soup.

"Good morning, Monique. It smells lovely as usual; oxtail and vegetable?"

It was Father Pierrot, a youngish priest who was the newest on the parish block, having been a Finger Bay father for only a month or so. Ever since his arrival, he had taken an interest in Monique and her life unlike no other priest before him.

As was his custom after his morning walk, he had broken away from the pack as they passed by the kitchen and was now looking over Monique's shoulder as she was stirring the pot.

"Thank you, Father. There's certainly nothing wrong with your nose, is there?" Monique replied, fleetingly turning her head around to acknowledge Father Pierrot's presence and forcing herself to smile to mask the nervous edge in her voice.

Looking at his boyish, innocent face, which belied his thirty-seven years of age, Monique couldn't believe that Father Pierrot was an abuser of young children. He was a handsome man, despite having prominent chubby cheeks speckled with freckles which were now glowing red, no doubt the legacy of the walk from the village centre under the hot mid-morning sun. He was grinning widely, salivating at the prospect of lunch looming. Monique had noticed he had a very healthy appetite and his girth had been steadily swelling since his arrival from his native France.

Father Pierrot always respected Monique's space, unlike the other priests who would sometimes walk up to her in the kitchen when she had her back turned and gently place their hand on her waist or shoulder in an almost loving gesture. She had become accustomed to this and had thought nothing of it until Gaston's tales of alleged sexual abuse. She then became more cautious and on tenterhooks when the priests were home and potentially able to invade her space in the kitchen.

But she let her guard down in the presence of Father Pierrot, particularly when he was dressed in his plain brown cassock, as he often was when he came into the kitchen at lunchtime. He then reminded her of Friar Tuck from the *Tales of Robin Hood*, who was one of her favourite storybook characters. Father Pierrot was naturally a bit younger than the various storybook and cinematic depictions of Robin Hood's faithful Friar and not quite as fat . . . yet. Also, unlike Friar Tuck, who had the standard tonsure haircut of monks, Father Pierrot had a healthy crop of thick red hair.

He seems so lovely; surely, he couldn't be involved in their disgusting antics? thought Monique.

Monique's feeling about Father Pierrot was right. He had always been true to his faith and vocation and had never been tempted to break his vow of celibacy. And the day news broke, just after lunch on a sunny Friday afternoon in Rome, that Catholic priests had been accused of sexually abusing young boys and girls in various parts of the world, Father Pierrot felt physically ill, and also angry that he'd been denied his usual pleasure of digesting the delicious spaghetti carbonara lunch from his favourite trattoria.

The Finger Bay fathers had been on their best behaviour since his arrival, but not because they sensed or knew of Father Pierrot's loathing of sexual misconduct among the Catholic clergy. Each time a new recruit joined their ranks, they would abstain from their abusive ways until they were certain the new recruit would be a willing participant in their sexual crimes.

Father Pierrot was the only priest to engage Monique in conversation which strayed beyond small talk, and this naturally made her even more relaxed in his company, although today she was struggling to remain calm and composed, but that had nothing to do with Father Pierrot's presence in the kitchen.

When not in the kitchen, she also seemed to run into Father Pierrot far more than the other priests, and that was no coincidence.

"Did I tell you about the delicious bouillabaisse my mother used to make, Monique?" Father Pierrot said.

"She made it nearly every Friday night when I was a boy, with wonderfully fresh seafood my dad would bring in; so fresh that the fish seemed to be still wriggling when my mum started cooking. Ahh, that was one of the highlights of my week as a child."

"I'd love to make that for you, Father; really, I would, but as you may have noticed, it's almost impossible to get fresh seafood here even though we live on an island. It's absurd, isn't it? But that's just how it is now when money rules, ehh? Most of the fresh seafood goes to the hotels, and the few rich island people buy the rest and we ordinary folk, well, you know . . ." Monique lamented.

"Yes, yes, I know. It's the same everywhere, Monique.

"Fresh seafood is pretty expensive in my village too now, even though my father is still a fisherman. But he now has to work for a big co-op. He can't afford to work on his own as he used to, so we hardly see any of his catch as we did when we were kids."

Father Pierrot had told Monique much about his upbringing in the French fishing village of Collioure. He was the son of a fifth-generation fisherman, his mother a hardworking housewife who raised four boys, none of whom showed any interest in continuing the family's vocational tradition, much to the parents' chagrin. One son had become an accountant after meeting the girl of his dreams and being lured to live just over the border in her native Barcelona; two others had moved to Paris and found jobs, one in a café as a waiter and the other selling tickets to tourists for the Eiffel Tower lifts. Although they continued to love all their sons dearly, Father Pierrot's career path was the only one that gained the respect and approval of the parents. They were, after all, devout Catholics and they felt such pride when Father Pierrot had announced that he was to be a man of the cloth. His parents both cried with joy, yet his calling had not been the natural evolution of the family's strict devotion to the Catholic faith as his parents had assumed.

In his teenage years, Anatole Pierrot had wanted to be a detective, drawing inspiration from his love of crime novels, initially Frédéric Dard's adventures of San

Antonio. However, as he approached his adult years, he wasn't overly fond of the adventures of Detective Superintendent Antoine San Antonio increasingly taking a satirical turn. He then discovered Agatha Christie and became convinced that he would follow in the footsteps of Hercule Poirot, the heroic detective who starred in thirty-three novels, one play, and fifty short stories written by Christie. The fact that their respective surnames were similar, Anatole interpreted as a sign of his inevitable career destiny.

Nevertheless, like his parents and two of his three brothers, Anatole was also a committed Catholic, firm in his conviction that the faith provided the only pathway to eternal life in Heaven seated at the right hand of God the Father, the Son, and Holy Spirit. And he didn't believe his faith would pose any barrier to his ambition to be a detective.

However, a family trip to Portugal when he was eighteen years old set him on the path to the priesthood. On an overnight train journey to Lisbon, young Anatole was sound asleep when he woke up with a start and felt a spiritual force guiding his hand to the train window to lift up the blind. The train had come to a halt and through the window he saw a large platform name board sign which seemed to fill up the frame of the window, indicating they were in the town of Fatima. Possessed instantly with an overwhelming sense of peace, love, and beauty, Anatole had stared for what seemed a long time at the sign, which then transformed into an image of the Virgin Mary, holding the hands of three children—surely the three who had witnessed the reported Marian apparition at Fatima in 1917—calling Anatole to join them in spreading the Gospel of the Lord Jesus Christ to the world.

It might have well been an illusion—a mirage, yet the episode was a life-changing experience for young Anatole. The family had planned to stop in Fatima on the way home after holidaying on the Algarve coast. That visit to the Sanctuary of Our Lady of Fatima a week later only confirmed his calling. He was filled with the same sense of peace, love, and beauty and a burning desire to spread the word of God that he had felt when looking out the train window.

Little did Monique realise that Father Pierrot had retained an interest in detective work throughout his theological training despite him becoming a priest whose devotion to Catholic duty and charitable works had seen his reputation spread all the way to the Vatican. As a result, he was summoned to the Vatican to undertake higher theological studies, apparently on the direct orders of the Pope himself.

Unbeknownst to the Finger Bay priests and parish community, this experience also had enabled Father Pierrot to combine his passion for both vocations.

"I'll see what I can do to get you some seafood, Monique. I've gotten to know some of the fishermen here quite well, and I'm sure they'll be able to get me some for a reasonable price. I'd be happy to pay. I've also written down my mother's recipe if you'd like it. You're such a brilliant cook, Monique; I'm sure you'll do it justice," Father Pierrot said, licking his lips subconsciously in anticipation.

"That would be no problem at all, Father; it would be an honour to make that for you," Monique replied.

"Excellent, I'll see what I can do tomorrow," Father Pierrot said as he headed towards the kitchen door without a parting greeting, which Monique found out of character for the usually very polite father.

But instead of walking out, Father Pierrot poked his head outside and looked up and down the corridor before gently closing the door and approaching Monique once more.

Startled by his actions, Monique started to feel a bit anxious.

Surely, he's not going to molest me! was her first thought.

He got closer and leant over as if he wanted to say something quietly in her ear, intensifying Monique's anxiety.

"Now, I was hoping you could help me with another matter . . . if you have a few minutes?" Father Pierrot began to say.

"Can it wait till after lunch, Father?" Monique said, intrigued, but simultaneously thinking, *What the hell can I help him with? Me, a humble cook?*

Her lingering anxiety melted away completely as a broad, comforting smile spread across Father Pierrot's face.

"Of course, of course, my dear Monique. Lunch is overdue, but can you come and see me in my office before you head home?" he asked.

"Yes, Father, happy to do that. Now if you'll excuse me, there are a few hungry priests waiting for this," she said, pointing to the bubbling pot with her large wooden spoon.

"I know exactly how they feel," Father Pierrot said cheerfully as he turned away once more and opened the kitchen door, but this time walking out whistling a happy tune as he headed towards the dining room.

CHAPTER XLI

A Saint among the Sinners

"What do you know about the death of Henri Laroche, Monique?" Father Pierrot was sitting behind his office desk, reclining back on his armchair and twirling a pen in his hand. His demeanour was markedly different from an hour or so ago when chatting to Monique in the kitchen, his tone of voice more earnest, the cheerful grin replaced by an expression of gravitas.

When she had walked in a few minutes earlier, he had been writing furiously in an official looking folder and had only fleetingly looked up and summoned her to take a seat on the other side of the desk with a wave of a hand.

Monique was feeling a little nervous again, even though the "spiked" lunch had gone to plan and had been devoured by the priests between the usual comments of "delicious" and "compliments to the chef".

Father Pierrot had kept Monique waiting for what seemed an eternity to her before putting his pen down and looking at her with a serious intensity she had never experienced before during their regular kitchen banter.

It suddenly occurred to her that she had never known an ordinary priest to be given his own office, which made her feel even more nervous. Father Pierrot must have sensed Monique's uneasiness and gave her a warm smile before complimenting her on the scrumptious lunch. But he resumed a more formal, solemn look and launched into the question about Henri.

"Err, you mean the altar boy who had the tragic accident at the wildlife park?" Monique asked, feeling somewhat flustered and previously unaware of the boy's surname.

Father Pierrot nodded, inviting Monique to answer.

"Well, err . . . all I know is what everybody else knows: that he accidentally fell into the crocodile pit after climbing over the safety barrier. But why ask me, Father? And what's this all about?"

Father Pierrot kept looking at Monique, who now had her head bowed.

"Call it a hunch, Monique, and perhaps you don't know any more about the poor boy's death than we all do, but I have a feeling you may possibly be aware of some unpleasant things going on around here which may have contributed to the boy's . . . err . . . 'accident'. After all, you're here every day, so . . ." Father Pierrot said, almost pleading.

"What do you mean, Father? What unpleasant things?" Monique interrupted.

She was thinking of Gaston and was unsure whether she should reveal what she indeed did know. She looked up to meet his gaze and sensed she was in the presence of a friend, not a foe. Nevertheless, she decided to remain silent until she knew for sure.

"Well, Monique, again, it's a gut feeling, but I am going to come clean and confide in you. I've been doing this for a while now and my gut feeling has rarely let me down," Father Pierrot said.

He smiled, then paused and got up abruptly from his chair, startling Monique somewhat. She had so many questions but held her fire.

Father Pierrot walked over to the door and checked outside his office to make sure none of the other priests were in the vicinity before he gently closed the door and resumed his seat.

He leant forward, causing Monique to instinctively bring her chair as close to the desk as possible.

"Now, you may have noticed that we seem to bump into each other quite a lot," Father Pierrot said, smiling.

"I've actually been watching you and noticed you've been hanging around the presbytery above and beyond the call of duty as our cook. And if I didn't know better, I would even say that you've been spying on the priests."

Monique expected a rebuke to flow, but the inquisitive tone in Father Pierrot's voice and the affable expression on his face assured her that none would be forthcoming.

"Well, Monique, if you have indeed been spying on the priests, you may just be able to help me. But first, I need to be absolutely sure that I can trust you and that everything I'm about to say to you stays between you and me and these four walls," Father Pierrot said.

Monique had no hesitation this time around.

"Of course, of course, Father, you can trust me absolutely, and if there's any way I can help you, I will."

"Thank you, thank you. As you may have guessed, I am no ordinary priest. I mean, I *am* a priest, but I have a much more important job in the church. I'm a member of a secret unit established by the Vatican not so long ago when a number of priests around the world were accused of sexual misconduct—you know, sexually abusing mainly young boys and girls in their care, but also taking advantage of vulnerable parishioners," Father Pierrot said, the disgust and distress visible in the contorted expression on his face as if he was about to be sick.

"I hope I'm not upsetting you by all this, Monique."

"No, no, not at all, Father. Please go on," Monique quickly replied, now confident she could reveal what Gaston had told her about the Finger Bay fathers. But she wanted to hear more of Father Pierrot's story first.

"Naturally, the Vatican—and the Pope himself—was disgusted by these allegations, so the Pope decided to put together a team of trusted and committed Catholic priests to go undercover, so to speak, to expose and get rid of those priests who are doing our fine church such great damage.

"I happened to be at the Vatican at the time, and also happen to be a bit of an amateur detective, and the Pontiff knew this, so he called on me to head the team. Since then, I've been posted to various parishes around the world and have had some success in exposing these awful priests. But unfortunately, there are still too many bad apples in the orchard. You can see what a big job we have when even a small community like Finger Bay has such wicked priests."

Monique took the opportunity to interrupt as Father Pierrot paused. There were so many burning questions she wanted to ask.

"But how, how did you know there was a problem here at Finger Bay, Father?"

"Ahh, that's a very interesting story, Monique, and one that I feel won't surprise you. Soon after Henri's death, his poor distraught mother found a series of drawings in his room, very dark and disturbing pictures of . . . err . . . well of priests in various states of undress doing ghastly things. Henri, it seems, was a very talented artist.

"Well, one of his drawings depicted a scene of a priest with a young altar boy doing something which was so distressing that the mother collapsed and had to be rushed to hospital. Fortunately, it was just shock, and she recovered quickly and was back home within a few hours."

Father Pierrot went on to explain that over the next few days, her immense grief gave way to an equally consuming anger when she realised that the priests of Finger Bay might not be as holy as everyone thought.

"A desire to avenge her son then took over, as you would imagine, so she wrote to a trusted relative—her cousin in Paris who happened to be a lawyer—and told him everything. She also sent him a copy of the drawings and asked for advice on what she could do, if anything.

"Her relative, also named Henri, thought the Catholic church surely must take action. He knew this sort of stuff was already on the Vatican's radar. He'd read recent reports of the Pope himself expressing grave concerns about the deviant behaviour of some priests.

"Henri is also a devout Catholic who has a close relationship with his local parish priest, a Father Mathieu, and, as luck would have it, Father Mathieu also happened to be a very close friend of mine. We studied at the same seminary in Paris.

"So, Henri went to see Father Mathieu and explained the situation. The drawings did that better than any words could, really, and my friend contacted me immediately. He knew of my work with the Vatican's secret unit, you see.

"When I too saw the drawings, I realised straight away something evil was going on here. They were so graphic. The boy must have suffered a great deal; so sad and such a tragic waste," Father Pierrot said, shaking his head, a tear trickling down his cheek.

"Anyway, there you have the full story, so now it's your turn. Do you know something that could help my investigation?"

"Well, Father . . ." Monique began to say, then checked herself suddenly, thinking that Patrick and Gaston would be better placed to enlighten Father Pierrot on the nefarious sexual activities of the Finger Bay fathers.

"I have heard stories about the priests but I really think you should meet my friends Gaston and Patrick. They know a lot more and I'm sure they would be more than happy to help," Monique said.

"So, there is something sinister going on here?" Father Pierrot said.

"Yes, there seems to be, Father . . . from what I've heard. But I really think you should hear the full story from Gaston and Patrick," Monique said.

"All right, Monique, but I must work fast before any other young boys suffer the same fate. When can I meet your friends?" he said.

"I'll try to set up a meeting as soon as possible. You're in luck. They both live in Palm Waters, but Gaston had a few days off so he's been visiting his mother who lives here in Finger Bay. I'll try to arrange a meeting with them tomorrow afternoon after work at the Tropicana Café. Can you make it?" Monique asked.

"Of course, of course, I'll make sure of it."

"That's great, Father. We'll be there around three p.m.," Monique said as she stood up.

"Thank you. I know Gaston and Patrick will be very happy to meet you and help you in any way they can," she said before extending her hand, which Father Pierrot, now standing, cupped in both his hands.

"It is I who should thank you, Monique. This is the first piece of joy I've had on this case since I've been here. I look forward to seeing you all tomorrow."

Monique smiled warmly at Father Pierrot before leaving and heading straight home as fast as her tired legs would take her.

CHAPTER XLII

Celebrity Ambush

As soon as Gaston walked out the front door of his mother's home, he didn't feel quite right. He had a strange feeling of being naked and vulnerable, yet he was fully clothed with no menace in sight, at least until he approached the front gate.

He heard the sound of leaves rustling and sensed some people loitering on the street outside the manicured bamboo fence which ran each side of a sturdy iron gate along the front of his mother's property.

Two young women poked their heads around the fence and stopped Gaston in his tracks with a sudden shriek as he reached the front gate. Following his appearance on the *Encounter* program a week and a half before, Gaston's celebrity had grown in all parts of the island. Whenever he was out in public since then, he had felt continually under the gaze of the people around him. At times, the gaze would transform into a verbal recognition of his heroic deed. Some people stopped him and wanted to have a chat and shake his hand. Some women were even more daring and stole a kiss on the cheek.

Naturally, the celebrity stalking was at fever pitch in Palm Waters, the scene of his heroics where he now also worked and lived after moving in with Patrick. National media had given the rescue and its aftermath saturation coverage, his photo seemingly permanently plastered to the front page of the local *Palm Village Gazette*.

After a week, he sought and was granted a few days' leave from work to visit his mother in Finger Bay, thinking he could find refuge from the constant intrusion on his personal space. Yet he quickly discovered that his popularity and degree of recognition among the folk of his home village were even greater. He was one of their own, as a letter from a Finger Bay resident to the editor of the national newspaper, the *New Express*, proudly boasted.

He'd even had a call from his former flame, Natalie, who had seen a report in the gossip column of the same newspaper saying that Gaston had been spotted around the village. She had immediately launched into a mea culpa and expressed her deep regret for her “immature and stupid” decision to break up their relationship and pleaded with Gaston to forgive her. But he, on the other hand, was not so immature anymore. The events of the past few months since the heartbreak had caused him to evolve emotionally, and he was quick to recognise the shallowness of her sentiments. The power of celebrity was her only interest, and if he had expressed any desire to resume the relationship, he knew it would once again end in heartbreak when that power diminished, as it inevitably would. Besides, he could confidently say that he was no longer in love with her. His heart had been taken prisoner by someone else in a more romantic, adult way. Nevertheless, he had been polite to Natalie and promised that he'd call her back to arrange a rendezvous, knowing full well he'd never follow through on that promise.

“Rescue me, Gaston, *pleaaaase*!” screamed one of the women as she attempted to open the front gate.

Gaston suddenly realised he had walked out of the house without the disguise which he had donned over the past few days when he could no longer bear being recognised wherever he went. He was surprised that the cheap, gangster-styled wraparound sunglasses he had bought at the local market, combined with a common baseball cap, had proved an effective disguise and given him some respite from the constant invasion of his personal space.

But now he was exposed and in no mood to be polite to anyone. He'd had a frantic phone call this morning from Monique asking him to meet her this afternoon at the Tropicana Café. The urgency in her voice had undoubtedly made Gaston anxious and perhaps complacent in adopting his usual disguise before going out.

Gaston rushed back inside the house and headed towards his bedroom but was drawn into Mario and Bruno's room as he passed by. His brother Mario was there as usual on a Wednesday afternoon, doing the ironing. But something was not so usual about Mario today. He was wearing Gaston's baseball cap and sunglasses, grinning widely and singing along to a hip hop song on the radio. Gaston was pleased with the small rupture in Mario's rigid routine and habits. Not only was he decked out in Gaston's disguise, but he was wearing different, modern “hip hop” styled clothing. (His life of routine had been so rigid that he usually wore the same clothes every week when doing the ironing.)

Mario looked up and smiled, then startled Gaston by singing along to a melody and “toasting” in tune with the rapper's angst-ridden voice blasting out of the radio.

Mario doesn't have a bad voice at all, thought Gaston, before realising that he was in a hurry.

"Hey Mario, take those things off and give them back to me," he had to virtually scream to make himself heard while nonetheless still grinning inside.

Mario stopped singing and turned the music down.

"I didn't know they were yours, Gaston. I found them on the kitchen table," Mario replied.

Gaston suddenly realised that he had had every intention of putting on his disguise before heading out earlier, but a call of nature had distracted him.

"Okay, okay. You look great, bro, just like a real gangsta, but I've got an urgent appointment so get them off," Gaston said.

"I'll get you your own set of shades and a cap if you like. Hey, since when have you been into hip hop?" he asked, contemplating what would be considered a radical change in Mario's life. Gaston couldn't ever remember him taking pleasure from anything like music.

"Wow, thanks, my bro, that would be awesome," Mario replied. "Bruno and I have been getting into this music for some time now. You wouldn't have known, though. You haven't been around much. I mean, I understand and all, but . . . and even when you were, you weren't really here. If you know what I mean?"

Gaston felt suddenly ashamed that he had been so thoroughly self-absorbed since the breakup with Natalie that he hadn't noticed that his little brother had grown up, on quite a few levels, it seemed. Mario was almost as tall as him now, but more importantly Gaston felt instantly heartened seeing the signs that he was emerging from his apartheid-induced shell. He hoped Bruno was following a similar path.

"It's not my kind of music, but I'm so happy that you're getting into it, Mario," Gaston said with much affection.

"Now, give me back my gear. I've got to go."

As Mario took off the cap, Gaston momentarily contemplated sending him out as a decoy, given he was of similar size and build. However, the dark chocolate skin would surely give the game away unless he covered him head to toe.

"What does mum say about all this—you and Bruno turning into hip hop dudes?" Gaston asked.

"Well, she's not too thrilled . . . keeps mentioning stuff about the 'devil's work' and 'how much more suffering can a mother bear'. You know the deal," Mario replied.

"Indeed, I do," Gaston said. "That explains it."

"Explains what, Gaston?" Mario asked.

"She's been complaining of sore knees," Gaston said. "She must be spending a lot of time kneeling in front of the Virgin Mary."

Gaston went over to the side window and peeped out. And sure enough, Harriet was there, kneeling, head bowed, and absorbed in prayer. She was dressed in the black widow's dress she usually wore when praying and tightly clutching her favourite big black rosary beads.

"It's good to share the black sheep in the family duties with my dear brothers at last," a smiling Gaston said, turning around and walking back towards Mario.

"Well, don't let mum get to you, Mario. She loves that martyr role. She'd be lost without it. As for you, my dear brother, I'm so sorry I have been a bit absent recently but I'll make it up to you. Why don't you and Bruno come and visit Patrick and me in Palm Waters one weekend? We'll take you to the local nightclub. It's full of hip-hop-type dudes like you. You'll love it."

"You really would do that, Gaston? Really?" Mario said in a tone of rising excitement.

"Of course, I would. Patrick would be thrilled to see you guys finally coming out of your shells. He could probably even find a couple of girls who'd be keen to meet two handsome, cool dudes like you. He's quite the ladies' man, that Patrick," Gaston said.

"Now, I've got to go. Tell mum I'll be having dinner out tonight and don't say anything about coming to visit me in Palm Waters yet. I'll raise it with her when the time is right."

Gaston living with Patrick was an obvious, almost unspoken move once he had settled into his new job, which was only a short walk from Patrick's flat. Even his mother Harriet had been able to put aside her own emotional anguish of him leaving home once again to acknowledge the logic in that. Patrick, after all, had a spare bedroom in his flat, albeit without a bed, but that issue was easily resolved. Best of all, this time, his flatmate was Patrick, not a woman who had led him down the path of being a sinner, and a mortal sinner at that. She still prayed every day that God would forgive Gaston for a decision that threatened his eternal life in paradise.

Gaston put on his disguise and went to the back door. He peeped outside and saw that the coast was clear. He was almost certain the girls would have given up by now, but he didn't want to take any chances and decided he would make his exit through a rickety old back gate nestled between two huge bamboo hedges which gave onto a smelly lane where residents piled their garbage in makeshift pits that often spilled onto the roadway. Needless to say, the gate and lane were hardly ever used except by garbage collectors.

As he walked towards the gate, he heard footsteps coming down the side of the house on the opposite side to where Harriet was praying.

"Surely it couldn't be the girls," thought Gaston. *"But who else could it be?"*

He instinctively ducked into an outhouse, which contained a squat toilet and bathroom, to hide from the incoming intruders. The ramshackle shed-like structure was constructed largely of corrugated iron and was rarely used these days, although the facilities were still connected and functional.

Gaston chuckled as he looked at the plaster wall full of holes that separated the bathroom section from the toilet where he was now waiting for the danger to pass.

Even when the outhouse was relatively new, the wall had holes in it and as a young boy, Gaston one day found himself in the toilet when a visiting young aunty went into the bathroom to have a shower. Being in the midst of the awakening sexuality of adolescence, Gaston couldn't resist peering through a hole and watching his curvaceous aunty take a shower. It was the first time he had seen a woman fully naked, and he was naturally very aroused.

"And what a lovely moment that was!" he muttered to himself as he had a vivid flashback to the aunty lathering and washing herself.

That was only a few weeks after he had been sexually initiated courtesy of Victoria, and the two episodes delivered him a masturbation muse that in his ensuing teenage years pleasingly reduced the frequency of his nocturnal emissions.

Immersed in a sexual fantasy, Gaston found that he was now getting an erection which, in turn, fuelled a memory of a strange advertisement he once saw in a soft porn magazine for an underwear brand called "Stiffies". The underwear allegedly featured an "erection direction" pocket which could conceal the embarrassment of an erection when in public, the ad had claimed.

He stifled another chuckle.

What an absurd idea, although such underwear would be handy in certain situations, he thought as the bulge in his pants grew and he had a vision of the building around him suddenly collapsing and finding himself confronted by his mother.

Gaston heard voices chatting outside, getting closer and therefore louder, which distracted him from this random and bizarre train of thought and into a reality where he was going to be late to meet Monique if he didn't get a move on.

Surprisingly to Gaston, they were male voices so he felt safe to push the door ajar slightly and peep outside. It was the gardener who, Gaston suddenly remembered, came around every Wednesday. He was chatting to a young assistant. Both were dressed in grubby khaki matching shirts and trousers and carrying various gardening tools.

Gaston flushed the toilet and stepped outside, greeting the two gardeners before heading out the back gate, holding his breath and breaking into a light jog.

CHAPTER XLIII

Déjà Vu at the Tropicana

"We think Henri Laroche committed suicide."

Gaston had no hesitation in his response to the same question that Father Pierrot had asked of Monique a day earlier.

In a scene reminiscent of the meeting following Henri's funeral a few weeks before, Gaston, Patrick, and Monique were hunched over a small circular table and speaking in hushed tones as far away as possible from the bar at the Tropicana Café in the cacophonous midst of happy hour.

But this time, Idris was absent due to yet another family drama involving his cousin Mariel, who had been in and out of mental institutions since being sexually abused as a teenager. Yet another unsuccessful suicide attempt meant she was about to once again enter an "in" phase of her roller coaster ride with mental illness.

In the chair Idris had occupied was Father Pierrot, who greeted Patrick and Gaston warmly, like two long-lost friends, and wasted little time in broaching the subject of Henri's death.

"How do you know this, Gaston?" Father Pierrot asked.

"Well, of course, we don't know for sure, but we have evidence to suggest that suicide was the most likely cause of Henri's death. And we think he was sexually abused by Father Terry, and maybe other priests, and this was what led him to take his own life," Gaston said.

Once again, Gaston found himself delving into a recent past he'd rather forget and relating to Father Pierrot the story of his brief encounter with a visibly distressed Henri emerging from Father Terry's confessional a week before his death and the bloodstained altar boy robe he had subsequently found in the church toilet block.

Naturally, Father Pierrot asked Gaston how he and his mother came to be at the church at a time that was outside normal church "business hours", and Gaston felt compelled to revisit the shame of his foolish drunken behaviour and the resulting arrest by the Finger Bay police.

Father Pierrot listened attentively, stroking his beardless chin and clearly making no moral judgment on Gaston's misdemeanours. He was only interested in establishing the facts surrounding Henri's death and investigating allegations of sexual abuse by the Finger Bay fathers. And Gaston was finally providing him with some shreds of evidence he had been seeking to justify his journey to the other side of the world.

Admittedly, the bloodied altar boy robe in the toilet wasn't conclusive proof of sexual abuse, nor was the sordid tale of Father Terry masturbating in the confessional, which almost made him choke on a half-swallowed mouthful of Fanta.

Gaston's lucky escape as a novice altar boy from the depraved clutches of Father Orton and the subsequent cover-up was also revolting, but another layer of circumstantial evidence. Surely none of the witnesses to these events would testify in an official church investigation, let alone a court of law—not even Gaston's mother, it seemed.

Father Pierrot still needed a "smoking gun".

"This is a good start, Gaston. If what you're telling me did indeed happen, and I have no reason to doubt you, then Father Terry and God knows who else—"

Father Pierrot realised he'd blasphemed, which caused him to pause and look up to the ceiling as if asking God for forgiveness before continuing.

Father Pierrot paused and blessed himself.

"Err . . . sorry. That happens when I get frustrated."

"What happens, Father?" Gaston asked

"Never mind," he replied.

"As I was saying, if Father Terry and the other priests sexually abused Henri and caused him to commit suicide, then they're heinous criminals, Gaston, but we just don't have the proof we need to convict them yet.

"So why didn't you report all these events to the police, who could then have investigated and turned up the evidence we're looking for?"

Gaston and Patrick fleetingly looked at each other in recognition that Father Pierrot was a relative newcomer to the island culture.

"I'm afraid our police are not much better than the priests when it comes to corruption and possibly criminal behaviour," Patrick chimed in.

"We think some of them know what's going on but turn a blind eye to it. Who knows, they may even be getting a kickback for looking the other way. The priests make a heap of money by renting out the church pews for their masses. All unofficial, of course. Haven't you noticed that the same people sit in the same pews week in, week out? That's no coincidence."

"I did think it was a bit odd, but then again, I just assumed people in this part of the world were even more creatures of habit than we are in Europe. That's outrageous," Father Pierrot said.

"Looks like I've got my work cut out," he muttered under his breath, then sighed heavily before continuing.

"All right, I'll have to investigate that as well, but of course, it's more urgent we get to the truth behind Henri's death. Think, my friends. Is there anything else, anything, any minor detail that could be more significant than you think?"

The table fell silent. Gaston and Monique furrowed their brows simultaneously as they raked over the detail of their respective recent encounters with the Finger Bay fathers. Gaston winced as he also had a flashback to Sergeant Cailason and the fear he had felt during the confrontation with him at the police station.

But nothing new emerged, and Gaston was the first to break the silence.

"Sorry, Father, I'm probably the one that's had the most to do with them, but really apart from what I've already told you, I really can't think of anything else."

"How about you, Monique? You've been working in the kitchen there for a while . . ." Father Pierrot said, a desperate tone in his voice.

"I've been there about a year, but I'm afraid I can't help either, Father. I rarely venture outside the kitchen and certainly didn't know anything about their disgusting behaviour until I spoke to Gaston at Henri's funeral," she said.

"As I said to Gaston, I did hear some funny noises now and then, which they told me was the television and that seemed perfectly reasonable. I'm not one to pry. I do my job and go straight home after.

"As you may have noticed, Father, since I found out what's been going on, I've been treading on eggshells around everyone except you."

With the table once again falling silent, Patrick decided it was time to let Father Pierrot in on their secret plan to stop the sexual abuse by "castrating" the priests.

Before coming to the Tropicana Café, Gaston, Patrick and Monique had met briefly at Monique's house, where she had revealed the details of Father Pierrot's mission. They had then decided that they would, at some stage, also come clean and tell Father Pierrot that they were lacing the priests' food with libido-reducing herbs.

"I understand your frustration, and we all felt really angry that they were getting away with this. In the end, the only thing we did come up with was a way of making them stop abusing the boys," Patrick said.

"Uh oh," Father Pierrot exclaimed.

"We've, or should I say, Monique has started putting some natural herbs in your food that reduces sex drive," he said.

"But rest assured, Father, she only started doing that yesterday, so you've really only had a couple of meals with the herbs in them. And now that we know what you're doing here, we'll make sure that Monique keeps food without the herbs aside for you."

"What? What sort of herbs are we talking about?" Father Pierrot said, somewhat alarmed.

Patrick immediately moved to reassure him.

"Don't worry, Father, I've thoroughly researched the herbs and they don't have any side effects, and as I said, you've only had a very small exposure to it, and if you say so, we'll stop doing it," he said.

"We were so upset by Henri's death, we *had* to do something, and do something quickly, to stop the abuse," Gaston chimed in.

Father Pierrot remained silent while contemplating what had just been revealed to him.

"It's okay, my friends. Certainly out of left field, but I am intrigued. So, Patrick, you say you've researched this and it works?"

"Well, some people think it doesn't, but overall, I found a lot more people who say it does and I was even told that some priests in Australia voluntarily took the herbs to lower their sex drive," Patrick said.

Again, Father Pierrot took a few moments before responding. He stared blankly ahead in a trance-like state of deep thought. Finally, he seemed to have a lightbulb moment, muttering something under his breath before breaking out in a cheeky smile.

"Well, well, well, my friends, this could be just the thing we're looking for to stop all this vile abuse," he finally said.

So many questions swirled in his head and when he managed to organise his thoughts, they came out like a burst of rapid machine-gun fire.

"Tell me more, Patrick. What are these herbs? Are they easy to get? Are they cheap?"

Little did Father Pierrot realise at the time that the conversation had taken an unexpected twist that would radically alter the course of his life.

CHAPTER XLIV

Anatole's Dance with the Devil

It would only be seven years later, as two naked "mermaids" were encircling his luxury jungle-style swimming pool and taking turns in performing fellatio while he reclined naked and spreadeagled on the pool steps, that Anatole Courtois, private and reclusive citizen of Terre de Bas on the Caribbean island of Guadeloupe, for the first time reflected on that defining moment at the Tropicana Café.

The most devout of Christians had changed his name and become a heathen, hedonist, and high net worth individual, as the US newspapers referred to him, even though no one in the media in recent times had been able to track down and talk to the reclusive chief executive officer (CEO) of Herbs R Us Pty Ltd.

And that conversation at the Tropicana had been the catalyst to his life taking a dramatic U-turn, hurtling him towards "the flames of Hell", his distraught parents would say of the son that they had had no option but to disown.

Following his return to the Vatican only six months after the Tropicana meeting, Father Pierrot was able to persuade the Pope to mandate the use of libido-reducing herbs in the diets of Catholic presbyteries around the world. This was even before there was any conclusive proof of their effectiveness in reining in the depravity of the Finger Bay fathers. Naturally, it was to be a top-secret operation with only the inner circle of the papacy in the know and trusted to put the plan into action.

To further deflect media or public scrutiny and minimise the risk of any link to the Catholic church, the Pope convinced Father Pierrot to leave the priesthood and take charge of the operation as a "civilian". Although reluctant at first, he could see the logic in this, and in any case, he hadn't been working as a conventional priest for some time.

The change of name was an extra precaution, and as Anatole Courtois, he formed and became CEO of Herbs R Us, which quickly cornered the world market on libido-reducing herbs. The sudden surge in demand for these herbs naturally created a scarcity in supply that sent the stock price of Herbs R Us soaring, making Anatole a small fortune in the process. Investors worldwide clambered for a share of the stock while scratching their heads trying to work out who was snapping up every ounce of the stock available and then demanding even more.

To further douse public or media suspicion, the company sold other medicinal herbs as well, but naturally not in anywhere near the same quantities as the libido-reducing variety.

Anatole moved back to France, but not to his old hometown. He set himself up in a luxury apartment befitting of a CEO of one of the fastest-growing and increasingly profitable companies in the world. Located in the Latin Quarter, the panoramic views of Ile de la Cite and Notre Dame through the large picture windows were an obvious drawcard to a man still devoted to his Catholic faith at the time of purchase.

But unleashed from the restrictions of clergy life, Anatole soon found himself calling his faith into question as the lure of material wealth became irresistible. Slowly, he was drawn into a hedonistic Parisienne social scene, initially through the demands of business, but soon attracted to the advances of the many beautiful women who attempted to work their way into sharing the lavish lifestyle of a still handsome bachelor and unlocking a libido that, unknown to them, had been closeted since his teenage years.

Anatole resisted for some time, still clinging to his long-held vow of celibacy until he locked eyes with the beautiful Jeanne de Buissy at a party to launch a new stock offering for the company soaring to even greater heights on the Paris Bourse.

She was so different from any woman he had ever met. She was eroticism personified. A brunette with thick shoulder-length wavy hair, make-up free, olive complexion bar for lipstick of an exquisite shade of red, which set off her deep blue eyes.

After the second date, they were locking lips and, after the third, locking limbs on the lounge room carpet with the gargoyles of Notre Dame looking on in displeasure at his libido being snapped off the leash. The sexual ecstasy experienced by Anatole by a woman obviously well versed in pleasuring a man only served to convince him further that priests needed the libido-reducing herbs to eliminate the risk of sexual abuse and misadventure. After all, how could anyone resist the sexual allure of women like Jeanne?

Anatole was soon in love. Or was it lust? Both were strangers to his emotional repertoire, so it was naturally difficult for him to discern between the two at first.

What he did know for sure was that with Jeanne he experienced a happiness that he had never felt as a man of the cloth. He felt absolutely no remorse, guilt, or sense of sinning. That did surprise him, as did, ironically, a conviction that he was continuing to serve the Catholic faith through his leading role in the Vatican's secret operation, which those in the inner circle had unofficially dubbed the "ball breaker" project.

Within weeks, Anatole was in a perpetual state of bliss when he was with Jeanne and gloom when he wasn't, which led him to conclude that he was indeed in love. And compounding his joy was the fact that Jeanne gave every indication that she reciprocated the feeling. He tried to imagine how he would feel if he were to lose her, and the immediate emotion to surface was one of intense grief. So, his next move was to minimise the grief and gloom by having her move in with him.

Before doing so, he perhaps should have pondered more on why such an intelligent, beautiful woman, in her mid-thirties, with a seemingly sunny disposition had yet to attract a life partner. In fact, she had confessed to Anatole that he had been her longest romantic relationship to date; "six whole months" she'd shrieked in wishing him a happy anniversary and popping a bottle of vintage Krug in celebration.

He really should have taken more time before plunging into the deep end, he was thinking, as he blankly watched mermaid number one swim towards him. She had a mischievous grin on her face, in contrast to the tears that were rolling down his cheeks. Not that she noticed as she "professionally" honed in on his penis.

He was indifferent to the physical pleasure she was bringing him, his mood still occupying the more solemn emotional space that had been the norm since that fateful day his life emotionally ended.

The wrath of God, no doubt! he had thought over and over again. *How else do you explain a life that plummets from heavenly highs to the depths of total emotional despair within the few seconds it takes to open a door?*

Bliss had continued to bless their relationship for nearly six months after Jeanne waltzed into his apartment resplendent in a casual red dress and declared excitedly that this would be the "first day together of happily ever after".

It was an unusually long time for Jeanne to experience such a bipolar high that falsely led her to believe she had conquered the debilitating disorder that had plagued her life. She had been able to manage the extreme highs and lows through medication since diagnosis in her late teenage years, but nonetheless, life had continued to be an emotional roller coaster characterised mostly by detachment at the peaks and bouts of manageable depression in the troughs. She would also experience moments of extreme highs where she felt she could conquer the world, but they never lasted that long.

Her relationship with Anatole had somehow engendered an extreme high that showed no sign of abating. She became convinced that as long as they remained together, she would be emotionally stable. He was the medication she had been seeking all her life, so she decided one day that she no longer needed the synthetic variety. The side effects—dizziness, nausea, migraines—could sometimes be just as bad as the extreme lows.

Love could conquer all, she'd heard. Even bipolar disorder, it seemed. Overwhelmed with joy and laughing hysterically (which should have been a warning sign), Jeanne ceremoniously dumped her medication in the Seine, her only concern being that it might poison the fish, which she heard had come back in great numbers in recent years. Once despatched, she stopped laughing, made a sign of the cross, and whispered a prayer as she looked up to the twin towers of Notre Dame baking in the late afternoon sun.

It didn't take long for the roller coaster to top the rise and plunge into the inevitable downward spiral. The most extreme of highs could only be followed by the most extreme of lows.

Only two weeks later, Anatole was climbing the stairs to their apartment when he felt an eerie chill, even though Paris was sweating under the influence of unusually high humidity. The sense of foreboding intensified with every step, causing Anatole to break out in a cold sweat as his trembling hand fiddled open the apartment door. The lifeless body of Jeanne hung at the end of a rope she'd ingeniously attached to the sturdy chandelier. She was framed in almost perfect symmetry by the large floor-to-ceiling window designed to extract maximum value from the view of the magnificent structures of the Ile de la Cite. She had a good sense of the aesthetic, even in death.

Shock paralysed Anatole. He just stood there looking at her still beautiful face draped in wild wisps of hair. The tears did not arrive for some time and when they did, he simply slumped into an armchair and howled in grief. He buried his face in his hands, but they did little to arrest the sobbing.

When he looked up again, he had a vision of a gleeful devil, horns glowing bright yellow. It hovered above Jeanne and swung around the rope, dancing on her head like a playful child in a park. Anatole closed his eyes but the image of the devil permeated the darkness.

Several years of tears while merely existing on emotional autopilot culminated in Anatole's self-imposed "exile" to Guadeloupe. Grief, by then, had thankfully given way to numbness as his default emotion.

By that time, the public hadn't even noticed that media reports of sexual abuse by Catholic clergy had reduced to a trickle, the fruitful legacy of a plan concocted at the Tropicana Café seven years before.

He would never have met Jeanne if it hadn't been for the chain of events set off by the meeting at the Tropicana.

As he reached the verge of orgasm courtesy of mermaid number two's luscious lips, his thoughts drifted away from the indifferent pleasure he was about to feel to the priest who had been brimming with optimism as he left the café.

CHAPTER XLV

The Button

The room had been left untouched since his death, apart from the odd incursion when she'd had a bit too much rum. The unrelenting grief blended with alcohol on one occasion to fuel a rummaging frenzy through Henri's drawers. She tossed everything out haphazardly between gut-wrenching sobs and uncovered a padlocked metal toolbox that made her gasp in dread. Henri had painted the box in army camouflage and tucked it away in the corner of the bottom drawer. Almost hysterical, she clawed at the sturdy metal padlock with her bare hands, trying to prize it open before some semblance of sanity prevailed that steered her to her husband's work shed. The pliers worked a treat, but the fleeting moment of triumph gave way to a shriek of sheer horror when she saw the drawings.

A month later, Henri's mother Josiane, still raw with grief, opened the front door to greet Father Pierrot, who had a copy of the very same drawings in his bag. He had left the meeting at the Tropicana feeling quite buoyant, thinking he had the final solution to the sexual abuse crisis plaguing the Catholic clergy around the globe. He had even muttered the words "final solution" a couple of times as he walked out of the café, then immediately chided himself for even thinking of an expression associated with one of history's worst mass murderers.

But his relatively good humour instantly evaporated in the aura of a woman dressed in regulation mourning black and clutching a handkerchief, a woman who was merely existing, her face gaunt, her demeanour broken.

"I hope I'm not intruding, Mrs. Laroche. I'm Father Pierrot, a Vatican investigator. It's because of your French cousin Henri that I am here," Father Pierrot said.

The mention of the name "Henri" made Josiane flinch. She opened her mouth to reply but nothing came out.

"I am so, so sorry for your loss, Madame; it must be the most awful thing . . . err . . . and I in no way wish to add to your grief," Father Pierrot said, he too struggling for appropriate words.

"Thank you, Father," Josiane said, finally finding a voice, albeit a subdued one crackling with sorrow.

"I have been expecting your visit. Hen . . . err . . . my cousin said an investigator would be coming to see me. Please come in."

Josiane led him into the lounge room, where a ceiling fan was whirring wildly, keeping the space refreshingly cool compared with the rest of the house. The room was sparsely furnished and the walls were bare, although showing evidence of recent wall hangings. Large square patches in the middle of three walls were cleaner and paler in colour than the rest of the wall surfaces.

The day after she had discovered Henri's ghastly drawings, Josiane ripped her most beloved artworks—a painting of Jesus Christ, one of the Pope, and a tapestry depicting the Last Supper—off the walls and shredded them with her dressmaker scissors. Her husband arrived home from work to find her on her knees, sobbing hysterically in the backyard while watching the remnants of the artworks go up in flames.

"Would you like a cup of tea, father?" Josiane said as Father Pierrot sat down in an armchair covered in a fabric patterned with bright red flowers set against a cream background. It looked out of place among the otherwise sombre old, dark wooden furnishings.

"No, thank you, madame. I won't keep you long," he replied.

"Please, Father, call me Josiane, and really there's no need to rush. I'm very pleased you've come. I really want to know the truth behind what happened to Henri even if it causes me great pain. It can't have been an accident. He's never been a risk-taker," she said, using her handkerchief to mop the inevitable tear or two.

"I'm sorry, Father. I wouldn't wish this on my worst enemy."

"No need to apologise, madame . . . err . . . Josiane . . ." Father Pierrot said before being once again lost for words and creating an awkward silence punctuated only by the sound of Josiane sniffling while trying to rein in her tears.

"Are you sure about the tea? It's really no trouble at all," Josiane said.

"I'm sure. I just had some at the Tropicana, and really, we should get on with hopefully finding some answers for you," he said.

"Now, I know this will be difficult, but I need you to tell me all about Henri and the lead-up to his death. Was there anything different about him? Did he change in some way?

"Given the nature of the drawings you sent and my investigations so far, I believe that one or maybe more of the Finger Bay priests may have abused Henri in some way before his death. I'm sorry to have to tell you that, Josiane, but I'm sure it's no surprise."

Josiane could no longer contain a sob and a trickle of tears called the handkerchief into action. She cleared her throat and composed herself.

"Well, he was a timid child, Father, and spent a lot of his time in his room—drawing mainly. He loved doing that. He was an only child, so we didn't think it was that unusual for him to spend so much time on his own.

"The one thing that was unusual was a couple of days before the . . ." Josiane's voice started crackling and she paused.

"Well, Henri was due to serve at mass a couple of days before his . . . well, I couldn't find his altar boy robes. He said that one of the priests had kept his old robe and told him he'd be getting a new one, and sure enough, he was given another when he went in that night for mass. The surprising thing was that it was a robe that looked older and in worse condition than the one he had before. I remember that well because it had a tear in it that I had to mend."

"That's interesting, very interesting," Father Pierrot said. "You see, someone who was at the church that day saw Henri coming out of the confessional and running out of the church looking rather distressed. Some moments later, that same man happened to go to the church toilet and noticed a discarded altar boy robe with a red stain. He was sure it was blood. Unfortunately, he left it there. He was wrestling with some personal problems and didn't want to get involved. He did, however, go back to the toilet later that day but the robe was gone."

Josiane gasped, and once again, the tears flowed.

"I'm truly very sorry to put you through this, Josiane, but this is all very important to my investigation. Would you mind if I had a look at Henri's room?"

Father Pierrot was sure Henri's room would have been left largely intact since his death. He had read case studies of children dying tragically and the grieving parents leaving their rooms untouched for many months, even years afterwards.

Josiane could only nod her consent before getting up and showing Father Pierrot to Henri's room which, as expected, was still set up in anticipation of Henri walking through the front door sometime today. Josiane's frenzied alcohol-fuelled rummage through Henri's drawers that had uncovered the drawings had been the only disruption to the room.

"Do you mind if I look through Henri's things?" Father Pierrot said.

"Of course not, Father," Josiane replied.

Father Pierrot started looking through Henri's drawers while Josiane just stood by the door leaning against the wall, staring at him but not seeing until she suddenly spotted a gold button on top of the chest of drawers.

How have I not noticed that before? she thought, even though she had no idea what relevance it would have until she looked at Father Pierrot's cassock that sported the very same buttons. Father Pierrot didn't usually wear a cassock when out in public or visiting parishioners. But he hadn't had time to change after celebrating mass in the morning. He had to rush to a series of meetings, including the rendezvous with Gaston and Monique at the Tropicana Café.

Josiane walked over to the chest of drawers and picked up the button and examined it as if hoping it was a clue to the answer she was seeking. Father Pierrot was focused on the items in the drawers and only felt Josiane's presence approach him. When he finally looked up from his foraging of the bottom and final drawer, he saw Josiane still looking at the button.

"What have you got there?" Father Pierrot asked.

He stood up and, when she nodded her consent, took the button from her hand.

"Standard cassock button," he said. "I imagine Henri would have picked it up at the church or presbytery. They're always getting caught in things and falling off. I don't think it's anything that can help us, unfortunately."

"Yes, yes, you're probably right, Father," she said. "Funny though, I've been in this room so many times since, you know, but I'd never noticed it before. Just thought it was a bit odd."

Father Pierrot put the button back on the chest of drawers and Josiane unconsciously picked it up again and held it tightly in her hand.

"Well, I can't see anything else here that could help us," Father Pierrot said after scouring Henri's wardrobe and a quick look under his bed.

"The drawings are the best bit of evidence we have, but that's not definitive proof of any wrongdoing by the priests, and it'd be impossible convicting anyone on that evidence."

They walked out of the room in silence.

"Thank you so very much, Josiane. I've taken up enough of your time," he said.

As they approached the front door, Father Pierrot took a business card out of his pocket.

"I know this is so difficult for you, but if you come across anything else or hear anything, please don't hesitate to call me—or if you just need someone to talk to," he said, handing her the card.

"Thank you, Father, and I will," she said.

As she closed the door behind him and turned to walk back inside, she suddenly remembered one of Henri's drawings that prominently featured a priest who had lifted his cassock to be "pleasured" by a faceless young boy. And she was sure the cassock had a button missing.

Sobbing once again, she rushed back to the bedroom and dug out the drawings she had kept in a sealed box. She quickly found the one she was looking for and her hunch was right. The cassock had a button missing, and she also hadn't noticed before that the priest bore a striking resemblance to Father Terry.

CHAPTER XLVI

The Banana Peel in the Belfry

Despite taking a couple of sleeping pills that technically induced slumber, Josiane woke up feeling like she hadn't slept at all. That had been the norm since Henri's death, but this morning she woke up with a suffocating anger to add to her usual heavy heart, lethargy, and deep depression.

She hadn't told her husband, Gerard, about the button and the drawing. She had wanted to, but through her grief she couldn't muster the energy and find the words to make her case for the prosecution of Father Terry.

Henri and his father had never been close. Gerard thought his son was a "mama's boy", weak and weird. He couldn't understand how Henri could be the product of his loins. Gerard was a "man's man" and very disappointed that his son wasn't the masculine boy that he had craved. Henri never wanted to wrestle with him as he was growing up. He didn't play sports, hang out with his friends and get into the rough and tumble of a normal boy's life. Henri was an introvert and spent far too much time in his room drawing and *God knows what*, Gerard thought. And when Josiane first showed him Henri's drawings of the priests and boys engaged in sexual activities, it only confirmed Gerard's inkling that his son was a homosexual-in-waiting. He dismissed the drawings as just a reflection of the boy's homosexual tendencies and perverted imagination and not proof of his abuse at the hands of the priests. Although he hated himself for it, some part of Gerard was relieved that his son would never grow up to shame the family.

Like many folks of his generation on the island, Gerard was deeply conservative and religious and would never entertain the thought that a priest could do wrong. Naturally, Josiane was aware of this and realised she faced a near-impossible task, convincing him that she had proof the Finger Bay priests were abusing altar boys.

Father Terry had murdered her son, her "heart and soul". She was sure of that now. And his tragic death had also murdered her will to live.

But as she got out of bed today, she first felt somewhat rejuvenated by the anger. Gerard was long gone, off before dawn to cut cane. The sugar harvest season was in full swing and Gerard was working twelve-hour days.

As she sipped her usual morning coffee, Josiane just couldn't expel from her mind the image of Father Terry's raised cassock and his face writhing in pleasure as a boy performed fellatio on him.

Was that faceless boy Henri?

The thought caused her to gag on her coffee. She had to scamper to the toilet, where she vomited and howled. A torrent of tears followed and persisted as she showered and got dressed in her Sunday best—an elegant maroon suit and silk blouse she hadn't worn for some time. Josiane had not attended mass or gone anywhere near the church since she discovered Henri's drawings.

She put on a hat with a meshed veil to cover her bloodshot, puffy eyes and put the drawing of Father Terry in her handbag. She took some deep breaths to compose herself before heading out to the Finger Bay church. She didn't have a plan except to confront Father Terry with the drawing. She had to do it for her boy. There was no other way.

Josiane had knots in her stomach as she entered the church gates and almost collided with Father Thibault, who was walking out, head bowed.

"Uhh, sorry, madame," he started saying and quickly realised it was Henri's mother.

"Oh, Mrs. Laroche, good to see you again. I am so sorry for your loss. I know it must be a very difficult time for you. But if it's any comfort at all, I'm certain that Henri is now in paradise looking down on us and waiting for you and your family to join him there one day."

"Err . . . that is reassuring. Thank you, Father," Josiane lied, her voice trembling.

"Rest assured, Henri's in our thoughts and prayers every day, and if there's anything we can do for you and your family, anything, please don't hesitate.

"But if you'll excuse me, I have an important meeting with the mayor."

"Yes, of course, I don't want to hold you up. Just one thing before you go, do you know where I may find Father Terry?"

"Yes, I do. He's in the bell tower, about to ring the bells," Father Thibault said.

"I'm sure he'll be pleased to see you. He was devastated by Henri's . . . err . . . accident. He'll have time to see you before he has to celebrate mass. Now, if you'll excuse me."

Josiane headed to the bell tower, a stand-alone, cylindrical structure made of stone and rising some ten metres above the back of the church. Just as she arrived at the open door of the tower, the bells started to chime.

Sweating and shaking, she waited for five minutes after they stopped chiming, but there was no sign of Father Terry descending from the belfry. She couldn't wait any longer.

She entered the tower and heard what she perceived as a moan. She climbed the spiral staircase entwined around a central concrete column that filled the entire narrow structure. As she reached the belfry, she could see Father Terry's slightly hunched back through the bells.

"Father Terry," she called out.

Father Terry took a few moments before turning around to face Josiane, who, by this time, had walked around the bells to be confronted by a startled, dishevelled priest.

"Uh oh, it's you, Mrs. Laroche. What are you doing here? Only members of the clergy are allowed in the belfry, you know. It can be a dangerous place when the bells are ringing," he said, clearly rattled by the intrusion.

"Well, well, I really needed to see you . . ." Josiane started saying but was rendered speechless as her eyes drifted to Father Terry's hands doing up a button of his cassock. It was the buttonhole above the one he had just done that left her dumbstruck. The button was missing.

"I'm sorry, Mrs. Laroche. What is so urgent that it couldn't wait till I came down?" Father Terry said.

Josiane tried to speak but nothing came out. She was numb with rage.

"Well, Mrs. Laroche, I am very, very sorry for your loss, and if I can do anything to help, I certainly will but please wait for me downstairs. I just have a bit of tidying up to do here, then I'll be right down," he said as he gently took hold of her elbow and guided her towards the stairs.

As he approached the top of the stairs, he released his grip and went ahead of Josiane as something on the ground caught his eye.

"This is so frustrating and very annoying, Mrs. Laroche," he said, clearly irritated.

"I've told them so many times not to leave their rubbish in the belfry, especially banana peels. I bet it's Father Pierre. He does it all the time. One of us could have slipped on this and done ourselves a lot of damage."

Up to that point in her life, Josiane had never ever harboured thoughts of criminal intent. But the sight of that missing button melded with the words "slip" and "damage".

Josiane later wouldn't remember gathering up all her forces and pushing Father Terry down the stairs as he bent down to pick up the discarded banana peel.

He tumbled down the steep gradient in almost perfect somersaults that didn't cause too much damage. But as he reached the first bend in the staircase, he went headfirst with a sickening thud into the stone wall, the impact cracking his skull and opening a large gash in his head. His mangled, lifeless body sunk on the stairs, leaving a deep red stain oozing down the wall.

Acting as if on autopilot and drawing on the subconscious experience of watching many television police dramas, Josiane used her handkerchief to pick up the banana peel. She then calmly walked down to Father Terry's body and smeared the peel on the heel of his shoe.

CHAPTER XLVII

Dinner Serves up Lobster, Hope, & Politics

The doorbell chimed.

Solange froze, an earring in her hand.

"I'll get it, darling," Tom called from the kitchen where he was overseeing final preparations for dinner. He'd managed to get his hands on some freshly caught, gargantuan lobsters the Indian cook was about to pop into a huge pot of boiling water after they were put to eternal sleep in the freezer.

Solange was relieved. She wanted to make a grand entrance and she wasn't quite ready. She had a soupcon of eye makeup still to apply and lipstick to re-apply.

Her hair was in a bun. She had considered leaving it loose and flowing. That definitely would have made her more alluring, but she didn't want to make her desire for Gaston any more obvious. The bun was also the best option for flaunting her favourite earrings, an Indian-style gold pendant pair sprinkled with dazzling, genuine red rubies that matched her cherry-red lipstick and provided an aesthetically sparkling contrast to her fair complexion and blue eyes. She loved the earrings; despite the fact they were a gift from Tom.

As she sat looking at her reflection in her mirror, doubt once again muddled her reasoning, as it had repeatedly since Gaston accepted the invitation to dinner. Would the desire she felt for him be reciprocated? And even if it were, would he be willing and able to help her escape this emotional mess of her own making?

She felt she'd been given a sliver of hope when Tom announced the night before that both Gaston and Patrick had not taken up the offer of a plus one and would both be "flying solo" for dinner. While this didn't guarantee that Gaston didn't have a girlfriend, Solange intuitively sensed it was the case.

It had been a long time since she'd gone to such an effort to dress up for a man, and she was hoping Tom wouldn't notice and continue to be the inattentive narcissist he'd been ever since he claimed his "trophy bride". To further ensure she didn't arouse any suspicion, however, Solange had asked him to help her choose an appropriate dress for dinner. Thankfully, he picked one of three she was considering herself—an elegant but simple, knee-length white dress patterned with tasteful Hibiscus prints that offered a titillating hint of her ample bosom and hugged her in all the right places.

She couldn't remember any occasion where she'd been excited and motivated to dress as seductively for Tom, even on the first few dates when she was still convinced he was her Prince Charming. There was a brief time she had been in lust with Tom, and as the thought of this spawned an image of him lying on top of her naked, she felt a touch nauseous. She gratefully found relief in a silent burp and a recasting of the lover in her sexual daydream. As she touched up her lipstick, the image of Tom had been replaced by Gaston, and this time, she was on top, grinding away slowly and relishing the sensation of her juices satiating his loins. She could feel her pulse quickening and sexual arousal brewing. It was yet another sensation she hadn't experienced for some time.

Solange was still a virgin, but that was more a consequence of a Catholic upbringing, fear of her father, and most pointedly, a dearth of sexually desirable boys rather than a lack of sexual appetite or desire. She had been masturbating since awakening sexually in her early teens, encouraged by a free-spirited mum who had even secretly gifted her a vibrator when she turned eighteen. Solange had put the sex toy to good use but rarely used Tom as her masturbation muse. Perhaps a few times in the very early days, but even then, it was a more stylised version, an avatar of Tom, really. Any lust for him had evaporated very quickly. She was certain it would be different with Gaston. *Maybe after tonight.* A mischievous smile breached her face.

I'll have to change my knickers if this train of thought continues! Her smile broadened.

A final flick with the mascara wand and Solange was ready. She stood up and walked over to the body-length mirror. She smiled at the reflection, staring back at her before twirling around to inspect the back of her dress and heading out into the hallway that led to the front reception room. To her surprise, she found Patrick alone engaging in small talk with Tom. Her broad warm smile subconsciously adjusted to lukewarm and she wanted to scream, *Where the hell is Gaston?* But Tom, turning away from Patrick to greet her, seemed to read her mind.

"Gaston's been held up at the office on an urgent matter, darling, and he should be here shortly," he said.

Patrick extended his hand to Solange, expecting a handshake but Solange instinctively kissed him on both cheeks as per the island custom.

"Gaston being late gave me the opportunity to solve the mystery," Tom said as he took Solange's hand and surprised her by kissing it and then holding onto it with a firmer than usual grip, seemingly to keep her by his side.

The gesture made Solange think that Tom maybe was a touch jealous and wanted to make sure that Patrick knew she was taken. After all, he was a very handsome man. *Almost as handsome as Gaston . . . but not quite,* Solange thought.

The hand-kissing also distracted Solange from what Tom had initially said, but suddenly she realised she had no idea what he was talking about.

"What mystery, darling?" she asked.

"Patrick's accent," Tom replied excitedly. "You don't hear too many Australian accents around here. When you've been out of the country for a while, Patrick's Australian accent really stood out, even sounded more 'strayan' than a true-blue Aussie."

"What's 'strayan' mean, Tom? And what's an Aussie?" Solange asked.

"Sorry darling, strayan is just how some Aussies, that is, Australians, pronounce Australian. Anyway, it turns out Patrick lived in Australia for quite some time and was even a bit of a celebrity there.

"Well, ain't life full of surprises? I remember all that palaver over that series of the *Chef Rules OK!* Not that I watched the show. Don't have much time for that reality TV crap, but it was all over the papers. I didn't realise it was you with that judge. *Wow,* mate, she was a bit of a babe; you lucky dog, you. I bet she gave you a ride to remember," Tom said, grinning and winking at Patrick.

He released his grip on Solange and gave Patrick a gentle poke in the ribs with his elbow. Even though Solange couldn't understand all Tom was saying, it was clear the conversation had turned sleazy, which was making Patrick visibly uncomfortable.

"Have you offered Patrick a drink, Tom?" she said.

Solange's attempt to change the subject didn't register with Tom, who ploughed on.

"Yep, no doubt about it, she would have been worth all that scandal. And even more surprising, darling, Patrick went into politics after that. He was just about to tell me about his time as a councillor. They do important work, those guys. Most Aussies . . . err . . . Australians don't realise the power local councils have over their lives, so often you get these radical nutters elected to councils.

"A mate of mine in Queensland told me about some crazy communist councillor who wanted to pass a local law that would have everyone earning the same wage no matter what job they did. Can you imagine? How bloody absurd is that?

"The guy's fucking loony tunes, obviously. Pardon the French," Tom continued, obviously enjoying his monologue and seemingly oblivious to a squirming Patrick and his disinterested fiancé.

"But how did this crazy idiot ever become a councillor? That's what I'm saying about people not caring about who gets into council. Who would ever have elected a bloke who's as mad as a cut snake? You know what I mean? Don't you agree, Patrick?"

A vivid shade of red was seeping through Patrick's coffee-coloured skin and he could only manage muffled agreement while looking away at the front door in the hope of salvation.

"Now, Patrick, what council were you on?" Tom asked.

"Oh, it was . . . err . . . hum . . ." a visibly embarrassed Patrick began to answer, still looking away, then cleared his throat before continuing.

"Err . . . it was a small council . . . err . . . in western . . ."

The discordant sound of the door chimes thankfully drowned out the rest of Patrick's response, the synthesised melody floundering in its attempt to echo a popular tune from the island's African musical tradition. At the same time, it caused Solange to take a sharp intake of breath and her heart rate to surge.

Oh my God, he's here! she thought, smiling inside.

"I'll get it, darling," Tom said.

Solange was once again grateful. She couldn't move, paralysed in anticipation. She bowed her head and closed her eyes momentarily.

When she opened them again and half looked up, a splendid bouquet of flowers was on approach and dominating her vision. It had gerberas blended with chrysanthemums, her favourite anthuriums and speckled with red and white roses. And offering her the bouquet stood a beaming Gaston. He was even more handsome than she had remembered. He was looking directly into her eyes, instantly dissolving any doubt in her mind she had found her "saviour".

Like Patrick, Gaston was smartly dressed in a dark blue suit but no tie. He naturally had wanted to make the best possible impression, not only with Solange but also with his boss. And compliments were in abundance every time he wore a suit.

"These are for you, Miss . . . err . . ." Gaston started saying before realising he didn't know Solange's surname. He certainly didn't want to risk causing her any offence by being overfamiliar and using her "beautiful" first name.

Tom immediately picked up on Gaston's awkward moment.

"It's Solange," he said. "No formalities here, mate. You're not at work, so relax."

Solange was surprised but also relieved by Tom's unusually convivial manner in welcoming Gaston. He surely wouldn't be so jovial if he was jealous or had any inkling of her desire for Gaston.

"I think we're paying Gaston too much, darling. Those flowers would have cost a packet. Not many of my workers can afford that," Tom said jokingly.

But Gaston didn't quite get the joke and went on the defensive.

"I have some contacts, Mr. Wright, so really, I didn't spend too much," he said.

"I'm only kidding, Gaston. You've been doing some great work for us and you deserve to be paid well. And please, as I said, you're off duty, mate, so call me Tom."

"Thank you . . . err . . . Tom," Gaston said shyly.

"No problems, mate, but you are showing me up looking so stylish in that snazzy suit," Tom said jovially.

"Can you please at least remove your jacket? You too, Patrick, and save me some embarrassment?"

Gaston this time did get Tom's intended jocularity. But he and Patrick also wasted no time in removing their jackets. Their brows were bathed in sweat, even in the air-conditioned room where the stifling humidity was still in control of the climatic conditions. A maid seemed to magically appear to relieve them of their jackets and hung them on the ornate coat rack in the hallway.

"I hope I've caused no offence in dressing up, and I hope I haven't offended your charming fiancé by bringing the flowers," Gaston said. "My mother thought it would be the right thing to do."

Gaston thought he probably shouldn't have mentioned his mother, who had indeed suggested the flowers. Then again, the mention of "mother" would help remove any suspicion that the flowers were an expression of his desire for Solange.

When he had bought the bouquet, he was indeed a lover buying them for his beloved and her alone. But he also made sure the local florist, a friend of the family, helped him arrange a bouquet that gave only a hint of his romantic intent with the roses.

He needn't have bothered. Tom was oblivious—ignorant even—to material expressions of romantic intent. He did shower Solange with gifts and, indeed, flowers when they were courting, but he had been working to a systematic, deliberate plan. The gift-giving binge was not driven by emotional desire, but purely designed to secure Solange's hand in marriage.

"Well, you're certainly looking much better than the last time I saw you," Gaston said still timidly, turning once more to Solange.

With his eyes again trained on her, she struggled to contain her joy, but managed to constrain it within a smile.

"Offended! Are you kidding me? The flowers are divine and surely your way of saying that you've come to rescue me from this hell hole. Just shoot these people—well, maybe drug your friend—and kiss me, you fool!" she wanted to scream out.

Instead, a polite, "thank you, Gaston, they're lovely", was all she could muster before once more bowing her head slightly to avoid a gaze that simply made her melt. She took the flowers gently from Gaston, and her fingers instinctively lingered and stretched to get the faintest touch of his. The touch was enough to make her swoon inside and send her imagination wandering once more into a zone of romantic desire.

Imagine those fingers caressing my body, she thought.

When she looked up again, Gaston gave her a wink that caused her to smile and blush at the same time. They were locked in an imagined embrace, like awkward love-struck teenagers.

She wondered if Tom had noticed.

He hadn't. Tom wasn't even in the room but had gone once again to answer the front door. Solange had been so absorbed in her flirtation with Gaston that she hadn't noticed the doorbell chime.

Patrick had wandered over to the glass sliding doors that gave onto a balcony and its panoramic views of the Palm Waters lagoon. He was alternating his gaze between a table on the balcony that had been lavishly set for dinner below shade sails glistening in the rays of the setting sun, and the lagoon rapidly shedding its exquisite turquoise colour as the light faded. He was hoping that the humiliation on the council floor and his subsequent exile from Australia wouldn't be revisited over dinner. He was still proud of what he had tried to achieve and continued to have faith in his FAIR doctrine. He just didn't want to embarrass Gaston, even though he knew Gaston was a "true believer" who would support him 100 percent.

The three were fleetingly cocooned from the uneasy reality of dinner "chez Tom Wright," each contemplating the object of their desires. For Patrick, it was putting his FAIR policies into action and, for Gaston and Solange, each other.

The approaching sound of voices broke their reverie and shifted their attention simultaneously to the hallway. A moment later, Tom emerged from the relative darkness, followed by Manilal and his wife dressed in a traditional bright red and gold embroidered sari.

Solange soon found herself draped in more flowers as Manilal's wife, Jasmin, stepped forward to hand her another bouquet dominated by Birds of Paradise, sunflowers and anthuriums. The bouquet was probably more impressive than Gaston's but certainly didn't pack the same emotional punch. Nonetheless, Solange reacted with similar gratitude before heading away to find an appropriate vase, only to be intercepted by the maid who relieved her of the task.

When she returned to the reception room, Solange found that everyone had already taken up their places at the dinner table on the balcony. The sun had set and the bamboo garden torches that lined two sides of the balcony were ablaze, casting shimmers of light over the guests in the prevailing evening breeze. The citronella scent dispersed by the torches also served to repel the mosquitoes, which seemed to magically come alive at that time of day. A couple of strategically placed fans were humming away in each corner and reinforcing the front line on any mozzie that managed to elude the citronella offensive.

The conversation stopped as Solange entered the balcony space and sat down at the only remaining free seat at right angles to Tom, who was at the head of the table. Next to her was Manilal. On the other side of the table directly opposite her was Patrick, with Gaston next to him and Jasmin at the foot of the table.

Solange turned to Manilal and Jasmin and thanked them for the flowers then hesitated before thanking Gaston as well, the tone in her voice noticeably becoming more timid as she said his name.

"Our pleasure, madame. We're delighted to see that you are fully recovered and, dare I say, looking very beautiful indeed. Mr. Wright is a very lucky man," Manilal said.

"Thank you, Edouard, you're very kind," Solange replied. "And yes, it's good to feel . . . errr . . . normal again," Solange replied.

"Here, here, my darling!" said Tom as he stood up, champagne glass in hand.

Riedel champagne flutes and wine glasses crowned the opulent table settings for each guest. A Krug Brut Blanc de Blancs Champagne Clos du Mesnil 1998, a champagne of a quality befitting the glasses into which it had been poured, emitted its dignified fizz in anticipation of a celebratory toast. And Tom obliged.

"Thank you all for coming, and I'd like to propose a toast to the future Mrs. Wright."

Tom's reference to "the future Mrs. Wright" didn't immediately register with Solange but when it did, it made her gulp and instinctively turn to Gaston sitting diagonally opposite her. He had a similar look of dread on his face that turned into a discreet smile as their eyes met and he raised his glass in her direction, a moment before the others around the table.

Solange glanced at Tom, wondering this time whether he had noticed the almost audible sigh of relief that greeted Gaston's smile.

"I want to take this opportunity to thank you, Gaston, from the bottom of my heart for rescuing Solange. Not just from that raging sea, but also from a very dark headspace," Tom said.

Turning to Solange, he continued in the genuine tone of a sinner asking for forgiveness.

"And for me personally, it's been a real wake-up call, my darling. As Edouard said, I am a very lucky man and I will do whatever it takes to make my beloved wife truly happy," Tom said.

Solange couldn't believe it. Tom actually sounded sincere. She even felt some guilt for not being able to return the love he was professing to have for her. But that lasted only a fleeting moment. The mention of her being his wife again stirred up a ripple of nausea.

A loud call of "to Solange" from Tom was echoed by all the guests as they each took a generous sip of the champagne in her honour. Solange was grateful for the champagne bubbles that triggered another subtle burp, which assuaged her nausea.

"Thank you, everyone, for your good wishes, and you can all rest assured that I am feeling well again, not 100 percent but almost there. And more importantly, I'm very much optimistic and looking forward to the future."

As Solange said this, she instinctively looked at Gaston, who met her gaze with a broad smile.

This time, Tom did notice. His unusually good humour dissolved instantly. She had left no doubt in his mind as to where that optimism lay. Gaston's smile said it all.

Tom felt an anger that quickly evolved into pangs of jealousy, an emotion previously alien to him. When Solange unlocked her eyes from Gaston's, she looked up at Tom, who couldn't hide the about-turn in his emotions. The aggravation visible on his face made her shudder and hardened her resolve to take drastic action tonight!

The other guests, in the meantime, were oblivious to the silent byplay between the trio. They were savouring the champagne and immersed in the magnificent view and luxury setting to which they were all unaccustomed.

Tom switched on a plastic smile and endeavoured to plough on as if nothing had happened. He had planned to propose another toast to Manilal for orchestrating Gaston's positive television performance, a veritable public relations coup for the Wright family and the resort development. But he couldn't bring himself to do that now while wrestling with his mounting anger.

I'll sort out the Gaston problem later, he thought.

Two maids made their way out to the balcony to serve the first course: barbecued locally harvested prawns known as "camarones" with a small serving of heart of palm salad.

The conversation was muted between mutterings of "delicious" and "compliments to the chef". Tom could not bring himself to look at Solange or Gaston and ate quietly, gulping the white wine which had been served with the entrée. He had polished off two glasses by the time the maids cleared the entrée plates. Getting drunk was the only way he could cope with the rest of the evening.

By the time they were halfway through the main course—steamed lobster with homemade aioli and a chayote (choko) gratin—he'd also consumed another three glasses of rose.

I should have punched the living daylights out of the fucker on the beach, he thought.

Released from his inhibitions, Tom could no longer contain his temper.

"So, what's this bullshit about you going into politics, Gaston?" Tom suddenly said in a loud menacing tone, looking daggers at Gaston.

Jolted from his Solange-induced reverie, Gaston was taken aback by Tom's outburst but remained calm. Solange and the other guests squirmed in their chairs while an uncomfortable silence reigned for what seemed an interminable moment.

Gaston combatively turned to look Tom squarely in the eye, only to find Tom staring blankly ahead wide-eyed with fury, his right hand firmly attached to his wine glass and sipping intermittently as he waited for Gaston's reply.

"Well, Mr. Wright, I can't deny that Patrick and I are thinking of taking the plunge into politics at some stage," Gaston said unflinchingly.

"As I mentioned on the TV, we think we have some good ideas for political change. We've had those ideas for a long time, some really simple ideas to make the island a better place for everyone and who knows perhaps set an example for the rest of the world to follow."

Gaston hadn't planned on revealing his political ambition to Tom until the time was right, and it seemed the right time had been forced upon him. He looked at Patrick and was greeted with a subtle nod and a smile that gave him the reassurance he was seeking.

Life on the celebrity treadmill over recent weeks, navigating the demands of media and dodging adoring fans, had toughened up Gaston and turned him into a more mature, self-assured young man.

Following his appearance on the *Encounter* program, he had received more positive media coverage and been deluged with fan mail from all over the island, including from several women who offered to bear his children.

Knowing all too well from personal experience that the power of celebrity can be fleeting, Patrick had convinced Gaston that they should "seize the moment".

"You're only as good as your last gig, mate, and your last gig was a ripper," a buoyant Patrick had said to a bemused Gaston.

"I have no idea what you're talking about, my friend, but I'm sure it's something good," Gaston replied.

"It sure is, mate. Look, what I'm saying is that everyone on the island thinks you're a hero for rescuing the damsel in distress. That's your last gig. Your last deed in the eyes of the island people, the voters. It's a deed that makes you very, very electable. And until you do something to fuck it all up, you'll remain Gaston, the hero.

"The fact that you're a handsome bugger helps a bit, too," Patrick said, grinning and affectionately putting his arm around Gaston. "To put it simply, mate, *now's* the time to get that Fucking Awesome Income Revolution out there."

They'd spent the past week mapping out a strategy for political power and decided to aim high. Gaston would contest the parliamentary elections that were due within the next six months and bypass the traditional pathway through regional councils that would take years. In the meantime, they would maintain Gaston's "hero" profile in the public spotlight by travelling to different villages on the weekends and hosting community town-hall style meetings where they would also promote their FAIR doctrine using the fine example of Choisyville as a prototype for their own vision of a fairer and more just society that, no doubt, the world would eventually emulate.

And Choisyville was uppermost in Gaston's mind as he waited for Tom's reaction. The village had adopted a way of life that was the antithesis of a society and lifestyle so prized by the likes of Tom Wright and his billionaire cronies.

Gaston was grateful for all Tom had done for him, but he also doubted that kindness and generosity were his default position. His alleged beloved was pushed to the brink of killing herself. Gaston didn't know what role Tom had in that or whether Solange's pending marriage to him was the catalyst, but it *had* to be a major influence. Her instant attraction to him was surely a "cry for help".

"Make life better for us all and set an example for the rest of the world. Well, la di da. Good for you, mate," Tom said in a mocking tone.

"How's a peasant like *you* going to make *my life* better? What a fucking joke!"

The raw, "vino veritas" version of Tom Wright was unleashed and Solange, the tears welling in her eyes, felt compelled to interrupt to calm the situation before it got out of hand.

"Tom, please don't. You're embarrassing me," Solange started to whisper to him while reaching for his hand, still locked firmly on the stem of his wine glass. But as her hand touched his, he pushed it away, causing some wine to splash onto her arm. She sat back and reached for a serviette to soak up the wine and a tear or two that could no longer be contained.

Tom paid no attention to her. His eyes were now fixed on Gaston, who defiantly returned the gaze. Manilal and Jasmin were shell-shocked—not daring to move or say a word, stiller than Cezanne's famous 1885 Basket of Apples.

Patrick alternated his gaze between Gaston and Tom while continuing to guzzle his wine. He couldn't resist, despite the looming drama. It was a robust Australian chardonnay with those intense oaky characteristics that he loved. The first sip had immediately transported him back to happy days, not so long ago, yet seemingly another lifetime, when similar wines had fuelled the sexual conquest of many an Australian lover.

Patrick was primed to leap to Gaston's defence. He even felt he had enough alcohol-fuelled bravado to expose and defend himself as that "commie lunatic" councillor who was exiled from Australia for his revolutionary political and economic plan, the very same plan he and Gaston would hopefully soon introduce to the island voters.

But Patrick was in no rush to enter the fray. Gaston had proven to be capable of defending himself and had become just as passionate an advocate for the Fucking Awesome Income Revolution. No surprise, really. After all, he was the architect of the revolution.

"Well, I really don't know why my plans for going into politics should make you so angry To—err—Mr. Wright," Gaston said calmly, knowing full well the reason behind Tom's anger.

He dared not look at Solange.

"Our political plans may not make *your* life any better, Mr. Wright, but there are lots of people out there doing it tough because society is not fair, and we think we can help them."

Tom resisted the urge to interrupt, even though each word Gaston spoke cut into him like daggers.

"Look, Mr. Wright, you probably own a hundred homes and many cars, but how many places can you live in at any one time, or how many cars can you drive while so many people are homeless or live in squalor and don't have enough food to eat? You've got to admit that that's just not fair. Actually, it's quite obscene. Don't you ever think about that?"

The question hung in the air for some time. The tension was palpable and evident on the grim faces of the party guests.

Tom hadn't been fully listening and didn't register at first that a question had been directed to him. The warm exchange between Solange and Gaston kept echoing in his mind, fuelling an anger that he had never experienced and wasn't quite sure how to deal with. No woman had ever betrayed Tom Wright in this way.

"No, Gaston. I never think about stuff like that," Tom barked.

"I've worked damn fucking hard for my hundred homes and flashy cars, while all those fucking lazy bastards you want to save sit on their fat arses and complain about how tough everything is and expect the government to come to their rescue or talk about taking money from the rich rather than getting off their fat arses and working.

"How many of your fucking island peasants are eating tonight because I've given them a job . . . including you, you ungrateful shit?

"I deserve every one of those fucking homes, and it gives me a lot of pleasure being filthy rich and I dare anyone to try to take that away from me, especially the likes of you."

Tom's tirade was bruising his calm, but Gaston managed to subdue the rage brewing inside. The situation called for coolness and composure. There was little hope of reasoning with Tom at this stage, but Gaston wasn't going to give up just yet.

"Look, Mr. Wright, I appreciate all you've done for me, but I—"

Tom cut him off brusquely.

"Just 'cause you've become some two-bit celebrity you think everyone's gonna love whatever fucking nonsense you and your mate are proposing. You are so deluded if you think you can make this world fairer. I've got news for you, mate; we're all still cavemen at heart, you dumb shit, and the law of the jungle still rules and always will.

"Why do you think America, China, and Russia rule the world? 'Cause they've got the biggest guns and most powerful armies. So, you'll have to get bigger guns if you want to change any of them with your naïve simpleton plans."

An increasingly distraught Solange once more tried to intervene.

"Please, Tom, stop. I can't take this anymore," she begged while once more attempting to latch onto his arm. Tom felt repulsed by her touch and withdrew his arm brusquely, causing Solange to almost fall off her chair. Gaston wanted to leap out of his chair to catch and console her as she stumbled.

He felt his patience quickly eroding then evaporating as Solange regained her balance and fled inside sobbing, but not before casting a fleeting glance of utter despair at Gaston.

Patrick sensed that Gaston was about to lose his cool and decided to intervene. He suddenly rose up, wiped his mouth with the linen napkin that had been perched on his lap and took one final swig of his wine glass.

"As delightful as the night has been," he started to say, turning to Gaston, "I feel it's time we made a move, Gaston.

"You have an early start in the morning," he lied.

Turning to Tom, who had resumed staring blankly ahead, one hand still cemented to his wine glass, Patrick thanked him for his hospitality and "delicious dinner" before grabbing Gaston by the arm and forcing him to his feet.

Tom was unmoved and silent. Manilal and Jasmin were seemingly paralysed by the drama too and remained speechless.

Patrick had to coerce Gaston, who seemed primed for a fight, into making a hasty retreat. They headed, unchallenged, towards the front door before realising they had left their jackets behind. On their way to retrieve them, Gaston caught a flash of someone scurrying into one of the rooms down the far end of the hallway. He was certain it was Solange and his instinct was to run after her. But Patrick, who sensed the danger, seized his arm once more and led him away and out the front door.

Outside, they both paused, put on their jackets and took a deep breath before heading for the bus stop, Patrick almost running, Gaston a more meandering pace behind. A nippy breeze had sprung up, causing their hands to chase the warmth of their respective jacket pockets. Gaston was surprised to feel a crumpled piece of paper in one of his pockets.

"Hey, hold on a minute, Patrick," he called out to his friend, who was already a fair distance ahead.

"What's up?" Patrick said. "We'd better get a move on or we'll miss the last bus."

"Wait, wait, have you got a torch?" Gaston said as he unruffled the paper.

Patrick ran back and handed him his more modern mobile phone with built-in flashlight.

Tuning on the ray of bright light in the pitch-dark night mirrored the emotional glow he felt as he read a note scribbled in lipstick on perfumed-laced paper:

"Meet me at the Fish Co-op at midday tomorrow—*please*."

CHAPTER XLVIII

In the Nick of Time

Gaston was barely recognisable. He had woken up early and spent some time building on the standard disguise he'd been using to ward off celebrity stalkers. He had procured an authentic-looking fake beard and moustache—from Idris's friend who was also a hairdresser and lived in Palm Waters—to add to the wraparound sunglasses and baseball cap.

He didn't want to attract any unnecessary attention at what was usually a very crowded Fish Co-op on a Saturday. He also didn't want any of Tom's thugs to recognise him. He was sure Tom would have Solange tailed if she had managed to get away from him at all. That thought suddenly made him shudder.

Maybe he'd assaulted her or imprisoned her in some way, Gaston thought.

Tom was certainly capable of violence. Gaston had experienced that firsthand. He felt a touch guilty that he and Patrick hadn't stayed on to assure her safety. No matter what happened, Gaston had made up his mind to resign on Monday morning. He clearly couldn't face Tom, let alone work for him anymore. It was probably a blessing. Running an effective political campaign would be a full-time job.

He arrived at the co-op fifteen minutes early. He wanted to survey the scene and check out whether Tom's bodyguards would be in tow when she turned up. He stood near a clump of large Casuarina trees that divided the beach from the street. It was a windless day so the trees were not whistling their traditional tune that Gaston loved so much. It was a sound that, more than most, evoked the fun times at the beach with his South African friend of his teenage years.

From his vantage point, he had a good view of the entrance to the Fish Co-op housed in a large, box-shaped, wooden building that backed onto the beachfront. It had seen better times but was ideally situated with a robust wooden wharf extending out from the beach where the fishing boats pulled in to unload their catch. A half a dozen of them were chained to their respective docks, stationary and still on a dead-calm lagoon. It was another clear sign that the wind was in hibernation.

Right on midday, Gaston saw Solange walking briskly towards him and the co-op. She was carrying a small suitcase and dressed in a smart beige suit. She would not have looked out of place in an airport lounge but was well over-dressed for shopping at the co-op. She, too, had made some attempt to remain incognito. Her face was adorned in big sunglasses and a large, bright red head-scarf enveloped her hair.

Gaston hid behind the trees and watched her through the branches as she walked by and headed into the co-op. He was relieved that she didn't seem physically scarred in any way. He'd convinced himself that Tom had hurt her, given how angry he was last night.

He waited a few minutes to make sure no one was following her. The coast was clear and he quickly made his way into the co-op. It didn't take him long to find her among the crowd. She was in the back corner pretending to be checking out the morning's Trevally catch. She still had her sunglasses on despite the dim light.

Gaston felt like he was in a dream that he was hoping wouldn't turn into a night-mare. The most beautiful woman he had ever met was, for all intents and purposes, in love with him as he was with her, and she was now waiting for him to make contact and rescue her. He suddenly realised he didn't have a plan and felt some panic that propelled him towards her.

He stealthily positioned himself beside her, pretending to be an interested customer.

"I love a good Trevally curry, don't you?" he whispered loudly but without looking at her.

She turned around to look at him and he felt her smile broadening with relief that he had shown up.

"Please, keep looking straight ahead and act as if you don't know me. I'm worried you may have been followed," he said, this time in a true whisper that she heard clearly despite the din of the crowd.

But in defiance of his own counsel, Gaston turned to face her, his eyes only fleetingly engaging with hers before his attention was drawn away to some commotion at the entrance of the co-op directly behind her. Two bulky men dressed in regulation gangster attire stormed in, causing the crowd congregating there to part as if sliced with a knife.

The fish that filled the fishmongers' trays were no longer the only fish out of water at the co-op. The black suit, white shirt, black tie, and wraparound dark sunglasses combo wasn't the usual outfit of a Finger Bay Fish Co-op shopper.

The men simultaneously lifted their sunglasses and began scanning the crowd. It didn't take long for Gaston to register what was going on. He tensed up, momentarily frozen by indecision in the face of impending danger. Solange was blissfully unaware of the intrusion, her eyes fixed on Gaston, silently imploring him to meet her lovestruck gaze.

How could I have missed them? thought Gaston.

But Tom's henchmen had outsmarted Gaston thanks to advice they had received from their boss. After last night's ordeal, Tom had immediately declared both Gaston and Solange dead to him. But he also wanted to plot his revenge carefully when he was sober and calm, so he had driven Solange home without a fuss and even offered an insincere apology for his behaviour. But he had no intention of forgiving her or Gaston, even if they came crawling to him on their hands and knees.

"Dead to me, dead to me," he kept mumbling on his way home until he found himself once again at the Angels Massage Suites, where he vented his anger and sobered up in a bout of violent sex with a hapless "angel". But immediately upon coming he felt some remorse for the poor woman pinned under him. Her face was gripped with panic, her legs trembling and still wrapped tightly around his waist. Her apparent distress caused Tom to withdraw abruptly, his penis still half erect. He got dressed almost in a frenzy before lacing a more sincere apology with a sizeable tip and leaving.

Once home, he had wasted no time in summoning his army of four loyal bodyguards—dragging two of them out of bed—to put in place a surveillance operation, but without a plan yet of what he would do with them. He was sure that Solange would try to make contact with Gaston sooner rather than later, so the job shouldn't be too onerous or drag on for too long. But he had also advised them to keep their distance when she headed for an obvious meeting place. They were to be patient and make sure Gaston didn't spot them first.

The boss's advice had reaped instant dividends when the two henchmen on duty saw Solange making a beeline for the Fish Co-op. Surveying the scene from their car, they had quickly spotted Gaston, despite his disguise, camouflaged among the casuarinas.

Now as they moved inside, the men quickly identified their target. Solange's outfit— like theirs, so unbefitting of the setting—shone like a beacon and drew them to her and Gaston like a magnet. One of the men reached inside his jacket to scratch an itch but it looked to Gaston as if he was drawing a revolver from a shoulder holster as cops classically do in the movies or on TV. It thawed him into action. He seized Solange by the hand without warning almost knocking her off-balance and causing her to yelp in surprise.

He steered her towards the back of the co-op, knowing there was an exit there, albeit restricted to staff. She was stumbling and struggling to keep up and keep hold of her suitcase. She remained unaware of the looming danger. It was only when they reached a wide, plastic-stripped curtain door leading to the loading dock that Gaston paused and pointed to the two bodyguards who, thankfully, were having trouble navigating through the crowd that was continuously swelling with peak hour imminent.

Solange gasped as she saw two men she instantly recognised emerging between a pack of tourists who were conspicuous with their cameras poised and without the traditional rattan shopping bag. The bodyguards' progress, however, was further hampered, this time by a local family. The matriarch was bravely brandishing her parasol and demanding they show more respect as they tried to barge their way through. They escaped just in time to see Gaston and Solange dash into the dock area, ignoring the large "staff only" sign and the lame protest of a cigarette-puffing fishmonger hanging out at the dock entrance.

A group of cleaners mopping the stone floor of the loading dock looked on, somewhat bemused (but largely disinterested) as the couple ran past them and out onto the wooden pier where a number of fishing boats were moored. With Gaston now carrying Solange's suitcase and holding her firmly by the hand, they looked like a couple running late and rushing to catch a boat that would whisk them away to an idyllic honeymoon destination.

Gaston instinctively decided to head for the pier rather than the beachfront that stretched for a long way perpendicular to each side of the co-op. The beachfront on both sides was exposed and provided minimal cover and opportunity for refuge. On the other hand, he was confident they could reach and hide on one of the boats moored at the pier before the bodyguards would be within viewing distance.

They bypassed the first boat, a traditional pirogue with a rudimentary white sail that was far too small to provide them with an effective hiding place. The second boat along, however, was a more suitable vessel. It was a wooden fishing trawler with an inviting open hatch to below deck. They jumped in, Gaston slipping and sliding on the deck that had been freshly hosed down, ready to accommodate another day's fruitful marine bounty. Solange managed to keep him steady on his feet and they headed to the hatch and scurried down the few steps to the lower deck,

"Monsieur Gaston, what are you doing here?"

A muscular black man, aged in his late forties, was seated at a small table in the corner, sipping tea and smoking a joint. He was dressed in an unbuttoned flowered shirt and denim three-quarter pants that had started life as stock-standard designer jeans.

"Vijay. Wow. Boy, am I glad to see you. We really could use your help, my friend," Gaston said.

Before Vijay could respond, they heard the sound of footsteps on the pier, causing Gaston to instinctively put a finger up to his lips to signal for everyone to remain silent. They could now hear voices close by and the sound of someone rummaging through the tarpaulins that were in the pirogue Gaston and Solange had passed earlier.

Moments later, footsteps on the upper deck of his boat seemed to spur Vijay into action. He put out the joint and held his hand up to Gaston and Solange, then gave them a thumbs up in a gesture that indicated he understood what was going on.

"Stay cool. I'll take care of it, Monsieur Gaston," he whispered.

As he headed up the steps, he turned around to Gaston, smiled warmly and winked.

"You have very good taste, Monsieur Gaston."

Loudly whistling his favourite island tune, he sauntered up the steps as if he didn't have a care in the world.

CHAPTER XLIX

A Safe Haven for Now

"Man, you're hanging out with some bad dudes, Monsieur Gaston."

Vijay had a smile on his face as he returned below deck, betraying the concern he had expressed in his comment.

"One of those guys is the brother of the biggest gangster on the island. I should know; he's my dealer, if you know what I mean."

Gaston and Solange had not spoken a word while Vijay was on the upper deck dealing with the bodyguards. And they remained silent as Vijay took up his half-finished joint and lit it up with a match that he used to also ignite a portable gas stove to put on the kettle.

"Cup of tea, my friends?"

Gaston nodded his assent while Solange whispered a "yes, please". They were both desperate to know what had transpired on the upper deck but were still somewhat frozen by fear.

"So, what did they ask you and what did you tell them?" Gaston finally managed to ask, despite knowing the answer to the first question and being very grateful for however he had answered the second.

"Well, it seems they were looking for a young couple who'd pissed off their boss. They wouldn't go into details. Now, you wouldn't happen to know who that might be?" Vijay said, broadly grinning.

"What could such a lovely couple have done to make someone so angry that he sends out the goon squad to look for them?"

A look of alarm suddenly wiped the grin from Vijay's face.

"Hey, it's not the gangster boss, is it?"

"No, it's not the gangster boss, Vijay. Relax. I'll tell you the whole story in a minute. But how did you get rid of them?" Gaston asked.

"Well, of course, I told them they're looking in the wrong place. No couple here. The other guy didn't believe me. He wanted to check the lower deck and started heading toward the hatch, even though I told him my wife was sleeping below," Vijay said.

"But fortunately, we still have honour among thieves. My dealer's brother believed me. I'm a longstanding, reliable customer, after all—not something I'm proud of, but we all have our vices, my friend."

The kettle started whistling and Vijay went to make the tea, the joint still dangling from his lips.

Solange loosened her jacket and sat down with a heavy sigh. It was an unconscious release of the past few hours (if not days, weeks, and months) of pent-up tension. She looked at Gaston as he sat next to her on the cushioned bench that ran the length of the boat's interior hull and burst out laughing. Another reflex release of emotion, but also a reaction to the fake facial hair that she'd only just noticed.

"Oh Gaston, I'm sorry . . . but the beard . . . it has to go," she managed to say through her laughter.

"I know, I know, it makes me look like a terrorist," he said, also laughing and tearing away the fake beard and moustache and leaving a trace of adhesive on his cheeks. Solange reached out to wipe it away with her fingers, their eyes meeting for the first time in a setting where their emotions were at last free to roam.

Solange took hold of both his hands and cupped them in hers. She looked deep into his eyes and whispered, "thank you". A tear escaped her eye to be met by his tender smile.

"The pleasure is half mine," Gaston whispered back, instinctively moving his face towards hers until he suddenly remembered they had company. That sumptuous first kiss would have to wait. Vijay was heading their way with two cups of tea in hand.

"So, how do you and Vijay know each other?" Solange asked as Vijay handed them the tea and resumed his seat at the corner table. He lit up another joint.

"My last for the day, I promise," he said, his eyes glistening, his face still grinning broadly.

"I don't mind, Vijay; it's your turf, my friend. We are just so grateful for what you've done for us," Gaston said.

"Vijay and our family go way back," he continued, turning to Solange.

"When I was a kid, he used to sell his catch every day at Finger Bay from his boat, and it was my chore a few times a week to fetch fish for dinner. Mum would come with me once a week to pay him. So over time, we got to know him pretty well.

"And when we were teenagers, he took Patrick and me out in his boat now and then during the school holidays. I haven't seen Vijay for some time, but boy, what a perfect time to renew acquaintances."

Vijay took a long slow drag on the joint and exhaled even more slowly. His eyes were sparkling and the grin now overwhelmed his face.

"Yes, it's lucky I was here. Those guys looked like they meant business.

"So, is this the woman you rescued? Good job. You've always had a good eye for a good sort if you'll pardon the expression, mademoiselle. I am not of the upper classes," Vijay said, once again breaking out in generous laughter as he attempted to imitate an upper-class British accent.

"Now, who was that old girlfriend of yours? Natalie, wasn't it? She was quite the dish but nowhere near as delicious as you, mademoiselle."

Solange forced a smile but remained silent and contemplative at Vijay's sexist remarks. She had quickly realised that he was of an older generation and set in his patriarchal ways. More significantly, Vijay was of the labouring classes, the bottom of the archaic social hierarchy that still lingered, despite colonial times fading into the past. Like most fishermen, he was likely to be ill-educated or perhaps even illiterate. His accent had given it away from the start.

To challenge him would be futile, a waste of energy, but also disrespectful given he had shielded them from a potentially dangerous situation. Emanating from the mouth of a more educated man, his remarks would have been met with a swift and scathing rebuke from Solange.

Besides, it wasn't Vijay's ill-educated comments that seemed to trouble her.

"It's not surprising she's fallen for you, Gaston. You've become quite the celebrity, my friend; if I can still call you a friend now that you're so famous?" Vijay continued.

"Yes, of course, I'm still your friend. I haven't changed at all, and the celebrity thing's not all it's cracked up to be. Frankly, it's a pain in the neck being recognised everywhere I go," Gaston said.

He turned to Solange expecting sympathy but was surprised to be greeted with a scowl. And it didn't take Gaston long to discover the cause.

Solange brought her mouth close to his ear and whispered, "So, who is this Natalie?"

Gaston blushed and felt flush with embarrassment that would surely have made his face glow red if he was white-skinned. He fumbled, trying to find the right words to respond.

Vijay picked up on the looming lover's tiff and attempted to lighten the mood and fill the awkward silence.

"A little trouble in paradise, my friends?" he said.

"Err, ahh . . . not at all, Vijay," Gaston said unconvincingly.

He turned once more to Solange, hoping to find the words to assuage her anxiety, but the stern look on her face once again rendered him momentarily mute.

"Natalie . . . err . . . she's an old flame—a very old flame. Long extinguished, I assure you she means absolutely nothing to me now," he finally blurted out.

Solange, for her part, was more curious than concerned or jealous. She was, in some way, "testing" Gaston. But he had aced the test with the obvious sincerity of his response and a congenial calm quickly returned to their conversation, or lack of conversation, as their eyes locked once more in mutual affection.

"So, now I know how you two met. Tell me, who is this boss?" Vijay said. "And what have you lovebirds done to upset him so much?"

Gaston recounted the aftermath of the rescue, and as he did, it dawned on him that he knew Solange barely more than Vijay did, yet with her hand still entwined in his, he felt the bliss of a happily married couple and the ecstasy of ardent lovers that he was certain they would become. He smiled warmly at her as he told Vijay about discovering the note which set up their first "date".

"So, you chose the Fish Co-op for your first date; not the most romantic setting. What were you thinking?" Vijay said, winking.

Gaston stood up and went over to Vijay. He gave him an affectionate pat on the shoulder.

"As for you, Vijay, you've obviously moved up in the world—a big new boat and now operating in ritzy Palm Waters. Business must be booming."

"Appearances are deceptive, Monsieur Gaston. Those greedy hotel dudes try to screw you every chance they get; then I see them flogging my catch to their rich guests for one hundred times the price they pay for it," Vijay said.

"Anyway, it doesn't matter to my family and me how much money I make. I live in Choisyville, so most of my income goes into the communal pot, if you know what I mean.

"But I can't complain. I get enough for my family and me to keep them happy and me in the drug habit that I've become accustomed to."

Vijay's grin turned into a hearty laugh.

"Choisyville must be a great place to live, from what I've heard," Gaston said.

"Yes, yes, Monsieur Gaston, I think it's a good thing. Or maybe I'm just lazy. I don't need to work too hard and we all have enough to eat and a place to live. And everyone gets a bit of pocket money.

"But I don't know if it suits everyone. We all seemed to be very happy with the change at first, but you're already starting to see some folks wanting more than others," Vijay said, adopting a more serious tone.

Gaston's thoughts turned to Patrick and their plans to have the whole island economy mirror the Choisyville experience. He felt concerned that there were already signs of decay in the system.

"So why do you think that's happening?" Gaston inquired.

"It's just normal, I guess—greed, human nature, and all that. I don't know. I'm no philosopher or economist."

Normal? Gaston had never considered that greed was "normal". And the thought now provoked an equal amount of concern and sadness which left him struggling to say anything in response. He looked at Solange, who gave him a reassuring smile.

"Or maybe I'm just a cynical bastard," Vijay said, once again smiling.

"But to more important matters, what are you going to do now? I have a feeling when they don't find any trace of this fugitive couple, they'll come back here."

Gaston sat down next to Solange and felt her hand glide naturally into his once more. Her other hand reached out and tenderly caressed his cheek, sliding down to his chin where it was met instinctively by Gaston's gentle kiss.

"I don't know, Vijay. I guess we need to find a place to hide out and have some time to think about it."

Silence interspersed with slurps of tea reigned while a trio of furrowed brows contemplated a plan of action.

"We can't stay in Palm Waters. I guess we're just going to have to risk getting to Finger Bay without being detected," Gaston finally said, letting out a sigh in exasperation.

"And it's not going to be easy. It's Saturday so the buses aren't running that regularly, and a taxi would cost a bomb."

"Ahh, it's Saturday. Of course, it is. I almost forgot. I must give up the evil weed. It makes me lose track of the days and my darling wife will never forgive me if—"

Vijay paused, the sparkle in his eyes turning into a blaze before he resumed his train of thought, this time speaking more slowly.

"If . . . if . . . I . . . don't come home . . . on a Saturday. It's your lucky day, my friends. I'm going home this afternoon, so I can take you with me. We'll figure something out when we get there. I have many friends who owe me a favour. And at least you'll be well away from the danger zone."

"You only go home once a week? That must be tough on you and the family, Vijay?"

"You haven't met my wife," Vijay replied jokingly.

"But seriously, it's only during the busy season, and that seems to be getting longer and longer these days because we need to go out further to get a decent catch. But that's another story for another time, my friend. We'd better get ready to vamoose."

CHAPTER L

Lust, Love, and Lightning

They couldn't believe it. He was looking deep into her eyes. She was immersed in his. And no one around to distract them from this moment of pure bliss.

The motion with her hips was slow and very deliberate but quickening in time with the increasing intensity of the storm. The lightning crisscrossing the night sky strobed through Solange's hair as she rocked back and forth on top of Gaston. She arched her back. It was sexually instinctive, natural.

Solange had been technically a virgin until a few minutes ago but having Gaston inside her, instead of her tried and trusted vibrator, and feeling an intense emotional connection as well, was so overwhelming, it brought her quickly to the edge—an edge she soon allowed herself to go over as he hit her G-spot. Her loud moaning was only audible between the frequent claps of thunder. A flurry of thoughts whirled through her mind as she came a second time, including one perhaps unexpected thought of her mother.

Solange was grateful that her mother—despite being a devout Catholic—never toed the traditional Catholic line that sex was only for procreation. She had always been very open about sex and sexuality. In fact, "too much information" was a phrase she had often uttered when her mum insisted on telling her in great detail about the carnal escapades with her father.

As she collapsed blissfully on Gaston's chest, Solange re-focused solely on the intense pleasure of the present. Meanwhile, Gaston's own thoughts had been oscillating between the sheer ecstasy of the moment and trying desperately not to come too quickly, and certainly not before Solange. But now that she had—and twice—he felt he had "permission". He had tried in vain to do so as she had her second orgasm so they could have achieved the alleged nirvana of lovemaking.

"I could do this all night," she whispered in his ear, still panting and trying to regain her breath.

"So could I," he replied, expressing a genuine pre-orgasm desire that would recede rapidly following the orgasm that was fast approaching the point of no return.

Oh, how he envied the ability of women to have multiple orgasms and engage in long sessions of lovemaking. Gaston could achieve the latter, providing he didn't come, because once he did, he just wanted to snuggle and immerse himself in the afterglow or just fall asleep. And he often felt frustrated that the ability to make love again sometimes didn't return until well after the desire to do so. When he experienced his first sexual encounters, he thought he wasn't normal but quickly came to realise that it was a common thing for men. And he would soon find out that when love was factored into the sexual equation, the time gap between desire and ability narrowed considerably.

"I can't hold on anymore, darling."

Solange didn't need any further prompting. She sat up and once again began swaying back and forth, her attention absorbed in pleasuring Gaston, who soon climaxed with a guttural moan that was consumed in a clap of thunder.

Solange once more collapsed onto Gaston's chest, now heaving with pants of pleasure. They turned on their sides, still entwined. Viewed from above, they looked like a living sculpture: two spent bodies oblivious to the warm tropical rain lashing them and the wooden deck. Just metres beyond the lovers, the rain pummelled the beach and the lagoon, the raindrops like spears churning up the sand and sea.

Gaston and Solange had arrived in Choisyville late in the afternoon to be blessed once again by good fortune. Through Vijay's connections with the village elders, they had secured a hideaway for a few days. And it was no ordinary hideout, but a beach cottage nestled among the only beachfront homes in Choisyville. A couple of shingle beaches, a deep harbour port and a steep cliff face shaped the rest of the coastline, making seaside development problematic, or nearly impossible, anywhere else in the village.

In holiday season, the prized row of ten communally owned homes would normally be crawling with local holidaymakers and their friends, or the odd tourist who'd managed to forge a link with a Choisyville resident.

Not without some dissent, the homes had been thrown into the communal pot of property and income in Choisyville's "Common Sense Collective Plan". Under the rules of the new regime, every year interested local families were allocated a weekend and a few days' stay during one of the school holiday periods in one of the homes, with a communal ballot held annually to determine the allocation dates.

Gaston and Solange were fortunate to have arrived at the peak of the cyclone season, during which weekend cancellations were common. Only two other cottages were occupied when they had moved in earlier that afternoon.

They had both been surprised how the thunderbolt on the beach (and rekindled at Tom's dinner) had evolved so naturally into romance and desire for each other. Surely that was the realm of Hollywood fiction and Mills and Boon novels; both had respectively thought—Gaston of Mills and Boon and Solange of Hollywood films.

They knew so very little about each other, yet as they settled into the two-hour boat trip to Choisyville, both had felt the intimacy and familiarity of long-time friends and lovers. When Vijay left them alone to set sail, they at last found the mental space to relax into a proper first date. And as conventional first daters would do, they took turns painting with a broad brush a picture of their respective life histories, each hanging on to every word and reacting instinctively with genuine emotion to the other's life experiences. The mood was buoyant, optimistic. They spoke with smiling voices. The conversation was animated as Gaston spoke of his political vision and found, in Solange, an instant disciple, eager and willing to join the cause for his and Patrick's FAIR doctrine.

Solange was studying at university and widely read and could see the logic in his arguments, although deep down, she remained sceptical that a world where everyone was economically equal would ever be realised. But for now, still caught up in a lingering wave of euphoria following her escape from a certain toxic marriage to Tom, she was more than happy to indulge Gaston and feed off his political fervour to embrace such a vision. And who knows? Look at the Choisyville experience! That seemed to be working more or less well, despite the doubts expressed by Vijay earlier. She might be proven wrong after all.

And wouldn't that be a historical moment to savour?

The fleeting thought of Tom caused Solange to shudder ever so lightly, but enough for Gaston to discern.

"Are you all right, darling?"

"Yes, yes, I'm fine . . . really, I'm fine," Solange replied, an endearing smile fortifying her reassurance but unable to prevent a tear escaping her eye.

"Do you want to talk about it?"

"About what? My stupidity in agreeing to marry Tom? It was my parents, you know, who really loved Tom, or should I say, they loved his money. I felt trapped. But in the end, I don't blame them, really. I wanted to do the right thing by them and never objected, did I? I tried *so* hard to convince myself that I would eventually fall in love with him. Then, they could have his money and we'd all live happily ever after. And you saw for yourself what that led to!"

Solange bowed her head and buried her face in her hands. It was more a gesture of relief, not shame or sorrow as Gaston perceived. She was liberated and all too happy. But he nevertheless took it as a cue to comfort her. He put an arm tightly around her shoulder and gently lifted up her head. He was greeted by more tears but ones of absolute joy. Her eyes were radiant and her lips inviting. They kissed with urgency—their first lingering, luscious, sensuous kiss that sealed their fate as lovers to be.

When they came up for air, the conversation moved on to the future, and one that was potentially trepidatious, yet they spoke with optimism and hope not only for their coupling but also for Gaston's plan to "save the world". A mutual yearning to consummate the relationship brewed throughout. However, when they had found themselves finally alone at the cottage, a surprising timidity had immediately subdued them, fully clothed, into slumber.

Now lying on his back in a state of bliss he had never experienced before, Gaston wanted time to stop. He couldn't actually remember who had made the first move that led them to make love on the back deck in the storm. It had started with claps of thunder, akin to bursts of cannon fire, jolting them out of a deep sleep and Solange immediately alluding to the intense heat that was lingering despite nightfall. Gaston had suggested a cold shower.

Still timid and drowsy, they had showered solo, but when Gaston emerged from the bathroom, he saw Solange through the glass doors on the back deck dressed in a loose white chiffon dress and dancing in the rain. Her arms were outstretched and she was twirling around. Now and then, she looked upwards to the night sky, deriving obvious pleasure from the raindrops showering her face.

He had watched her, entranced, for a few minutes before walking out onto the deck with only a towel draped around him. She seemed consumed with joy and oblivious to Gaston's presence for some time. She might as well have been dancing naked. Her dress was soaked and she was wearing no underwear.

Gaston had moved slowly towards her and gently took hold of her hand as she attempted a pirouette-style move that caused her to stumble and stop. Nothing was said as they embraced for what seemed an eternity, both longing to be absorbed into one body. The raindrops, warm and sensuous, seemed to wash away the past and give life to nascent love. They were soon naked and writhing in a cocoon of pleasure as intense as the tropical storm pounding the deck.

CHAPTER LI

An "Angel" Caught in the Line of Fire

Tom took a swig of wine straight from the bottle while fighting the haze brewing in his head to remind himself that he'd like to be sober enough to keep his appointment at the Angels Massage Suites later in the evening. He was determined to carry out a plan to undermine the brothel's new edict to enforce the use of condoms. Even though the wearing of condoms had been mandatory at all reputable brothels on the island, exceptions were made for regular clientele, particularly the son of a foreign billionaire.

It had been more than three months since Solange had run away with Gaston and Tom was beyond angry, not so much at the loss of his bride-to-be but, at the humiliation he had suffered when she and Gaston had seemingly vanished off the face of the earth. He had never experienced such a catastrophic blow to his ego. He had scoured the island several times over to find the pair, but all to no avail. The one place he didn't search, however, was Choisyville. The authorities he had consulted—high-powered politicians and police officers whose palms Tom and his father had liberally greased to secure consent for their resort development—all assured him that they couldn't possibly be hiding out there. The town was only accessible by sea or by one treacherous, winding mainly gravel road, prone to rock falls that hugged the most rugged mountain peaks on the island. Besides, the rest of the island now treated Choisyville like a foreign pariah state since its economic revolution. The town's residents were considered lunatics by non-residents who only ventured there when absolutely necessary.

But a few weeks later, just as Tom was coming to terms with his loss and refocussing on completing the resort development, Gaston and Solange surfaced on the television news, glowing with happiness and flaunting their love to announce that a new FAIR political party—with Gaston and Patrick at the helm and Solange, the party secretary—would contest the national elections a month later.

They became untouchable as opinion polls pointed to a landslide victory for the party, given Gaston's lingering hero status that had been only enhanced by positive media reporting of his fairy tale romance with the damsel in distress he had rescued, not only from the raging sea but also from the foreign "ogre" who, the tabloid press claimed after testimony from her parents, had tried to buy her heart.

When the happy couple appeared on the *Encounter* program in the lead-up to the election, it was the highest rating program of all time on island television. Patrick had also been invited, but he had the political nous to decline, knowing full well that the Solange-Gaston love story was the ticket to an election victory, and he didn't want to confuse the electorate.

It only got worse for Tom as the opinion polls proved right on the money and the FAIR party claimed every seat in parliament at the elections.

He felt nauseous when he saw Solange on television beaming a smile and clutching Gaston's hand as the party celebrated the historic victory and an overwhelming mandate to implement its FAIR doctrine. Patrick was also in the frame, arm in arm with a woman whose beauty almost matched Solange's . . . almost.

"How absurd! The Neanderthals have prevailed," he had uttered in disgust many times since.

To compound his misery, during his victory speech, Gaston announced plans to marry Solange, which drew rapturous applause and cheering from his supporters. Tom had thrown his glass towards the television screen in drunken disgust but fortunately missed the target. The glass had shattered on the wall to the left of the screen, causing a red wine stain to spread in a spider-like pattern across the lime-coloured surface. Emotionally broken, he had curled up on the couch, bawling like a newborn until fatigue subdued him to sleep.

In the aftermath of the election result, Tom and his father felt they had no option but to abandon the resort development and flee the island. The new government had promised to seize and nationalise all commercial property assets, including all hotels, with little to no compensation.

Tom's belongings were now all packed up. The substantial lease on his substantial house (that would soon have no value under the FAIR regime) had been cancelled and Tom was on the sofa, a nearly empty bottle of wine in hand and surrounded by a mountain of cardboard boxes. He was contemplating his visit to the Angels or more precisely, the busty, strawberry blonde known as Yasmina, who had only recently started working there. Tom had been simultaneously turned on by her exceptional ability to massage his penis to orgasm between her breasts and turned off by her Nazi-style adherence to the mandatory use of condoms.

The other sex workers—and he'd sampled most of the Angels' personnel—had always relaxed the condom rule for a client who always left a very generous tip. But not Yasmina.

"If it's not on, it's not on," she had said the first time he tried to penetrate her with his naked penis, and that led him to discover the arousing joy of her breasts. But the novelty had worn off after a few visits, and he was now determined to have condom-less sex with her in what would probably be his farewell performance at the brothel.

Tom took it as a personal insult that a "whore like Yasmina"—through her surrender to the brothel's condom regulations—was somehow insinuating that he could infect her with a sexually transmitted disease. She should consider it a privilege to receive his sperm, he thought, and concluded that she was probably just too lazy to be on the pill and was relying on her clients' use of condoms for contraception, not protection.

But Tom was determined to teach her a lesson and, if she got pregnant due to her indolent ways, that would be just tough luck. He would be thousands of kilometres away from "this godforsaken island", expunging the horrid memories of the recent past and getting his life back on track.

An hour later, a naked Tom was sitting on the edge of Yasmina's bed, very glad that he'd resisted a strong urge to open that second bottle of wine. Normally, just the sight of her voluptuous breasts would have instantly had him at "half-mast" but not this time.

Nevertheless, he didn't panic and allowed Yasmina to take control. She undressed him and sat him on the bed before teasingly removing her sexy lingerie and kneeling down on the ground between his legs. She stealthily reached over to the bedside table and, in the blink of an eye, had a condom on before Tom had a chance to protest.

Her head was soon bobbing up and down; her mouth working overtime and gradually getting the desired result. He picked up the scent of strawberry *"from a flavoured condom, no doubt"*. And despite his indignation, it wasn't long before Tom had a viable erection.

Mission accomplished, she stood up, expecting to straddle Tom, who was still sitting on the edge of the bed.

"Now you will be a very good boy, and keep the condom on when you fuck me, Monsieur Tom, won't you?" she said.

"Of course, of course, my darling Yasmina," he reassured her. "But would you mind if I took you from behind?"

Without waiting for her assent, he stood up off the bed and moved behind Yasmina before bending her over the bed and gently easing into her. She was surprisingly wet.

And it doesn't feel like a lubricant, the thought heightening his horniness that only intensified further when she started moaning.

Tom's smug smile at her being genuinely sexually aroused was somewhat justified. He was one of the few clients she actually enjoyed fucking.

But as his orgasm began to brew, he slowed down and then withdrew, which took Yasmina by surprise.

"What are you doing, Monsieur Tom?" she said.

"Just making sure the condom is still on, Yasmina darling," he said.

He coughed to mask the noise of him removing the condom before re-entering her and driving even harder to hasten his orgasm.

"Ahh, just a little more gentle, please, Tom!" Yasmina said as she instinctively brought her hand around to his penis in an attempt to slow him down.

She let out a shriek when she realised he was no longer wearing a condom.

"Ahhhh Tom, please . . . you mustn't! It's forbidden," she said, screaming for him to put the condom back on.

Her fingers clawed around the base and her nails dug into the throbbing flesh as she tried frenziedly to extract his penis.

"Please, Tom. *Stop, I beg you*!" Her voice crackled with anger.

But Tom remained oblivious to Yasmina's pleas. He was like a dog on extreme heat. He reached out and gripped the back of her neck and pushed her face into the mattress to muffle her cries for help. He pumped faster and harder until he came with a triumphant shrill.

It was only later that evening while he was showering that Tom noticed some dried blood mixed with Yasmina's equally dried juices at the base of his penis, and as he washed it off, there were also some raw cuts that could only have been inflicted by her nails.

CHAPTER LII

The Angel's Revenge

"I'm afraid I've got some bad news for you, Tom. You're HIV positive."

Dr. Lim paused, waiting for a reaction, but Tom was dumbstruck. A range of emotions was assailing him all at once and bundled within an overarching state of shock.

It was meant to be an unexceptional visit to the doctor a week before, to be formally diagnosed with some sort of flu virus. Even when the doctor had insisted on running comprehensive blood tests that included testing for sexually transmitted infections as a precaution, Tom wasn't overly concerned.

He'd only decided to visit the doctor because of a recalcitrant fever that made him think he'd picked up some strange bug from the island as a parting gift. But nothing that wouldn't be cured with the right medication, which would be readily available now he was back in "civilisation", he had thought.

The Depeche Mode song "Blasphemous Rumours" kept churning in his head throughout the week as he waited for the blood test results. It was an earworm that was to be the harbinger of bad news. He had been a big fan of the band back in the day.

As Dr. Lim dropped the bombshell, the song was still floating between his conscious and subconscious; in particular, the lyrics about God having a "sick sense of humour" and the songwriter expecting God to "laugh" when he dies.

Tom still thought HIV was a death sentence and one that would be swiftly executed. He had an image of God, in Jesus Christ mode, rolling around on the floor laughing.

"So how long have I got, doc?" Tom said in an anxious, whispered tone.

"What do you mean?" Dr. Lim snapped back with genuine surprise.

"I mean . . . err . . . I mean, you can be straight with me, doc; I don't want you to beat around the bush. How long do I have to live?"

Dr. Lim stifled a chuckle, not wanting to mock Tom's ignorance at a time of great distress. Instead, he got up from behind his desk, went over to Tom and placed a reassuring hand on his shoulder. Tom cupped his face in his hands.

"I know, it's a shock, Tom, but HIV is not the dreaded killer that it once was," Dr. Lim said.

"Most people with HIV these days lead more or less a normal life as long as they take the medication and do all the right things with their health—you know, eat well, don't abuse the alcohol, etcetera, etcetera. You know the drill.

"It can be a chore having to take those pills every day, and you'll have to take them for the rest of your life, but it's better than the alternative."

Dr. Lim's silver lining did little to lift the veil of doom and gloom that had descended upon Tom, coupled with a rising anger.

Since arriving back in Australia two months ago, he'd been on a mission to alleviate his lingering heartache and erase any memory of his time on "that cursed island". And he had made great progress. Solange and Gaston were quickly fading into an innocuous memory. Their command of his emotional state was extinguished.

He and his father had landed in Brisbane but soon after moved north to Central Queensland, where they went on a property buying spree around the coastal town of Seventeen Seventy (1770).2 They had picked up on a rumour circulating among their reacquainted property developer mates that a new airport would be built in the region, leading naturally to a surge in both the tourist trade and property values.

What a joy it would be to develop tourism infrastructure in a civilised part of the world not governed by the "law of the coconut tree" or "greasy palms", they had thought.

Their property purchases also included two lavish homes within a gated community—Sunrise at 1770—an eco-friendly, sustainable residential community from where they also intended to run the business. Their decision to buy there had nothing to do with a desire to jump on the environmental bandwagon but everything to do with isolating themselves from intrusion by "riff-raff" who might disrupt their renewed development ambitions.

Tom had even managed to wean himself of his daily morning habit of perusing the island news online, a habit that was only compounding his angst and delaying the mending of his broken heart. Most days, he'd be confronted with stories

---

[2] Seventeen Seventy, known by locals as 1770, is a small town on the Central Queensland (Australia) coast. It was originally named Round Hill after the creek on which it lies. On 24 May 1770, James Cook anchored his ship near Round Hill Head and went ashore with his botanist, Joseph Banks, and assistant, Daniel Solander. The town's name was changed in 1770 to commemorate the 200th anniversary of Lieutenant James Cook landing his ship, the *Endeavour*, in the area.

about the "popular" new government and the success of its FAIR policy program. The island economy, it seemed, was making a rapid and smooth transition to one where everyone was paid the same wage, and the government was now negotiating bonuses for the workers who "made a difference".

More often than not, when he clicked on an island news website, he was assaulted by a striking picture of the "ideal couple" illustrating the lead story. Solange and Gaston were in power and in love, beaming joy and obvious affection for each other and for their constituents. Tom knew it was torturing him, yet, a masochistic streak continued to lure him to the website, like someone who's hypnotically drawn to rubbernecking at the scene of a horrific car crash.

A promising first date with a local woman, Vanessa, broke the spell. Tom had sought out women to date very soon after arriving in Australia in an attempt to rapidly exorcise the ghost of Solange past. However, the two women that he did date in Brisbane before moving up to 1770 both had a lukewarm response to his advances that miraculously sizzled hot when they found out he was wealthy.

Beautiful, long black-haired, bikini-model body Vanessa, on the other hand, was keen on Tom the man, not Tom, the property tycoon. That was obvious from their first chance meeting on the beach as he emerged from the sea after a surf. She had been sitting watching him for some time, he later found out. Her piercing deep blue eyes had stopped him in his tracks as he jogged up the beach with a surfboard under his arm. They had shared a flirtatious chat and a joint before arranging to meet up the next day. They had dinner at the bistro in the iconic 1770 pub watching the dipping light of sunset cast romantic red and orange hues over the gentle surf. All was suddenly well again in Tom's world. Dinner ended with a promising kiss and a plan to meet again a few days later.

Between dates, Tom only logged on occasionally to the island news website and when he did, he didn't care. The second date confirmed the promise of the first, and the third, Tom was convinced, would definitely have sex on the menu. The visits to the island news website stopped completely. Then the flu-like illness struck and he had to postpone the "sex" date.

And now here he was, confronting the island demons once more. Or one in particular—Yasmina.

His head was still buried in his cupped hands, but not in sorrow. He was livid.

That fucking dirty whore. She's given me a fucking life sentence. I should have smothered or strangled her that night and done the world a favour, Tom thought, oblivious to the fact that he had been the architect of his own HIV destiny.

Tom left the doctor's surgery clutching prescriptions tightly in his hands. He wanted to head straight to Vanessa, fuck her and infect her too. If she insisted on using condoms, he would prick holes in them. Then, when she got HIV, he would be indignant and feign being outraged that she might have infected him too. No doubt, she would have had a few lovers in her time.

She had called him earlier in the day to wish him well for the doctor's appointment. She had sounded concerned even though she really didn't know him.

Did she suspect something? How could she? Anyway, that concern could work in my favour when I accuse her of giving me the virus.

The thought cheered him up somewhat as he walked back to his car in the hot afternoon sun. He was still very angry, but he now had a plan of action. Dr. Lim's assurances that he could live a normal life were also beginning to sink in. He sat in his car in the surgery carpark for some time.

He wouldn't stop with Vanessa. Although he was fond of her, it was pure lust at this stage. Love might have evolved, but not now. He would infect as many women as he possibly could. Revenge seemed justified given the misery women had caused him in recent times.

As he finally reversed out of the car park, he couldn't help again conjuring a vision of Jesus Christ laughing heartily at the pun, but this time he smiled. And he was still smiling when the gates of the Sunrise at 1770 community compound closed behind him as he drove in.

A few weeks later, Tom was on the medication and contemplating his seduction of Vanessa while holding her hand and toasting his return to health over a glass of wine at the pub.

At about the same time, a few thousand kilometres away, four pallbearers speckled in the heavy morning light percolating through a clump of flame trees were lowering Yasmina's coffin into a pauper's grave at the Palm Waters cemetery. Only a church minister and three colleagues from the Angel's Massage Suites were present at the funeral service.

Yasmina had officially died of complications resulting from a bout of pneumonia, but her few friends knew "complications" was a euphemism for the HIV that she had contracted some five years before during a time when heroin ruled her world.

The owner of the Angels Massage Suites had saved her life following pleas for help from one of her sex workers who was also Yasmina's only close friend. The brothel madame had supported her rehab and initially paid for her HIV medication, expecting Yasmina to show her gratitude by joining the ranks of the Angels.

When Yasmina gratefully accepted her offer, the madame stressed the importance of enforcing the mandatory condom regulation given her condition. The Angels Massage Suites was a high-class brothel with a stellar reputation. That's why the establishment attracted high-powered, high-profile clients like Tom and a regular cohort of politicians from across the political spectrum. A client contracting HIV would be very bad for business.

And Yasmina didn't disappoint on all counts. She took on her new job with a zeal that soon made her one of the most popular working girls at the brothel, despite her rigid enforcement of the mandatory condom rule.

But the allure of heroin continued to torment her and she succumbed to the occasional "bender" when she had a few days off. As a result, she was often negligent in her medication regimen, which kept the virus active in her body and worse still, left her prone to a potentially life-threatening illness. If pneumonia hadn't claimed her life, it would have only been a matter of time before full-blown AIDS did.

The encounter with Tom hastened her downfall. In shock, for a few days after, she had carried on working in a zombie-like state before disappearing. With heroin in increasingly short supply, Yasmina had turned to crystal meth to assuage the trauma of Tom.

A week later, her comatose body was found dumped outside the island's new mental hospital and drug rehabilitation centre that was housed, ironically, in Tom's former resort development. It had been ready for internal fit-out and exterior cosmetic work when Tom and his father had fled the island, so the hotel rooms were simply converted into hospital suites while the planned grand ballroom became the main hospital ward.

Gaston's new government had wasted no time in turning the site into the urgently needed hospital where mentally ill and drug-dependent patients were given the best care available on the island. By first-world standards, that was still well below par. Nevertheless, the move only boosted the popularity of the new government; the only note of dissent being over the differing bonuses awarded above the standard wage to each level of health professional working there. All were eligible for a bonus given the vital service they provided, but some believed they were "more eligible than others" it seemed. Gaston and Patrick had decided to personally take charge of negotiations to resolve the issue.

Yasmina, meanwhile, was nursed back to some semblance of health but discharged far too early. A few days later, her frail immune system proved defenceless against an attack from a man's cough on a bus. The resulting flu virus quickly transmuted into pneumonia that, in a healthier individual living in a more advanced nation, would not have been life-threatening.

As for Tom, the seduction of Vanessa was about the only thing that went according to plan. His delayed third date delivered on the promise of sex, and Tom was prepared. As he had suspected, Vanessa insisted on him using condoms and was heartened to find that Tom raised no objection and had even brought some of his own. But if she had examined them more closely, she would have found them riddled with pinpricks. Nevertheless, her immune system proved remarkably resilient to Tom's infected sperm and she failed to contract the disease.

But Tom had revenge ambitions beyond Vanessa. He was keen to infect as many women as possible before the antiretroviral treatment reduced his viral load to a point where it would be difficult for him to pass on the virus to others. He began making regular alleged business trips to Brisbane on a mission to avenge the "injustice".

His first two trips proved unsuccessful, as the brothels he visited were strict in policing their regulation of clients only using condoms supplied by the establishment. On his second trip, Tom tried in vain to pierce the condom while the prostitute wasn't looking but only managed to prick his finger and draw blood. Realising another opportunity to infect her, he attempted to put his blood-soaked finger in her mouth, thinking the dark-lit room would provide cover for his nefarious deed. However, she was awake to the danger and managed to dodge his finger before reaching into a bedside drawer for a tissue and Band-Aid, then insisting she would not continue until he covered the wound.

On the third trip, he decided to try his luck finding a willing woman at a pub that, a mate had said, was a "dead-set meat market". And he was right. Tom was only there half an hour when he locked eyes with an attractive thirty-something blonde named Sylvia. She was dressed in a buttock-hugging mini skirt and a low-cut blouse that accentuated her ample bosom. A perfect complement to the smutty outfit were fishnet stockings and stiletto heels with glistening steel tips that showcased her shapely legs. *She wouldn't have looked out of place starring in a porn film's opening sequence,* Tom thought.

Had they been more conversational before rushing to bed in Tom's nearby hotel room, he might have discovered why Sylvia had spent most of her life searching in vain for a long-term lover. He was totally caught up in the sexual desire of the moment and didn't ask any questions or make much conversation as they eagerly clawed each other's clothes off.

Sylvia kept her stilettos on until the last moment, tossing them up carelessly into the air but leaving her stockings on before jumping into bed and spreading her legs wide. To Tom's great delight, there was no mention of a "condom", so he climbed on top of her and ploughed right on in.

But joyful lust soon turned to misery for Tom when Sylvia suffered an epileptic seizure which caused her to lurch forward unexpectedly, throwing him off the bed. He landed heavily on his back and on an upturned, razor-sharp stiletto heel that pierced the thoracic region of his spinal cord between the T3 and T5 vertebrae, leaving him a paraplegic.

CHAPTER LIII

Trouble in FAIR Paradise

The body of the headless chicken was still experiencing postmortem spasms. Blood was spurting out at regular intervals and dripping over the hand of Mireille, a patient at the Palm Waters Mental Hospital.

Middle-aged Mireille was serving one of her regular "sentences" (and her first at the new hospital) after yet another psychotic episode courtesy of the chronic Schizophrenia that had plagued her life.

Waking up after a restless sleep on her second night at the hospital, she had a sudden childhood memory of eating freshly killed poultry that sparked her hunt for chicken. She had sneaked out of her room and somehow managed to procure a scalpel from an operating theatre before venturing outside undetected, where she captured one of the chickens that regularly strayed onto the hospital grounds.

The skills she'd acquired in catching and butchering the family chickens as a teenager instinctively resurfaced as she imprisoned the bird's legs with her bare hands and conveyed it to a makeshift chopping block, a stone slab usually used to scrub dirty clothing. She quickly and efficiently decapitated the chicken, despite the squawking and its wings flapping vigorously in protest to the bitter end. She then headed back indoors on a mission to find the kitchen, where she was convinced her mother would be waiting to cook up her favourite chicken curry.

She struggled to maintain her grip on the chicken torso. The blood was spilling liberally over her hand as she stomped down the main hospital corridor. Mireille made it all the way to the reception, torso still in hand, without encountering any other patients or staff.

Patients had been confined to their rooms while staff were gathered excitedly around the front doors to herald the imminent arrival of the new leaders of the island nation.

To their astonishment, the staff caught their first glimpse of Gaston and Patrick standing at the bus stop across the road in the wake of a bus that had just dropped them off. The hospital workers might have missed them entirely if it hadn't been for the thundering cheers and whistles of the passengers as the pair alighted and the driver sounding his horn as the bus drove away.

The howling chorus of approval only intensified as Gaston and Patrick crossed the road and entered the hospital grounds. Doctors, nurses, orderlies, admin workers, and cleaners applauded as one, united in near veneration of their new leaders, despite the recent division the bonus negotiations had created among staff.

The applause continued as they climbed the stairs to a faux sandstone landing where the head doctor and hospital manager were poised to greet them, surrounded by a bevy of starstruck staff members crowding the entrance of the hospital.

A scream from indoors instantly arrested the applause and drew the attention of the crowd away from the VIPs. Many gasped in horror at the sight of a wild-eyed Mireille with a scalpel in one hand, bloodied chicken torso in the other and heading straight for them.

A copybook rugby tackle from a quick-thinking orderly sent Mireille crashing to the ground, sending both scalpel and chicken torso somersaulting into the air. The scalpel tumbled towards a cluster of nurses and caused them to shriek and scurry in different directions. It fell harmlessly on the tiled floor but with a clang that reverberated throughout the reception area. The torso, meanwhile, as it fell, scattered its last few droplets of blood onto another group who hissed in disgust at their clothes being soiled.

Mireille offered no resistance as another orderly came in to help his colleague take her away. But they had only gone a few steps when both Gaston and Patrick, concerned for her welfare, dashed in and parted the entourage of "worshippers" in the process.

"Stop, stop!" Gaston said.

They turned around, surprised to see the new leaders of the nation running towards them. Each orderly had one of Mireille's arms draped around his neck and shoulder. She was limp, her feet lifted off the ground and motionless.

"Are you oka—" Gaston began to ask, only to be confronted by Mireille's vacant stare and drooling mouth.

"I'm sorry, your Excellency, but we need to get her to the doctor," one of the orderlies said.

"Yes indeed, I don't want to hold you up. I didn't realise . . ." Gaston replied, suddenly lost for words.

"Thank you, sir," the orderly said. "Now, if you will excuse us."

"Of course, of course . . . but please call me Gaston."

As he and Patrick walked back to the reception area, the staff once again cheered and broke out in gentle applause. They were obviously touched by their leaders' show of concern for the hapless Mireille.

It was very early days in the new government's quest to create a status-less Utopia and, despite their best efforts, Gaston and Patrick continued to receive celebrity treatment wherever they went. And the visit to the hospital was proving to be no exception.

They had ditched the flashy cars and police escorts and earned the same basic wage (and a modest bonus as leaders of the new island order). But they were still feted and fawned upon wherever they went.

Marx might have been right about the need for a "dictatorship of the proletariat" in the initial phase of a communist revolution, but Gaston and Patrick were determined that their control over the island's socio-economic and political life, which was a far cry from a dictatorship, would not last long. They would devolve the powers to implement the FAIR doctrine to the communities as soon as possible. This had already happened in Choisyville, and Gaston's own Finger Bay community was almost there. It was no surprise that the wealthier communities, like Palm Waters, were putting up some resistance.

So-called communist regimes had failed to get beyond what Marx had always designed to be a short and purely transitionary phase of the revolution. Perhaps that's why they've all failed, the pair reasoned. They were not going to make the same mistake. Not that Gaston and Patrick thought of their government as communist. Theirs was a "common sense" management of the economy type of government.

At the same time, they were not naïve and fully aware of the human flaws that posed a potential threat to their common-sense government. But were greed, power, and competition traits of human nature or nurture? They had based their philosophy of government on the latter, and the rapid and broad acceptance of their FAIR plan seemed to vindicate the faith in their theory, that is until this doctor's dispute had thrown a spanner in the works.

Gaston was particularly troubled because the first serious ructions in the new economic regime were emerging among a cohort of workers that had inspired a core tenet of the FAIR doctrine. Members of the medical profession were to be the superstars of the new order and bonus payments needed to reflect that. That's why he and Patrick had decided to personally intervene and take charge of negotiations.

The psychiatrists were demanding a significantly bigger bonus than the non-specialist doctors, who, in turn, were seeking an outrageously larger bonus than the nurses. Gaston and Patrick could see merit in each side's arguments. After all, it did take greater skills, acquired over many more years of work and study, to become a specialist, as it did to become a doctor when compared with nurses. Nevertheless, an accomplished nurse was an invaluable part of any medical team and worthy of a reasonable bonus too. But the disparity in bonuses being proposed was anything but reasonable, particularly between the doctors and nurses.

Disturbed and distracted by the episode with Mireille, the motive for their visit to the hospital momentarily eluded Gaston and rendered him deaf to apologies from the head doctor. There was already little sign of the disruption to what had been expected to be a jubilant, choreographed welcome for their new political leaders. The chicken carcass and its residue had been cleaned up and the panic-stricken crowd was now a sea of smiling faces.

Patrick, however, was keen to get down to business. They had limited time and he knew that negotiations at the hospital would be challenging and protracted. And the incident with Mireille had been an unwelcomed delay to proceedings. Unlike Gaston, he was not optimistic of a quick resolution, despite them having hashed out a plan to help all the medical staff boost their standard income.

The new government had always intended to help professions that had lifesaving ability to earn sponsorship income in return for businesses having their logos emblazoned on uniforms or any printed materials attached to the organisation. The medical profession was the obvious first cab off the rank.

Gaston was convinced this would help resolve the issue quickly; Patrick was more pessimistic and found immediate vindication for his sentiments. Gaston's outline of the sponsorship plan at the start of negotiations was met with derision and scorn from all parties. Lobbying for sponsorship would only increase the respective workloads that they considered already overwhelming.

The mood at the meeting had quickly deteriorated from one of hope and festivity to a room full of furrowed brows and sighs of exasperation.

"With all due respect, Your Excellency, we believe we have a right to a bigger bonus without having to work harder, doing something we know nothing about," the head of the hospital's specialist team said.

"We're not marketing people; we're highly qualified medical specialists working in extremely difficult conditions, as you saw yourself today. Many of us are on call twelve to fourteen hours a day. You call your system FAIR, and that's exactly what we are demanding, a FAIR income for what we do."

"Please, please, it's Gaston, not Your Excellency. We . . ." was all Gaston could muster before he and Patrick fell silent in contemplation.

They could only nod in sympathy. But, as if to hammer home the Head Specialist's argument and before they could fashion a satisfactory response, a woman patient dressed in a standard hospital gown burst through the double doors of the meeting room. She athletically bounded onto the large oak conference table, where she launched into a virtuoso performance of the cancan with equally accomplished vocal accompaniment. As she lifted her gown, she couldn't help but flash her densely woolly genitals at the meeting participants. Gaston and Patrick were aghast, but the hospital staff was unfazed. One of the doctors then bizarrely started a countdown.

"Five, four, three, two, one . . ."

And right on cue, another patient, this time male, surged through the doors and joined the cancan dancer on the table. He started crooning a rendition of the jazz standard, "Fly Me to the Moon," that would have impressed Frank Sinatra and Michael Bublé.

But instead of summoning the orderlies, as Gaston and Patrick would have expected, the hospital staff started clapping in time with the tune.

As their routine drew to a close, a couple of orderlies did walk in, each taking the hand of a patient and calmly escorting them off the table and out of the room.

Gaston and Patrick could hardly believe what they'd just witnessed.

"But what . . ." Gaston started to say before the head specialist cut in.

"Ahh, happens every week when we have a meeting," he said. "Michel there has a good repertoire of songs, you know.

"We haven't heard that one for a while. I wonder if his name is really Michel. He does a lot of Michael Bublé numbers, you see. Maybe he adopted the French equivalent.

"You must admit, he's good. Demented, but a fine singer, so we indulge him and the cancan girl every week. Caterina is her name, I think. I keep forgetting to tell the nurses to give her some underwear. Sorry, Your Excellency, for that."

"Please, it's Gast—oh, never mind!" Gaston said. "Shall we get back to business, ladies and gentlemen?"

Immediately, a veil of gloom once again fell upon the ambiance that had momentarily lightened with the intrusion of Michel and Caterina. And it prevailed for the next two hours, as no compromise could be reached.

In stark contrast to their arrival, there were no cheers, crowd, or admiring smiles as Gaston and Patrick left the hospital. The stalemate was reflected in the solemn faces of the hospital manager and a few senior doctors who escorted them out. A commitment to further discussions did little to lift Gaston's spirits.

As they were walking out of the hospital, an ambulance, siren wailing, pulled into one of the emergency unit bays. Intrigued, Gaston and Patrick walked towards the ambulance to watch the paramedics unload the patient. It was obviously an urgent case, given the sombre look on the faces of the paramedics and confirmed by a doctor rushing out to take charge of the patient. It was a woman sporting breathing apparatus and motionless on the ambulance stretcher as she was wheeled passed Gaston. He instantly recognised her as his old flame, Natalie.

CHAPTER LIV

The United Nations Refuses to Play Fair

His face was nestled in her ample bosom, his penis deep inside her as she straddled him on the armless dining chair.

Gaston was not fully focused on the obvious physical pleasure that his gentle thrusts were creating and causing Solange to drip juices liberally over his groin.

Despite his best efforts to be fully in the moment, his thoughts were distracted by a vision of a comatose Natalie and a letter the government had received from the United Nations addressed to *"Gaston Le Clezio—the President of the Island Republic"*. This had caused some friction between him and Patrick, as they had decided that neither of them would be the outright leader of the government. Leadership would be a collective endeavour and duties shared until, of course, all power was devolved to the communities. Representatives of the United Nations had no doubt seen the ubiquitous images of Gaston (mostly embracing a beaming Solange) that illustrated media stories about their rise to power and assumed he was in charge.

As for Natalie, Gaston discovered that she'd tried to commit suicide and four days later, was still in a coma. He was surprised to still have some feeling of care for her despite her betrayal seemingly a lifetime ago. He also couldn't help but wonder whether his elevation to power and the bombardment of pictures of him and Solange in the media—in love and exuding happiness—had somehow traumatised her to the point of taking her own life.

Solange's moaning intensified, which made her struggle to find the right key. To Gaston's delight, she'd taken to serenading him whenever they made love straddling him this way. She had a lovely voice and she'd sing in a loud whisper into his ear while they rocked gently. Normally Gaston was so turned on by this that he would have to concentrate hard to not come too quickly. But today was different, even though she was singing one of his favourite tunes, "Ave Maria".

She'd already come twice, the first orgasm almost immediately after Gaston had penetrated her. Solange had always found it easier to have an orgasm during intercourse when she was ovulating. As her third approached, the squishy sounds of their swaying loins, coupled with the heady mix of moaning and song in his ear, brought Gaston back to the moment. And soon after, over the edge of an orgasm that not only brought him the usual sensual pleasure but one that nine months later would also produce their first child—a son, Gabriel—named after the archangel, the "perfect balance of masculine power and feminine nurturing", according to Christian doctrine.

They lingered entwined in a post-coital embrace for some time, both longing for time to stop. But gradually, despite his best endeavours, Gaston's thoughts drifted away and back to the dispute with Patrick the day before. It was the first time he could remember that they'd had anything resembling a disagreement.

The letter from the UN was an invitation for Gaston to travel to the UN headquarters in New York for a "please explain" session. It hadn't taken long for the island's velvet revolution to come to the notice of the world's politicians, press, and, in turn, the United Nations. The island leaders were universally condemned by western media for the "obvious communist ideology that gave the FAIR virus life". They branded it a threat to the capitalist world order, should the "contagion" spread. But the panic was largely confined to hysterical media reporting at a time—the lead-up to Christmas—when news outlets traditionally suffered from a dearth of compelling stories.

The world's political leaders in general were much less concerned. The heads of the major capitalist nations publicly laughed off the threat and openly described the FAIR doctrine as "primitive" and the island population as "uncivilised peasants" who would no doubt soon "come to their senses". The president of the USA was even caught—off the record—describing the island folk as "savages".

Nevertheless, they were still quick to invoke the help of the United Nations to help contain the FAIR economic system within the island borders. During a debate at the UN, the British prime minister added; "This insane economic system now in place in our former colony would have frightened even Karl Marx and must never be allowed to infect the civilised capitalist world order".

The UN debate ended with a resolution to give the island leader an opportunity to front the UN and explain the implications of the FAIR plan for the island's relationship—particularly its trade relations—with the rest of the world. More importantly, they expressed their wholesale disapproval of the FAIR system and resolved to provide an incentive, in the form of economic sanctions, for the island to return to a more conventional capitalist economic system.

A few hours later, the bliss of the morning love-making session had evaporated and Gaston found himself once more face-to-face with Patrick at Government House, discussing the UN invitation. The mood was tense, a far cry from their joyful reunion only a few months before. They sat perpendicular to each other at a conference table, sipping on mineral water.

They were due to have a formal meeting with the full leadership group at the same venue in the afternoon to get their approval for one of them to travel to the UN in New York. The question was who was going to go, and for the time being, the question remained unresolved.

"How dare they call us savages? It's the UN that's ruled by savages," Gaston said, fuming and hoping to delay letting the elephant in the room.

"These countries have the biggest guns and aren't afraid to use them, usually in proxy wars that kill millions of innocent people thousands of miles from their own land. Now that's primitive. Really, we've barely progressed from the days of the caveman."

Gaston stood up, glass in hand, and walked over to the window. He looked out over the still water of the harbour, the harsh midday light dancing on the surface.

"What we're doing here is how human beings should behave towards each other: care, compassion and making sure everyone is able to have a good life. Our system gets us closer to planet Utopia. Do you remember that, Patrick? My story of David Beckham and planet utopia?"

Gaston paused, smiling at the fond childhood memory before turning around and heading back to the table, where he looked Patrick in the eye.

"But it's also the only way this planet's ever going to survive, my friend.

"And don't get me started about the US fucking A. They're such fucking hypocrites. They bang on about human rights and democracy, yet they turn a blind eye to their mates in the Middle East repressing their people and literally getting away with murder."

Gaston banged his fist on the table to emphasise his point.

"Look at their best friend Israel; they're constantly ignoring and violating UN resolutions, yet they're never punished. When Iraq defied UN resolutions, they got invaded.

"Fuck the UN. They can all go to hell! We can survive . . . no, thrive . . . without the lot of them."

"No, we can't, Gaston," Patrick said calmly, even though he was annoyed by Gaston's naivete.

"The world isn't that simple anymore. Just a small example, how on earth can we make our own medicines here, Gaston? You know, the ones we need to save lives," he said sarcastically.

"You really need some lessons in diplomacy, my friend, and that's precisely why I should go to the UN. We simply can't afford to piss off the rest of the world. We have to make them think that FAIR is a better way to live, yes. But make them angry? No."

Infuriated at being talked down to, Gaston got up once more and took a deep breath. He walked to the window, trying to maintain his cool.

"Come off it, Patrick. I'm not that stupid. We still have many friends. I get lots of letters from people from all around the world—America even—praising us for the revolution, and one accomplished with no bloodshed.

"As for the United Nations, it's time for some straight-talking, not diplomacy, Patrick. That's why I should go. Besides, I had the idea for FAIR. And the other thing is that the voters would expect me to go. They love Solange and me.

"We wouldn't have won the election without my celebrity factor. You know that, given your experience in Australia. That'll help us attract media attention when I'm there so I can spread the message about how wonderful FAIR has been for the island and why it should be adopted by all civilised nations."

Sarcastically, Gaston concluded, "I don't see *your* face much in the press or on social media."

Clearly irritated, Patrick snapped back, "You certainly are the show pony, Gaston. Sure, it may have been your idea, but that's all it was, my friend—a skeleton of an idea that I fleshed out into a Hercules-like plan and know all the intricate details of how it works.

"And I've been in the hurly-burly of politics before. They're likely to eat you up and make a fool of you at the UN. I don't want us to be the laughingstock of the world.

"Bottom line, mate, I've done all the hard yards and worked so much harder than you on this and now you want to take all the glory."

"Higher inequality begets more crime, less happiness, less trust, and more violence. Inequality contributes to the deaths of at least 21,300 people each day."

—Nabil Ahmed. "Inequality Kills: The unparalleled action needed to combat unprecedented inequality in the wake of COVID-19." *Oxfam.* 17 Jan 2022.

About the Author

Pascal Adolphe was born on the Indian Ocean island of Mauritius but has lived most of his life in Sydney, Australia.

Pascal is a writer, television producer, journalist, and versatile media professional with more than thirty-years' experience working in a variety of roles across a range of media in Sydney, Australia.

He's been able to adapt his considerable storytelling skills to television production, newspapers, digital media, public relations, radio and now in writing *Gaston Saves the World;* his first novel that was inspired by his Mauritian ethnic heritage.

www.ingramcontent.com/pod-product-compliance
Lightning Source LLC
Chambersburg PA
CBHW061054190726
48286CB00006B/1741

* 9 7 8 1 9 5 6 0 1 9 6 8 1 *